Praise for the novels of Kathryn Shay

NOTHING MORE TO LOSE

"Hidden Cove tales continue to provide superb romantic suspense thrillers . . . Terrific." *—Midwest Book Review*

"The talented Shay offers another heartwarming tale of brave men and women." *—Booklist*

"Another moving novel from an author who is a sure bet for a good read." *—Huntress' Reviews*

AFTER THE FIRE

"This powerful, emotionally realistic book is the first of Shay's new trilogy about the men and women who put their lives on the line every day and how that dedication and commitment affect all those around them. Poignant and compelling, this novel reinforces Shay's well-earned reputation as a first-rate storyteller." *—Booklist*

"Powerfully written . . . genuine . . . Shay pays homage to rescue workers with this exhilarating tale that demands a sequel." *—Midwest Book Review*

continued . . .

TRUST IN ME

"[This] powerful tale of redemption, friendship, trust, and forgiving shows once again that Shay knows how to pack an emotional wallop."   —*Booklist*

"An unusual and compelling tale . . . I don't know when I have become more involved in a novel's characters and story."   —*The Romance Reader*

"A master storyteller . . . Don't miss this book or you will be sorry you did."   —*Reader to Reader Reviews*

"Each one of [Shay's novels] is a moving tale of friendship, the truest form of love."   —*Huntress' Reviews*

PROMISES TO KEEP

"A wonderful work of contemporary romance. With a plot ripped straight from the headlines, *Promises to Keep* evokes genuine people confronting a genuine crisis with all the moral, ethical, and emotional struggle in between."
   —*New York Times* bestselling author Lisa Gardner

"Emotion, romance, realism, and intrigue. A love story that you'll never forget. *Promises to Keep* is romantic suspense at its very best, with a dynamic cast of characters, a plot that will hold you on the edge of your seat, and an ending that you'll remember long after you turn the last page."
   —*New York Times* bestselling author Catherine Anderson

"Shay does an admirable job with a difficult subject, writing . . . with sensitivity and realism."   —*Booklist*

TIES THAT BIND

KATHRYN SHAY

BERKLEY SENSATION, NEW YORK

THE BERKLEY PUBLISHING GROUP
Published by the Penguin Group
Penguin Group (USA) Inc.
375 Hudson Street, New York, New York 10014, USA

Penguin Group (Canada), 90 Eglinton Avenue East, Suite 700, Toronto, Ontario M4P 2Y3, Canada
(a division of Pearson Penguin Canada Inc.)
Penguin Books Ltd., 80 Strand, London WC2R 0RL, England
Penguin Books Ireland, 25 St. Stephen's Green, Dublin 2, Ireland (a division of Penguin Books Ltd.)
Penguin Group (Australia), 250 Camberwell Road, Camberwell, Victoria 3124, Australia
(a division of Pearson Australia Group Pty. Ltd.)
Penguin Books India Pvt. Ltd., 11 Community Centre, Panchsheel Park, New Delhi—110 017, India
Penguin Group (NZ), Cnr. Airborne and Rosedale Roads, Albany, Auckland 1310, New Zealand
(a division of Pearson New Zealand Ltd.)
Penguin Books (South Africa) (Pty.) Ltd., 24 Sturdee Avenue, Rosebank, Johannesburg 2196,
South Africa

Penguin Books Ltd., Registered Offices: 80 Strand, London WC2R 0RL, England

This is a work of fiction. Names, characters, places, and incidents either are the product of the
author's imagination or are used fictitiously, and any resemblance to actual persons, living or dead,
business establishments, events, or locales is entirely coincidental. The publisher does not have
any control over and does not assume any responsibility for author or third-party websites or their
contents.

TIES THAT BIND

A Berkley Sensation Book / published by arrangement with the author

PRINTING HISTORY
Berkley Sensation mass-market edition / June 2006

Copyright © 2006 by Mary Catherine Schaefer.
Cover illustration by Franco Accornero.
Cover design by George Long.
Interior text design by Stacy Irwin.

ISBN: 0-425-21053-7

BERKLEY® SENSATION
Berkley Sensation Books are published by The Berkley Publishing Group,
a division of Penguin Group (USA) Inc.,
375 Hudson Street, New York, New York 10014.
BERKLEY SENSATION and the "B" design are trademarks belonging to Penguin Group (USA)
Inc.

PRINTED IN THE UNITED STATES OF AMERICA

10 9 8 7 6 5 4 3 2 1

TIES THAT BIND

ONE

WHEN REESE BISHOP approached the front door of his ex-wife's chic condo, and it swung open to reveal her young lover, he felt like he always did when he encountered Tyler Sloan—old!

"Sloan," Reese said tightly.

"Bishop." The guy always seemed uncomfortable around Reese, which gave him some satisfaction. "Is Kaitlyn expecting you?"

"No." And she wasn't going to be happy, he thought, gripping the newspaper he held in his hand. "She's here, isn't she?"

"In the shower." Tyler scowled as he shrugged into a casual, unconstructed jacket. His hair askew, his clothing rumpled, it was obvious how he'd spent the night. "I'll let you inside," he said tightly, "and wait till she's finished showering and dressed."

"That won't be necessary. I'll be fine. I'll wait downstairs until she's done."

As he watched the other man trundle down the slate walkway in the warm April sunshine, Reese sighed. It came as no surprise that Kate had a younger man in her life. Though she was forty-five, and had never been drop-dead gorgeous, there was a vibrancy about her, in the snap of her dark eyes, in the glow of her complexion. Hell, even her rich, mink-colored hair shimmered. Men had never been able to stop staring at her. He'd been smitten himself the first time he laid eyes on her, while in law school at Yale. But that had been a lifetime ago. Now, when he thought about the past, he remembered only the fights and the pain of their permanent split. It had ripped him apart.

Reese stepped inside the condo and closed the door. Most everything was white in Kate's house—walls, carpets, leather furniture. The stark décor was accented by black-and-white prints that decorated the walls, black geometric-shaped pillows, and black vases sprouting white flowers. So different from the warm wood-and-earth tone furnishings of the home they had bought just before Sofie was born. A sprawling cedar-sided farmhouse just on the outskirts of town, they'd lovingly restored every single room. Some of the work they'd contracted out, but they'd done much of the renovation themselves, which had made it *theirs*. He'd bought out Kate's half during the divorce, but had been unable to live there without her. Though he couldn't sell it then—it was on the market now—he'd used the rental money to pay the mortgage on his current, simpler ranch house.

Reese was examining a photo on a coffee table and turned when he heard Kate speak behind him. "Ty? Is that you? Did you bring back that buff bod to—" She broke off when she entered the room and found Reese.

For some reason, her sexy tease irritated him. Whenever he was around Kate, Reese felt like there was a coil inside him that was ready to spring at the slightest provocation. So there was a clip in his voice when he said, "Sorry, my *bod* doesn't appeal to you anymore."

Her dark eyes fired at his retort. "What are you doing here?"

"I need to talk to you. Sloan let me in."

Rubbing the towel on her wet hair, she shook her head. Wrapped up in a red satiny robe, even her dishabille was attractive. *Damn her.* Though he hated her for what she'd done to their marriage, and worse, had lost respect for her as a person, the physical spark between them had never quite been doused. "Look, Reese, I don't have time for you this morning."

"Well, make time, sweetheart."

Her whole body tightened. "Oh, my God, is something wrong with Sofie?"

He softened his tone. "Not the last time I spoke with her. Our daughter's fine. Well, as fine as a sixteen-year-old can be living a hundred miles away from her parents in that private school."

The cool façade, the one Kate adopted with him routinely now—she was none too happy about his part in their breakup—replaced the worried mother. "Then can't this wait? My day's packed. I'm running late already."

"It can't wait. And you may have to alter your schedule."

"Really, Reese." She hated being told what to do and always needed to be in control. Then again, so did he. The combination had worked surprisingly well for them for almost fifteen years.

He handed the newspaper to her. "You won't be in any hurry to get to the courthouse after you see this." His heart beat faster. He still couldn't believe what he'd read in this morning's *Herald.*

She dropped the towel onto the floor; he remembered how much she cluttered things up . . . and another towel she dropped years ago.

My messiness is part of me, love.

You're lazy, Katie, admit it.

However, at the time, since she'd bared her luscious body to him, and she'd plastered the whole length of her against him, he hadn't cared that she was a slob. He'd taken her against the wall, if he remembered correctly.

Ruthlessly, he shoved the reminiscence back into the

compartment where it belonged. Those memories only caused his anger at her to seep out. "Read the headlines." He'd memorized them. LONGSHORE FEDERAL CORREC- TIONAL INSTITUTION INMATE DIES OF DRUG OVERDOSE. And beneath it, *Local judge and lawyer blamed in suicide note.*

Kate's hands gripped the paper. "Not us," she whispered.

He fought hard not to be moved by her vulnerability. "Yes, us. A woman we defended years ago, Anna Bingham."

"Tell me. My glasses are upstairs and I haven't put in my contacts."

He eased the paper from her hands. "We defended her on credit card fraud." Which wasn't the kind of case they usually represented in the law firm they'd started together here in Westwood, New York, but they'd taken on a lot of pro bono work that year and needed more paying clients. "She was running a dot-com scam and got caught. She ended up in a federal prison camp." The level of incarcera- tion for white-collar crime.

"Longshore's not a prison camp. It's medium security." She referred to the New Jersey prison, two hours from Westwood.

"Apparently, she did her time, got out, and repeated her offenses. Twice. She was sent to Longshore six months ago."

"Read me what it says about us."

"This is her suicide note. 'I had an affair with Reese Bishop during my trial. When his wife found out, they didn't do enough to keep me out of jail. After that experi- ence, my life went downhill. Now, I'm in for ten years. I can't handle the bars, the cell, the other inmates. I don't want to live.' "

Kate's entire body stiffened. Her dark eyes lost their hot-chocolate warmth and turned frosty. "I see. Is it true? Did you have an affair with Anna Bingham?"

He reined in his pique. "No, I didn't. It's all a lie. You know we didn't act unethically because of some ridicu- lous allegation that I screwed her and you wanted her out of the way."

"You could have told her I knew."

"Accusations again, Kate?"

"Well," Kate said in her best judge voice, "it wouldn't be the first time, now would it?"

Reese stared at the woman he once loved to distraction, unable to believe she could still drive him crazy. "You forget, darling, I was provoked."

Her face turned ashen but she regrouped quickly. "There's blame on both sides, Reese."

Slowly folding the paper, he pulled himself up to his six-foot-plus height. She was five-seven, so he had an advantage. "Could we for once try to be civil to each other?" His tone was sharper than he intended, so he calmed himself and finished, "This is going to cause havoc in both our jobs. We have to put our animosity aside."

Crossing her arms over her chest, she tossed her head back. Her hair had started to dry, and without the blower to tame it, the thick locks were curling around her face. These days she wore it straight or in a knot at her neck. He preferred the wild tangle it used to be. "Give me a minute to put some clothes on. And call my assistant. Then we can talk this out."

He merely nodded.

"There's coffee. Tyler made it."

"Of course," he muttered. "Tyler—the incarnation of Mr. Wonderful." Damn, he hated that talking doll who quipped all the things an ideal man should say.

With one last flinty look, Kate headed out the door and up the stairs. Reese drew in a heavy breath. She made him crazy *and* reduced him to making nasty comments. He couldn't think clearly around her now.

Not that he ever could, he reminded himself as he found her all-white, sterile kitchen and grabbed for the pot of coffee her lover had brewed. From the day he met Kaitlyn Renado, his life had been a roller-coaster ride. Only after their divorce had it evened out.

One broken heart was a small price to pay for being off that ride.

* * *

TWO HOURS LATER, in her sunny breakfast nook, Kate
sat across from her ex-husband, and tried to study the file
before her. Earlier, she and Reese had had a phone conference with their attorneys, who planned to talk to the New
Jersey police regarding the investigation into Bingham's
death, then contact the prison to see what they could find
out. Because it was Friday, they weren't sure how far
they'd get.

Kate and Reese also had some tasks. Their first step was
to analyze the law office's file on Anna Bingham. They
each had a copy of it, thanks to Reese's efficient secretary,
Yolanda, who used to be Kate's secretary, too. The woman
had mothered them both when they started their firm and
hired her. Kate and Reese, each having been motherless for
years, had loved it. Kate now stared down at file, blocking
the nostalgic memory, shutting out the sight of Reese,
wishing she could shut him out of her life completely.

It had been five years since their divorce, and, thank
God, she'd gotten a handle on her feelings for him. For the
first year or so, she'd cried at night because of what happened those last few months, but gradually she'd begun to
heal. The following two years included days and weeks
when she didn't think about him at all. Eventually, her life
was fine without him. But at times like these, when she
came face-to-face with him, or especially when what had
happened in the past reared its ugly head, her resentment
toward him and the hurt he'd caused her surfaced abruptly.

Thank God no one except her dearest friend, Jillian
Jenkins, knew how being with her ex could still affect her.
Tyler had some stupid male insecurity about Reese, so
Kate never admitted to him how hard it was to have contact
with Reese, nor how much their split had hurt. Only Jillian
was privy to the fact that losing the only man Kate had ever
really loved, and the horrible way they treated each other at
the end, could still cut her heart to ribbons.

Damn it. She had to concentrate on the matter at hand. She could work on this until one p.m., then she had to take her afternoon cases. Family court judges heard an average of fifty to sixty cases a day and had no room for absenteeism. That she'd shuffled her load to someone else this morning didn't sit right with Kate. But she'd had no choice. They had to get to the bottom of this mess.

She sneaked a peek at Reese; he was due in court, too, for a pretrial hearing at three. He wore a beautiful pinstriped suit but had removed his tie and jacket and rolled up the sleeves of his shirt. His dark hair fell onto his forehead, which was tanned. He'd probably spent some vacation time in the Caribbean, his favorite place now, with his own private beach bunny. His sage-green eyes were intense even through the glasses he wore only when he was tired. Absently he rolled a pen between his palms, something he often did when he was thinking. For a brief minute, she remembered what those hands felt like on her bare skin.

Really good.

Her cell phone rang, dragging her from her memories. Reese scowled at it, but said nothing as she picked it up from the table. "Hello."

"Hey, gorgeous. I was just calling to see how it went with the ex." Tyler's voice pitched sexily low. "And protecting what's mine."

"I'm at home, and Reese is still here. Something's happened." Briefly she explained, in case he saw the paper.

"Kaitlyn, honey, I'm so sorry."

"I'll call you when I have more information."

Reese glanced over when she clicked off. His mouth thinned. "Lover boy checking up on you?"

"He's concerned." Her eyes narrowed. "Does your little sweet thing know about this?"

"Not yet." He closed the file and held it up. "I don't see anything here, do you?"

She shook her head. "It's pretty cut and dried. Anna Bingham came to our firm ten years ago, and we defended her for fraud. She was guilty as hell. Only your expertise got her self-surrender at Danbury, and a stint of sixteen months with time off for good behavior. I heard that at some point she got a prison advocate to help her through the process."

Frowning, he sat back in the chair. "I wonder why she didn't come back to us when she got in trouble again."

Kate's jaw clenched.

He noticed. "What?"

"Nothing. Unless what she says is true."

Slapping the file on the table, he leaned forward. "Fuck it, Kate! If you're not going to believe me, no one else will. We won't have a shot in hell of coming off innocent if my own partner-at-the-time doesn't stand behind me."

He was right. She hated when he was right. "I know. Swear to God you're not lying in this. If you are, it's okay. Just tell me. We'll go from there."

The corner of his mouth turned up in a begrudging grin. It had been one of many private things between them, for big and little testimonials . . . *Swear to God you like this dress and aren't just saying you do . . . Swear to God you don't think I was wrong in that case . . . Swear to God you still love me like you did when we were first married.*

"I swear to God," he said, his tone sincere. "I never had an affair with Anna Bingham." Slashes of scarlet appeared on his high cheekbones. "I strayed *once*, and you know why."

Kate's own face burned. She remembered the day she caught her husband of fourteen years with another woman. His car had been parked in front of the young woman's building, in the middle of the day, for all to see. It had been as if he was flaunting his indiscretion. Jillian had driven past the vehicle and called Kate. Raw from their prolonged emotional distance and the yelling matches that broke out routinely, she'd gone over to the house and confronted the Malibu Barbie, who answered the door in a skimpy robe. Kate had barged through the entrance and stalked up the stairs. Reese had been naked in bed, smoking a cigarette.

"All right," she finally managed now. "I'll believe that."

"You don't sound convinced." His voice was still tight. "Again, if you aren't . . ."

"No, I am." She bent back the corner of the file and felt that old vulnerability to Reese, and only to Reese, overcome her. "Truthfully, I was shocked that you went to someone else. Regardless of what happened, we'd always been enough for each other."

Removing his glasses, he braced his arms on the table. They were muscular and strong, sprinkled with dark hair. "You were enough for me, Kate. Maybe too much." He sighed, suddenly seeming weary. "It was the other stuff."

Her heart beat at a clip. "You mean you did it to punish me?"

"Partly, I guess. But mostly, I did it to stop the pain."

"Did it? Stop the pain?"

"Some." He scrubbed a hand over his face.

She shook her head. "This is old ground."

"I know." Again, he held up the file. "Resurrected because of Anna Bingham."

"Let's bury it back where it belongs."

"Agreed. So, we're square that I didn't do what she accuses?"

"We're square. But hell, Reese, how are we going to prove it? Come out from under it all? This kind of scandal could ruin both of us."

"You got that right. My credibility as a lawyer will be shot. If people believe I behaved unethically, I'll be lucky to hold on to the clients I have, let alone bring in new business."

"I'll be called before the Judicial Conduct Commission. A judge can't have her ethics questioned like this."

"No sense in panicking," he said gruffly.

"I agree. We have to just plow through it all until we find the answers."

In this, as in so many other ways, they were perfectly matched: They were perfectionists who took charge, were self-disciplined, and had high expectations of themselves and others. They didn't wallow in worry, but took action.

"We'll do what the lawyers said," he went on. "Now that we've scrutinized the file, we'll look at the trial transcript. And I already have Yolanda downloading any information from the Internet on Anna Bingham. There's some reason the woman lied about us in her suicide note, and we'll find it. I promise."

Kate swallowed back the doubt. He'd made promises in the past that he had been unable to keep.

She only hoped to God this time his words held quarter. Kate didn't know if she could handle losing her beloved profession. It was all she had left after Reese divorced her and her daughter stopped talking to her.

AS DRAY MERRILL ducked into Starbucks and headed toward his table, Tyler studied her. A blue-eyed blonde, she was lovely. But she held no appeal for him. When had he become so drawn to luscious dark hair and the supple body of mature womanhood? Dray owned a gym, The Iron Butterfly, and was toned and fit. But she lacked Kaitlyn's sensuality. And her strong, forceful personality. Where Kate was a blinding diamond, Dray was a soft moonstone.

"Hi," she said as she took a chair. She wore a lightweight sweatsuit that matched her eyes; he guessed she was on her way to work. "What's up?"

Tyler felt himself flush. "They're together as we speak." He was always self-conscious talking like this to Dray. And she had voiced similar feelings of discomfort. But the situation they found themselves in was unusual, and they'd unexpectedly discovered an ally in each other.

A frown marred her brow. She was a few years younger than he, and the bloom of youth still went unhampered on her face. "Why aren't they at work? Reese said before he left this morning that his day was crazy."

"There's trouble, which is going to cause havoc for us, I think." He explained what Kaitlyn had told him a couple of hours earlier, about the newspaper article. All morning, he'd refrained from calling back to check up on her.

"Damn it." Dray sipped her coffee. He'd ordered it, knowing what she liked. This wasn't the first such meeting, though each time, Tyler hoped it would be the last. "Well, we can't keep them apart forever," she added.

They'd done a pretty good job of that. "I . . ." Tyler ran a hand through his hair. "We shouldn't have to. If she'd just marry me, like I asked. And if he'd let down his walls with you, we wouldn't have to go through this anxiety."

She smiled softly and squeezed his hand where it rested on the table. "I'm not sure any of that would make a difference. They're connected, Tyler. Try as we might, we haven't been able to break that bond. That tie between them."

"Sofie's the tie."

She shook her head. Streaked blond hair escaped from a ponytail and glistened in the overhead lights. "Not just their daughter. There's something between them. They're so alike—competitive, take-charge, ambitious. Reese told me once that even though similar personalities often clashed, for some reason his and Kate's meshed and brought out the best in each other."

"I guess we should be glad they fight so much when they're together now, so that the bond gets masked." The caffe latte he was drinking tasted bitter. "We're pathetic."

Dray shrugged. "Yeah. I wish there was a twelve-step program somewhere for insecurity."

He relaxed. She always made him feel better. He was in a hell of a situation. Thirty-six, successful pediatrician pioneering a new Well Child Project in his medical practice, attractive enough. And in love with someone who wouldn't commit to him. All his life he'd nurtured significant relationships in the hope they'd work out, like his parents' solid, happy marriage, but he'd never found anyone he could connect with. Now that he had, he'd chosen a woman who wouldn't have him.

He was very afraid she was still in love with her ex-husband.

"What are you thinking?" Dray asked him. "You've got this horrible look on your face."

Tyler shrugged. "Just what we've talked about before. I think they still love each other."

Dray watched the man seated across from her. He was a nice guy, real eye candy, smart to boot. And, she thought wryly, totally in love with Kate Renado. What was with guys and that woman? She was a man magnet. "If they do, it doesn't matter. They spar like cats and dogs whenever they get near each other. He won't admit it, but he still feels a lot of anger toward her. They couldn't live together again even if they wanted to. Reese has said *that* many times."

"You talk about Kaitlyn with him?"

"Sometimes." When she was really insecure. "He admits he loved her to distraction. But he also says she drove him crazy at the end."

"He's the crazy one, to have let her go."

"Well, lucky for us that he did." She stirred her latte. "So, do you think we should do anything about this newest situation?"

He shook his head, his slate blue eyes sad. "No, I just thought you'd want to know."

Again she squeezed his hand. "I do. And I appreciate you thinking of me."

"Hey, I got a lot to lose."

"So do I." The only man she ever loved in her life. "I hope—"

"Uh-oh." Tyler's face reddened.

"What?"

"Kaitlyn's best friend just walked in. And saw us." His eyes got a bit panicky. "Will she know you?"

"Is it Judge Jenkins?"

"Yep."

"She'll know me."

"Brace yourself." He pasted on a phony smile. "Hey, Jillian, how are you?"

Jillian Jenkins resembled Susan Sarandon, and just like the gutsy, outspoken actress, was a force to be reckoned with. As was Kate. Dray had heard they were called the dynamic duo of family court. "Hi, Tyler." She turned shrewd brown eyes on Dray. "Hello. Dray, isn't it? Reese's friend."

"Yes." Her smile was as phony as Tyler's. "How are you, Jillian?"

"I'm good." The judge glanced from Dray to Tyler. "What's going on here?" she asked in her trademark no-nonsense manner.

"Dray and I bumped into each other getting coffee. We were just shooting the breeze." He frowned. "Did you see the paper today?"

Jillian waited a heartbeat, probably assessing Tyler's story. "Yes, I tried to get Kate, but she isn't answering her phone."

"She and Reese are meeting with their lawyers this morning."

"Ah, I see." Jillian checked her watch. "Well, I'm on a break, so I'll be going." Her smile was innocuous, but her words weren't when she said, "I'm sure you two have a lot to discuss," then walked away.

"Hell," Tyler said scowling into his coffee.

"Think she'll tell Kate?"

"As soon as she can. Wouldn't you?"

"Probably."

"Will you lie to Reese about meeting me intentionally?"

"I wish Reese would care enough so that I had to lie."

"You live with the guy, at least. Kaitlyn won't let me move in."

"No, I think you two are closer than Reese and I are." Reese always maintained a subtle distance from her, one she'd bet her new elliptical equipment on that he didn't have with Kate when they were together. "Despite the living arrangements." She gathered her things and stood. "I have to go. I have a class to teach at noon. Stay in touch."

"Yeah sure. And thanks, for listening to my ranting."

"We're on the same side."

"I wish there weren't sides."

"I know, me, too."

As Dray turned, she caught sight of Jillian Jenkins sipping coffee at the sidebar. The woman made no pretense that she was doing anything but watching Dray and Tyler. Dray nodded to her and headed out the door.

She felt like an idiot. She felt deceptive. She felt worthless. But she loved Reese Bishop, and she knew in her heart that her only competition was his beautiful, smart, well-respected ex-wife.

Who'd practically destroyed him. Dray would be damned if she let Kate Renado get another chance to finish the job. With that unselfish thought in mind, she walked toward her car.

SOFIE BISHOP SLID to the floor of her closet and buried her face in her hands. The nightmares she was having sucked and had kept her up until five this morning. She'd zonked out after lunch, missing classes. Her stomach hurt and even her skin burned. The hole she was digging for herself was deep and she couldn't climb out.

For a minute she considered calling her father. But he'd rush up here like a knight in shining armor and a) force her to go home with him or b) make promises to her he couldn't keep.

Go home. What a flamin' joke. She didn't have a home anymore. Not since the big D. Not since her mother ditched the coolest man in the world, forcing her dad to hook up with some bimbo. Now the illustrious judge had a young lover, an ult pad and a new life. No room there for a daughter who hated her guts.

Well, fuck her. Sofie crawled over to a box on the floor, opened it and pulled out a reefer. She lit it, sucked in the mellow pleasure and, after two more puffs, could finally breathe again. Nope, Sofie wouldn't call her parents. She'd have to drag herself out of this pit all by herself. And she would. Much as she hated to admit it, she had her mother's grit. She'd survive and be a success in life.

And probably, despite what everybody else thought, she'd be as unhappy as Kaitlyn Renado was. Her mother hid it well from the world, but Sofie knew the real truth about the woman who had given birth to her.

Two

"ALL RISE. THE Honorable Judge Kaitlyn Renado presiding."

Kate entered her courtroom to the familiar announcement, forcing herself to concentrate on the case she was to hear and not think about Reese and the deathbed charge by a federal inmate. From day one, the courtroom had been her refuge. She remembered that first morning she was to preside; she'd been furious with Reese for not being there the night before to help her cope with the anxiety of her debut on the bench. Not only wasn't he there to give support, but their final divorce papers had been served that afternoon. She vowed then never to let thoughts of him enter the courtroom.

Portia Elliot, her assistant, sat off to the side. She was a feisty black woman who was studying for her law degree at night, and managed Kate's caseload with the skill of a magician. Kate glanced at the folders stacked on the bench. They were color coded by type of case: blue for domestic violence, yellow for custody and visitation, green for neglect and abuse, black for paternity. She noted a red one:

surrender of parental rights which, for a myriad of reasons, everyone in the New York justice system dreaded.

Action on all cases would range from brief proceedings to short hearings to full-blown trials, with the judge as the only decision maker. There were no juries in family court. It was one o'clock in the afternoon, and by five she might hear thirty or more cases.

Somber faced, she looked out at the assembled cast for a brief proceeding on an order of protection. The caseworker from CWA, Child Welfare Agency, stood and made a presentation requesting that a boy of six be taken from the home of a single parent until a complete evaluation could be performed.

Kate studied the overworked woman. "And your reason for this, Ms. Smith, is"—she glanced at her notes—"bruises identified by the school nurse."

"Yes, Your Honor. We have reason to believe they were inflicted by the older brother."

"And that's because?"

"The boy told us. But the mother can't be reached. And the brother was too busy at work to come here today."

"Are you saying the child is living with just his brother?" Again, she checked her notes. "Who is sixteen years old?"

"That's what we want to find out. Meanwhile, we're worried about Sammy. We need time to unravel all this."

"Then do so. Temporary order of protection is granted. Ms. Smith, I'll see you back here . . ."

Kate looked at Portia who said, "Three days from now at three o'clock."

Kate pounded the gavel that she'd bought herself, along with a formal judicial robe, when she was appointed as a judge. Traditionally, a spouse or significant other gave the two items as gifts, but Reese hadn't been around to bring presents—something she still resented.

Kate spent two hours dispatching cases—foster-care arrangements, neglect hearings, domestic-violence incidents.

At nearly three o'clock, Portia leaned over. "Judge Renado, you should take a break before the next one. It's time for the termination of parental rights case."

Moaning, Kate shook her head. "No, let's do this first. Then I'll *need* a break."

Portia glanced at Lucy Linstrom, Kate's clerk, and Robert Cannon, her stenographer; all of them knew Kate was a stickler with these types of cases and lingered over them more than most judges.

"All right, Mr. Vance. You're the Legal Aid lawyer for the petitioner, Ms. Monica Leahy?" A beanpole of a girl, Monica wore her hair cut short and a sullen teenage scowl. One Kate was all too familiar with. It was Sofie's favorite expression these days.

"Yes, Your Honor," the lawyer replied.

She glanced at the respondent. "Ms. Leahy, are you Monica's mother?" The woman looked about thirty. "Yes, Your Honor."

"Do you have counsel?"

"Um, no."

Glancing to the back, where a redheaded man sat, Kate nodded to him. He was an 18-B lawyer, named for the statute that provided for a court-appointed attorney. They earned fifty dollars an hour and waited to be appointed by the judge.

"Mr. Simons, can you step up?"

"Yes, Your Honor."

"Let's begin. Ms. Leahy," she said to the mother, "do you understand what terminating parental rights means?"

"I won't be Monnie's mother no more."

"Correct. Legally, you will have no say over anything she does."

"She ain't got no say anyway," Monica spoke out.

"Mr. Vance, please inform your client that she isn't to speak out of turn." Kate glanced back to the mother, who was worrying the strap of her purse. "Ms. Leahy? I'd like to ask you some questions." Kate always fired off at least a dozen questions before she even considered terminating parental rights. "Has anyone coerced you, made any threat or used any force to bring you to surrender?"

"No, Your Honor."

"Has anyone promised you anything in return for this surrender?"

"Just some peace of mind." This from Monica.

A few snickers.

"Excuse me?" Kate said in her stern judge voice.

"I'm incorrigible," Monica spoke again. "She don't want me."

"You're not to speak, young lady, unless asked. If you continue to do so, I will take punitive action. Do you understand that?"

"Yeah."

"Ms. Leahy, are you surrendering this child of your own free will because you want to, and for no other reason?"

"Yes, ma'am."

God, how could a mother surrender her child?

"Monnie'll be better off with a mother who can handle her."

Out of nowhere, came Sofie's enraged face and spiteful words, three years after the divorce. Kate had been seeing Tyler for a while, but their relationship had just begun to get serious. *I'd be better off with a different mother. I don't want to live with you. I hate this stupid condo and that jerk you date. You ruined my life.*

"Do you understand that if I accept this petition, your surrender will be effective immediately and will be irrevocable? By that I mean, never able to be changed. You will never be her mother again."

For one brief moment, Mrs. Leahy faltered. She looked longingly at the girl. The daughter was swallowing hard. That was all Kate needed.

She often postponed these kinds of cases. Sometimes the reason was one party's confusion over what was happening, sometimes it was signs of hesitation. Sometimes, it was just a gut feeling. But surrender of parental rights was serious business and no judge did it capriciously. She almost always adjourned the first time to give everybody a chance to think over such an unalterable move. The hesitation she saw in the two women prodded her to do just that.

"I am not fully convinced this is what either of you wants. I'd like to see you both back here in six weeks. If you're here, and fully convinced surrender is what you want, then I'll terminate rights."

And, as always happened, Kate couldn't help the impromptu lecture that came from her mouth. Some people said her tendency to give advice made her a great judge and some people warned that it made her look like a sap. She wondered what Reese would think. "Ms. Leahy— Monica. I urge you to try to make peace with your mother." Easier said than done, Kate knew. "The bond between a mother and child should never be severed."

Please, Sofie, don't insist on this. I can't bear for you to be living away from me.

She turned to the other woman. "Ms. Leahy, try to reconcile with your daughter. The court can provide counseling for you both to see what's best for you. You're breaking the natural order of things if you give her up."

The mother nodded. The girl looked down.

When she pounded the gavel, Kate was drained.

"I'm calling for a fifteen-minute recess."

As the burly, uniformed court officer, Carlos Rayes, left to notify those in the waiting area, Kate headed to her chambers. Once inside she closed the door and let her own, private domain calm her. The room was elegant and classy. Enclosed in frosted glass and rich oak, it had a secure yet professional feel to it. She crossed to the small fridge she kept in the corner and removed a bottle of water. She retrieved her cell phone from her desk, sank onto the soft leather, chestnut colored couch, and checked her voice mail. Two messages from Tyler. One from Sofie's school. Three from Reese. One from Jillian asking her to have a drink after work.

She dialed Sofie's school, only to be told her daughter had missed classes again today. She tried Sofie's cell, but there was no answer. She closed her eyes, breathed slowly and let in the thoughts of that fateful day when her only child had demanded to go away to school . . .

Reese had tried to convince his daughter otherwise. "Sofie, honey, your mother and I love you. You need to be with us."

Still, Sofie remained stone faced. "That's the last thing I need. I don't want to be with her."

Ah, the awful truth. *Her*, Kate, not *them*.

So Kate had swallowed her pride and squelched the horror of Sofie's statement. "All right then, you can live with your dad full time. At least you'll be with one of us."

But Sofie surprised her. "I don't wanna live with his bimbo." Dray and Reese had just moved in together. "Anyway, I wanna be away. From both of you."

And so, the child of her heart had been enrolled in a private school a hundred miles away. Kate had not only lost the man she'd loved more than God, but also the daughter she cherished more than her own life. Looking around at her chambers, she thought about the Leahys and wondered, starkly, how different her own family was from them.

With that depressing thought, she headed back to the courtroom.

"DRAY? IT'S REESE." Sitting back in his office, he propped his feet up on the desk and anchored his cell phone between his ear and shoulder. "Sorry, I didn't get to call you sooner."

"That's okay. Rough day?"

"The worst. Did you see the paper?"

She hesitated. Damn he should have contacted her right away to tell her himself about Anna Bingham's accusation and the ensuing publicity. "Yes, I saw the paper. I'm sorry you have to go through this."

"Thanks. How's your day?"

"Fine. Busy."

"Look, I'm not going to be able to make it tonight." She

always cooked on Friday nights and they shared a romantic meal alone. After which they'd make love. It was a special time for them as a couple.

"I can wait if you're going to be late."

"I have no idea what time I'll be done here. Kate's coming over after she finishes at the courthouse and we're getting started on some things suggested by the lawyers."

"You already met with your lawyers?" There was a little bit of pout in her voice at having been kept in the dark.

"A conference call this morning. I'm sorry, honey. I know I should have filled you in on all this."

"It's okay, Reese. You have a lot on your mind. We can catch up this weekend."

Uh-oh. "I'm going to see Sofie tomorrow."

"Did you tell me that?"

"I might not have." He knew he hadn't. Sofie had specifically asked that his young bimbo—her words—not come with him to visit.

"Hmm." She waited. When it became apparent he wasn't going to invite her to go along, she said, "Well, Sunday maybe."

"Yes, of course. Why don't you call one of your girlfriends and do something tomorrow?"

"Maybe."

"All right. Well, don't wait up for me."

"We'll see. At least get something to eat."

"I will." He clicked off, feeling like a first-class jerk. Sometimes, he just didn't think about Dray, about calling her or confiding in her. He and Kate had worked hard at talking to each other, recognizing they both had a tendency to keep to themselves. But it had been easier to bare his soul with his ex-wife. With Dray, he couldn't seem to open up. He had to do better. He hated hurting her. She was a beautiful woman, generous to a fault, and very much in love with him; his friends envied his relationship with her. He needed to be more appreciative of her devotion.

He glanced at the clock. He and Kate had played phone tag all day; finally, she'd left him a message saying she'd be at his office by seven. He'd order food to be delivered. Kate loved Italian cuisine, so he'd get her favorites: gnocchi, green salad and cannoli. Chocolate. He was dialing for the takeout before he cursed himself for remembering what the woman—who had hurt him more than anyone in the world, and whom he was glad to have out of his life—liked to eat.

His relationship with Dray was so much simpler. He was indeed a lucky man.

"TYLER, IT'S ME."

"Hi, doll. Where are you?"

"I'm waiting at Gavels to meet Jillian for a drink."

A long hesitation. She wondered why. "Will you be out late?"

"Yes. I'll be quick with Jillian, but I'm going over to the law offices to work with Reese on this Bingham thing. He got more documents during the day for us to review."

"I see. I'll be done at seven. Want some help with that?"

"No, I think Reese and I need to hash this out together."

"Whatever you think is best. Come here after?"

"It'll be late."

"I don't mind."

"Maybe. I'll let you know."

"I'll count on you."

Kate clicked off with a heavy heart. Tyler was unhappy, she could tell by the tone of his voice. But she needed to do this investigation with Reese, and truthfully, having Tyler around would make things more tense. Already, she was stressed, not only because of the accusation and publicity, but about being with her ex-husband again. Hell, she didn't have any choice! They had to figure out this whole Bingham thing—and fast, before their reputations were destroyed. So she'd bite the bullet and spend time with Reese again. She vowed to be better around him, not sniping and sarcastic. Maybe he would, too, though she sensed a seething anger in him when they were together. For both their sakes, they needed clear heads, unclouded by the past, to save their jobs.

Problem was, the past was like a tangible presence in the room whenever she was with Reese. It was a past that had almost destroyed them both, but there had been so many wonderful years, that were almost impossible to forget . . .

She'd met Reese that first, harrowing year at law school. Kate had secreted herself away in a cubicle in the Yale library, studying for her International Law course when a shadow fell over her desk. She looked up to see a shaggy-haired guy in disreputable jeans and flannel shirt standing over her. He had startling green eyes. "Hi, Kate Renado," he'd said in a low, smirking tone.

"Do we know each other?" she asked.

"Not yet. But we will."

"Excuse me?"

"You got a higher grade than me on that last International Law exam." IL grades were posted for all to see.

"I beat everybody," she said, matching his tone.

"This time. I'm going to be valedictorian of our class."

"Salutatorian, maybe. I'll be number one."

He grinned then. She didn't know it at the time, but that grin would get him into her pants, literally, and into her life sooner than she could blink. "No way, sweetheart. But I need somebody to study with."

"No study group for you? What, didn't they want someone with such a humble attitude?"

"Most of them go too slow. I figure you could keep up with me."

"I could run over you, hotshot. What's your name anyway?"

"Reese Bishop."

"Hello, Reese Bishop. Now go away." She glanced back down at her book, hoping he didn't leave. Even then she'd wanted to be with him.

"You don't have a group, either. For the same reason." Again the grin. "You might as well give in now. You'll succumb eventually."

"Modest aren't you?"

"Modesty doesn't get you valedictorian, a good clerking position, your own firm, then a judgeship."

"Is that what you're shooting for?"

"Yeah. Though I'd do pro bono stuff, too, to help poor people like me. What about you?"

She wanted the exact same things. "Maybe."

"Come on, Katie."

She scowled. "Nobody calls me that."

"Good. I'm special."

"Go away."

"I'll be back."

"Like the Terminator."

He winked at her and then swaggered down the aisle. He pestered her for a few weeks until she finally gave in.

She had no idea that fateful Friday would change her life forever . . .

"Kate? Hi, sorry I'm late."

Startled, Kate looked up. It took her a minute to realize who spoke to her, that she was at Gavels, in the present time, and that she'd been thinking about when she and Reese met.

"Where were you?"

"Oh, God, in the past."

Jillian's expression was sympathetic. "As well you would be. I'm so sorry about those allegations in the paper."

"I can't believe it, Jillian. And I'm scared to death all of it's going to hurt my career. A federal judge can't afford this kind of scandal."

Sliding into the booth across from her, Jillian removed her coat, revealing a dynamite red cashmere sweater. "Innocent until proven guilty, girl," she said, signaling the waiter, ordering a Manhattan and folding her hands on the table. Jillian was the most efficient person she knew. And the most loyal. She would stand by Kate during anything, especially so after she'd contracted breast cancer three years ago and, during the months subsequent to her surgery, Kate had moved into Jill's house—lock, stock and barrel—to take care of her.

"I certainly hope so." Kate sipped her apple martini. "I can't understand how this happened."

"He didn't cheat on you with pretty Anna Bingham?"

No need for names. "Not with her. Actually, he contends Malibu Barbie was the only one he cheated with. And then it was because of what I did."

"Speaking of Malibu Barbies, I saw Dray Merrill today."

Reese's young lover. Slender, fragile, nurturing in a way Kate had never been. And a good thirteen years younger. "Where?"

"Starbucks, across the street."

"Hmm. I think her gym is near here. If I recall, that's how she met Reese. He worked out there on lunch hours."

"She was with Tyler."

"Tyler? *My* Tyler?" At Jillian's nod, Kate said, "Why?"

"I marched right over and asked them."

Kate chuckled. "You would. What did he say?"

"That they'd bumped into each other and stopped to chat."

"Sounds odd."

"He was lying."

"How do you know?"

"Judge's instinct."

"Hmm. Circumstantial evidence at best." Her heart started beating a bit faster. "I can't believe anything's going on there. Dray Merrill thinks Reese walks on water."

"So did you, at one time."

"He has that effect on women."

"In any case, Tyler wouldn't cheat. He's crazy about you."

"So why were they together?"

"Observation of their body language tells me they were talking about you and Reese."

"Really?"

"Maybe they're worried this case thing will throw you two back together and you'll realize you're still in love with each other."

A huge gaping hole made itself known in Kate's heart. "You know how I feel about him." During those long periods after her surgery, when Jillian couldn't sleep, she and Kate had talked about everything. "I've gotten over him, don't think about him all that much, but he still has some kind of . . . power over me." She thought of his cutting words this morning, and how they'd thrown her emotions into a tailspin. "I have some residual feelings for him."

"Which, as you know, I've always thought are returned."

"I doubt it. Even so, I'll never let myself in for that kind of pain again. Neither would he, I'd guess." She thought of her daughter. "Mostly though, we didn't put Sofie through the horror of a divorce to fool around with something best left alone."

"I'm worried about your spending this time together."

"Me, too." She shrugged. "I'll just have protect my heart."

"I'm here if you need to talk."

"Thanks."

"What are you going to do about Tyler?"

"Nothing. He's a big boy, and has his own life."

"He'd love it if you were jealous."

"I'm not."

"Too bad. He's a great guy."

"That he is. Now, tell me about the great guy in your life. I have a half hour before I meet Reese."

"Okay, just be careful. With him."

"Always am. Now, let's change the subject before I start to panic."

Her friend smiled, and Kate counted her blessings that she had people in her life like Jillian and Tyler. She didn't need Reese Bishop anymore.

"LIGHT PINK SAUCE on the gnocchi. Peppercorn dressing on the salad. Garlic bread. And chocolate cannoli. At the office. Thanks, George." Reese hung up the phone and stared at it for a minute. "You're a idiot," he said aloud. How could he remember such minute details about his ex-wife?

And it wasn't just the food. He remembered sensory things—the way her lotion tasted on her skin, the coarse texture of her hair as it wound around his fingers, the sounds she made when he was inside her.

Fucking son of a bitch. He didn't want to recall any of that.

Rising, he strode to the bathroom off his office and changed into jeans and a sweater. It was almost seven and they'd be working for a while. At the end of the day, he and Kate had always had their fill of being dressed up and put on sweat suits or jeans as soon as they could. Arrgh . . . what the hell was going on here with all these flashes to the past?

Back at his desk, he pulled out the information he'd had his assistant gather today: a full transcript of the trial they conducted for Bingham, all of the Internet articles on the woman—regarding that trial and subsequent others where they were not her representation—and what was publicly know about her prison history.

But instead of seeing the words before him, Reese thought about casual clothes again, and ordering late night dinners when he and Kate were in law school. One time in particular . . .

"Food's here," he'd remarked one night when the doorbell to his tiny studio in New Haven rang.

Stretched out on her stomach on the floor, wearing a baby pink sweat suit, Kate glanced up at him. "Okay." She reached for her purse. "My treat." Since they were so poor and had gone to school on loans and scholarships, money was tight for both of them.

"No, I got it, Katie."

"No way, then this'll be like a date." She scowled. "And don't call me that."

He'd smiled, though weakly. They'd been spending all their free time together studying and sometimes discussing their futures; he was able to talk to this girl in a way he couldn't with other people. They still sparred verbally, but the teasing about being mortal enemies was wearing thin. He liked her and he got turned on by the subtlest of things. He took her money, though. She had an Italian temper and could go off like fireworks when somebody didn't listen to her.

They ate in the living room; she was seated on the floor, he was on the couch, both up close to the scarred coffee table. For some reason, her mouth drew his attention. He watched her munch on the bread with relish. Stuff down the pasta. Take sips of the cheap wine he had provided. "How come you don't gain any weight when you eat like a lumberjack?"

"Please, I'm way over my weight limit. I just don't care about it."

"I think you look great."

She must have caught his sincere—and interested—tone. "Thanks." She eyed his muscular body. "You do, too. Because you work out so hard." In exercise, like everything else, Reese was driven to be the best.

"I do. Gotta keep up my manly appearance," he joked.

She studied his unshaven jaw, his shoulders with utter seriousness. "You're the most *manly* guy I know."

"Really? You been hanging out with law students too long."

He thought he saw vulnerability in her eyes and regretted his taunt. "Maybe." She wiped her mouth and stood. "I'll clean up. We still have a lot of studying to do for the test."

When she came around the table and reached for his plate, he grabbed her hand. "Katie, I—"

Looking down at him, her eyes flared. He'd never touched her before. Her hand was warm, smooth, feminine. She cleared her throat nervously. He knew girls well enough to recognize her nervousness and the source of it. So he tugged.

She tumbled into his lap, and tossed back all those glorious curls. "What are you doing, hotshot?"

"Something I've wanted to do for weeks."

Tensing, she sucked in a breath. "This isn't a good idea."

He'd rubbed his thumb over her bottom lip. "You can sue me for forcing unwanted attention on you, but I'm going to kiss you, Katie. Right now."

"They're not unwanted, Reese," she whispered softly.

His body went from zero to sixty in seconds. "Katie . . ."

He'd kissed her then. Again and again.

They'd torn each other's clothes off.

And when he thrust inside her, he knew he'd never get enough of Kaitlyn Renado . . .

A loud knock jolted him from the memory of the first time they'd made love. Kate stood in the doorway. "Reese? Where were you?"

He shook his head to clear it. "Daydreaming. Come on in."

She hesitated at the entryway. Dressed in a beautiful peach suit and crisp blouse and heels, she looked every inch the intimidating judge. Yet somehow she looked feminine, too. A hell of a combination.

"What are you staring at?" she asked.

"It's odd seeing you here again." Once named Renado and Bishop, now called Bishop Associates, she'd helped design the layout, picked out colors, furniture and equipment along with him. It had been a heady time.

"It's odd *being* here."

"I'll bet." He stood. "Not painful, I hope."

"Nah. I got over you a long time ago."

Today, her barb felt like a slap in the face. "Ah, I see. Well, come on in. I hope you're hungry."

"Starved. Do you want to order dinner?"

"I already did. It should be here any minute."

"Good." She threw her stuff on a chair, slid out of her jacket and kicked off her shoes, then scanned his jeans and shirt. She drew sneakers out of her bag. "I wish I'd brought clothes to change into. I only had my running shoes in the car."

He watched her. "I have a sweat suit in the closet. Socks. You can borrow them."

She seemed surprised by his offer.

"Then again, if you want to plow through Italian food and files in a pretty little outfit, go ahead."

"Sure, I'll change. Thanks." He told her where the clothes were and she headed for the bathroom. While she was in there, the food arrived. He set it on the coffee table and snagged some water from the fridge.

When she came out, he had to bite his tongue at the sight of her in his clothes again. All those years ago, after they'd admitted their feelings for each other, they'd moved in together right away, and she often wore his stuff. At that time, neither could afford nice clothes, or enough clothes, really. She looked good in his navy fleece that drooped off her shoulder and had to be rolled up at the sleeves. Tearing his gaze away, he glanced down at the food and said in a voice that was way too hoarse, "I hope you still like this."

"Oh, God."

He chuckled. "I take that as a yes."

"Are you kidding? I love gnocchi." She dropped down on the floor and dug in. He sat across from her, on the couch. They enjoyed the spicy sauce and gooey potato-based macaroni in silence for a few minutes and he wondered what she was thinking.

When she finally took a breather, she cocked her head at him.

He said, "Just like old times, isn't it?"

"Not quite."

He stiffened. "No, of course not. What was I thinking?"

Her dark eyes sparkled with mischief. "We're twenty years older and at least fifteen pounds heavier."

Relaxing at her attempt to tease, he smiled. "You look great."

"You too. Do you still work out everyday?"

"Most days. Do you still run?" She'd been on the track team in college and had passed that love to her daughter.

"As often as I can."

"Does Sloan run?"

"Yep."

A subtle tension invaded the air. She rubbed her arms, encased in his sweat suit. "Let's get to those files."

"Fine by me."

They made quick work of cleaning up the food, then tackled the transcript of the trial. It was painstaking work, rereading everybody's testimony, going over their own notes on the proceedings. Painstaking, with little to show for it.

At midnight, Kate yawned. "I'm fried, Reese. I can't think clearly anymore." She glanced over at him. He looked tired, too, though even with the tiny lines around his eyes and mouth more visible now with fatigue, he was sexy. Life just wasn't fair.

"Me, too. We didn't make much progress, did we?"

"No, there's nothing in the transcript that I can see might help us. It's pretty routine." She bit her lip. "We've got to get to the bottom of this quickly."

Leaning back onto the sofa, he scrubbed a hand over his face. "You have no idea."

She frowned. "Is there something you're not telling me?" Maybe he was getting married. Or—Oh, God— Sandra Dee was pregnant.

"I found out today that my name's been submitted for a judgeship in criminal court."

"Reese, how wonderful."

"Is it?"

"What?"

"Nothing."

"No, what were you implying?"

He sighed. "Your judgeship drove us apart."

"No, no, it didn't."

"Yes, we couldn't withstand that competition."

"We thrived on that competition for years. We loved having the same goals and seeing who could reach them first."

"I couldn't . . ." He drew in a breath, and swore. "Never mind. Let's table this discussion." Rising, he crossed to his desk, and checked his calendar. "When can we get together again? We should go over the articles Yolanda got on Bingham, and what she put together on the woman's subsequent crimes and prison history."

Glad to let the personal conversation go, Kate reached for her purse, whipped out her PDA and checked it. "Are you free tomorrow? I can make myself available." She darted a glance at the files on the table. "We could finish up with these."

He was watching her. "No, I'm not free. I'm going to see Sofie."

Her throat clogged. She'd spoken to her daughter on the phone last night. Sofie hadn't said a word about Reese's visit. Nor had she asked Kate to drive up to see her. "Oh."

"I badgered her into letting me come. She's got a track meet, and I insisted."

"I'd love to see her run."

He waited a beat, then for some godforsaken reason said, "Come with me."

Sighing, Kate felt like a pitiful mother. She *was* a pitiful mother, *now*. "No, Sofie wouldn't want that."

"The child doesn't know what the hell she wants. She runs hot and cold with both of us."

"Mostly cold with me."

"No, she warms up to you more than you realize. Besides she's none to happy with me a good deal of the time."

Kate leaned back against the couch. "Sometimes I can't believe it's come to this. My little girl . . ."

"If we told her more about why we divorced, maybe she'd be better."

"Oh, God, no. She'd be worse. And we both have too much to lose. Not only would it worsen your relationship with her, but then we'd have to get into stuff about me that's best left unsaid."

"Well," he said curtly, "that's certainly true. Then we'll just have to do what the therapist advised—keep battering her defenses."

"I'm trying."

"Drive up with me."

Kate frowned, still not convinced.

"We can go over the files in the car. Four hours of work time is a lot."

"Isn't Gidget going with you?"

"Gidget?"

"Oh, my God, did I say that out loud?"

He shook his head. "You're a piece of work."

"I'm sorry. She's a nice woman."

"Yeah, she is. And no, she's not coming."

"Why?"

"Sofie asked me not to bring her."

Hmm, that was good news. If her daughter got close to Dray Merrill, Kate didn't know what she'd do.

"Reese, Jillian saw Dray today."

"So?"

"She was with Tyler."

"Sloan?"

"Yeah. At Starbucks."

He arched a brow. "Good God, there's nothing going on between them, is there?"

"No. I'd be shocked if there was. Tyler wouldn't cheat. He knows how I feel about that kind of thing."

Reese looked like he was going to comment on that, but instead said, "Why the hell would they be together?"

"Tyler told Jillian they'd bumped into each other."

He ran a hand through his hair. "They probably did. Proximity to her gym and his hospital."

"What would they have to talk about?"

He arched a brow. "Us, I would guess."

She frowned. "I'm not sure I like it."

"Talk to the good doctor." His words were sharp. Gone was the sensitive man of a few minutes before. "I'm sure he'll cave on anything you want."

"No need to get nasty."

"Isn't it boring having somebody so smitten?"

His sarcasm ignited her temper. "You should know the answer to that question."

Shaking his head disgustedly, he said, "Don't mock Dray."

"You threw the gauntlet, Reese, like you always do." She stood. "I'm going." She looked down at her clothes. "I'll change."

"Don't bother. Give them back to me some other time."

"Whatever you say." She gathered up her suit and shoes and got to the door before he stopped her with his words. "Kate."

She turned back.

"I . . . didn't mean to get into old stuff."

She sighed. "Me, either. We just can't be together without reacting like this."

"We have to be together. We need to make a pact to stop sniping at each other."

Ah, the infamous pact . . .

Let's make a pact. No matter what happens, we'll always love each other, treat each other well. Even if we get divorced.

Don't talk about divorce on our wedding day.

I mean it. You're my best friend, too. I couldn't bear to lose you . . .

She smiled sadly. "Agreed. We'll make a pact to be better with each other."

"And come with me tomorrow. We'll get a lot of work done and you'll get to see Sofie."

"Oh, Reese . . ."

"There's something else. We need to tell her about this thing with Bingham."

"I suppose we do."

"Best we present a united front."

"She'll believe I did something wrong."

"I'm the one accused of adultery in the note."

Kate sighed. She was so weary she weakened. "I'd really like to see her." A hesitation. "Okay, I'll go."

"Should I pick you up?"

"Oh, sure. Fine."

"Where?"

"My house."

"You and Sloan don't spend your nights together?"

"That's not a question you get to ask, Reese."

"You're right. How stupid of me."

She ignored the sarcasm. "What time were you leaving?"

"Nine-ish."

"Fine, I'll see you then."

"Good night, Kate."

"Good night, Reese."

Kate held her head high as she left the office and the building and the man who had once been hers. But the weight of all that loss was heavy on her shoulders.

THREE

WHEN REESE ARRIVED at Kate's condo the next morning at nine o'clock, he found her waiting at her door, dressed in jeans, low-heeled shoes, and a pretty red cotton long sleeve shirt that made her eyes liquid and . . . enticing. Hell. He'd spent an uncomfortable night, with Dray asleep next to him and his ex-wife drifting in and out of his consciousness. One day in Kate's presence and he felt that stinging attraction to her again. But he'd learned his lesson. Though the physical thing between them had always been good, he needed to remember the emotional damage they did to each other that ended their marriage. And summon the anger, if necessary.

"Hi," Kate said coming down the walk, backlit by the early morning sun. She was holding a newspaper. "Did you see this?"

"Yeah, not too bad."

The *Herald* had run much the same story as yesterday, except for an update from the police to say they were checking into the *alleged* suicide and talking with pertinent people. It briefly mentioned Reese and Kate, who had each responded to the reporter's call with *no comment*.

He nodded to the paper. "It'll get worse, though, if we don't come up with something."

"I know." She took in his outfit and pointed to his navy Yale Law sweatshirt, that he wore with jeans and a Yankees baseball cap. "Where'd you get that? It looks brand-new."

"A reunion. I went to our twentieth."

"I see," she said tightly. "Was it fun?"

"Except for having to answer questions about us from our old buddies, it was."

That was an understatement. The comments had ranged from, *Man you two were made for each other*, to *Never thought I'd see the day. You were sides of the same coin.* Of course, Reese had always thought that, too. So had Kate.

Circling around his sporty yellow Mustang convertible, she slid into the passenger side as he took a seat behind the wheel. "They were surprised we were divorced?" she asked, once they were in seatbelts.

"Shocked. Especially since we were the envy of all of them at our tenth."

A small smile broached her lips. They were unpainted and she wore little makeup. She'd never needed it. "That reunion was fun." They'd thought, at the time, the world was theirs for the taking. Everything had clicked into place by the time they were thirty-five. "Sofie was only six, remember?"

"Yeah," he said as he started the car and headed down her street. "She stayed with my sister for the weekend. The boys weren't even born yet."

"How is Emily? I haven't talked to her in a couple of weeks."

"Still trying to find her sea legs."

Emily was Reese's sister, whom he'd helped raise because his mother had been diagnosed with Hodgkin's disease when Emily was ten and Reese was fifteen. Even after his mother died, and his father had more time for his kids, Reese had watched out for her. It nearly killed him when she'd married a loser, and divorced him six years ago when Jason and Jimmy were three and four.

"Not to be callous," Kate put in, "but she's definitely better off without Charlie Gates. He drank like a fish."

"Yes, she is." He shot her a glance. "I think it's nice you still have contact with her. I never told you that."

"She's like another sister to me."

Reese knew that. Kate had three sisters of her own, all older, who lived in different parts of the country. Though she talked to them each once a week, on different days, she missed them; his sister had filled part of that void.

He smiled. "Remember how we used to have the boys stay with us every summer?"

"Yeah. You built that tree house in the old oak behind the farmhouse, and even when Sofie got older, the three of them spent hours together in it."

A farmhouse that had broken Kate's heart to part with.

"Emily said the boys still come to stay with you on occasion."

"I couldn't give them up, Reese. Besides, Sofie loves it." She glanced over at him. "You see them a lot, don't you?"

"As much as I can."

"You're still sending her money."

Emily had set up an online T-shirt company, but it was in the early stages and she was having trouble making ends meet.

"Some."

"You were always so generous, Reese. It was such a good trait in you."

"So were you." He kept his eyes on the road, but his thumb rubbed the wheel. This conversation was starting to stir things up inside him again. "Interesting coming from two kids who had nothing."

Because they'd grown up in lower-income families, Kate and Reese both had to work for everything they got. Along with scholarships and loans, they paid for their own college, law school and every material thing they possessed by taking jobs, sometimes two at once. It took them ten years to pay off their debts, but it had been worth every penny.

"Yeah, I guess you go either way. If you grow up with nothing, you get stingy or you figure, hell, I never had any, might as well spread it around."

"Want to stop for coffee?" he asked as they approached Interstate 90.

"Not now. I had some already. I'll need a snack in an hour or so."

"You always needed to eat every two hours."

"Still do." She patted her tummy. "It's hell on the abs, especially since they've never been the same since I had Sofie."

She'd complained bitterly about her stretch marks and rounded stomach after the baby, and he'd always called them battle scars, well worth the sacrifice. "I told you last night, you look great, Kate."

She shifted uncomfortably in her seat. "Should we start with the articles?" The subtext read, *And get off the personal stuff*. Damn, either they were yelling at each other, or the good things about their relationship surfaced. He didn't know which was worse. He *did* know it wasn't healthy to be reminded of what had gone right in their marriage.

"Maybe we'd better."

She opened her briefcase and pulled out a sheaf of papers. He'd had his secretary duplicate all the information she found on Anna Bingham and had given Kate her own copies.

"How do you want to do this?"

"You read, I'll listen while I drive, and then we'll highlight the salient points."

She dug a pink highlighter out of her bag. He chuckled. *So girly,* he used to tease when they were in law school. *You love my girly-ness.*

He had, right down to the nail polish she wore on her toes and the thongs she scrimped to buy just to torture him. Briefly he checked out her jeans and wondered if she wore the naughty underwear for Sloan now. For some reason, that notion brought his anger to the forefront, and he had to work at containing it.

Kate focused on the material in front of her. "All right. This is an article on her from a society page. Christ, it was when she came out at a debutant ball." Kate rolled her eyes. "Do they still do that?"

"I guess."

"Did Dray?"

Dray's parents had money and she and her sister—and later an adopted sister—had been spoiled little princesses. Which would be evidenced in the fancy and, in Reese's opinion, ostentatious wedding of the younger sister planned for the end of April. Dray was maid of honor, and she and Reese were spending a long weekend in the Hamptons.

"I don't know, I never asked."

She began to read again. "Blond hair and blue eyes."

His preference until he'd met Kate.

"Only child. Father stockbroker, mother dealt in antiques." She studied the article. "There's a picture of her. Now I remember her."

Kate continued reading the bio information. He smirked a couple of times over the private schools, the horseback riding competitions and other activities reserved for the very rich.

So did she. "Remember how we used to mock the rich kids at Yale?"

"Who made up the majority. Yeah, I remember." Again, he threw her a knowing look. "Of course, you didn't mock Max."

Kate chuckled. Maxwell Thurman Jacobs the Third. "God I hadn't thought of him in years."

"He was at the reunion."

"Really, what happened to him?"

"Working for his father, managing the Jacobs Foundation. You could have had all that, Kate."

"I didn't want it. I only dated him because I knew you hated him and you broke up with me . . ."

"I didn't break up with you."

"Oh, no, wait. I forget. You wanted to 'see other people. To be sure.'"

"Well, hell, it worked. After a week of watching him squire you around, I came to my senses." A small smile. "You made me sweat, though."

"Why not? I never wanted the separation."

"You didn't tell me that. I thought you agreed."

"I do have some pride."

Reese was shocked by the revelation, but when he thought about it, a young Kate Renado would do just that. It made him wonder what else she'd kept—or was keeping—from him.

"So, did he ask about me?"

"Uh-huh. He wanted your phone number."

"He never called."

"I didn't give it to him."

"Why?"

"Damned if I know. I guess I never liked seeing his hands all over you." Reese gripped the steering wheel, remembering all too well how he'd had to fight to get her away from Jacobs.

She sighed. "How did we get on this?"

"I don't know. Read the next article. I think there's one in there on white-collar crime. It uses her as an example, and gives some of her adult bio."

Kate rustled the papers, her hands shaky. She wished she and Reese hadn't gotten off on that personal tangent. It unnerved her. And he seemed more uptight now than he was when they began the trip.

"Here's one from when she was released from Danbury. And there's a picture with her prison advocate."

"Yeah? He turned out to be a nice guy."

Prison advocates were hired as consultants by criminals facing federal incarceration to *ease the way* and *show them the ropes* in their down time.

"I still think those people prey on others in a bad time."

Reese frowned. "Maybe. Make a note to check if he was her advocate at Longshore."

"Done." She pulled out another article. "This one was written after her third indictment. It's about repeat offenders. I'll just read it. 'Anna Simpson Bingham is a debutant gone bad. Her first foray into crime was credit card fraud. As revealed in court testimony, the bogus dot-com company she set up sucked in Net surfers to purchase vitamins online, then sold their credit card numbers; she was caught in 1989. Bingham's lawyers were unable to keep her from jail. They did, however, play the system.'" Kate scowled. "I resent that. We defended her as well as we could."

"Don't take it personally. These writers have an ax to grind."

And just like in the past that they were trying to ignore, Reese centered her. He'd been able to cut through the crap and see what was important. If her concern wasn't warranted, he convinced her not to worry. If it was, he told her so.

She continued to read. " 'In 1996, Bingham was sent to Danbury Federal Prison Camp, often snidely called Club Fed.'" Kate shook her head. Though there was no Club Fed atmosphere anymore in minimum security prisons, federal prison camps weren't your traditional prisons, either. Martha Stewart–type offenders got to live in dormlike housing, and there were no razor-wire fences around. But they had to wear prison clothing, eat terrible food, work at a tedious job and suffer a kind of boredom that can drive you crazy. Being in a prison camp was certainly no vacation.

"Here's more of her history. 'While inside, she was disciplined for black-market trafficking and failure to abide by prison rules.'" Kate frowned. "How would they know this?"

"I'm not sure. We'll have to get a court order to get her records if it comes down to that. The newspaper couldn't have subpoenaed them though. Legally the press can't get those records."

Kate continued to read. " 'After Bingham's release to a halfway house, where she spent three months, she returned to the outside world in 2000. From there, she was charged with tax evasion, and sent to low security prison.' "

These institutions had strengthened perimeters, higher guard to inmate ratios and greater internal controls.

"Where'd she go?" Reese asked.

"Tallahassee, Florida."

"Who was her attorney?"

"Benning and Benning."

"Okay, keep going."

" 'Finally, Ms. Bingham violated probation and, given her history and behavior inside, was sentenced to five to ten years.' " Kate lowered the paper. "This was written at the end of 2005 when she went to Longshore."

Reese shook his head. "She doesn't sound like a woman who would commit suicide."

"I know. She seems too self-absorbed."

He looked thoughtful. "Kate, what are we hoping for here? With the police investigation?"

"That they find out why she lied in her suicide note."

"Or there's another possibility we haven't mentioned yet. Think about it." They always used to quiz each other like this. Make each other stretch in their thinking.

She stared out the window as the countryside sped by. Absently she noted the just-budding trees and green grass along Interstate 90. "That it wasn't really suicide. That someone inside killed her and made it look like a suicide." She shook her head. "Murders happen in prison, though not often in medium security. Are we stretching too much here?"

"Look at the facts in evidence: She died in prison and she lied in her suicide note. Those are the only two things we know for certain. So if someone else killed her, that person lied about us."

"What could they hope to gain?"

"I don't know. We'll find out though. We have to wait for the police report, which should be available by the end of next week. If they rule it a suicide, we investigate further. If they rule a homicide, they'll want to work with us, since we're named, to solve the mystery."

She blew out a heavy breath. "This is a lot to take in."

He glanced at her. "We're on top of this, Kate. We'll figure it out. Especially together. We did it all the time in our practice—got to the real story. We're good together like that."

They were. In some ways the thought comforted her. And in some ways it scared her to death because it meant spending even more time with Reese. Which she didn't want right now. All night she'd tossed and turned because of him. She hadn't gone to Tyler's and had instead slept only with the ghosts. What on earth would happen if this investigation went on too long? Could they endure each other indefinitely?

"What's wrong?"

"Nothing."

"You moaned."

"My mind drifted, I guess."

His green eyes narrowed. "Where?"

"To . . . Sofie."

"Want to talk about her?"

"What's to say? I am anxious to see her, though. It's been a month." She sighed. "I can't believe I haven't seen my little girl for a month."

"I used to think that about you. After we divorced."

"Reese . . ."

"Shit. I didn't mean to say that." He hit his fist on the steering wheel as he made the comment. "Replaying the past doesn't help. Let's concentrate on Anna Bingham and Sofie."

"Fine by me."

"Look, there's a breakfast place off the interstate. I'm going to stop. I need some space."

"Me, too."

Forcefully Kate squelched all her fears about being with Reese, about doing everyday ordinary things with him like driving in a car and eating together again. It would take their combined intellect, insights and professional competence to ferret out exactly what was going on with Anna Bingham. If they didn't, they'd have a lot more to worry about than their reactions to each other.

With that sober thought in mind, she turned back to the articles until she could escape from the confines of the car—and Reese—for a while.

"HEY, THERE'S MY girl."

Sofie looked up from where she sat on her bed and found her father standing in the doorway. For some reason, the sight of him brought tears to her eyes. She bolted off the bed and flung herself into his arms. "Daddy." His strong hands gripped her tightly. She headlocked his neck.

"How are you, princess?"

"I'm okay," she lied, burying her head in his shoulder. He smelled the same—of some nice soap, an aftershave she forgot the name of and just *her dad*. Drawing away, she said, "I—" then stopped when she saw her mother standing a few feet away. For a minute her heart leaped at the sight of the woman she once thought hung the moon. Then Sofie's insides went cold. "What's she doing here?"

The phony smile disappeared off her mother's face. For a minute, she got a glimpse of the real woman inside of the tough cookie that she meanly dubbed, Judge Judy. But then Kaitlyn Renado threw her head back and stuck out her chin. "I found out your father was coming up and asked if I could tag along. I hope that's okay."

Sofie stepped back from her dad. "Whatever. You'll get to see me run."

Something they'd shared. Her mom had been a runner, too. Despite her resolve to stay distanced, Sofie remembered things: *That's it baby, jog with Mommy . . . Okay, little girl, let's race to the swing set . . . Come on, Sofie, a teenager should be able to keep up with an old lady like me.*

If nothing else, her mother had given her the desire and helped her develop the ability to run. In some ways she was like her parents and in others, she was so different. Like, *duh*, in needing a stable home life!

"I'm anxious to see one of your meets." Sofie hadn't invited her up for any of them this year. "But I'm more happy to spend some time with you."

She nodded to the bathroom. "I gotta get ready."

"Fine." Her dad dropped down on her bed. "We'll wait and walk with you to the field."

"Take that silly hat off, Daddy. You'll embarrass me."

He tugged on the bill of the cap. "No way. It makes me feel like a jock again."

Her dad had been a star pitcher in college and still played summer ball. Sofie had liked to watch him play. Her mother used to scream like a banshee cheering him on.

Sofie smiled softly at her father, the man who loved her unconditionally. Always had. "Be right back." She didn't even glance at her mother.

Inside the john, Sofie sank onto the toilet and buried her face in her hands. She hated seeing her mother. Already, Sofie was looking for some summer program up here so she didn't have to go home and live with her. Or with her dad and his bimbo. Jesus, wasn't he too old to be thinking with his dick? She glanced at the sink. Behind its pipes was her stash of uppers. She considered taking one. But she hated to compete when she was on anything. It didn't seem fair. And she was still hungover from trying some blow with Jax last night. Oh, just wait until her mother got a look at her new boyfriend. Would she freak. As Sofie dressed in her track clothes, she remembered her mother's advice on guys: *Don't fall for any sweet words, honey. Guys will have them all . . . First find out what kind of person he is . . . When the time's right, you'll know.*

Did you with Daddy? Sofie had asked.

Uh-huh. I knew he was the one for me before we made love.

How'd you know, Mama?

I just did. You will, too. When you meet a wonderful man like your dad.

Ha! Sofie tied the laces of her track shoes. Her mother had been lying through her teeth. Not long after, they had another conversation.

Sofie, your father and I are separating . . . We have some things we can't work out . . . No, it's nothing we care to discuss with you . . . People grow apart . . . they lose the feelings they have for each other . . .

Sofie had known her mother wasn't telling the whole story. So she'd gone to her dad . . .

We can't live together anymore, princess. We don't agree on so many things . . .

Later, when she remembered the fights she wasn't supposed to hear, she started piecing it together, and realized her dad wanted another kid and her mother didn't. It was then that the thought took hold, and like the evil monsters from her childhood story books, got their talons in her. If Kaitlyn Renado had really liked being a mother, she would have had another baby. Especially since her dad had wanted one. Ergo, he loved Sofie with his whole heart and her mother didn't.

That was why Sofie forced herself to start hating her mother. When she got a new boyfriend, and her dad had gotten a girlfriend, Sofie had realized there was no room in either of their lives for her, and insisted on going away to school.

She came out of the bathroom to find them talking softly. "This is new."

"New?" her mother asked from where she sat at the desk.

"Usually you two are yelling at each other when you're within fifty feet."

"We're trying to do better with that, honey," her mother said.

"Yeah, sure."

"We are, baby." Her dad stood. "We'll show you today. We're all going out after the meet."

"Terrific." Sofie crossed to the mirror and pinned up her

straw-colored hair. Now *that* had gotten a reaction out of both of them when they first saw it at Christmas . . . *Oh, Sofie, what did you do to your pretty dark hair?* Her mother had unconsciously touched her own. Why wouldn't she? Sofie's had been the exact texture and color of hers. Even her dad had commented . . . *Oh, baby, it just doesn't look like you.*

They made small talk on the trek to the fields. Sofie asked about Emily and the boys, whom she loved like brothers. At least she still got to see them. Her parents made up questions to keep the conversation going, and Sofie was glad when they reached the track so she could get away from them. She bounded toward the teammates without a word. She heard her father call good luck after her, but didn't turn around. She kept on running, like she had since they got their divorce. Too bad she couldn't cut them out of her life like they cut out each other.

"I SHOULDN'T HAVE come," Kate said as she walked toward the stands with Reese. Her hands were shaking and she felt ill. How could this have happened to her life?

Reese stopped, forcing Kate to halt, too. "Of course you should have. Sofie needs to come face-to-face with her problems with us."

"With me."

"No, Kate. You don't see it, but she's mad at me, too."

"She hugged you and wouldn't come near me."

"I'm sorry. That must have been hard."

His kindness brought tears to her eyes. She'd forgotten how they'd always tapped into each other's softer side. Since they'd split, she'd squelched that part of herself and wondered if he had, too.

A tear trickled down her cheek. Disgusted, she swiped it away.

He said, "Don't cry."

"I . . ." She sniffed. "I just can't believe that's my little girl. Scrawny as hell. Hair out of a fright flick. And an attitude that's impossible." When Reese didn't respond, his face a mask of pain, she asked, "How did this happen to our baby?"

His hands fisted at his sides. "When your world caves in, and you hurt so much, you strike out at the nearest target. Or the people who caused it."

Kate watched him stare out at the field.

"I did. When we divorced." His voice was gritty with the admission.

"You did?"

His piercing green gaze locked on her. "Yeah, didn't you?" His tone was accusatory.

"Yes, I just didn't know you did."

"You were my world, Kate."

Because she was hurting, and because being with him made her confront what she'd lost, she conjured facts that made the spilt happen in the first place. "Not quite. What we had wasn't enough. You wanted more."

"I wanted another child." His words were curt, and the snap of them made her think he was coming from the same place as she.

"Things went bad before you started singing that tune."

He sighed. "Sometimes, you know, I can't figure out how."

"The competition started wearing on us."

"We thrived on that competition from day one."

"No, it got to be too much. We couldn't deal with it any longer."

"I—"

Just then the whistle blew for the start of the match. She straightened. "Let's go sit. I hate rehashing this."

"Good idea." He strode ahead of her, and they found a place on the bleachers.

Kate watched her little girl warm up. She watched her take her position on the field. She watched her gear up for the hundred meter dash. And she watched her come in seventh.

"Jesus, what's the matter with her?" Reese asked. "She's slow and breathing hard."

"This is so not her."

They said the same thing after the two hundred yard dash and the five hundred meter relay. Sofie performed terribly. It was so unlike the star athlete she'd always been.

"Damn it . . . she's pale and exhausted, and obviously isn't sleeping. Something's going on." Reese stared out the field, then pointed off to the side. "Kate, look."

Sofie jogged over to the sidelines, opposite of where they sat.

If parents could paint of picture of the worst candidate to court their daughter, the guy Sofie ran to was it. He was too old for her. He wore a leather coat, even though the weather didn't call for it. And he was smoking a cigarette. Kate bet they'd find tattoos and piercings if they were up close.

"Oh, my God," she said when the guy leaned down and gave Sofie a very adult kiss.

"Great." Reese yanked off his hat and threw it on the ground. "Another thing to deal with. Damn it, is nothing going to go right with this kid again?"

Kate didn't respond to that query. She was feeling even more like a terrible mother. Though Reese had often seen her at her worst, this was taking the cake.

WHEN SOFIE BOUNDED downstairs after getting cleaned up, Reese groaned, then rose from where he sat on the couch in the common room of the Connor Prep dorm. Kate had gone to use the ladies' room, thank God. He crossed directly to his daughter.

Kissing her on the forehead, he made sure his tone was soft and coaxing. "This isn't going to happen, honey."

She pointed her chin in a gesture very much like her mother affected when she was feeling contrary. "What do you mean?"

"I've never seen you dressed in all black like this when I came to visit before." He swiped at the inky lipstick on her mouth. "Or wearing this crap."

"I . . . it's a new style."

"Adopted just for your mom, I'd guess."

Her eyes—his color—flamed. "What do you care, after how she hurt you?"

"The divorce was mutual."

"My ass."

"Sofie . . ."

A mutinous teenage glare.

"I mean it, Sof. Go change into something normal."

She stomped away. He watched her go, remembering when she was little and they'd dressed her in pink dresses and lacy bonnets. Her dark curls had peeked out from under the brim.

In a few minutes, Kate returned. "Isn't she back yet?"

"No, not yet."

"What were you thinking about? You had an odd expression on your face."

"When she was little."

A smile. "She was so beautiful."

"I know. I thought—"

"Okay, I'm here." Reese turned to find Sofie dressed in jeans and a Calvin Klein T-shirt under a baggy blazer. "I'm hungry," she said, her tone surly.

"Me, too." Kate leaned over and slid an arm around Sofie's shoulders.

Their daughter stiffened and drew away. Kate's face fell, and once again Reese felt compelled to comfort Kate as he had earlier. This time, though, he refrained.

After a stilted meal of hamburgers and French fries and cokes, Reese broached the subject of Anna Bingham. "Sofie, we need to talk to you."

For a minute, the little girl of his heart returned. Her face suffused with such naked vulnerability, he reached for her hand. "It's not that bad, honey."

"You're not sick, Daddy?" Her gaze swung to Kate. "Mama?" Yes, there was the real Sofie.

"No, honey, we're not sick." From the other side, Kate briefly squeezed her shoulder. "But we have a professional problem that you need to know about."

"You don't work together anymore."

"No, it's from when we did."

Reese told her about the case.

"That sucks," she said after he finished. "And it's stupid. You wouldn't cheat on your wife."

How to answer this? Though he was innocent on *this* charge, he *had* been unfaithful.

Kate stepped in. "Your dad did not sleep with Anna Bingham. Her accusations are a lie. This has hit the papers, honey, so we didn't want you to hear about it from anybody else. Or wait till you came home next weekend for your birthday."

"Are your jobs gonna be all right?"

They'd always tried to be honest with her. "We're worried about the damage to our reputations. What could happen with our careers."

She looked at her father. "I'm sorry, Daddy."

"Us, too. We don't want you to worry about it. We just thought you should know."

"Okay."

His daughter turned to Kate. The hopeful look on Kate's face practically broke his heart. But Sofie didn't seem affected. Instead, she went on the offensive. "So, you gonna use this against him?"

Kate jolted back from the emotional slap.

Reese said, "Sofie . . ."

"No, I'll answer. I wouldn't use anything against your father, Sofie."

"Oh, come on. You took him to the cleaners in the divorce."

Kate sent Reese an accusatory look. "Did you tell her that?"

His hand hit the table, making the dishes dance. "Of course not."

Sofie rolled her eyes and gave that infuriating teenage cluck of her mouth.

Reese said, "Let's not go over all this again. We've been through it so many times. Can't we get past the blame?"

"Sure, fine." Sofie glared at *him* now. Then her face brightened. "Oh, look, there's Jax."

"You invited him to join us?" Kate asked tightly.

"Yeah, sure. Why not?"

Reese stared at the boy as he approached them. He had a tattoo on his forehead, and several earrings in his ears. When his jacket pulled away, a studded dog collar became apparent.

Just what they needed. The ending to a perfect visit.

KATE STRODE AHEAD of Reese to car. She couldn't deal with the fact that her own child hated her. And right now she was very afraid that she was going to turn to her ex-husband for comfort, which would be a total disaster.

When she reached his Mustang, Reese came up behind her. It was dark out now, but the parking lot was illuminated by lamps. Kate shivered into the cold April evening, despite the wool blazer she'd donned. He didn't touch her, thank God, but tried to soothe her with words. "Sofie'll come around."

Kate felt tears moisten her eyes. She fought them back with the verve of an emotional gladiator.

"It's a phase," he continued. "She's mad at us, she'll get over it."

His words calmed her. Finally Kate gained some control, turned and looked up into his sympathetic face. "I'm sorry. I don't know why I'm so emotional about this. I thought I was dealing with it better."

"Things have been tough lately, with this Bingham accusation. Sofie's behavior just makes everything worse." He moved closer. She would have stepped back but the car was behind her. Slowly, he raised his hand and brushed a thumb under her eye. "Didn't sleep much last night, either, did you?"

Her breath caught at his touch—so slight, but the very first one since the divorce. She had to clear her throat before she could answer. "N-no."

"Me, either." He was staring down at her.

She stared back at him. Suddenly, a different kind of tension rose between them.

He focused on her lips.

She licked them.

He froze.

So did she. *You don't want to do this,* she told herself.

His face darkened and he moved forward a millimeter. Still he said nothing. She watched him for a minute, forcing herself to remember those last few years were horrible. The final one hauntingly grim. She couldn't bring that darkness back to their lives. She couldn't risk hurting her daughter even more by acting foolishly. She was needy, but she would *not* seek solace in Reese. Who knew where that would lead?

So she straightened her shoulders and sidled around him, circling the hood of the Mustang to get to the passenger door. Reese stayed where he was for a moment, then slapped his hand on the hood, making her jump. She didn't look at him as he fished out his keys and popped the locks. Kate slid inside the car, wordlessly, as he did. And when he started the engine, his scent surrounded her. She forced herself remember that scent, during one of the blackest, bleakest moment of their lives together. . . .

"I have to tell you something," she'd said that night she'd confessed all, erroneously thinking he would forgive her. She should have known, because things had been so bad, baring her soul was the wrong thing to do.

"Let me guess." They were in their bedroom, in the farmhouse she'd loved, and he yanked off his tie mercilessly. "The judgeship came through." The infamous judgeship that had proved to be the last wedge between them.

"No, it's too soon for that."

His eyes narrowed. "Something with Sofie?" She'd been almost ten at the time.

"No, Reese, it's about us."

He'd cocked his head. He'd looked haggard already. Just wait.

"I did something today." She'd started to cry then. Tears she'd suppressed all afternoon coursed down her cheeks.

She watched him try to resist. Finally, he crossed to her and took her in his arms. He felt so safe, so secure. The smell of his woodsy aftershave calmed her. "It can't be that bad."

"It is."

She felt him stiffen. Then he asked wrenchingly, "You didn't go to another man, did you?" They hadn't been getting along for months.

She shook her head. It was beginning to pound with migraine force.

"Then it'll be okay. I know things between us have been bad. I've been thinking we should get that counseling you suggested. I was being pigheaded about it."

"If you still want to, after I tell you."

His hand had caressed her hair like she was some rare and precious artifact. "I will."

Pulling back she faced him squarely. She remembered now how his sage-colored eyes were soft and loving. How his mouth gave her an encouraging smile. He wore his hair shorter then, but it complemented his exquisite, angular face.

She said starkly, "I had an abortion today."

It took him a minute. His brow furrowed and his chin angled. With a lawyer's calm, he whispered, "You were pregnant?"

She nodded.

His hands gripped her shoulders. "You didn't *tell* me."

"After I found out, I tried to talk to you. On several occasions. We just started yelling at each other, and I couldn't bring this up then."

"I don't believe you."

"It's true."

"Even if it is, you went ahead and killed my baby?"

"I—" She started weeping then. "I was so angry at you for pushing me. For saying those awful things."

"I was *pushing* you to have another child with me. All the while you were pregnant."

She just stared at him. And she'd known, in that instant, things would never be the same again.

"How far along were you?" he asked.

"Just a few weeks."

"I can't believe you're capable of doing something like this."

What could she say? A good lawyer went on the defensive. But when you'd already tried and convicted yourself, it was hard to feign innocence. "I was confused. Hurt. But I knew as soon as I did it that it was a mistake not to have talked to you first, worked it out with you before I . . ."

He'd gripped her hard enough so that he'd left bruises; she discovered them the next day. "This was not a mistake. This was a crime."

"I know it hurts. Please, give me a chance to make it up to you. Maybe . . ."

"You can't make up for this. You committed a heinous act that you can never—"

"No, Reese, no. It didn't seem like that at the time. You yourself have argued that. Have fought for women to have the right to choose."

"That's not the same thing. You *knew* how I felt about this issue for us."

"Reese, please . . ."

He stepped back then, shrugging her off like a leper. "I will never, *ever*, forgive you for this." He'd turned then, and walked out. He'd stayed away for three days. It had been the beginning of the end. . . .

FOUR

TYLER SIPPED HIS coffee as he stared out the window of his clapboard house and watched the wind whip around his small backyard, making the newly budded leaves tremble. In downstate New York, April could be mild or brutal, depending on her whim, and this Sunday morning, she'd chosen not to be kind.

Just like Kaitlyn. Damn her. She knew he wanted to see her, knew he wanted a call or, better yet, for her to spend the night with him when she returned from seeing her daughter. But she'd done neither. He guessed she went home and crashed. He hoped nothing of significance had happened between her and Bishop. That was something he feared every single time she and her ex had cause to be together.

"You're pathetic, Sloan," he told himself. Why didn't he just ditch this relationship? He could find a dozen women who would treat him better.

Hell. Dropping down into a chair at the butcher-block table by the window, he picked up today's *Herald*. He was drinking his coffee when he turned to the local section and sputtered the brew all over the paper. He had to wipe off

the article to read it. There were headlines: BISHOP AND
RENADO HAVE NO COMMENT. Beneath that banner were
head shots of Kaitlyn and Reese, retrieved, most likely,
from the paper's files on newsworthy people in Westwood.
Then there was text, which didn't say anything new, just
that the New Jersey police were investigating the incident
and neither Reese nor Kaitlyn would talk to reporters.

But it was another picture of them that grated on Tyler's
already raw nerves. Apparently taken when they were still
together: They were dancing; he could identify Westwood's
Civic Center in the background. Bishop wore a tux and
looked young. Kaitlyn sported a form-fitting black beaded
dress that made Tyler's mouth water. The two of them were
staring at each other like they were alone, in love, and
couldn't care less about what was going on around them.

Fuck!!!! He wasn't going to do this! To get her out of
his head, he picked up the phone. After three rings, a sultry, cultured voice answered, "Hello, darling."

"Hi, Mom. Caller ID?"

"For my only son, of course. How are you, Tyler?"

He thought about lying. But he never could dissemble
with this woman, not when he hid frogs in his pocket,
when he skipped school in junior high or even when she
asked, while he was in high school, if he was sexually ac-
tive. "I am not good, Mom."

"Tell me." He pictured Susan Sloan at the breakfast
nook of the Connecticut home, sipping her herbal tea.
She'd be dressed in exotic nightclothes, and her beauty
would shine through naturally, without any makeup.

"It's Kaitlyn. Promise you won't criticize her, and I'll
tell you."

An exasperated sigh. "I promise, even though Kaitlyn
Renado isn't my favorite person."

He explained the predicament with Anna Bingham.

"Is she guilty?"

"No. Kaitlyn would never do anything unethical."

"Then I'm sorry for her." His mother waited. "Is this af-
fecting the relationship between you two?"

"Yeah. She's spending time with her ex-husband, trying to uncover the truth."

"And that hurts you."

"I guess."

"She's hurt you a great deal with her inability to commit to your relationship."

"I know. I'm just so frustrated."

"You should talk this out with her."

"I have. She gets angry at my insecurity about Bishop."

"I'm biting my tongue, dear, so I don't criticize."

He chuckled. "I love you, you know that."

"I do. And I love you *more*." The familiar retort from his childhood lightened his mood.

"Let's change the subject. Fill me in on how Dad is and about you and that art gallery of yours." His mother owned a gallery in Manhattan that featured new artists.

And so his mother was off on her two favorite topics. When Tyler hung up, he felt better. He stood, stared at the phone and decided he wasn't going to mope around waiting for Kaitlyn to call. He'd do something fun on his day off. He was passing the foyer on the way to his bedroom when the front door opened. There she stood with the keys to his place in one hand, carrying a white paper bag in the other.

For a minute he just watched her, the cool morning air swirling around his ankles. Then he said, "Hi, stranger."

Giving him an small smile, she eased inside and shut the door. She wore deep red knit pants with a matching T-shirt and light zippered jacket. Sneakers graced her feet. "Hi, handsome." She crossed to the living room table and set down what smelled like coffee and pastry. Turning, she stepped close to him.

He put his hands on her hips and pulled her closer. "I missed you."

"I know." Her arms slid around his neck. "I'm sorry about the last few days."

Don't say it. Don't whine. "You could have come here last night."

"I was whipped. Sofie was awful and it was an emotional day."

"Emotional just with her?"

"No, of course not. With this Bingham thing hanging over my head, I have to fight not to give in to panic."

"That's not what I meant."

Tossing her head back, she stared up at him. Her deep brown eyes flashed with . . . resentment? "What did you mean?"

"Is it emotional being with Bishop so much?"

"Oh, Tyler, don't start that again. I know you don't like me seeing him, but I have no choice."

For some reason, her irritated tone and dismissal of his feelings annoyed him. "You know very well how I feel about this. I'm afraid something will spark between you two again." She tried draw away, but he held her in place. "I'm afraid you're in love with him, still. That he'll get you in the sack, then take you away from me."

"We agreed we'd be exclusive. I wouldn't cheat on you."

"Like he cheated on you. Best you remember that."

Her face drained of color and he regretted his words.

"Look, I'm sorry. That was mean. But I worry, Kaitlyn. About us. About your inability to commit to this relationship."

"You know I care about you."

"And you know I love you." He waited a beat, then added, "I hate the fact that your feelings haven't caught up with mine."

This time she managed to step back. "Look, maybe I shouldn't have come over today. I didn't sleep well and I'm exhausted. I don't have the energy to argue with you."

So much for taking his mother's advice and bringing all his feelings out in the open. He didn't mean for this to go south. Though he knew he was acting like some Neanderthal, he bent down, swung her up in his arms and headed for the bedroom.

"What are you doing?" she asked, half in surprise, half in amusement.

"Ending this argument." He strode down the hall and kicked open his bedroom door. "We won't fight if we're busy doing other things."

Dumping her on the huge four-poster bed, he dragged his shirt over his head and, never taking his eyes off her, he began to unfasten his jeans.

She stared at him a moment, then reached for the zipper of her fleece. "Works for me."

REESE BRACED HIS arms on either side of Dray and kissed her nose; he was trying to pretend what they'd just done wasn't the worst sex they'd ever had. The lines around his mouth and eyes gave him away, though. When he started to move off her, she gripped his shoulders. Strong and muscled, they bunched beneath her fingertips.

"You're not doing well, are you?" she asked gently.

"No, I guess not. This thing with Anna Bingham has me preoccupied. I'm worried."

"About the judgeship nomination?"

"Hell, about my practice. A scandal like this could ruin Bishop Associates."

He did move away then, settling onto his side of the bed, linking his hands behind his head, and staring up at the plaster ceiling. He'd told her once—without meaning to, she guessed—that in the farmhouse he'd shared with Kate, they'd put in an oak ceiling with skylights in the bedroom. Wistfully, he'd said he missed looking up at the stars at night and the sun during the day, and hearing the wind chimes tinkle outside their window.

Dray turned to her side and came up on her elbow, anchoring her head in her open palm. "Is that all, Reese?"

"Isn't that enough?"

"Are you upset by being with Kate?"

"I'm upset about the reason I'm forced to be with Kate."

"Did you argue?"

"We always argue, though it isn't as bad, now that we have something in common to fight for." He never admitted the anger and resentment that was still there on both sides, but Dray could sense the emotions inside him. "And then there's Sofie." He'd already explained last night what happened with his daughter.

"I'm sorry." Dray ran a finger down his chest. "She's so mean to you."

"She's hurting."

"And being a typical teenage brat."

He chuckled. "That, too. And now this guy, Jax. My Lord, he's bad news."

"Did you talk to her about him?"

"Kate and I both tried to. Sofie said we couldn't keep our marriage together so any advice on relationships that we had to give her was useless." He expelled a heavy breath. "Maybe she's right about that. She's never going to get over the divorce."

"Neither are you."

He turned his head to the side, his green eyes glittered with questions. "What do you mean by that?"

"Just that you're still hurting from the divorce, too."

"Dray, please, let's not get into that again. I've got a lot on my mind."

Hurt by his careless dismissal of what she needed to talk about, she sat up, stayed there a minute then swung her legs over the side of the bed. The window was cracked open and she shivered a bit. Rising from the mattress, she walked to the bathroom. When she got to the doorway, Reese called out, "Dray, I'm sorry."

Turning, she looked at him; her heart swelled at the sight of everything she'd always wanted in a man. Still she had some pride. "You're sorry for what, Reese? For dismissing my feelings? For making love to me like you weren't even there?" She lifted her chin. "Or worse yet, like you wished I was someone else?"

He just stared at her. No denial came from his mouth. She shook her head, then stepped inside the bathroom and closed the door.

She'd be damned if she cried in front of him. Facing

herself in the mirror, she also made a promise. "And I'll be damned if I let you have him back, Kate Renado. Not without a fight, at least."

BY TUESDAY, WHEN they'd wrangled an appointment to meet with the warden at Longshore Federal Correctional Institution, Reese felt better about facing Kate again. He'd managed to put her out of his mind, make up to Dray for his thoughtlessness, and spend an even-keeled two days away from his ex-wife. They hadn't seen each other since Saturday, but had spoken on the phone about the press the case was getting, the progress the cops had made, and any new information that had come to light. Yesterday's newspaper article had been mostly about the police investigation into Bingham's death. The New Jersey cops had spoken with the warden and some of the inmates, which was exactly what Reese and Kate planned to do today.

Once inside the Longshore facility, the four met up outside Warden Evans's office. Kate's lawyer greeted them first. "Bishop. Marcia."

"Carl," Reese said. "Nice to see you again."

Kate greeted Marcia.

All four of them were on friendly terms, even though the other two attorneys had represented Kate and Reese in their divorce proceedings. Ironically, given how angry they had been at each other, neither he nor Kate had wanted to cheat the other out of anything. The settlement had been amicable, making the whole thing even more heartbreaking.

A tall gray-haired man, with a kind smile and a shrewd mind, Carl Wakefield crossed to Marcia Schmidt and began a quiet conversation. Reese's lawyer, Marcia, only came up to his shoulder but matched Carl's intellect and sophistication easily.

Reese took the opportunity to study Kate. Her peacock-blue suit set off her dark coloring, though she was a bit pale today and her brown eyes were muddy with fatigue. He knew he didn't look much better even though he'd put on a blue power suit. "Come sit, Kate." When she did, he asked, "You okay?"

"No. I'm a wreck. This is going so slow. I want it over."

He sighed. "Me, too. It's been a rough few days."

"Do you think . . ." She stopped speaking when a female inmate opened the door to the warden's office. "Mr. Bishop? Judge Renado? Warden Evans is ready for you."

They both rose, and he felt Kate lean into him. He grasped her arm. "Easy." They walked into the office, close together, seeking the comfort of the other's nearness.

The warden's private domain was paneled and held a wall full of books. The room smelled faintly of furniture polish. There were pictures on a desk, behind which sat a very attractive woman. She reminded Reese of a young Mary Tyler Moore. Her smile was pleasant. "Hello, Judge. Mr. Bishop. Nice to see you again," she said to their lawyers. When all were seated, Evans nodded. "You want to talk about the Anna Bingham case."

Reese's lawyer. "My client fully denies the allegations in her alleged suicide note."

Kate's. "Mine, too."

"Yes, I expected that. I imagine you have questions for me."

Kate leaned forward. "Warden, do you think Anna Bingham committed suicide?"

Lauren Evans sat back in her chair. She folded her hands over the gray suit she wore. "Hard to say. Prison does things to people's minds. You can never rule out ending all this." She gestured toward the window where cinder-block buildings with bars, surrounded by barbed wire, could be seen. Inmates dressed in khaki milled about the recreation yard, some smoking cigarettes, some tossing a ball. An occasional bark of a guard could be heard. "And Bingham was inside twice before, but in a prison camp or low security facility. This is the first time she's had to deal with being in a cell, with razor fences on the ground keeping out the world." Evans's gaze transferred from Kate to Reese, back to Kate. "But my gut tells me she wasn't the type to take her own life."

"What type is that?" Reese asked.

"I've had suicides on my watch before. The prisoners who try it or accomplish it are usually depressed, sullen, introverted. They don't participate in any part of prison life. They're . . . waiting to die, I guess."

Kate and Reese exchanged a quick glance. This had come up on their way to see Sofie. "And Bingham wasn't like that?" Reese asked the warden to confirm their previous speculations.

"No, she wasn't. Her cellie said she was the belle of the prison ball, so to speak."

The warden's phone buzzed. "Hold on a second." She spoke into it. "Yes, Mary. Wait just a minute though." She faced them again. "To speed the process along, I thought you'd want to talk to the cellmate, Lena Parks, as the police did. I sent for her."

Marcia Schmidt exchanged glances with Carl Wakefield. The latter asked, "Warden Evans, you're being very cooperative. It strikes me as odd. If Bingham didn't commit suicide, then you've had a murder in your prison. That would be far worse than the suicide, wouldn't it?"

Evans leaned forward, her expression hard. This was a glimpse at the warden inside the woman. "I don't give a rat's ass what would be better. I want the truth, and if the truth is murder, I'll deal with it. Besides, all this is conjecture. Let's see what Parks has to say."

LENA PARKS WAS a diminutive woman with straight black hair dyed blond and looking worse than Sofie's; she had a bony frame on which her drab prison khakis hung. She entered the warden's office as if she was coming to a party. "Hey, Warden Evans." She scanned the room, let her gaze linger on Reese, like most women did, and finally looked back to the warden.

"Hello, Lena. Sit down." When the woman took a chair, Evans addressed her. "These people want to talk to you about Bingham."

Immediately, Lena's shoulders tensed. "Like I told the cops, I didn't do nothin' wrong. I didn't see nothin', either. I was working in the laundry when she offed herself."

"We know that," the warden told her. "These are the people named in the note, Lena. They want your opinion on the type of person Bingham was."

Relaxed by the warden's easy manner, Lena sat back. She addressed her comments to Reese, of course. "She was a pistol, that one. Always organizing things. Always talkin' about what she was gonna do when she got back in the free world."

"Did the other inmates like her?" Reese asked.

"Most of 'em."

"She have any enemies?"

An almost imperceptible hesitation. "Don't know of any."

Kate knew there was a strict prison code on ratting. You never did it. Lena Parks wouldn't let slip if Bingham had enemies.

"Did she have a lot of visitors?"

"Yeah, I guess."

"Men?" Reese continued with a syrupy smile on his face. "Or women?"

Parks laughed. "Men. She was real popular."

Marcia intervened. "Why do think she'd commit suicide?"

"Maybe 'cuz her walkaway date was years from now." She picked at a patch on her khaki pants. "That's alotta hours down, ma'am." "Down" meant behind bars.

"Did you two talk about things?"

"Cellies usually do," she answered casually.

Frustrated, Kate sat forward in her chair. "Is there anything you can tell us about her that would help us understand why she might have committed suicide?"

"She, um, she gave that reason in the note, didn't she?" Parks glanced at the warden, surprise suddenly lighting her face. "You think maybe somebody took her out?"

"We don't know," Evans said easily. "We're just after the facts."

"Is there anyone else we should talk to?" Marcia asked.

"Got me."

The warden stood. "All right, Lena. You can go now." When the woman left, Evans sat back down. "That wasn't very helpful. The police said they didn't get much out of her, either. Though she seemed more unnerved with you."

"What's next?" Reese asked his lawyer.

"Well, we need to delve into Bingham's life inside the prison, and determine on our own whether we think this was a suicide or not. In any case, somebody was out to implicate you." Carl faced the warden. "We need records of her activity, visitor lists, who she phoned, that kind of thing."

"The only way you can look at those documents is with a court order. The police had to get one, too." She frowned. "Why aren't you working with them?"

"We prefer to conduct a simultaneous investigation of our own."

"Fine by me," the warden told them. "Get the paperwork and you can take a closer look at Anna Bingham."

REESE AND KATE had always had a lucrative law practice, with a satisfying number of pro bono cases added to the mix, but when Kate left, Reese worked like a demon to grow the firm from what it was when she was on board. Freud would have a lot to say about that, but Reese didn't care. When he'd acquired more clients than he could handle, he'd taken in three other lawyers and they were now bursting at the seams and making plans to move to bigger accommodations. The only downside was he'd let the pro bono cases they accepted dwindle in number.

Due in court in two hours, Reese sat down to review his notes on the upcoming hearing. Ted McAlister had been arrested for a second DUI. The first time around, the man had been fined a grand, given ninety days restriction of his license, and attended a mandated drug and alcohol program.

After this second offense, the penalties would be harsher. At the very least, Reese hoped to keep him out of jail.

As he always did before a court appearance, alone in his office, he leaned back in the chair, closed his eyes, and went over his arguments in his head. It used to drive Kate crazy that he didn't write them out. But he worked better when his thoughts were fresh in his brain. As planned, his assistant, Yolanda Price, knocked on his door a half hour before he was due in court.

She entered his office and found him with his feet up on the desk, hands linked behind his head, eyes closed. The lights had been dimmed, so he was in shadows. "Ready, Reese?"

"Yep." He righted himself in the chair and stood.

"You okay?" Yolanda asked.

"Sure, why not?"

Her brows furrowed. Trim and fit at almost sixty, Yolanda ran his office efficiently, taking care of details with seeming effortlessness. Often she still mothered him. It appeared that this was going to be one of those times. "You don't have to pretend around here that nothing's going on. We all know. We're all worried."

"I called that meeting to discuss this with the staff. They seemed reassured."

"That's not what I mean. We're worried about you personally."

He shrugged into a lightweight heather-brown pinstripe suit jacket. "That's nice, I appreciate it."

"You've had to deal with *her*."

No antecedent to the pronoun was needed. Yolanda had been with them from the beginning, but had taken his side in the divorce, believing Kate had been at fault. Reese knew that was because his assistant witnessed firsthand how angry and hurt he was after the split, and Kate was gone from her viewfinder. Reese suspected Kate suffered as much, maybe not for as long, as he did, but he couldn't convince Yolanda that they were both to blame.

"I have to see Kate. But I'm dealing." He snapped his briefcase closed. "I wish you didn't blame her so much."

"Wish all you like," she said sniffing.

He squeezed her arm as he said good-bye. He walked the short distance to the courthouse in downtown West-wood, appreciating the warm spring sunshine, trying to concentrate on the case, and not what Yolanda had said. He wouldn't think about his ex-wife, or anything that might taint his concentration. Now, more than ever, he had to be at the top of his game.

Entering the courthouse, he passed through the security detector. The low din of conversation and the occasional beep of the machines filled the huge reception area. The checkpoint was slower than usual, and he thought he heard behind him, among the guards, snatches of talk mentioning his name. On his way to the elevator, several attorneys passed him. Some greeted him normally. A few smirked. More than one averted his gaze.

There was silence when he stepped into the elevator.

Guess innocent till proven guilty didn't apply to lawyers. Fuck them, he could deal with it.

He met McAlister outside the courtroom. "Ted. Hi. Ready?"

"I hope you are, Bishop." His client's tone was gruff. Ted McAlister was a prominent businessman in Westwood, had a nice family, a girl on the side and a big drinking problem.

"Of course I'm ready. Why would you doubt that?"

The guy ran a shaky hand through his thin, graying hair. "I read the papers, boy."

"Are you referring to the allegation by Anna Bingham?"

"Of course. You up to this today?"

Reese bit back a retort. "I assure you, Ted, I'm fully prepared to argue your case."

"People are going to know about your situation. Will that hurt my defense?"

A valid question, still it stung. "No."

"Hmm."

"If you'd like to seek other counsel, I understand."

"No, no, too late in the day for that. I want to get this over with."

"Fine," Reese said curtly. "Let's go."

Struggling not to be paranoid, Reese entered the courtroom. The mammoth space consisted mostly of wood-high ceiling, paneled walls, tables and spectator seats. When the opposing counsel gave him a second look, and the judge seemed to peer down, narrow-eyed, from the judicial bench, Reese refused to read anything into their actions.

He wondered if Kate was getting the same kind of vibes.

JUDGE LAWRENCE LARKIN always reminded Kate of Barry Krumble on the TV show, *Judging Amy*. Bearded, with a full head of just-graying hair, he was about fifty, in good shape and had a sharp, all-seeing gaze that intimidated most people.

Not Kate, though. As she waited in the conference room for the ranking judge in charge of administration for family court, she remembered their first few dealings . . . *You've made some rather . . . creative decisions, Judge Renado . . . I hope I don't have to tell you again that your theatrics in the courtroom are not well accepted . . . Superb work on the adoption, Kate. I'm not sure I would have seen through the father's façade . . .*

"Sorry I'm late," Larkin said striding into the conference room. "Did you get coffee?"

"No, thanks, I've had plenty."

Sitting across from her, his gaze was direct. "You look tired."

"As you might expect." She wasn't going to pretend the last six days weren't wearing on her.

"Been tough, I imagine."

"Yes."

"Give me a progress report."

She sat back and smoothed down the skirt of her sage-green suit. "Actually, the newspapers are doing a fairly good job with the facts. The alleged suicide is being investigated. The New Jersey cops are getting a court order to release Bingham's records. We've got our lawyers on it, of course, and have gone to Longshore to talk to the warden. She let us speak with Bingham's cellmate, too. Everything's still in the investigative stages."

"Fact-finding is important." He cleared his throat. "I need to ask you some things. If they offend you I apologize ahead of time."

"Go ahead."

"Did you act unethically?"

"No."

"Did Bishop?"

"No. At least I believe he didn't. He says Bingham's allegations are preposterous."

Larkin leaned forward, bracing his arms on the table. "Kate, rumor has it Bishop was unfaithful to you in the past. With another lawyer, Lindsay Farnum. And that caused your divorce. This Bingham woman charges him with an affair, too."

She tossed back her hair. "He did cheat right at the end of our marriage. But he had reasons. And I think it was the only time."

"You aren't known for getting along that well now. There have been strained moments at social events and professional meetings when you've met up. People still smirk about that time you were trying your hand at criminal court and filled in for another judge, and Reese substituted for another lawyer. There were fireworks then, and you had to recuse yourself."

"People talk, Larry. I can't help that. But I believe Reese when he says this allegation isn't true. And I know, of course, that I didn't do anything wrong."

"What could be this Bingham woman's motive for lying?"

"I have no idea. If the police don't find anything, we'll dig on our own."

"Maybe you should be looking for an investigator now. In case it doesn't go your way."

"Good advice."

"Well," he said pushing back his chair. He didn't stand to leave, though. "I won't keep you. I hope you understand I had to touch base on this."

"Yes, thanks for being so understanding about it." She didn't know exactly what she'd expected.

"I want to be fair. As you know, I've been prompt to chastise some of your actions, but I think you're a good judge." Briefly, he squeezed her shoulder. "And I had hoped to see you rise in the ranks quickly."

"*Had* hoped?"

"This could hurt you professionally. Try to resolve it quickly."

"I will. Do you believe me, Larry?"

"Yes, I believe *you*. I don't, however, have the faith in Bishop that you do. A bit more advice?"

"Of course."

"Don't have too much confidence in your ex-husband. If he goes down, you go down with him."

"Are you saying I should take sides against Reese? That I should blame him?"

"I'm saying you have to protect yourself, Kate. Let him sink if he's guilty, but don't let him pull you under with him." Larry stood, said good-bye, and strode out.

Well, this was a surprise. An unpleasant one. Suddenly, she wondered if she'd been too quick to believe Reese.

With that thought still fresh in her mind, she went back to her chambers and called her lawyer. "Carl," she said, leaving a message on his voice mail. "I just spoke with Judge Larkin. He had some disturbing things to say about Reese. It makes me wonder if I'm going about this in the right way. Call me asap."

Sitting back in her chair, she thought about Larry's words. Everything inside her told her to believe Reese. Other than the infidelity, engendered by her abortion, she had truly believed everything he said. God, could she be wrong?

* * *

REESE WAS PISSED off by the treatment he'd received in court today: real from Ted McAlister; imagined, perhaps, from the judge and other lawyers. Because of that, instead of leaving the courthouse after the hearing, he headed to Kate's chambers on the first floor. She probably wouldn't be here, but if she was, she might be experiencing the same thing and they could commiserate.

He'd only been to her chambers a few times since the divorce. He didn't like going there. As he waited for the elevator with a crowd of people heading home for the night, a fragment of memory hit him. They'd always thrived on competition, until she'd been nominated for a judgeship and he wasn't—something that had been a goal for both of them from day one. Since the baby thing was also between them, their relationship had already been strained . . .

You're jealous of this nomination, aren't you?

No, of course not. I just don't want it to be an excuse not to have another baby.

I'm not sure I want another baby.

You said you did.

Before our life gelled like it did. Look, things are perfect. Why upset the balance?

Because I want another kid. And Sofie shouldn't be an only child. We always agreed on that.

Sofie's ten. She's fine as she is. It's probably worse to have a brother or sister now.

She might be too old because you've hedged so long.

Leave it, Reese. You're becoming really tedious about this.

Oh, excuse me for being tedious about my life!

Recalling that conversation made him uneasy, for reasons he didn't care to explore, so he quelled it as he exited the elevator and headed for her office. Sometimes he wondered why he'd pushed Kate so hard. Was it jealousy of her success? No, he did want a second child. Still he could have lived without one; in the end, he had anyway. He stopped at her chambers and stared at the inscription on the frosted glass: *Judge Kaitlyn Renado.* Shaking his head, he knocked.

"Come in."

He opened the door to find her seated behind her desk, writing on a legal pad. She looked up, wearing her glasses. Her eyes were probably tired. The smudges under them testified to the fact that she was. "Reese, this is a surprise."

Checking his watch, he said, "I just finished upstairs. You done for the day?"

"Yes." She leaned back. She'd removed her suit coat and wore a sage-green silk T-shirt that molded to her breasts. She appeared—what?—stiff with him, stiffer than usual. "Is there something specific you wanted?"

He closed the door and sat down on the opposite side of her desk. The room smelled nice—like perfume and pot-pourri. Framed by diplomas and accolades on the wall behind her, she seemed every inch the successful judge. He cleared his throat. "I wanted to talk to you about something."

"Shoot."

"Did you get any negative reaction at the courthouse these past few days?"

Her pause was meaningful. "Like what?"

"People say anything? Look at you funny? Whisper behind your back?"

She shrugged. "Probably. I tried not to pay attention. Did you get those reactions?"

"And worse." He told her about his client.

"Shit. What happened in the case?"

"As favorable an outcome as possible. I could tell the judge didn't like McAlister's attitude, but I managed to avoid jail time. He got the max fine and a year suspension of his license. Next time this happens he's in deep shit."

"As he should be."

"Agreed."

She sighed.

"What about you?"

"I was called in to meet with Larry Larkin."

"How did that go?"

"He says he believes me."

"You?"

"Excuse me?"

"Your emphasis was on the *me*."

Her face reddened. She squirmed a bit. The subtle reactions might go unnoticed by the casual observer, but he knew this woman inside out. Though they both often played things close to the vest with others, he could always read her face better than anyone. "Was it?"

"You know it was. Doesn't he believe *me*?"

Her cell phone rang. She pulled it out from her pocket, and scowled. "I'll let it go." She glanced back up at him. "I didn't say Larry didn't believe you."

"You didn't say he did."

"Reese, please, don't start on me." She checked her watch. "Why did you come here?"

"For reassurance. That I'm not getting, Kate."

"I—" This time her office phone rang. She ignored it but an odd expression passed across her face.

"Kate, talk to me. Tell me what's going on."

Before she could answer him, the machine picked up. "Kate, this is Carl. I got your message about Reese. Call me."

Reese felt his blood pressure rise. Along with a swift kick to his heart. "About me? What message about me?"

She bit her lip.

"Larkin doesn't believe me. Why?"

"He said there were rumors about you and Lindsay Farnum." She swallowed hard. "Rumors, of course, that were true."

"Which makes me guilty with Bingham? Jesus, he's judge."

"It goes to pattern, Reese. He's right to be worried."

"And did he convince you to be worried?"

"He said I should watch out for myself."

"By what?" He glanced at the phone. "By blaming me openly. Clearing yourself and implicating me?"

"No! I'd never do that to you."

"Is that why you called your lawyer?"

"I wanted to talk to Carl about it all." She raised her chin. "There's nothing wrong with that."

How could she even consider turning against him publicly? He was so angry he threw back his chair and stood. "I can't believe you'd do this to me. We were married for fifteen years. We meant everything to each other. The divorce was both our faults. And you're *considering* hanging me out to dry and saving yourself?" He shook his head. "Why the hell was I thinking that we could work together without this animosity flaring between us?" He gave her one last scathing glance and stormed out of her office.

Shocked, and stupidly, *stupidly* hurt by this new development, Reese found his way to the exit of the courthouse.

FIVE

HER BREATHING LABORED, Kate nevertheless kept running in the cool, Friday morning April air. She'd awakened at four and had been unable to go back to sleep, so she decided to outdistance the demons by pounding the pavement.

Demon number one, though, kept up the pace she set as she jogged down her tree-lined street, two miles outside of town. The police reports weren't looking good for her and Reese. The cops were close to ruling Anna Bingham's death a suicide. And they hadn't been pleased with the interference Kate and Reese had brought to their investigation. The seasoned captain in charge had told their lawyers he knew how to do his fuckin' job, and to back off.

She speeded up and took a slight incline. Her calves began to ache but she kept going, letting the breeze ruffle her hair and revitalize her. Demon number two was right on her heels. A reporter from the *Herald* had been hounding her and Reese for a statement about their response to Anna Bingham's charges. Eddie Wick had taken an interest in the case and had speculated in yesterday's paper why

Reese and Kate wouldn't talk to the press. The editorial had a negative slant, asserting that the public had a right to know their response. It implied they were hiding something.

Kate reached the top of the hill and slowed down a bit. No sense in killing herself. Since she hadn't been sleeping or eating right, she shouldn't overdo the exercise. Catching her breath, she set herself an easier pace. Demon number three—the head honcho—came out and ran right alongside her. Reese. He'd been so angry about her misgivings. He'd stormed out of her office on Wednesday, full of righteous indignation. Though she'd known he'd always been angry with her, the vehemence of his reaction to her talk with Larkin had almost frightened her. Damn it, nothing was easy about that man. He messed up her thinking. He gave her headaches. He caused an insomnia that was driving her crazy. Maybe it *would* be best to take sides against him. That way, she wouldn't have to work with him anymore and this disturbing contact with him would stop. Judge Larkin had given her that advice. So had Carl and Tyler . . .

Her lawyer hadn't had to think too hard about it. "We should listen to Larry Larkin. He has his pulse on the legal world in Westwood. He'd know if associating with Reese, siding with Reese, will hurt you. Remember, I mentioned this line of defense earlier and said we'd wait for the police report to take a position. If Bingham's death is ruled a homicide, you're off the hook. If it is indeed ruled a suicide, you have to make a choice. I vote to blame Reese, if it comes to that. After all, *he's* accused of the affair."

Kate had felt a sinking in her stomach. "The note says I was in collusion with him."

"We can imply that Reese lied to her about that."

"I don't know, Carl. I simply don't believe it of Reese."

"He had another affair, Kate. That gives you the upper hand."

"I know. But that was right before the divorce. The thing with Bingham was supposed to have happened when Reese and I were both thirty-five. We'd just celebrated our tenth wedding anniversary. Things couldn't have been better between us."

"You've got a way out of this. Think about taking it."

So Kate had talked about it to Tyler . . .

"I think Wakefield's right," he'd said over dinner two nights ago at La Dolce Vita, her favorite Italian restaurant. She used to dine there with Reese. Tyler's blue eyes were sober and he'd looked like he hadn't been sleeping well, either.

"You think he's guilty?" she asked.

Ever fair, ever the good guy, his face had flushed. "I didn't say that. I think blaming him can clear *you*, which is what I want."

"Don't you want the truth?"

"Maybe not." He'd sat back and sipped his wine. Shook his head. "I can't believe I'm jealous enough to say this, but I'd do almost anything to get you away from that guy. If you thrust this off on Reese, that would solidify your break with him."

"Tyler, the *divorce* solidified it."

"No, it never did. And now, you're getting drawn back into his life. I can feel it."

Because Tyler might be right, because the notion scared her, she'd given a lot of thought to turning on Reese Bishop.

Only Jillian had suggested any reason to think she shouldn't . . .

"What was going on in your marriage at the time?" Jillian had asked at Gavels where they met for a glass of wine after work last night.

"Oh, Jillian. It was a heady time. We'd opened the law firm and were doing great. We'd just gotten those classy offices. We couldn't handle all the clients we had. Sofie was six and had started school. She was a happy, sunny child, and loved life then. And we'd bought and renovated that farmhouse just outside of town; I loved that place so much it broke my heart to sell it."

"Doesn't sound like he had time to cheat, even if he did have the inclination."

"I can't make myself believe he'd want to. We were so close. I would have known if he was seeing someone else, like I did with Malibu Barbie."

"Well then, there's your answer. If you do believe him, I know you won't turn him over to the sharks to cover your own ass . . ."

Still running, Kate had made her way to town and stopped at a bench near the coffee shop on Main Street. She checked her watch. The place was due to open in ten minutes. Maybe she'd grab some coffee and then head home. Dropping down on the bench, she knew she had to make a decision. And she knew she could only find the answer in her heart. Would Reese really have screwed their client ten years ago? *Think, Kate, think.* All of what she'd told Jillian was true. And so much more.

They'd gone on a trip to celebrate their tenth wedding anniversary that year, right before they took on Anna Bingham's case. They'd returned to Florida, to Siesta Key, where they'd spent their honeymoon . . .

"Look, Reese," Kate had said staring out of a penthouse condo window on Siesta Key Beach the first morning they were there. This time of day the sun gilded the water and the *whoosh* of the waves was soothing. "That beach is so beautiful." It was advertised to have the best sand in the world.

"Not as beautiful as my wife of ten years." He'd come up behind her and circled her waist with his arms. He was nuzzling her neck.

"Remember our honeymoon here?"

He'd grinned. "We had that shabby hotel room, six blocks from the beach. It was sweltering hot at night, and was smaller than a postage stamp."

"It had a bed. That's all we cared about."

His lips had traveled from her ear to her neck and she luxuriated in the feel of his mouth on her.

"Remember the plans we made out there on that very sand, the dreams we had?"

"And we've gotten it all, sweetheart."

She'd pivoted in his arms. "It can't get any better than this, Reese."

He started to unbutton her blouse. "Hmm. Let's see what I can do about proving that statement false, Counselor."

Gently, she'd stayed his hands. "I'm serious. I love our life. I love you, so much. Promise me it'll always be this good."

His face lost the sexy tease and sobered. His green eyes had glittered like polished jade. "I promise it'll only get better. I love you, too, Kate. I'll never do anything to hurt you . . ."

Her eyes began to mist. Those had been the vows they'd made at their wedding. Sappy. Sentimental. Emotional as hell.

"I'll protect you from others who want to . . . I'll give you everything I have and always put your needs above mine . . . I'll stay with you no matter how tough life gets and rejoice in the good things . . ." By the time he'd finished reciting those precious words they had written ten years before, she'd been sobbing . . .

Sitting on the bench, Kate sighed. She'd forgotten they'd renewed their vows again, in the privacy of their suite overlooking Siesta Key Beach, as the sun rose into the pink and white sky over the gulf, on their anniversary.

Now, as she looked at another sunrise, this time over Westwood's horizon, Kate knew the truth. A man who vowed all those things on that beautiful, sunny morning, wouldn't have an affair with a client the next month.

When the coffee shop opened, Kate stood, crossed the road and entered it. There were no customers inside yet; the pungent smell of strong coffee suffused the small space, and a waitress was behind the counter sipping from a steaming mug. Before Kate could close the door, someone came in behind her.

A delivery boy for the *Herald*. Turning, she saw him place a stack of the morning papers on the counter.

From where she stood, the headline leaped out at her.
NEW JERSEY POLICE DECLARE DEATH OF ANNA BING-
HAM A SUICIDE.

REESE OPENED THE door to his house and stepped out
into the morning air, cool at seven a.m. He shivered in his
pj's bottoms, having not thought to put on a shirt because
his mind was muddled from tossing and turning all night;
finally he'd given up on sleep at five. He'd downed a pot of
coffee by the time he heard the newspaper delivered.

At the mailbox, he snagged the *Herald* out of its metal
cylinder and turned to go back to the house, when his gaze
caught on a cab coming down the street, unusual for this
hour, on this quiet suburban street. He was further surprised to see the taxi stop in front of his house, and
shocked to see his ex-wife climb out of the car—dressed a
black-and-white running suit. His pulse began to thrum.
He was still furious at her for doubting him. He'd met with
his lawyer and they had a strategy all planned if she sold
him out.

Which he guessed she would. Maybe that's what she'd
come to tell him. Kaitlyn Renado never backed away
from a fight and he knew she'd inform him of her decision face-to-face.

She paid the cabbie and approached him. For a minute
he was taken aback by her appeal—the sun rising behind
her, the flush on her face from running, some of that glorious hair escaping from a tie of the ponytail. "Hi."

"Kate." He said her name stiffly. He wasn't about to be
bulldozed by her beauty when she was going to bury him.

Nodding to the paper, she asked, "Did you read that yet?"

He shook his head and opened it; the headline jumped
out at him. "Terrific." He glanced up at her. "How bad is it?"

"Bad. The reporter who's taken an interest in us—Eddie
Wick—peppers our name through the whole thing."

"Fuck!" He skimmed the article. " 'No response from

the judge and lawyer . . . police say Bingham's note is genuine . . . don't lawyers and judges have an ethical responsibility to their clients . . .' "

He lifted his chin and looked at her. He'd never been one to back down, either, even when the odds were against him. "Do I even need to ask if this means you're going solo? I'd guess that's the advice from everybody in your life."

Cocking her head, she gave him a sad smile. "Since when did I listen to advice?"

He frowned. "What are you saying?"

"I'm not going to clear myself at your expense."

"Why?"

"Because it wouldn't be right. I've been doing a lot of thinking and I remembered where we were in our life together at the time we took on Anna Bingham."

Still he said nothing. Didn't even move.

"Do you remember our tenth wedding anniversary?"

Of course he did . . . the warmth of the sand, the salty scent of the gulf, the hot, sultry night air . . . "How could I ever forget Siesta Key?"

"Things were good then, Reese. Better than ever. At that time, you would never have cheated with another woman, let alone a criminal like Anna Bingham. Even if I hadn't remembered that second honeymoon, I should have known, given the fact that she broke the law you love, that you wouldn't hook up with her."

Reese had to swallow hard. His emotions were running high because of the case and because of Kate's previous suspicions. "Thank you for that." He averted his gaze from hers. "I was having a hard time with your doubts."

She squeezed his arm. "I would have felt that way, too, if I thought you were going to hang me out to dry."

"So," he said, embarrassed by how good it felt to have her faith in him. "Want to come in and talk about what we're going to do now?"

She checked her watch. "I don't have to be in court until ten." She glanced at the house. "Won't Little Miss Muffet mind?"

"Be nice," he said, easing a hand to her back and nudging her toward the door. "And I'll refrain from bad-mouthing Peter Pan."

It was a silly conversation, but it lightened his heart.

Once inside, he poured her some coffee and flavored it himself with hazelnut creamer. She looked around at the sunny, oak paneled interior. "This is lovely," she said nodding to the room. "It reminds me of our kitchen on Old Town Line Road."

He hoped like hell that wasn't unconsciously why he bought this house. "I like it."

Grabbing his own coffee and a legal pad and pen, he sat next to her. "First off, we have to hold a press conference, preferably today, to publicly deny Bingham's allegation and present a united front."

"Agreed."

"Then we have to investigate two threads. The first is that Bingham did commit suicide and lied about our role in it for some reason."

"Right, then we'd have to determine why."

Heads bent, they began making a list of their moves: hire a private investigator to look into Anna Bingham's life in and out of prison; study her phone calls, disciplinary action, etc., through prison records, which they'd already filed for; talk to her lawyers for the subsequent crimes; get a look at her personal effects.

It took an hour to finish the list. When Reese pushed away the pad, he sighed. "Then there's thread number two—that she was murdered and the note is false. Someone else planted it and made her death look like a suicide. And"—he shook his head—"blamed us for it."

"I've been thinking about that since we brought it up on the drive to see Sofie. It still means somebody is lying about us? Why?"

"I've given it a lot of thought, too. I can only come up

with one reason. That the person who did it has an ax to grind with us."

"Are you saying she was killed to get to us?" Kate asked.

"I'm saying it's a possibility."

"Oh, my God, Reese. I don't know what I expected, but it wasn't this. It's so vicious. And dramatic."

Reaching out, he took her hand. "I had the same reaction. But, I'm damned if I can think of another reason the note would implicate us. She falsely accused me. Either she killed herself to get back at us—for no reason, which is far-fetched—or someone used her to get to us. We'd need to determine why."

The thought was stark. Kate shifted subtly, leaned in and pressed her head onto his shoulder, as if she needed the contact. He did, too, so he moved closer, laid his cheek on her hair and a hand on her back.

He was about to say something when he heard behind him, "What's going on here, Reese?"

Dray's voice. Rightfully suspicious and annoyed, given the tableau he knew he and Kate made.

AT HER GYM, Dray closed herself in her office and picked up the phone. She dialed her adopted sister's cell, a special one that accepted overseas calls. Phoebe Merrill was in France searching, Dray knew, for something she'd never find. She hated to bother her there, but Lacey, her other sister, was busy planning her wedding, and Dray didn't want to dump something this depressing on her.

"Phoebe Merrill." Hearing her sister's voice was calming.

"Hey, Phoeb, it's Dray."

Though Phoebe had special problems, or maybe because of them, she always sensed when someone—especially one of her sisters—was hurting. "What's wrong, honey?"

Dray battled back tears. "I just needed to talk to you. Where are you?"

"At the Institute."

Every few years, Phoebe went back on the road. She was a physical therapist, who'd gotten into what Tyler had been doing in his Well Child Project—music and dance therapy. Right now, she was at the Institute for Autism in Paris, studying selective mutism in children. She and Dray had gone to college together after Dray and Lacey had literally found Phoebe on the side of the road when she was sixteen, and Dray was seventeen. Beaten and battered, Phoebe had sustained an injury to her brain that led to amnesia. Though it sounded melodramatic, there was scientific evidence that she would probably never regain her memory of life before they found her.

"Good classes?"

"Yeah, you should come over to France."

"Not now."

"Because of Reese?"

"Oh, Phoeb, things are bad." She explained the situation.

"Dray, you deserve better than he's ever given you, which is only half of himself. Now he's withdrawing even more. It sucks."

"I love him."

A silence. At thirty-one, Phoebe had never let herself love anyone. "I'm sorry. I know it's not easy. But I worry about you. I need to see you."

"You'll be home in a few weeks for Lacey's wedding."

"Still, I wish I could come there right now and take care of you."

"That means a lot."

"Honey, did talking to me make it worse? If it has, I'm sorry. I just want you to be happy."

Dray drilled a pencil on the tabletop. "Nothing you do could make it worse. I'll feel better when I see you again."

"I hope so. Meanwhile, remember, you deserve better than this."

"Yeah, I do. But I'm not giving up on Reese yet."

Dray hung up. She'd lied to her sister. She did feel worse. Because Phoebe was right. Dray shouldn't put up

with Reese's distancing. She could still see him hugging
Kate in the kitchen this morning. And she knew in her
heart, Reese wasn't distancing his ex-wife physically or
emotionally. Instead, they were growing closer.

Damn it. Damn *him*. Dray really didn't know what to
do. She glanced at the clock. Right now he and Kate were
in a press conference with the reporter who'd been after a
statement from them. Hell of a thing, she'd probably find
out more about what Reese was thinking by reading the
newspaper tomorrow morning than what he himself would
tell her.

EDDIE WICK FIT the old-time newsman stereotype to a
tee: rumpled clothing hung on a lanky frame, sandy brown
hair casually mussed, and cigarettes stuck proudly out of
his shirt pocket, just waiting to be lit. His Columbo-like
appearance immediately put Kate on edge.

"Thanks for seeing me, Bishop." He nodded to Kate.
"Judge Renado."

"You're welcome, Mr. Wick." Reese's tone was polite,
but authoritative. Dressed in an impeccable gray suit, surrounded by the elegance of the conference room at his offices, he looked confident and in control.

Kate had put on a navy suit, and kept her own body language neutral. "May I ask you why you've taken such an
aggressive interest in this story?"

A slash of eyebrows shot up. "John Q. Public has a right
to know if a local attorney abused a client, before he hires
on with the firm. And if a judge here in River City did something this unethical, should she continue to adjudicate?"

Kate stiffened. Reese frowned.

"Besides, you're news. Westwood's *Herald* has covered
you since you settled here after law school. We got bulging
files on you, your cases, some social things. One article
called you the 'Cinderella Couple'."

Their attorneys, seated at the table, glanced at each

other. Then Carl said, "I hope you aren't out to destroy the fairy tale, Mr. Wick."

"Fairy tale took a nosedive when divorce came into the picture." He checked his notes. He even had one of those flipping pads, though he was taping the interview. As was Reese. They wanted a record of exactly what they'd said in case they were misquoted. "When was that?" Wick asked.

"Five years ago."

The reporter arched a brow. "Comin' up on your twentieth anniversary."

Damn it. Kate hadn't thought about their wedding anniversary. Not that she ever did. She ruthlessly blocked it from her radar screen every single year. Christ, this was just what they needed now.

"Filed for irreconcilable differences?"

"Yes." Reese's voice was still even. Kate wondered if he was as affected by what Wick had pointed out as she was.

"No piece on the side causing the split, Bishop?"

Kate assumed the reporter had heard the rumors about Reese and Lindsay Farnum somewhere.

"That is a totally inappropriate comment, Wick," Marcia told the guy. "If you're going to take this tack, then the interview is over."

"Sorry if that offends anybody's sensibilities, but Bishop here is accused of infidelity in Bingham's suicide note. If he got some on the side before, it would be more proof of your guilt."

"As far as I know, Eddie," Reese said, "there is *no* proof of our guilt at all."

"Right." He turned to Kate. "So you didn't divorce him because he cheated?"

At least that could be answered truthfully. "No, I divorced him because we wanted different things at that point."

Again, the reporter studied his notes. "Hmm. You two applied for a judgeship at the same time and you didn't get it, right Bishop?"

"That's correct."

"That drive you apart?"

Kate saw Reese swallow hard. He took a bead on Wick. "Can we get off the divorce? It happens to more than fifty percent of the population."

Wick shrugged. "Do you agree with the police's findings that Anna Bingham committed suicide?"

"We think," Carl put in, "that's one possibility. We *know* the note falsely accuses Kate and Reese. We're going to find out why."

"One possibility? You thinkin' somebody took her out in prison and faked the note?"

Kate wondered what it said about herself that she hoped that was true. "We have to explore every possibility."

"Somebody who wanted to discredit you two, maybe?"

Marcia said, "Lawyers make a lot of enemies, Wick."

He smirked, then his brow narrowed. "Can you think of any cases where a client was mad enough at you to nail you this way? It's a big leap, but having suspects might lend credibility to the story."

"We know it's a big leap," Reese answered honestly. "But something isn't right in Denmark, since her accusations are false. We intend to prove that."

Wick went on to ask them about the prison, the possibility of assaults and murders occurring, and some speculation on white-collar crime. Then he went back to their bio. "I see you both come from modest backgrounds. Went to Cornell and U of R respectively, and Yale, all on scholarships. Your rise in the legal world was equally impressive."

They explained how they'd clerked for very prestigious judges, given Kate was valedictorian of their class and Reese was salutatorian; how they'd landed great jobs in a fast track law firm, made partners there at a young age and finally went out on their own.

"Harrumph, that really is storybook material."

"Yes, well, we had a nice life." Kate's voice carried harsh overtones she hadn't meant to be there. It was just that hearing how good she and Reese had had it, and lost it, upset her.

"Got a kid, right?"

"Yes."

"She goes to Connor Prep?" His expression asked why.

"She's very bright." Reese smiled at Kate. "Takes after her mom."

"And talented. Like her dad."

"Aw, isn't that sweet." He shook his head. "All this solidarity, this niceness, makes me wonder how you ever got divorced."

Kate sighed. She glanced at Reese. His expression mirrored what she was feeling. How *had* they let the Cinderella story end so badly?

"WHERE HAVE YOU been?" Kate asked, right at the very end, when Reese rolled in just as the grandfather clock his dad had given them chimed 2:00 a.m. She'd been waiting up for him and confronted him in the den.

"What does it matter?"

"If you've given up on this relationship, I have a right to know."

Crossing to the sidebar, he poured himself a scotch that he didn't want. He'd already had too many. Pivoting he sipped it and studied her. She wore ice-blue satiny pajamas and her hair was loose around her shoulders. Even with what was between them, she stirred him. "I have given up on us. Finally."

Her face drained of color. "When did you decide this?"

"How about when we started sleeping in different rooms? When we stopped eating together, talking about our jobs, fighting so badly that Sofie wants to stay at her best friend's house all the time?" Which is where their child had gone that night.

"That's been going on for months. What brought your decision on now?"

"I'm sick of pretending. I want it done."

"Were you with Lindsay Farnum tonight?" Her voice trembled.

"Yes."

"Well. That says it all, doesn't it? You can have your divorce. I won't be made a fool of."

"Of course not, the soon-to-be Honorable Judge Kaitlyn Renado wouldn't allow that."

He'd seen something he hadn't expected then. A weakening. A vulnerability. "Reese, if it's mostly my appointment to the bench, we can deal with that. We've competed for years, beat each other out, silently lauded the other when they won. You'll get your judgeship."

Stalking over to her, he'd gripped her arm. "Maybe if you hadn't had an abortion I would have been able to weather it. This divorce is your fault."

"No, it's yours, too. All the accusations, the bickering, the whoring around that you did brought us to this point."

"I wouldn't have whored around if you hadn't walked into a clinic and had our child's life sucked out of you."

His crudeness made her go on the attack. "Admit it. You only wanted another child so I'd have a harder time handling a judgeship."

It was at that moment, standing in the living room, that Reese realized she was right. Oh, sure, he'd always planned on having another kid. Vaguely though, without the importance he attached to it when she got closer to the brass ring. And once he realized that was the kind of person he'd turned into, that's what their wonderful, exciting glamorous marriage had become, he'd said the words that he knew would cause the permanent split—and had.

"You're right, Kate. I pushed hard for another baby because I didn't want you going for this appointment. For the first time in our lives together, I didn't wish you well."

Since that said it all, he'd left the next morning and filed for divorce.

SIX

SOFIE TRUNDLED DOWN the staircase in her father's house, wearing a black skirt and a striped blouse. She'd taken off the T-shirt she first put on that read, *In my world, you don't exist,* because she knew her father would make her change. He was tougher than her mother, who Sofie could bulldoze with her outrage. Besides, he'd be hurt and she hated to make him feel bad. Judge Judy had done enough of that. But especially today, after he'd driven up to school to get her yesterday and put on this party for her, she wanted to be nice.

Off to the right of the steps, the family room had been decorated with balloons and crepe paper—compliments of the bimbo—and a big sign that read, *Happy Birthday, Sofie. Sweet Sixteen.*

There was nothing sweet about being sixteen in Sofie's world.

From the archway, her gaze fell upon a photo album that had been set out on the coffee table. She didn't want to look at it because she knew what it contained—baby pictures of her. When they were a family, the album got dragged out every year on her birthday. Her mother would insist they go through it together, and both parents would get all misty-eyed. Sofie had loved looking at the album with them. Now, the pictures just reminded her of all she'd lost, so she left it untouched.

A stack of presents filled the corner and she crossed to them. Some from her dad, three from her aunts on her mother's side who were out west. Judge Judy was close to them, and they'd visited Arizona often; and every time her mother talked to them on the phone, they'd want to speak to Sofie. But she hadn't seen the Renado sisters in a long time. Hell, she barely saw her mother, who'd wigged out big time when Sofie told her she was staying with her dad for this weekend.

"Hey, no peeking," she heard from behind her.

Turning, she saw the bimbo had come into the room. Christ, the woman looked about Sofie's age with her long blond hair streaming down her back, tight tan jeans, pretty white top, and perfect makeup. Trying to sound bored, Sofie said, "I don't care enough to peek."

Dray frowned. She came to stand before Sofie. "Your father went to a lot of trouble for this party today. He's excited that your grandfather, aunt and cousins are coming to Westwood. Even if you're determined not to enjoy it, please don't spoil it for him."

Sofie's heart ached, but she'd be damned if she let this chick see it. "Chill, lady. I won't spoil anything."

Dray lifted her chin. "Can I ask you something?"

"Knock yourself out."

"Why do you dislike me so much?"

"Start with the fact that you're closer to my age than my dad's."

"That's not true. I'm thirty-two. You know that."

"Still too young for him."

"Would you feel differently if I was older?"

Sofie shrugged. The answer to that was no, so she kept her mouth shut.

"I didn't think so." Dray folded her arms across her big boobs. "I'm in love with your father. I want to marry him."

"He had a wife. Didn't work out. I wouldn't count on a happily-ever-after if I were you."

"Are you hoping he'll go back with your mother?"

Yes. "Nope. Judge Judy's too busy for Pops. And me."

"Five years is a long time to be so bitter."

"So sue me. No wait. You're the jock, dad's the lawyer."

Dray touched Sofie's arm and squeezed it. "I'm sorry you feel this way about your life. But please, don't take it out on your dad, at least today."

Was she for real? When Sofie's conscience forced her to admit the woman was being genuine, and she herself was being a shit, she felt bad. "Sure, okay. I won't." She'd go after her mother instead.

From the doorway, Reese took a bead on the two women in his life, hoping they could get along, at least for today. "What's going on in here? You aren't peeking at presents, are you?"

"Sofie tells me she doesn't peek," Dray told him, with a phony smile.

"Ah. She used to. When she was little, she'd sneak around every holiday or birthday and try to find presents. Once, she climbed into our closet and accidentally locked herself in. Cried bloody murder till we got her out."

Sofie smiled at the memory.

"Well, that's nice to see."

Dray headed out. "I'm going to check on the food." She touched Reese's arm as she swept by him. Some pretty perfume followed in her wake.

Reese crossed to his daughter. He brushed back her strawlike hair, wishing like hell he'd find a way to reach her. "Happy about today?"

"Sure. Especially since I get to see Grandpa, Aunt Emily and the boys. What time are they getting here?"

"Any minute. You haven't seen them in a while."

She shook her head, her hand creeping to her hair. "Grandpa won't like this."

"No, he won't." He cocked his head. "Why'd you do that to yourself, Sof?"

Because my hair looked too much like Mom's. "For a change."

He waited a beat. "Do me a favor, princess?"

"Yeah, sure."

"Be nice to your mother today. She's going through a lot, and it still stings that you wouldn't stay there this weekend."

"You're having the party."

"I know. Just be nice to her."

"Why do you care, Daddy?"

"Because it hurts you as much as it does her when you go on the attack. Or worse, when you ignore her."

"Give me a break. Nothing penetrates Judge Judy's armor."

"It does. In any case, humor me."

Sofie nodded. "Whatever." The doorbell sounded, and Reese said, "That's probably my family." He held out his hand. "Let's go, birthday girl."

She leaned into her dad, and he slid an arm around her shoulders. "Thanks for the party, Daddy. I love you."

"Ah, I like hearing that." His daughter had no idea how much he meant that. Those words, which used to come naturally and often from her, had been absent from her vocabulary for months. He kissed her hair. "I love you, too."

"I'm gonna hit the bathroom before I go out there." She nodded to the foyer.

He squeezed her fingers and watched her head down the hall, then he walked into the foyer in time to see his dad, sister and nephews step inside and greet Dray.

In a few seconds, towheaded Jason caught sight of him. "Uncle Reese!" he shouted and flew across the tile.

Reese barely caught the boy before another ball of fire hurled himself after Jason. He hugged both guys. Jimmy wailed, "Uncle Reese. It's been forever."

Reese chuckled. He'd seen them just last month.

"Hey, how are my best guys?" He'd fallen for Emily's

kids hook, line and sinker when they were born. Since her divorce, and the death of her ex, Reese had tried to spend as much time with them as he could.

Standing, with a boy hanging on to each leg, he said, "Hi, Pa."

At sixty-eight, Bill Bishop was still a strapping man. His shoulders were as wide as Reese's and his height the same. Always demonstrative, he hugged Reese. Drawing back, he ran a hand through his still thick head of white hair. "Good to see you, Son."

Emily came closer. Her face was lined with fatigue. "Hey, big Brother, how are you?"

"Great." What a lie. He hadn't told his family about Anna Bingham. He'd been hoping the case would be solved before he had to fill them in. Hugging Emily, he noticed she felt thinner than just a month ago. And her jeans and blouse hung on her. "How's my favorite sister?"

"Great." She was lying, too, of course.

"We'll talk later," he whispered to her. With Kate out of the picture, Emily was the one person he confided in, especially in recent years since things had gone badly for both of them.

"You betcha."

"Where's the birthday girl?" his dad asked.

"Right here." Sofie came up behind him.

Reese had to give his family credit. Both his dad and Emily only missed a beat before they said, "Hey, girl, give Grandpa a hug," and "There she is. Come to your aunt."

However, the boys were not so circumspect. "Holy cow," Jason blurted out, "What happened to your hair?"

Jimmy followed up with, "It looks like straw."

Sofie scowled and Reese prayed she didn't blow. After a moment's hesitation, she bent down, hugged each boy and ruffled their blond heads. "I'm trying to look like my only cousins," she said, smiling.

"Cool," Jason told her.

"Yeah, cool," Jimmy parroted.

Way cool, Reese thought. Letting out a breath, he caught

Sofie's gaze and got a glimpse of the little girl that once in a while peeked out from behind the sullen teenager. Maybe today would go well after all.

KATE GRIPPED TYLER'S hand as they took the brick walkway to Reese's backyard. It had warmed up for mid-April and she could hear voices coming from the behind the house. They must have set up outside for the party. The party she'd had no part of. Her baby was turning sixteen and not only wasn't Sofie staying with Kate, but she hadn't helped plan the event. When Dray Merrill had called to ask if she wanted input, Kate had curtly refused. She'd regretted it later.

"Looking forward to this?" Tyler asked, leaning into her.

"Sure."

"Liar. You're dreading it."

"I'm dreading whatever new kind of torture Sofie's conjured up for me."

"She's really been out of line lately," he said as they rounded the house.

Reese's property was lovely. A half acre of spring-green grass, big oak trees, a two-level deck, a couple of umbrella tables, strategically placed. Though Kate doubted he picked out the mauve-and-blue theme. Little Mary Sunshine probably did the decorating. They'd crossed to the deck when his family saw them.

Immediately Bill Bishop stood and Kate braced herself. Though she spent some time with Emily and the boys, she'd had little contact with Reese's father since the divorce. "Well, there she is. Come here, Kate, my girl. I want a hug after all this time."

And just like it was yesterday, she walked into the older man's arms. The smell of Old Spice and the hint of tobacco catapulted her back to the past . . . *My boy loves you and now I know why. Thank you for my grandchild, honey. She's as beautiful as her mom . . . Oh, no, Kate, my girl, you gotta work out these problems with Reese.*

"Hi, Pa," she whispered, holding on tightly.

His hug was lumberjack strong and Kate reveled in it. Her father had died five years after she and Reese were married, and Reese's dad had neatly stepped in to fill that void. When Bill drew back, his eyes were moist. Unlike Reese, he'd always worn his emotions on his sleeve. "You look like a million bucks, honey."

She tossed back her hair, which she'd let hang loose today, and smoothed down her red polka dot capris and blouse. "Thanks. You always were good for my ego." When Tyler moved beside her, she said, "I don't think you've met my friend, Tyler Sloan."

It was brief. Just a flash of disapproval in Pa's eyes, which were a shade darker than Reese's. "Tyler." Pa held out his hand. "Nice to meet you."

"You too, sir."

Over Bill Bishop's shoulder, Kate saw Emily emerge from the house through the French doors. Reese's sister looked much older than her thirty-nine years. Her hair was limp, her eyes dulled with fatigue; her posture spoke of weariness. When she saw Kate, though, her whole face perked up. "Hey, Kate."

Crossing to Emily, Kate hugged her warmly. "Hi, honey. How are you?"

Reese's sister returned the embrace. "It's so good to see you."

Kate closed her eyes, remembering Emily's total acceptance of her. *I always wanted a sister . . . You're so cool, Kate, you're the only one good enough for Reese . . .* And she'd cried when she called Kate after Reese told them about the impending divorce.

"You okay?" Kate asked.

"Yeah, I'm fine."

"I—" Just then, Sofie appeared in the doorway, looking almost normal in a nice outfit and no makeup. With her were Jason and Jimmy.

"Aunt Ka-te," they said in unison as they flung themselves at her.

Bending down she grasped onto the little boys, basking in the feel and smell of their sturdy little bodies. "How are my guys?"

"We're big. I'm fifty-one inches and Jay's forty-nine."

"Almost fifty," Jay said, burying his face in her shoulder. "You smell good, Aunt Kate. Want to push me on the swings?"

"Sure. Let me say hi to Sofie first."

Her daughter, who'd been leaning against the door, straightened when Kate came toward her. "Happy Birthday, sweetie," Kate said. She reached out, despite the fact that she knew Sofie could embarrass her in front of everybody. But she'd be damned if she'd not hug her child on her birthday.

Sofie went into her arms almost willingly. Kate enveloped her, breathed in her scent. She remembered the feel of her child exactly sixteen years ago today, how she'd clutched the naked, wet newborn to her chest, and stared down at the miracle she'd created. Later, she'd done the clichéd thing of unwrapping her infant, counting her fingers and toes, marveling at how small and beautiful she was.

As if Sofie sensed something, too, she held on longer. "Thanks, Mama."

It was such a little thing, the warmth. But it meant more to Kate than winning a Supreme Court judgeship.

"Come *on*, Sof," Jason said, now tugging at his cousin's hands. "You said you'd play croquet with us."

"Okay." Pulling back from her mother, she didn't meet Kate's gaze as she skipped away with the boys.

Kate took the opportunity to slip into the house to compose herself. She crossed the tiled area where she'd sat with Reese just yesterday and went into the family room. She spotted the photo album lying on the coffee table, and couldn't resist picking it up.

Inside was the story of Sofie's life. Sinking onto the couch, she laid the precious volume on her lap and looked at the first picture. It was the sonogram, taken when Kate was four months pregnant. Kate remembered the thrill of seeing that little heartbeat on the monitor. Reese had cried. On the next page were shots just minutes after birth. Kate—sweaty and exhausted, Sofie wailing, Reese, appearing dazed.

"Kate, what are you doing in here?"

She looked up at the sound of Reese's voice. Standing in the doorway, he jammed his hands into the pockets of the nice gray slacks that he wore with a silk T-shirt. "I'm . . . catching my breath."

He came close enough so she could smell the aftershave he used. It was different from the one he used to wear, the one she'd loved. "Was my father all right to you?"

"Are you kidding? He treated me like the prodigal daughter. He's so kind, Reese."

"He always loved you." A smile broached his sculpted mouth. "I'll bet the boys gushed at their favorite aunt."

"Yeah."

His face turned soft. "Too much?"

"No, it was great. And Sofie actually hugged me. Was nice to me."

He squeezed her shoulder. "I'm glad." He noticed the photo album on her lap, and after a brief hesitation, squatted down. "I love looking at this thing."

"Me, too." She turned a page. A picture of her breast-feeding Sofie had been blown up.

Reese reached out and traced the outline of Sofie's nose. Somehow, maybe because Kate's breast was exposed, the gesture seemed intimate. "I loved watching you feed her. It was sacred, almost."

Kate cleared her throat. Emotion welled inside her as Reese continued to turn the pages—Sofie coming home from the hospital, at her baptism, wearing a tiny white dress with a white bonnet. When a picture of Reese, holding a diapered infant on his bare chest, rocking her, appeared on the next page, Kate closed her eyes.

"Hey, what's this?"

She looked down to see his finger on the page, tracing a wet spot. Swallowing hard, she swiped at her cheeks. "Nothing of consequence."

"You were always sentimental on her birthday."

"I know." She closed the album, and shoved it into his hands. Taking the hint, he rose. She did, too, and wrapped her arms around her waist. In an effort to change the subject, to run from the poignancy of all she'd lost, Kate raked back her hair and faced him. "Have you told your family about the Bingham thing?"

"Yeah, I corned Pa and Em for a few minutes. They're mad as hell."

"The support must feel good."

He cocked his head. "Did you call your sisters about it?"

"No. I don't want them to worry."

"Well, you shouldn't deal with all this alone."

"I've got Tyler."

His features lost their softness. "Ah, yes, of course."

"Let's not discuss this now. We'll deal with it when we meet with the private investigator on Monday. Let's just have fun today." She started to walk away. He called her back.

"Katie?"

She turned to him. He'd picked up the album and held it out in front of him. "There were a lot of good times. Especially when she was born. When she was little."

Again, her eyes misted. "I know. It seems like a lifetime ago."

Unspoken was the fact that they could have repeated the experience—had another child together.

He sighed. "How did we . . ." He stopped, watched her for a minute, but shook his head and didn't continue.

She didn't ask what he was about to say. What ever it was, it was better left unsaid.

DRAY WATCHED THE French doors from the lower deck, where she'd gone to check on the snacks she'd put out. She bit her lip, telling herself not to be so insecure.

"They've only been inside a few minutes." She turned to find Tyler had joined her. Dressed in cargo pants and an oversize brown-and-white shirt, he looked good, as always.

"I know. Nothing compared to the hours they now spend together." They sat down at the table simultaneously. Tyler sipped his beer. She nibbled at a chip.

"So, how we doing, do you think?" he asked.

"I have no idea. Reese says he's fine, but things between us are stilted." She thought of the unsatisfactory lovemaking last weekend, and the absence of any contact since. "You?"

"Kaitlyn's putting up a good front."

"I found them . . . touching . . . hugging . . . *something* yesterday morning. She came over here, apparently after a run, and after she'd found the morning paper. You should have seen them, Tyler, they looked so much like they belonged together. Two halves of the same whole. It startled me."

"Maybe they were like that before." His tone had hardened. "But not anymore."

"You know," she said staring out at the sunny day, "I was hoping they'd turn on each other over this Bingham thing. Take sides. Blame each other. Not very nice of me, I admit."

"I advised Kaitlyn to do just that. So did some other people."

Tyler watched Dray's face pale, wishing he'd been more careful with what he said to her. She was so lovely, with eyes bluer than the sky that was a backdrop for her. What the hell was wrong with Bishop? "Really? Does Reese know people told her to turn on him?"

"Yeah. He and Kaitlyn had quite a row over it."

"He didn't tell me."

And that hurt, Tyler could see.

"I think Kate only told me because she was so torn."

"Why did she decide not to?"

"Who knows? She said things were good between them ten years ago."

"Damn it. I knew this would conjure good memories of the past." Dray blew out a heavy breath. "If he'd only confide in me."

"Kaitlyn told me once she always had trouble getting him to open up when things were tough."

"Yeah, well, he seems to open up to her just fine."

Kate and Reese emerged from the house together. They were walking close, shoulders touching. He grasped her forearm when he leaned over to whisper something in her ear. She gave him a grateful smile and squeezed his hand.

Tyler felt as if the sun had gone behind the clouds.

"SO, LITTLE SISTER, tell me how you really are." Reese had cornered Emily in the den, where she'd gone to use the Internet.

From behind his desk, she blew out a heavy breath. "You always did know."

Hitching a hip on the edge of the desk, he watched her sit back and fold her arms over her waist. He asked, "How's the business going?"

"Slow. I'm still not making a profit."

"Need some money?"

She shook her head. "You already gave me too much. To start this online T-shirt company, and to keep the boys in toys."

"I don't mind. I have it."

Wearily, she shook her head. Now that he had a chance to study her, Reese worried even more that she wasn't taking care of herself. "Is Pa helping with the boys?"

"Yes, but he's too old to keep up with them. And having them every day after school, while I take that shift at the diner, really cramps his retirement." She looked around the den desolately. "I hate my life, Reese. I'm trying so hard to get some momentum going, but ever since I divorced Charlie, I've been stuck."

"Divorce can be immobilizing." He stared over her

shoulder for a moment. "The boating accident that killed Charlie didn't help."

"No, the boys have suffered."

"You could move here if you want. Your company can be run from anywhere. We'd have time as a family."

"Your girlfriend might not like that."

"She'd do it for me."

"I think she'd do anything for you." Emily watched him. "She's not Kate."

His hands curled and he consciously forced himself to relax. Every time he thought about the good times, he wanted to punch something. "No, she's not. Thank God. Kate and I practically destroyed each other."

"Only in those last few months." Emily smiled sadly. "It was the abortion." His sister was the only one Reese told about what Kate had done. He'd never forget how Emily had comforted him, had talked to him on the phone some nights into the wee hours.

"And my infidelity. Which very well may come back to haunt me because of this Bingham thing."

"Is Kate on your side?"

"Miraculously, yes."

"Not so surprising. Up until the end, she was there for you in everything."

Loss, huge and heavy, descended on him. "I don't want to talk about Kate."

"Because you've never really gotten over her."

"Of course I have. She's got a young stud sniffing after her."

"He is yummy. Does he want to marry her?"

"Why wouldn't he?"

"What about you? Are you going to marry Dray?"

"Not anytime soon." Maybe never.

"She's a nice girl. And she loves you."

He leaned over and tugged on a piece of her dark hair. "How did this chat get on to me?"

"Your life is more interesting."

"My life is a mess." He heard Dray's voice in the kitchen, calling to him. "Looks like I'm needed." He stood. "You sure I can't help you out, honey?"

Tears moistened his sister's eyes. When she was little and unhappy, she used to come to him with that same misty look. Then, he could clean up a scrape or offer to beat up a boy. Now, he couldn't seem to make things better for her no matter how hard he tried. He vowed to find more time for her, despite the Bingham case.

She said, "No, I'll be all right. I need to stand on my own two feet."

"Okay, but if you change your mind . . ."

"I know. You'll fix everything."

"Hey, I'm a guy. That's what we do."

He was glad to see the smile on her face as he left to find Dray.

"WHAT'S THE PLAN now?" Jillian asked, seated beside Kate under one of the oak trees. A breeze ruffled the branches above them and the smell of rich loam and budding flowers filled the air.

Sipping a gin and tonic, Kate watched Sofie with Emily's boys. They were more like siblings than cousins when they got together. "On Monday, we're meeting with a private investigator." She snorted. "His name is Chase Sanders."

"Chase? Oh my, that's corny."

"It's as bad as the vasectomy doctor named Dr. Stoppe."

"You made that up."

Kate chuckled. "No, Tyler knows him." Then she sobered. "Next, we're getting the court orders to subpoena Bingham's prison records. Hopefully our man Chase can start interviewing her family and friends. Reese and I are meeting with the lawyers she hired for subsequent arrests."

"You two are? Why not the PI?"

"We think we can deal with the lawyers better, being a part of their breed."

"Probably." Jillian squeezed her arm. "I've heard talk, Kate."

"I'm not surprised, after what Larkin told me." She winced. "Is it all bad?"

"No. You've made friends in the court system. And you're well respected. Still, there's the jealous element. The one who wants to see the mighty fall."

"The mighty has fallen *hard* with this turn of events, and"—she gazed longingly at her daughter—"by other things."

"Is the little monster still beating up on you?"

"She hugged me today."

"Will wonders never cease. Maybe she's punished you enough."

"Maybe."

Reese came out of the house with his sister and father, carrying presents. "Looks like it's gift time," Jillian commented.

"Hey," Reese called out after he set the presents on a picnic table. "Come over here, birthday girl."

From the yard, Sofie smiled at her father like she never smiled at Kate anymore. It cut to the quick. She raced over to the presents with the boys on her heels. Kate watched Sofie hug her father, and start to sit down in front of the presents, tugging him with her. Somehow, Kate been reduced to looking in at her daughter's life from the outside, like a spectator. Her throat constricted at the obscene thought.

She watched Reese whisper something in Sofie's ear. Sofie frowned, then her expression lightened; she scanned the yard, and her gaze landed on Kate. "Hey, Mom, come on. Help with the presents."

Tears welled in Kate's eyes.

"Go on, honey," Jillian said. "Join your family."

Her family. Seeing father and daughter watch her expectantly, Kate drew in a breath. Sometimes, she'd give anything in the world to have *her family* back.

SEVEN

IT WAS DIFFERENT between them, somehow. For years, in self-preservation, Reese had cut Kate out of his thoughts. Now, seeing her almost every day precluded that tactic for survival. And after their talk, when she'd come to tell him that she wouldn't turn on him, and that half-hug in the breakfast nook, and after Sofie's party where Kate had seemed so vulnerable, Reese was feeling less animosity for his ex-wife. Sure, the anger at her for what she'd done still seethed inside him. But it was diluted by their shared experiences, and that damned closeness between them was coming back. All of which was not good. They'd gone through hell to get this divorce, and put their daughter through the tortures of the damned; second thoughts had no place in their lives at this late date.

As they sat in the law office conference room, across from Chase Sanders, the private investigator they'd hired, Reese ruthlessly squelched his renewed feelings for Kate. Sanders, however, couldn't seem to take his eyes off her. Her dark hair was loose today, and fell onto the shoulders of a yellow linen suit, contrasting the pale color. With the sun streaming in behind her, she did look good, Reese thought it was unprofessional for Sanders to eye her like he did during their recitation of the course of events that had brought them there.

"Thanks for the information," the private investigator said, sitting back into his chair, which he'd pushed away from the conference table to accommodate his long legs. The guy was tall, with a runner's body. Kate's type. He wore a high-quality suit and a silk T-shirt. "So, specifically, what's your plan of action?" he asked them.

Kate shot a glance at Reese, an eyebrow cocked to ask who should answer that. Mildly noting how they could still communicate without words, Reese nodded for her to go first.

She faced Sanders. "We know the note is false. There are two ways to look at this, we think. One is that Anna Bingham lied when she wrote it. But that doesn't make sense, because a person about to die doesn't usually lie. That's why dying declarations are accepted in court."

"So, maybe it wasn't a suicide." Sanders said the stark words matter-of-factly.

"We know that's a possibility," Reese put in. "But we think that should we we should keep all the options open at this point, to make sure."

"I'll talk to her family, friends and as many people at the prison as I can. We'll look for evidence of both—was it a suicide, and if not, who killed her, and why would they implicate you." He didn't take any notes, just watched them with shrewd eyes. "You know that if it was homicide, we're saying somebody murdered her to get to you."

"That seems equally implausible," Kate said, frowning. "It's hard to believe we made that kind of enemy. Done something that egregious."

"Not so unbelievable. People retaliate for all kinds of offenses, real and imaginary. Meanwhile, you're getting her prison records, which I'd like to see when you're done with them, and you're talking to her other lawyers, right?"

"Yes, Wednesday night. I think we'll get more insight into all this after examining those records."

"And talking with inmates." He grunted. "They say a lot more than they mean to." In a welcome no-nonsense manner, the private investigator stood. "I'll be in touch after I contact Bingham's family and friends. I'll let you know when I go to Longshore. Keep me up to speed on the records." He extended his hand to Reese for a quick shake, but held Kate's longer. "I'll be in touch."

When he left, Kate sank down onto a chair. She leaned back against the leather and closed her eyes. "This is hard."

"I know. And so damn slow. It's only been eleven days but it seems like we've been under this cloud forever." He rubbed the bridge of his nose with his thumb and forefinger. "It's wreaking havoc with my concentration. I just got a new case that needs my full attention."

"On what?" They used to discuss every single case, inside and out, for hours, even if one of them was working alone. It was exhilarating to match wits with her.

"A school shooter. He's seventeen, so he's going to be tried as an adult."

"The one that happened over in Allenstown?"

"Yep. The family contacted Bishop Associates because of our success with the shooting you and I handled."

"That was six years ago. One of the last cases we did together."

"Well, at least we won."

She stared off as if she was seeing something. "Are you doing this one pro bono, too?"

"Yes. I haven't done as much of that as I'd like to since you . . . since I took over as sole partner."

She smiled. "That case was a success story. I read where Jamie Ryan's back from upstate. And on the right path."

"He got a lot of counseling, finished high school in detention, and is at a SUNY college." Reese sighed. "The new one looks like another bullying situation."

"It's criminal that bullying still goes on in schools. My

caseload would be a lot lighter, if it didn't." She sighed. "I wish I could do some pro bono work, like I used to with you."

"Your job as a family court justice is community service, Kate. More so than any other judgeship."

"Still, I'd like to do more."

Rising, he poured them coffee. "We never got a chance before things fell apart between us to discuss how you liked being a judge." And to his amazement, he really wanted to know.

She took the coffee and sipped. "Thanks. I love the job. Many appointees just use family court as a stepping stone. We're low on the totem pole with civil and criminal courts." She sighed. "I tried my hand at criminal court for a few weeks. It wasn't my thing."

"I remember all too well."

She looked puzzled. Then awareness dawned. "Oh, yeah, that time we met up on either side of the bench. What a fiasco."

"The opposing counsel had a field day with it."

She shook her head. "The whole courthouse joked about it, so I hear."

"Forget it. They fed off our splitting. What were you saying about family court?"

"Just that when people like Judge Judy write that we're too lenient, it doesn't help the image of family court."

"I can't believe you're too easy on your cases."

"I'm not. There's a difference between empathy and leniency. I'm tough when I need to be."

"I can attest to that."

Giving him a weak grin, she hesitated before she said, "At the risk of breaking this . . . truce, your nomination is for criminal court, isn't it?"

"Yes."

"Are you excited about that?"

"I'm not letting myself be. Every day I fear that phone ringing, telling me my name is being withdrawn."

"Do you still want it?"

"Truthfully?"

"Of course."

"I haven't gone after it until now because I lost some of my drive when we split."

"You built this firm up a lot, Reese."

"Yeah, but as far as going further, I don't know, Kate, the magic was gone."

She smiled wistfully. "Same here. I have no desire to go any further than where I am."

Nostalgia hung heavily in the air. They just stared at each other. There were shadows in those pretty brown eyes of hers. He wondered if she was thinking the same thing as he. They'd lost so much.

A knock on the door precluded any comment. "Come in," Reese said, annoyed by the intrusion.

Yolanda strode into the conference room. She nodded to Kate, who arrived for the early morning meeting before his assistant had gotten in. "Judge Renado."

Kate frowned. "Yolanda, we've been on a first-name basis forever."

Yolanda sniffed, and Kate's gaze swung to Reese.

He shrugged.

"Greg Abbott's waiting for you." His colleague and maybe soon-to-be partner. "You need to be on your way to Allenstown." She angled her head to Kate. "Are you done with her?"

The words echoed in the air. For five years, Reese had thought he *was* done with Kaitlyn Renado. It was more than disconcerting that the notion didn't seem true anymore.

And it sure as hell didn't feel good.

HER PRETTY YELLOW suit was hidden behind her judge's robes, which was unfortunate because Kate needed the pick-me-up of the cheerful color. The meeting with the private investigator had been unnerving, but nothing compared to the trial that was just beginning.

She looked to the petitioner's table.

"Mary Lank, from the state's attorney's office, Your Honor."

Standing also, the other lawyer stated, "Eric Benson, for the respondent."

Kate turned her attention to the fourteen-year-old girl accused of second-degree murder and swallowed back the feeling that always surfaced with what she secretly labeled *baby cases*. "Ms. Lank, would you give your opening statement?"

"Elsa Golindez is charged with second-degree murder. Her infant son was found dead in the toilet of her home, after her sister called 911 saying Ms. Golindez was bleeding and in need of medical help. Firefighters found the newborn facedown in the toilet. Medical personnel confirm that Ms. Golindez did indeed give birth to the child."

Kate steeled herself to hear the gruesome details. "Mr. Benson?"

Eric Benson was a distinguished lawyer, who did more than his share of pro bono cases. "Your Honor, Elsa Golindez has an IQ of eighty. She contends that she didn't even know she was pregnant until the baby . . . came out."

"That testimony was in the hearing. We're here to proceed to fact-finding." Which in family court meant the trial.

First up on the witness stand was the sister who called in the emergency. Dark and pretty, she resembled Elsa in size and coloring. The state asked, "Ms. Golindez, did you know your sister was pregnant?"

"I thought maybe, but I asked Mama and she said Elsa couldn't be because she wasn't married."

Mama sat behind the respondent's table, a big woman, dressed in black, her hands fumbling on rosary beads. She stared down, not at the goings-on in the courtroom, nor at her daughter.

"Why did you call nine-one-one?" Benson asked.

"Elsa was on the toilet, and there was blood all over her legs."

"Did you check inside the toilet?"

"Ew . . ." the young girl said. "No way."

"Was your sister dating anybody?"

"No, but . . . there were boys, who . . . liked her, who wanted to walk her home, be with her."

Oh, dear, Kate thought. No question as to what they were after. A young, retarded girl, abused by boys at school. Where the hell was the supervision?

After the sister, the mother was called to the stand. She needed an interpreter. Her testimony revealed that she didn't know how her daughter could be pregnant, she was a good girl, not too smart, but good. The prosecution asked the mother questions that indicated she was irresponsible and should have known her own child was pregnant. The woman seemed confused by that. When it came out that the mother and aunt were in the living room when the girl gave birth, Kate had to bite her own tongue not to rage at all of them.

By noon, Kate had heard from doctors and caseworkers as well. "All right, we'll adjourn until after lunch when I'll hear testimony from . . ." She looked at the respondent's lawyer.

Benson said, "Ms. Golindez is our only witness."

Kate returned to her chambers exhausted. As usual this baby case made her think of the baby she and Reese didn't have, and her actions to bring that about. For all her life, she'd fought for a woman's right to choose, sure that, if an unwanted pregnancy happened to her, she wouldn't choose abortion, but believing women had the right to their own decisions. Why, she wondered as she took off her robe, had she changed her mind and gone ahead with her own abortion?

To get back at Reese for hounding her, his jealousy, his destruction of the perfect marriage? No, there was more to it than that. She hadn't really wanted another child, and it *would* have interfered with her career. She wasn't going to apologize for that. Still, in the dark of night, she did wonder if she'd acted rashly. If things had been better between them would she have had the child? The night she'd told Reese what she'd done, she'd been stricken with remorse. After time had passed, she didn't feel guilt over her actions, but questioned if she'd made the right decision for herself. And, of course, it had damaged their marriage beyond repair.

Damn it, why was she thinking about this again? She'd dealt with her feelings about it all long ago.

A quick knock on her door brought her out of the uncomfortable reflection as her assistant, Portia, stepped inside. The woman's sympathetic smile was soothing. "Tough one today, huh?"

Kate sighed. "Yes. That poor family. Still, something has to be done."

"I know." She plopped down in a padded chair. "I hate these cases though. How can anybody destroy or allow a child to be destroyed?"

"There are always circumstances." She glanced at her calendar. "How's the docket?"

"Packed. We'll run late. You should finish this one as soon as you can."

Kate nodded.

"You all right, Judge Renado? That suit's a knockout, but it can't hide how tired you look."

"I'm not sleeping well."

"I'm sorry. Anything I can do?"

"No, but thanks for being concerned."

"Hey, am I interrupting?" Tyler poked his head through the open doorway, his hands filled with white cartons.

"Not if that's food."

"It is—chicken Caesar salad and hot croissants."

Portia gave Kate a *lucky you* look, stood and greeted Tyler. "I'll be back in twenty. Enjoy the respite."

All smiles, dressed in beltless jeans and a navy T-shirt, Tyler crossed to the desk, set the food down and kissed Kate on the cheek. "Hi, gorgeous."

"Hi, handsome." She was glad to see him.

"Hungry?"

"Always." She nodded to the table. "Let's sit there."

As they ate, she asked about his day off, and he told her he was playing golf that afternoon. "However, I made your recipe for spaghetti sauce and put it in the Crock-Pot this morning, in hopes of luring you over tonight for dinner."

"That would be nice." She squeezed his strong, doctor's hand. "And you don't have to lure me over, Ty."

"You look tired."

She hadn't gone to his house the previous evening, nor invited him to hers. "I know. It's why I didn't call you last night."

"How did the meeting with the private investigator go?"

"Nerve racking." Her office phone rang. "Let the machine pick up. I turned off my cell."

"I'm sorry you're going through this. I wish you'd let me help."

"You can help tonight. Dinner would be terrific."

His eyes turned hot. "And maybe . . . other things . . . will be just as terrific."

A beep . . . She glanced at the phone as the voice came on. "Hi, Katie." It was Reese. Too late she recalled the last time she'd gotten a call that the person with her shouldn't hear. "I tried your cell. It was off, so I'll just leave a message now. I'm on a break, but I wanted to tell you the prison records came in. Since we're meeting with Bingham's lawyers tomorrow evening, and I've got a full load today, I think we should get together tonight and look them over. My office? About eight?" He chuckled. "I'll even order you Italian food again, and let you wear my sweat suit. Call and tell me if this works for you."

Chagrined, Kate swallowed the bite she'd taken of her salad and met Tyler's gaze. His had turned hard. "Ty, I'm sorry. He . . ."

"Didn't even identify himself. He didn't have to."

Of all Tyler had to object to, Kate was surprised he chose that. "I . . ."

"You wore his clothes?"

She just stared at him. "It's not what you're implying."

"No? Then exactly what is it?"

"It's two people forced to work together for a common good."

Tossing down his napkin, Tyler stood. "I'm sick of this."

"It's only been a few days. I need to be with Reese to get to the bottom of this accusation."

"You could have done that without him. Hell, you could have implicated him and been out of this mess."

"I thought we rang that bell. I won't do something I don't believe is right."

Pacing now, he didn't look at her. "I don't like it. Any of it."

She stood, too, with anger accompanying her. "Neither do I. But there's not much I can do about it."

He gestured to the phone. "Are you going over to meet him?"

"I think I should."

His gaze narrowed on her. "You want to, don't you?"

"Tyler, I can't answer that because you'll take it wrong."

"Don't play lawyer with me." He shook his head, ran a hand through his wheat-colored hair. "I was always afraid of this."

"There is no *this*."

"Yeah, keep telling yourself that, *Katie*." The name only Reese called her. "Then one of us will believe it."

Turning abruptly, he stalked out of the office. Before the door could close, Portia was there. "It's time to go, Judge Renado."

"Thanks."

"It's going to be a tough afternoon."

Which would only match the rotten morning that she'd had. Crossing to her closet, she removed her robe and slipped into it, seeking refuge in being Judge Renado, hoping it would take her mind off her problems.

It always had.

* * *

DISTRACTED, KATE LOCKED her office and headed for
the elevator. Juggling her briefcase, carrying a light rain-
coat and a stack of books, she played back the scene in the
courtroom today. God, she hoped she'd made the right decision. The attorneys had been surprised, which always
made her wonder if she was on target.

As she rode the elevator to the ground level, she reviewed her findings: She'd assigned probation to the young
mother, supervision by Child Welfare for two years, counseling for the whole family and two follow up sessions
with Kate, one in six months, another in nine, to make sure
things were going in the right direction. It seemed to her
everybody had suffered enough, though she'd take some
knocks for being too lenient with her decision.

At ground level, the elevator pinged open and she made
her way to her reserved parking space, her heels clicking
on the cement floor. It was almost eight and she was going
to be late getting to Reese's office. As she headed for her
red Eclipse, she whipped out her cell to call him.

It was darker than usual in the parking garage. Mist had
covered the city all day and it had crept into the cinder-
block structure, making the air heavy and intensifying the
oil and gasoline odor. She punched in her speed dial, re-
gretting that Reese had claimed a spot on her phone again,
and in her life. Tyler would be upset by that. Poor Tyler.
He'd been angry about Reese since Anna Bingham had
died. He was insecure, and though she felt bad about it,
truthfully, she was getting tired of reassuring him. Her life
was a mess and he needed . . .

A low, husky voice on the other end of the cell interrupted her thoughts. "Reese Bishop."

"Hi, it's me. Kate. I just left the office and am in the
parking garage. I should be there in . . . Oh, my God,
what . . . Reese, *help* . . ."

The phone flew out of her hand as Kate was shoved up
against her car.

"Shut up and don't say nothing, lady."

The man smashed her face into the window, and vicious pain shot through her body; she whimpered when he jerked her arm up behind her. She managed to get out, "I have money in my purse. You can have it all . . ."

Again, he rammed her into the car, and said in a gravelly voice, "Don't want no . . ."

Feet clattered on the pavement. "Judge Renado, is that you? Are you—"

Suddenly Kate was released; she slid to the cement floor, her knees scraping the rough surface. Her vision blurred and her head pounded.

The voice of the security guard . . . "Judge, are you . . . shit, you're hurt."

It took her a minute to respond. She looked up into the craggy face of the guard she spoke to almost every day. "I'm okay, John. Thanks to you."

Slumping, she leaned against the car, swallowed back pain-induced nausea, and tried to gather her wits. "Did you see who it was?"

"Big guy, dressed in black. Couldn't see if he had a weapon." John studied her as he picked up her cell phone. "You should go to the hospital."

Sirens sounded outside. "Let's see what the police and the medics say. The person I was calling must have contacted them." She gripped his arm. "Thanks."

"Don't mention it. This kind of thing doesn't happen much, but women have to watch out down here."

She closed her eyes as she heard a siren get louder and then a car screech to a halt a few yards away.

Kate thought, *What next?*

"WHAT INGREDIENTS DID you put in this?" Dray stood over Tyler's counter and tasted the marinara sauce. "It's delicious."

Tyler answered from the other side of the room. "Just spices Kaitlyn uses—oregano, garlic powder, parsley. And pepperoni. Most people don't put that in sauce, but her mother . . ." He trailed off. "Shit."

Dray turned and picked up her glass of wine. She leaned against the counter and watched him. His face had darkened. "We have to handle this right, Tyler."

He sighed and sipped his Merlot. "I'm blowing it. I got furious at her today."

"That won't help."

"What did you say to Reese when he called?"

"I kept my temper. But I told him I didn't like his spending so much time with Kate. Again."

"What did he say?"

"That he didn't need to be hounded about this. He was doing the best he could."

Tyler ran a frustrated hand through his thick hair. It was a bit long, and curly. "Do you think that's true?"

"I'm not sure. I afraid they're using this Bingham thing as an excuse to be together."

"At least Reese is."

That irritated her, but she spoke calmly because she liked Tyler and he was obviously upset. "I think that's a little unfair, Tyler. Kate's as much to blame as Reese is."

Tyler sighed. "You know what? We need to get a life."

She laughed. "You know what? You're right."

"How about we eat and go to a movie? Kaitlyn never has time to do that."

"Sounds good to me. What do you like?"

Crossing to the sink, he ran water into a big ceramic pot and when it was filled, he went to the stove, set it on a burner and adjusted the temperature. "All kinds of movies. How about you?"

"Romantic comedies are my favorite."

"Yeah? Kaitlyn hates those."

"So does Reese."

"I'd go see that new one about the girl who hires the escort for her sister's wedding. The writer's from my hometown."

She smiled over at him. "On one condition."

Cocking his head, he arched a brow at her. "What?"

"We don't talk about Reese and Kate. I'm sick of moping about them. It makes me feel like such a loser."

He frowned. "Should I not have called you?"

"No, no, I'm glad you did. I'm only tired of commiserating. Let's really do something shocking and have some fun together."

"It's a deal." He nodded toward the other side of the room. "Now make the salad."

Dray went to the refrigerator and opened it, but glanced over at Tyler. "You're a nice guy, you know that, Dr. Sloan?"

His grin was stellar. "Aw, that's what all the girls say. How about sexy, mysterious and exiting?"

"I imagine you're all that, too."

He chuckled, she laughed, and the evening seemed a bit brighter.

"KEEP THAT ON your face, Kate." Reese nodded to the ice pack she held in her hand. "It'll reduce the swelling."

Heeding his directive, she lay back onto the cushions of her soft leather couch, and adjusted the compress on her face. She glanced down at her clothing. "I loved this suit."

Watching her from his stance by the sidebar, he shook his head. She was something else. Though she was pretending to be calm, he could see through the bravado. When he arrived at the parking garage, she'd been trembling and still shaky. The police and medics had already gotten to the scene, so all Reese could do was stand by and watch. His heart had rammed against his rib cage when, as they spoke on the phone, he'd realized something had happened to her and called 911. "I'm sorry about this. It was the last thing you needed."

"Just my luck."

He crossed his arms over his chest and frowned. "Maybe it wasn't bad luck."

"What do you mean?"

"Maybe it wasn't a random mugging."

"Well, the police said that was a possibility. Judges are sometimes targeted because of their unpopular decisions and I've made my share. One today, as a matter of fact."

"I know. But I didn't mean that it was court related."

She watched him. "What are you getting at, Reese?"

"An alleged suicide, a false accusation and now an attack on one of the people involved? If you weren't in the center of this, what would your sharp mind tell you?"

"Oh, God, do you think this is related to Anna Bingham?"

"Truthfully, I don't know. I think it's a possibility."

As if dislodging the thought, she shook her head fast. "Jillian was stalked two years ago by someone she put in jail; he'd recently been released on probation."

"I remember reading about that."

"It happens all the time."

He noticed her hands were shaking again, so he pushed away from the wall, crossed to her and sank down onto a couch cushion. She just sat there, a bump the size of a walnut on her forehead, her cheek badly bruised, her eyes wide with fear. He reached out and smoothed down hair that had gotten messed from her ordeal. "Look, I'm not saying I think this attack was definitely related. I'm just saying we shouldn't ignore that possibility."

She bit her lip. Kate was so rarely vulnerable, he was moved by this display. Picking up the hand that wasn't bandaged, he squeezed it. "I'm sorry, Katie. I hope they're not connected."

She gripped his fingers. Her deep brown eyes misted. "I guess I'm scared now." She leaned in. "Could you . . . could you hold me for a minute?"

His heart leaped into his throat. But as natural as summer rain, his arms circled her and drew her close; he felt her hands press into his back. He anchored his hand at her neck, and she tightened her grip. "Katie . . ."

She buried her face in his shoulder and inhaled the scent of him. As she did, Reese closed his eyes. He remembered the feel of her so well. Every angle and plane and curve. He remembered how he'd relished her scent. And when she hung on, when he drew her as close as they could get, he realized he was scared, too. But not just of what was happening with Anna Bingham, or whoever was in that parking garage. He was afraid because something was happening between him and his ex-wife. Try as he might, he could no longer deny that reality.

EIGHT

"IF YOU DON'T sit down on that bed and get undressed, I'm going to take your clothes off myself."

Although the medics had given her pain medication, Kate's bruised knees stung, her head still pounded a rapid tattoo in her brain, and the coppery taste of fear was still in her mouth. Yet she smiled at Reese's command. "Back off, hotshot. I'll do it."

He stilled.

For a brief moment, she didn't know why. Then she cringed at her use of the old nickname. "Sorry about that. A blast from the past. I'm not thinking clearly."

He reached out and tousled her hair. "It's all right, Katie. Our lives are so screwed up. Neither of us has it together."

Things were way off track if she was allowing his touch. Reveling in it. The embrace downstairs had broken through some emotional dam and everything between her and Reese seemed to be flooding out.

He crossed to the bank of dressers on the side of her huge bedroom. "Where are your nighties?"

"You can get plain cotton pajamas out of the bottom drawer." Her tone was dry. "Plain ones, Reese."

He smirked. "Yeah, like you wear those." Over his shoulder, he arched a brow. "At least you didn't used to."

Oh, Lord, he was flirting. She'd forgotten how attractive—and sexy—the playful side of him was. "I have some demure Victoria's Secret pajamas I bought for comfort. Just get them, and leave so I can change."

He crouched down and drew open a drawer. Taking his time, he sifted through the contents leisurely. Mesmerized, she could only stare at the sight of his big hand on lace and satin and silk. Finally, he picked out her favorite pj's— white background, covered with hot pink hearts. At least they were modest. He stood and brought them to her. "Not your usual style, but they're cute."

She grasped the clothes, and looked up at him.

"You thinking what I am?" he asked, his voice hoarse.

"About your favorite pastime?"

"I used to love prowling those stores, searching for just the right thing for my bride."

God, she remembered—satiny tap pants and tops, eyelet nightgowns, indecent wisps of black lace. "You were so lascivious." For a brief moment, she wondered if he bought lingerie for his own personal baby doll. The thought stung.

"Yeah, I was." His level stare was meaningful. Finally he broke it and stepped back. "You have to eat. Still want Italian?"

Her hand went to her tummy. "No, please. I'm feeling sick."

"From fear and the bumps on your head. We'll forgo the Italian. Got any canned chicken soup and crackers?" What he used to feed her when she was first pregnant with Sofie.

"I think so. In the pantry. But really, I'm not all that hungry."

"Doesn't matter. Change, and I'll bring fresh ice with me."

"Always the boss."

"Best you remember that." He headed for the door.

Though she was sore all over, she managed to get into her pajamas while still on the bed and prop herself up with pillows. Picking up the remote, she turned the news on the TV. The routine actions helped her to block what had happened earlier in the dank garage. And what it all meant. She didn't want to think about that now.

Thankfully, Reese returned soon. Carrying a tray with crackers, two bowls, milk for her and a scotch for him, he set the tray down on her lap, and took his meal off. Her stomach growled at the aroma of the hot broth. "Eat, and then put the ice pack back on those bruises."

"Does it look bad?" Hating the quiver in her voice, she asked anyway.

He ran a finger down her cheek where it wasn't bruised. "Not your usual gorgeous complexion, sweetheart."

"I hope it's better by tomorrow. All my reputation needs is for me to go into court looking like I went a few rounds with Mike Tyson."

"If you use the ice, it'll keep the swelling down. Now eat."

He took a seat on the couch across from the bed, and ate while she managed to down the soup, nibble on salty crackers and drink the milk. When they were done, he cleaned things up then returned to the bedroom. "What else can I do?"

Wearily, she glanced to the side of the room. "I have to use the bathroom." Because she was woozy, she hadn't wanted to get up without him there. Slowly, she eased her legs off the bed, set them on the floor and stood. Dizziness struck her like a lightning bolt, and she started to sway. He caught her before she dropped and her entire body sagged into his. His hand slid around her and rested just below her unfettered breast. Though the contact was intimate, his strong fingers clutching her felt safe and solid. She leaned into him as he got her to the bathroom.

He asked, "Can you manage by yourself? Or should I help?"

She looked up at him. There was a twinkle in his green

eyes, so like the boy she used to know, her own eyes misted. "No, thanks. I'll be fine."

He was at the door when she came out with a freshly washed face, brushed teeth and combed hair.

"What do you think?" he asked.

"That I look like somebody used me as a punching bag."

"It'll be better tomorrow."

Though she was more steady, he took her arm and guided her back to the bed. When she was settled, he picked up his drink and turned to the TV. "*New York Law* is on," he told her, smiling. The long-running legal drama was something they'd enjoyed watching years ago, if only to mock some of its lack of realism.

Remote in hand, she switched the channel, just in time to hear the familiar refrain of the opening.

"Stay. Watch the show with me." She bit her lip. "Just for a while."

"Sure, if you want me to." Reese glanced from the couch to the bed. Since the couch was out of viewing range, he nodded to the other side of the mattress. "May I?"

"Yes, of course." Her pulse began to quicken.

It beat faster when he kicked off his shoes, rolled up his sleeves, and made himself comfortable; he dropped onto the bed, his weight heavy on the other side, so familiar yet so strange.

And, like the "old married couple" they used to be, they watched the show, in bed at ten o'clock at night, bemoaning some of the protocol and rolling their eyes at the histrionics of the characters.

Kate was amazed, after all that happened, how it could feel so right to be with him like this again.

HE SHOULD GO home, he thought, watching her sleep. She'd dozed off right at the end of the show, and he'd eased her down onto her side. Stretched out on the bed, watching her, he marveled at the turn of events in their lives. After all the animosity, after all the bitter words and accusations, they came together when things got tough, and she let him take care of her when she was hurt.

From his vantage point, he studied her room. More white—a painted oak headboard and built-in dressers to match. White walls with peach accenting framed pictures. At least the carpet had some blue in it. Again, he thought of the farmhouse. Their bedroom was filled with real wood, skylights and a jungleful of live plants.

Turning to his side, his head propped up in his hand, he watched her chest rise and fall. Her unbound breasts swelled against the cotton. He'd forced her to take pain medication at the last commercial and it had kicked in. From where he lay, he could smell the scent of soap and the perfume that clung to her pillows. Reaching out, he tucked heavy hair behind her ear, stealing a touch—just a brush of his knuckles down her cheek where it wasn't injured. The bruises there and on her forehead were nasty. They would still look bad tomorrow. He wondered if she'd want to go to work. If she was still his, he'd insist she stay at home. They'd fight about it, but those were arguments he would always win.

Groaning at the memories that had haunted him all night, he turned over on his back and linked his hands behind his neck on the pillow. What the hell was happening to them? He was beginning to feel the pain over losing her again. He'd been afraid that this would happen. Dreaded it, actually. But he hadn't been able to prevent it. They'd only been together eleven days and already he ached for his ex-wife and what they had had together.

He should leave. But he hesitated to do so, since she'd been so weak.

Poor excuse, Bishop.

Okay, hell, he wanted to stay a little longer. The eleven o'clock news was on and he tried to tune it in.

The next thing he knew, Kate was screaming. He woke up to the jolt of the terrified shouts. "No, no . . . get away . . . Reese, help . . ."

"I'm here, Katie." He bundled her up in his arms. "Sweetheart, shh, it's just a bad dream."

"No, no." She buried her face in his chest.

"It's over. Shh . . ."

She inched in even closer; then gradually she calmed. "Oh, Lord." In the glow from the TV, which was still on, she gripped his shirt. "Don't go."

He kissed her hair. "No, I won't. But you're safe. You're fine."

She slumped into him, and he brought her gently back to the pillows. His head rested right next to hers and they lay together, the darkness broken by the eerie light of the TV, and the silence interrupted by the set's low din.

In minutes, she turned in his arms, fitted her back to his chest and her backside to his groin. They used to sleep in this spoonlike position, every single night until the end. Her curves aligned him, and her womanly scent rose up to meet his nostrils. The proximity made him hard, but also, caused an ache in his chest that might be mistaken for a heart attack. Still he didn't move, and like he promised, he didn't leave, either.

AT SEVEN A.M., when Tyler drove down Kaitlyn's street and caught sight of Bishop's car in her driveway, he felt a clutch in his chest. She hadn't called last night, and he'd decided to stop over before he went to the office. He glanced at the Starbucks coffee on the floor of his SUV. He hadn't brought enough for three.

Pulling over to the curb a short distance from the driveway, he hit the steering wheel with his fist. Damn it. Despite the worry he'd voiced with Dray last night, he didn't really believe Kaitlyn would betray him. He thought they'd at least hash out any feelings she had for her ex before they ditched an eighteen-month-old relationship, one that had gone along just fine until Anna Bingham's death. He cursed like a sailor, then lay his head back on the leather seat of his Blazer. Should he leave? Barge in? Hell, this was like a bad movie. But he'd be damned if he'd just turn tail and run.

He whipped out his cell and dialed Dray's number, faintly surprised he remembered it. She answered on the first ring. "Hello."

"It's Tyler."

"Oh. I thought maybe . . ."

"It was Reese? I know he didn't come home last night."

"You know? How?"

"I stopped to see Kaitlyn on my way to work. His yellow Mustang is in the driveway as we speak."

A quick intake of breath. "Oh, no."

"I'm on the road now, but I'm going inside."

She didn't say anything.

"Do you think I should?"

Muffled sounds.

"Aw, Dray, are you crying?" Bishop was such a bastard.

"I'm all right."

"I'm sorry."

"It isn't your fault." She waited. "Maybe it's not what it looks like."

"Maybe." But he didn't think so.

"What will you do?"

"Go inside and see what the situation is. I'm tired of letting them call all the shots."

"Be careful, Tyler. It could backfire."

"I don't care. She gave me a goddamned key. I have rights."

"Of course you do."

"I'll call you back."

"Okay." She waited. "Tyler, I'm sorry, too."

Squelching his doubts, he pulled the truck into Kate's driveway, threw open the door, and stalked up the sidewalk to the stoop. He should ring the bell, he knew, but hell, he was working himself up into a fine fit and didn't stop to consider his actions. Instead he let himself in.

The house was quiet, except for the refrigerator turning

on, the faint sound of an ice machine. Drawing in a heavy breath, he glanced upstairs. Should he go up? What if he found . . . Fuck it! He took the steps two at a time. Stared down the corridor to her bedroom. The door was open, so he strode to the archway.

He didn't know exactly what he expected, but it wasn't this.

They were indeed on the bed together. Kaitlyn was dressed in pajamas and Bishop was fully clothed. She was under the covers and he was on top of them. But they were entwined in a way that made Tyler's throat feel like a sock was stuffed in it. The fact that Kaitlyn liked her space in bed when Tyler stayed with her, and never once had they cuddled through the night together, made his stomach roil. He leaned against the doorway.

And watched Bishop rouse. Maybe Tyler had moaned and awakened him.

His arms tight around Kaitlyn's waist, Bishop lifted his head off the one pillow they shared, glanced down at her, then looked up right into Tyler's eyes. "Oh, shit," he said, but softly.

Kaitlyn stirred and nestled in closer.

Tyler saw red. "Get out of her bed."

Bishop's eyes narrowed. "Hold on, it's not what it looks like. And be quiet, she needs her sleep. She had a rough night." Lithely, Reese disentangled himself and slid off the mattress. He looked rumpled, tired and grungy. "It's not what you think," he repeated. But there was an undertone in his voice, something resembling smugness.

Tyler came into the room and crossed over to them. "Oh, my God, what happened?" He gaze flew to Reese. "Who the hell did this? You wouldn't . . ."

The guy recoiled with a stunned look. "Like hell I would. Or ever did." He angled his head to the door. "Out there."

Both men left the room.

Stomped downstairs.

And squared off in the foyer. Tyler clenched his fists in

an effort to control himself. He was a healer, had taken an oath never to harm a human being, but God help him, he wanted to beat the shit out of this guy.

"Kate was attacked last night in the parking garage of the courthouse. A mugger, we think."

"Jesus Christ. What happened?"

"Somebody came up behind her, pushed her against the car."

"Did they get him?"

"No. He ran when the security guard came on the scene."

"Did they call the cops?" His brow furrowed. "And how the hell did you get involved . . . She called *you* and not me?"

"She was phoning me when he attacked her. To tell me she was running late."

Oh, well, that was better.

"The police arrived just before I did." Bishop ran a hand through his hair. "Look, I'm going to make some coffee and we can finish this discussion when I'm not so fuzzy."

Tyler stared at him, then headed for the kitchen. "I'll do it."

They talked about the attack while the coffee brewed. Tyler leaned up against a counter, arms folded over his chest, and Bishop dropped down in a chair. "What do the cops think?" Tyler asked.

"Could be your run-of-the-mill mugger. Could be somebody who has a grudge against Judge Renado."

"That happened to Jillian."

"I know. But I have another theory." He glanced at the pot, got up, fixed his coffee and sat back down. The strong scent filled the air; Tyler poured a mug for himself and joined Reese.

"What other theory?"

"Maybe the assault was related to this case."

"The Bingham case? Man, this just keeps getting worse."

"It's hard *not* to see it that way. Too many coincidences.

Bingham's note is false, Sloan, I swear. So that means someone's lying. If so, then our investigation into her death wouldn't sit right with them."

"Someone who what? Faked the note? Killed Bingham? Christ, Bishop, do you know how far-fetched it sounds?"

"Then you think this is all a coincidence?"

"It could be."

"That's naïve. And I'm not willing to risk Kate's well-being because of your Pollyanna view."

"*You're* not willing to risk it? Since when did you get rights back with Kaitlyn?"

"Since we were thrown together into this thing! Don't get your jocks in a twist, Sloan."

Tyler slammed his coffee cup down on the table. "Don't you dare speak to me like that. I walk in here and find you groping the hell out of the woman I love, and I shouldn't be upset?"

"I was *not* groping."

"Why the hell did you stay all night?"

Bishop looked away. Meaningfully, as if deciding what to say. "I, um, was worried about her. When I brought her home from the courthouse, she was shaky. I fixed her soup, made her eat, got her settled."

"Got her settled?"

"In bed. Nothing untoward happened. She was scared, couldn't calm down, so I hung around. I was going to leave when she fell asleep."

"Why didn't you?"

"She had a nightmare, and woke up screaming."

"So you took advantage of her and stayed."

Bishop let out a disgusted sound. "No. I didn't take advantage."

"You son of a bitch. I don't believe you."

Kaitlyn's ex leaned forward. "I didn't. She *asked* me not to leave."

His anger deflating at those words, Tyler sat back in his chair. "Shit."

Bishop sipped his coffee.

Over the rim of his own mug, Tyler watched him. Then, very quietly he said, "You can't have her back, Bishop. I won't let her go."

The other man watched him with a lawyer's blank expression. Then, he pushed back the chair, stood, and walked out of the room. Tyler heard noise in the living room, the front door open and close. He sat in the kitchen, alone, pondering the notion that Reese Bishop hadn't denied that he intended to take his wife back.

REESE LOOKED LIKE he'd spent the night in another woman's bed. Dray would have thought that, even if Tyler hadn't called her. She wondered if he enjoyed himself. Right now, he'd come to the doorway of the kitchen and found her there. Without preamble, he said, "I can explain."

Holding a cup in one had, and her arm around the waist of her terry robe, she said, "Why don't you do that, Reese? Explain it all to me; make it clear why you spent the night with your ex-wife."

He scrubbed a hand over his face. "I'm getting tired of this."

"Oh, excuse me if I have some qualms about why the man I've lived with for two years didn't come home last night."

"I'm sorry. I didn't mean it that way." He crossed to the coffeepot, poured a cup for himself, and sipped from it. Even in wrinkled clothes and a heavy beard he looked good. She wondered if Kate had thought that when she saw him this morning.

Dray shook back hair she hadn't bothered to comb. "So, did you sleep with her?"

"Technically, yes."

Dray was sure she could hear her heart breaking. She didn't know why she was so shocked, and hurt, by the confirmation. She'd been up all night wondering where he was, what he was doing. "I'm moving out." She set her coffee down on the counter and brushed past him.

"Not so fast." He grabbed her arm. "If you want to leave after I clarify this, fine, but I won't have you storming out on false pretenses."

"False pretenses? You cheated on Kate, too, didn't you? Why did I think you wouldn't do it to me?"

He recoiled back as if he'd been slapped. "Only once, and there were reasons."

"Reasons that I don't know because you never talk to me about things."

"It's hard for me to open up, Dray."

"You seem to open up just fine to your ex-wife."

Sighing, he drew her to a chair. "Sit, please. I won't let you go thinking what you do."

Hating herself for capitulating, she sat across from him at the table. She picked up a napkin and twisted it at the edges while he talked.

"I spent the night with Kate because she was attacked in the parking garage." He told her the entire story. Briefly, as if he was arguing someone else's case. Passion was there, but not emotion.

"Are you saying you stayed in the same bed with her and nothing happened?"

"I'm saying exactly that."

"And you expect me to believe that?"

He was offended. "I've never lied to you. It's the truth."

"You've never lied to me? Okay, then tell me the truth about this. Do you still have feelings for Kate?"

"What kind of feelings?"

"Don't hedge, Reese. Don't play lawyer with me. Are you still in love with Kate?"

"I've always cared about her. Even after we divorced."

"You're mincing words. Let me be clearer, Counselor. Are you having renewed feelings for her, the kind you had before things went bad?"

He took in a deep breath. His green eyes darkened with something that looked like fear. "Yes, I am."

Tears misted her eyes. Tracked down her cheeks.

"Oh, honey, don't cry. It doesn't mean what you think."

"You don't want a relationship with her? Like you had?"

"It doesn't matter what I want, Dray. It only matters what I do. I can't control the feelings I have for Kate, but I *can* control what I do with them." He drew in a breath. "Our relationship almost destroyed us, and our daughter. I won't let that happen again."

"Then you don't want me to leave?"

"Lord, no. That would be the worst thing you could do now. I need you to keep . . ." His voice trailed off.

Briefly, she closed her eyes. "Do you have any idea how insulting what you just said is? And how hurtful."

"That came out wrong." He raked a hand through his hair. "Look, I'm exhausted. I'm not saying what I mean. I don't want you to leave me. Unless you're too uncomfortable with what I said."

"I hate what you said, and didn't say."

"I'm sorry."

Dray watched Reese. He seemed to be telling the truth. If she ignored the innuendo that her leaving would throw him into Kate's arms, she could believe that he was telling the truth. God, she'd always hated women who chose to believe what they wanted instead of what was staring at them in the face.

How on earth had she become one of them?

NINE

PROPPED UP IN her pillows with the April sunshine streaming in through the blinds, and the still-crisp air tickling her skin, Kate sipped her coffee and watched the man across her bedroom. From his seat on the couch, Reese drank from his own Starbucks cup, which he'd bought for both of them this morning. He seemed to tamp down a grin. "You took this better than I thought you would."

"After Tyler called my doctor, and you called Judge Larkin, I'd have a right to be furious at both of you."

"If you won't take care of yourself, we will."

We. Uh-oh. That didn't sound good. Still, she appreciated all Reese had done last night. And the fact that, since she was off work for two days, he'd cleared his schedule as much as possible so they could delve into the mountain-size pile of prison records they'd obtained from Longshore. Best to concentrate on that. But something needed to be said first.

"Reese?" Her voice had turned soft and feminine. He glanced up sharply from the papers he was scanning. "Thanks for all you did last night."

A smile turned up the corners of his mouth. The green knit polo shirt he wore with khaki chinos deepened the color of his eyes, which warmed when his gaze landed on her. "You're welcome. Scared the shit out of me, though, when I was on the phone and heard you scream in that garage, for God's sake."

"I'm sorry I scared you."

"I'm sorry somebody assaulted you."

"But I meant that I'm grateful for what you did in the aftermath—taking me home, and staying all night."

"I was worried about you."

"I know. And I appreciate it." She sighed. "You always took good care of me."

"Back at ya, sweetheart."

Sweetheart. Second uh-oh. Time to get their minds away from what was between them. She picked up papers which were duplicates of his. "We should go over at these."

"You sure you're up to it?" He studied her bruises. "You're pretty banged up."

She touched her face. "Does it look awful?"

"Bad enough. The doctor said in two days it'll be a lot better." Anger lit his eyes. "I could kill the bastard for doing that to you. Whoever he was."

"The police are on it. Did you call Chase Sanders?"

"Yep, this morning. He's going to stop by here this afternoon. I hope that's okay."

"Of course it is."

Reese swallowed hard. "I called Sofie but her phone's off again."

"Oh, Reese, no, we can't tell Sofie about this."

He nodded to the morning paper. "Have to. It's in there. Something about beleaguered judge haunted by her past."

"Great." She laid her head against the pillows.

He got up, crossed to the bed and dropped down on the edge. He seemed so big sitting there, his wide shoulders straining against the knit of his shirt. And he smelled so male, like he always had in the morning. Way too naturally, he grasped her hand in his. "We'll get through this, Katie. I promise."

She gave him a weak grin.

"Maybe you should rest some more. I can start reviewing the files myself."

"No, our minds always worked better together. You have an insight and I run with it. We cover more ground that way."

"All right." He checked his watch—a new one that she didn't recognize. At one time, she knew everything about him. But now, he had a life very separate from her. "We've got a couple of hours until lunch. We'll see how it goes."

Before he stood, he leaned over and brushed his knuckles down her uninjured cheek. "At least it's better between us."

She grasped his wrist. "I know. I'm glad.

As he went back to the couch, though she meant what she said, she also worried that this truce of sorts would push them somewhere they didn't want to go. Tyler had concerns, which he voiced before he left this morning. She'd awoken to find him there, and not happy about Reese having spent the night. After the debacle in her office yesterday, things were clearly going downhill with him. Kate imagined Dray grilled Reese when he returned after spending the night, too. She'd give anything to know what he said to Dray, but kept herself from asking—for both their sakes.

His feet propped up on a hassock, Reese put on his glasses and picked up a file. "How do we do this?"

"Just plunge in, I guess." She opened a full folder. "Holy hell, look at the paperwork." There was a hefty stack, about two thirds the size of a ream of computer paper.

"We'll have to organize it to make any headway." He leafed through the material. "You take the first half. I'll take the second. After we group it, we'll comb through each one."

An hour later, having read their sections, without a word spoken, Reese said, "I'm ready."

"I am, too."

"I'll write." He stood and crossed to the window, where he'd set up an easel he'd brought from the office. On it was a hanging pad about two feet by four feet; he'd also brought markers. This was the way they worked best.

Reese wrote: *Unit Team Orientation.* He reviewed aloud that each inmate, upon arrival, was scheduled into a team consisting of a unit manager, case manager and corrections counselor. After the initial orientation, the team met with each inmate on their unit every six months. "Then there's disciplinary reports, called Incident Reports. Visitor lists and videos—we don't have the tapes, though. Phone call list, mail received and medical records." He looked over at her. "That's all I have."

He recorded her input as she gave it to him. "I've got her activities: recreation, hobbies, religious and other organizations she joined. Counseling visits. Library books checked out. Commissary reports. And forms called Call Outs—mandatory appointments; Cop Outs—request forms; and Counts—a roll call of sorts taken several times a day." Kate reached out for the bottle of water on the side of the bed. "Can you imagine living like this? It would kill me to live under such scrutiny."

"I know. You love the outdoors so much."

She grinned, remembering the camping trips they took before Sofie was born. They'd loved to sleep under the stars. It seemed like a lifetime ago.

"Okay," he said, studying the board. "Her Unit Team. The prison orientation is first. Three documents were prepared," which he recorded on the board. "Judgment and Commitment, Inmate Financial Responsibility Program, and Sentence Computation." They scanned the forms for the salient points, without even discussing how to do this. Old patterns apparently never died. "Looks like our girl got off to a bang. She'd challenged the sentence computation and claimed she had no financial restitution to make because she was put in Longshore for parole violation."

Kate narrowed her eyes on the paper. "They didn't let

the latter go, though. She was forced to make restitution for the bribery that she didn't finish paying in Tallahassee."

Reese recorded the information.

"Interesting, isn't it?" Kate noted. "Her family had the money to pay back what she stole. Yet she balked. Hell, why'd she steal in the first place?"

"For the thrill of it all." Reese glanced down. "She won on the sentence computation. They were off a whole fourteen days. Didn't count travel time."

"I imagine fourteen days is a lifetime behind bars."

"Hmm. Here's her job—prison laundry initially, but she got into the library somehow. Must have had some pull for the cushier job. She was assigned quarters with Lena Parks, right away. There's a list of clothing she was given."

Cocking her head, Kate thought back. "Clothing? I think I saw a complaint about her having too much underwear."

"You're kidding."

Kate leafed through. "Nope, it's under 'Shots—the disciplinary incidents'." She read further. "Usually those kinds of complaints aren't written up, but hers was."

"Probably pissed off a guard one too many times."

"The guard who wrote her up is Nell Sorenson."

"A picture's already starting to form, isn't it?"

He nodded. "Uh-huh. Anything else on the Unit Team?"

"No. Bingham was supposed to meet with them the week after she died to assess her first six months, but obviously, she didn't make it to the meeting; there's no summary of her progress or lack of it. We'll have to do everything ourselves."

"Lucky us."

"What's next?" she asked. "Logically?"

"Let's do the Incident Reports. You read them and I'll write up here on the easel."

"For someone incarcerated only six months, she has a hell of a lot disciplinary referrals."

By noon they'd listed Anna Bingham's disciplinary record. Even writing small, Reese filled the whole easel with her screwups. Listed were major and minor infractions. Reese picked up a bottle of water and drank, while he and Kate studied the list. Commissary infractions abounded: making a stink after she signed a receipt for goods; apparently it was a big no-no to accept what you ordered and then complain the order wasn't right. Contraband found in home-cooked meals: Only certain items were available at the commissary; if food was cooked with other stuff, it was black market. If you got caught, you were written up.

Reese said, "She liked the black market. She was reported for possessing steaks, marijuana, hiring somebody to paint her cell and do her ironing. Some hooch. Everything's available, I guess, for a cost. Oh, and she got caught for gambling on football. Looks like she was into sports."

Reese continued to read the list and check with the file papers. "She had a violation of medical status conditions— seems she was put on medical confinement and left the area. Oh, man, six or seven altercations with the guards. Sorenson's name is here a lot. Missing counts." She shook her head. "Little Anna was one busy girl."

"I'm surprised they kept her in medium security."

"There aren't a lot of high-security prisons for women. I read some stats. Only seven percent of all prisoners are female, so they group security levels together more for them than for men."

Reese put down his marker and raised his arms over his head and flexed his back to stretch. He seemed tall and very imposing. Until his stomach growled. "Guess I'm hungry. Let's eat and talk about the meaning of this part, before we go on."

"I agree." Kate started to get out of bed. She'd managed to shower this morning and had put on a black warm-up suit with peach accents. When she bent over to put on sneaks, though, she got dizzy. Reese was beside her in seconds. "Here, let me do this."

"I can tie my own shoes," she said dryly.

Batting her hands away, he knelt in front of her. "I *used*

to do it." He picked up a sneaker. "When you were pregnant with Sof."

"I couldn't bend over that far at the end."

He glanced up. His color was high this morning, even though he couldn't have slept much. "I loved how you looked at that stage."

"I know you did. It's what got me through those last few weeks."

He held her ankle, caressed it really. "There were so many good times, Kate."

She didn't shrink from the touch or the remark this time. Placing a hand on his shoulder, she whispered, "I know. We forgot about them during that last year."

Sighing, he held her gaze a bit longer, then he finished up with her shoes. He stood and put out his hand. "Come on, let's eat. I brought stuff."

"Ah, a man after my own heart." She placed her hand in his before she realized what she'd said. And how that statement had once been so true.

REESE STUCK THE Brie in the microwave and cut the bread, but let Kate mix the salad. He could only keep her down so long, and it was an easy task she could do from a seat at her bar. "So," she asked, "what's the picture we have of Anna Bingham?"

"A bad girl, prone to leaving trouble in her wake."

"Which means she might have made a lot of enemies."

The microwave beeped and Reese brought the cheese to the breakfast nook. "But enough for someone to kill her?"

Kate slid off the stool and carried the salad over to the table to join him. "Maybe not. Maybe it would be enough to make her so unhappy that she'd kill herself." She thought for a moment. "On the off chance that it's a homicide, why on earth would a fellow inmate implicate us? How would they even know us?"

"I can't answer that, Kate."

On that disturbing note, they sat and dug in. After a while, Reese shook his head. "They say prisoners form their own support groups. They get each other through their downtime. If she couldn't do that, didn't have those connections, maybe she would be depressed enough to kill herself. Which will put us up the legendary creek without a paddle."

Kate shook her head. "Parks said she was the belle of the prison, Reese. These records don't show that."

"Parks lied?"

"Good thing to note."

He grabbed the legal pad he'd brought with him and jotted the point down.

"And if she was always in trouble with the guards, wouldn't it go to pattern that there would be fights with other inmates, too?"

"I'd guess."

"But there were none in the Incident Reports. Put that down."

"Done." He scribbled some notes, then said, "What we've done in our first line of investigation is her internal world." He bit into the Brie, enjoying its tart taste. As he took an apple to dunk in the cheese, he said, "This afternoon maybe we can do the external world. Visitors, mail, phone calls. If it wasn't suicide, those will be really indicative of what was going on."

Kate nibbled on a pear. "When we meet with her other lawyers tonight, we'll get more information."

"Um, we're not."

"Not what?"

"Meeting with her lawyers. I canceled it."

"What? Why did you do that?"

"You'll be exhausted by then."

He could see pique deepen the brown of her eyes. The reaction happened when she was aroused, too. "Reese, don't presume to make these decisions for me. You no longer have a right."

"A fact which I'm beginning to regret again. Unfortunately." He didn't mean to say it, but it slipped out.

Her face, even with the bruises, drained of color. She just stared at him, then shook her head. The curls were back today and fell into her face. "Don't go there."

"All right, but leaving things unsaid doesn't make them disappear."

She sighed. He noticed her hand shook when she put down the chunk of bread she'd just dipped into the Brie. "Tyler was angry about last night. That you stayed."

"Don't I know it. I still have the skid marks from this morning when he confronted me."

"He . . . found us together."

"I'm sorry, that was my fault. I dozed off, was just about to leave at two and you had a nightmare."

"You stayed because of that?"

"And because you asked me." He thought, what the hell, "And because I wanted to."

Her gaze darkened. "This isn't good, Reese."

He raked a hand through his hair. "I know. Dray was hurt." He stared hard at Kate. "She asked if I was having renewed feelings for you."

"Now that's a question I'd like to hear the answer to."

Both Kate and Reese startled. They looked up to see Sloan in the doorway. Neither had heard him come in.

Kate slumped back in the chair. Damn, she didn't need this today. She said, "I didn't know you were coming here for lunch, Tyler." She indicated the cartons he carried. Looked like lover boy had brought her lunch, too. Why in hell did Reese feel triumph that he'd beat the guy to the punch?

Sloan was none too pleased, either. He nodded to their food and snarled, "I guess I didn't get the memo on this tête-à-tête, either."

Kate shook back her hair. "We've been working all morning."

"And talking about personal things, I gather." He straightened. "Tell me. Are Dray and I are going to have any say in all this, or are you two going to decide arbitrarily where these relationships go?"

Kate stood and anchored her hand on the chair. "No decisions are being made without you and Dray. Nothing's changed."

Sloan watched Kate, then arched a brow at Reese. "I don't hear a denial from you."

"I don't have to answer to you, Sloan."

"Like hell." He set the food he carried down hard on the counter and swept the area with his hand. "How long do you plan to continue this?"

"I cleared my schedule for the afternoon." Reese raised his chin. "And tomorrow morning."

"I'll just bet you did." Sloan sent him a furious glare. "I want you gone by supper."

"You don't get it, do you? We're no longer just trying to save our careers. We're looking for a reason why Kate was attacked."

"The police can do that." The other man's voice rose a notch. Reese was determined to keep his cool.

"Tyler, please, calm down."

"Yeah, okay." He took his keys out of his sports coat. "I'll be at work until seven, and all day tomorrow." He held Kate's stare.

She said, "I'll call you."

"You do that."

He stalked out of the room. Kate sank onto the chair again. She said nothing, just stared after Sloan.

Reese let the emotion hang in the air. Then he asked, "Are you in love with him?"

Her gaze swung to him. "As I said before—"

"Yeah, I know. That's not a question I get to ask."

Looking very weary, she briefly closed her eyes. "We need to regroup here, Reese. This is all getting way too personal. I want a pact that we won't rehash the past, we won't talk about it. And that we won't get into what either of us is feeling now."

Standing, he felt the old anger bubble inside him again. It had been squelched for a while, but now it was back. "Yeah, whatever." He gathered the dishes and took them to the sink, then faced her. "I'm going out for a walk to clear my head. I'll be back in a bit. Go on upstairs and rest for a while, then we'll continue with the papers on Bingham."

"Reese—"

"Drop it, Kate!" His voice rose and his tone was clipped. "I'm feeling none too stable myself right now. We'll just concentrate on Anna Bingham today." He left her gaping. But he had to get away before he said something he regretted.

ALLISON PETERS, A friend of Sofie's from Westwood, caught up with Sofie in the hall where she was on the way to her American History class. She smiled anxiously. "Hey, Sof, hi."

Sofie smiled back. She liked Allison, who was as normal as apple pie. "Hi. What's up?"

Allison frowned. "I take it you didn't see today's *Herald*?"

"From Westwood?"

"Yeah, remember my mom got me a subscription?"

They started to walk to class. "Something interesting in it?"

Her friend's face scrunched up. "Um, yeah." Stopping, she handed Sofie the paper, folded open to a section. Sofie glanced down. The headline leaped out at her. "Beleaguered Judge Attacked in Garage." Her heart started to gallop. She read further. Her mother had been attacked in a parking garage by a mugger. Judge Renado was doing fine . . . out for a few days to recover from bruises. Sofie clapped a hand over her mouth. "Oh, no."

Allison grasped her arm. "I'm sorry, Sof. I thought they would have called you by now."

Shaky, Sofie fished out her cell. It was off. When she got it booted up, she found two messages from her dad. Stumbling to a bench in the hall, Sofie punched in his cell. No answer. She punched in her mother's. No answer. She called her mother's house. Same. Then she tried Jillian Jenkins, her mother's best friend. Nobody was home anywhere!

"Damn it." Tears formed in her eyes.

Allison sat beside her. "The newspaper says she's all right."

"I know." She bit her lip. "But I . . . how do I . . ." She closed her eyes. "I need to see her."

"Wait till you call your dad."

"No." She glanced at her watch. "I'm going home."

"Okay. Let people here know, first. So you don't get in any more trouble."

"You do it for me, okay?" Sofie was already turning away. She hurried to the front of the school to catch a bus to the train station; on her way, several things haunted her.

Her mother had been attacked.

No one was home.

Her father wasn't available.

And they had kept things from her before.

"I STOPPED BY the police station and got their report." Chase Sanders's tone was matter-of-fact, soothing Kate. That, and because she'd slept for an hour, made her ready to take on the afternoon. And sane enough to be with Reese again.

He'd looked better after his walk, too, though he was still tense.

Now he sat across from Sanders, his ankle crossed over his knee. "Do they have any suspects?"

"Nope, and don't expect any. They're running the judge's description, and dusted everything for prints, but no luck." He sighed. "Think it's related to this stuff?" He indicated the files on Anna Bingham that Reese had gotten from the bedroom, along with the easel, and set up in Kate's den.

Steepling his hands, Reese scowled. "We don't want to

believe that. But we have to look at everything objectively. If I were on the outside of a situation like this, I'd definitely consider the possibility. Actually, it would be good news."

Sanders took a long look at Kate's bruises, making her self-conscious. Her face was more swollen this afternoon. "How do you figure?"

"If the attack is related to this case, it confirms we're on the right track. It gives credence that Bingham was either lying, or murdered in prison and somebody else lied about us, though we can't fathom why."

Kate tried to keep a lid on her emotions. "I do have enemies, Mr. Sanders."

"You need to start making a list." He glanced from her to Reese. "And at some point, you're gonna need to start thinking about any client you defended in your law practice who would have it out for the two of you. Go back into those files."

"Hell, we haven't even dented that pile." Reese nodded to the Anna Bingham's papers.

Kate could see the restlessness brewing in him. In the past, at about this point in a case, he'd get frustrated at the lack of progress. He'd start to pace, move about, coil up tight inside like he was ready to spring. Sometimes, they'd made love to get rid of his tension. She banished that image.

Glancing at his watch, Sanders said, "I got an hour. I can help."

"Good." Kate picked up some files. "We're going to look at her external world. Visitors, mail and phone calls." She glanced at Reese. "We can each take one section."

By four, they had more lists. These Reese had typed into his laptop so they could cross-reference them on the computer. His fingers flew across the keys. When he finished, he ran off the document on Kate's printer.

They studied the stats.

"Jesus, she was one popular broad," Chase said.

"Lena Parks told us she had a lot of male visitors. Look at these two men. They came often, she phoned them each twice a week, and got mail from them regularly."

Shaking his head, Reese sighed. "She kept two guys on a string from prison? Doesn't sound likely to me."

"Musta been good in the . . ." Chase stopped his comment and shot glances at both of them.

Kate chuckled. "Yeah, but nobody had sack time for six months. Maybe when she was out, though, she kept up the relationships."

"So why would she violate probation, if she had such a great sex life?" Typical male response from the private investigator.

"Sex isn't everything," Reese said, his gaze straying to Kate. "Sometimes, people just can't solve their issues outside of bed."

Kate was bombarded by a memory. Of a time she and Reese had sex. It was angry sex, months after the abortion and the discovery of his affair. They'd both known the end was near . . .

Holding her under him, gripping her shoulders hard, he'd thrust inside her; she'd groaned. Not in pain. "How could you give all this up?" he asked, fury in every movement of his body.

She clenched her inner muscles around him. "I didn't. *You* gave up on us."

He'd growled, bit her shoulder. She raked his back with her nails.

He'd made her come three times, before he finally let himself go . . .

"Kate," he asked. "Are you all right? You're flushed."

She cleared her throat. "I'm fine."

Sanders stood. "I gotta book. Can I get a copy of these records? I'd like to read through everything myself."

"Already done. I left it in my car." Reese stood, too. "I'll walk you out to get it."

Sanders crossed to Kate and stood over her. "I'm sorry, Judge. Try to get some rest."

"Call me Kate. And thanks."

Kate watched the two walk out of the den to the foyer.

And was shocked, after Reese opened the door, to hear him say, *"Sofie?* What are you doing here?"

Then came a shaky voice. "Is she okay?"

"Yes, honey . . ."

Her daughter appeared in the doorway. Her lithe form wavered a minute, and then she flew across the room. "Mama," she said stopping in front of Kate.

Kate opened her arms, and, just like when Sofie was a little girl, she fell into them. "Shh, baby, it's okay. I'm okay." She kissed Sofie's hair, overwhelmed with emotion.

Kate had the fleeting thought that all the aches and pains and ugly bruises on her face were worth it if they brought her child home, really home, even just for a little while.

She caught Reese's profound gaze across the room; his expression mirrored her thoughts.

THE AIR WAS filled with the homey smell of oven-fried chicken and French fries—and a calmness that had been missing for a long time whenever Sofie was in the room. Reese watched her push her empty plate away and smile up at him. "It was great, Daddy. Thanks for cooking."

Grinning, he ruffled her hair. "Lucky for you, Mom had chicken to defrost." After the initial tearful reunion, he'd cooked her favorite meal.

Sofie sniffed the air. "I love that smell." She turned to Kate, no animosity on her youthful face. Reese suspected the truce was temporary, but he was enjoying it while it lasted. Sofie was in control now that she'd seen Kate was all right. On the phone earlier, he'd made that case to her principal at school, hoping to avoid punishment for her leaving without permission. It was decided she'd stay overnight here, and Jillian, when she called to check on Kate, had volunteered to drive Sofie back to school tomorrow.

Sofie said, "Go rest, Mom."

Kate smiled softly at her daughter. "I'll help clean up."

"No, I'll do it." Reese stood. "Sof, why don't you take your mom upstairs and lay in bed with her. Like you used to."

For a minute, Sofie stiffened. Reese sent her a stern, *Don't you dare start again* look. "Sure, okay." She stood, too. "Come on, Mom."

"Go on, Kate."

Kate stood, circled the table and put her arm around Sofie's shoulder. "You're on, honey."

"*Jeopardy!* is gonna start soon."

"In ten minutes." Kate glanced at Reese. "Come up when you're done. Join us. We'll all play."

Left unsaid was *Just like old times*.

The girls left Reese alone, and he made quick work of the dishes and storing food. It was so odd cleaning up Kate's kitchen. He didn't like the place much; it just wasn't her. She should have some warmer colors, plants in the corner, copper pots hanging from the ceiling . . . Hell, what was he doing mentally redecorating her house to resemble the one they used to live in?

Trying not to deal with your feelings, Bishop.

Yeah, he knew that. Things were happening fast here. So fast he couldn't keep up emotionally. That's why he had taken the walk. Why he was glad when Sanders showed up.

Sofie's presence, however, brought back those feelings of loss. Simultaneously, the appearance of their daughter made him affirm that they hadn't put her through a divorce only to be having second thoughts at this juncture; he had to play this right now.

"Dad-dy!" he heard from upstairs. He'd lingered too long with the memories. "Come on, the show's starting."

Setting the dishwasher, switching off the lights, Reese made his way upstairs to join them, like he'd done a thousand times when they were a family. He braced himself for what he'd find, and good thing. The sight of his wife and daughter, snuggled in bed together, Kate propped up on pillows, Sofie cuddled into her chest, could have coldcocked him if he hadn't been prepared. "Now there's a nice picture."

Sofie patted the other side of the mattress. "Missing one person. Come on, Dad. Hop in."

Reese hesitated.

"Da-ad!"

Slowly he crossed the room. He kicked off his shoes and slid onto the bed. Sofie moved over and plunked herself on his chest this time, just as the familiar strains of the game show began. Reese held her close, rubbed her arm up and down, and breathed in the wonderful scent of his baby girl, momentarily close to them again.

Afraid to look at Kate, he tried to concentrate on the show. But after a while, she was so silent, so still, that at last he glanced over to check her out. She was staring at them, not the TV. In her eyes was a yearning so potent he almost gasped at it.

He looked down when he felt Sofie tremble. Then heard the sniffling. His arms tightened around her.

Moving closer, Kate brushed back her hair. "Sof, are you okay?"

No answer. More sniffles. "Sofie?" Reese added. "Honey, what is it?"

"I want it to be like this again," she said burying her face in his chest and gripping his shirt. "Just the three of us. In our old house together."

Reese's gaze connected with Kate's. He didn't flinch from it. And though she didn't say anything, he'd swear on a Bible that the same the words formed in her brain as his.

So do I.

TEN

THE LAW OFFICES of Benning and Benning were smaller than those of Bishop Associates, but just as classy. Their firm consisted of a paralegal, an assistant and a husband and wife team. The assistant showed Reese and Kate into a conference room. She gave them a pleasant smile. "Julia will be right with you, Judge. Mr. Bishop."

Reese pulled a chair out for Kate, then sat. He ran late picking her up after lunch, as he'd been in Allenstown all morning, where he'd gone for some pretrial work on the bullying case. His body was tense in his light gray pinstripe suit, which he wore with a snowy shirt and paisley tie. He shifted in his seat.

"Can I get you some coffee?" the assistant asked.

"No, thanks." Reese's tone was cold. "I've had too much caffeine already today."

"I'll have some, if you don't mind," Kate said.

As soon as the woman left, he opened a file. He was all business today; they'd discussed nothing personal on the trip over, just what newly discovered facts Kate had discerned that morning while reading over Anna Bingham's prison files. She recognized his demeanor as the mode he went into when something was really bothering him.

While he ignored her, Kate studied the nicely decorated conference room. Grass-cloth walls. Teak bookshelves. Her gaze landed on one of the many pictures displayed there. Julia and James Benning with a small boy. Her heart stuttered at the sight of it. She remembered other pictures—of a newborn child, a happy couple smiling for the camera; she and Reese had displayed their photos at their law firm, too.

Thankfully, Julia Benning entered the room soon. She was about forty, with pretty gold-red hair, a friendly smile and an easy manner. Kate appreciated the tailored beige suit and guessed it was Ann Taylor.

"Hello, Reese. Judge. We haven't met formally, but I'm Julia Benning. James will be joining us soon."

"Thanks for changing the schedule, from last night," Reese told her as he stood and shook her hand.

Kate shook hands, too. "Call me Kate, please."

Julia inspected Kate's bruises. "Reese told me about the mugger when he called to reschedule. Have they found him?"

Smoothing down the skirt of her severe black suit before she sat again, Kate shook her head. "No, and I'm thinking they don't expect to."

"This is all you guys need, isn't it?"

Kate smiled at the woman's candor. Liked it. "It's been tough enough as it is."

"Then let's see what help I can be."

Reese leaned forward, his shoulders stiff. "We need some insight from you about Anna Bingham when you defended her." He held up the file marked Legal Visits. "We've subpoenaed her records and see that you had contact with her while she was in Longshore. We're not asking for details that would violate lawyer/client privilege"— which in most cases continued after the death of the client—"but more about her state of mind, and your visits to jail."

"I think I can tell you that without crossing the line." Julia shook her head. "We try not to take such blatant fraud cases, but we needed to balance out our caseload at the time."

Just like she and Reese used to do, Kate thought.

"So we took her on. She was a character, I'll tell you that much."

"How so?"

"I never saw a bit of remorse in her. She did time, got out and went right back to her old ways. The only thing that seemed to sober her was being sentenced to a higher security facility."

Reese fired questions at the lawyer as if he was interrogating a witness. "Was she depressed about her situation?"

"More worried, anxious."

"Enough to cause her suicide?"

"Objectively, yes. When she committed the last crime— it's public record that she went in for tax evasion—she didn't expect what she got. The bars, the razor wire, the incarceration with drug addicts. It wore on her."

Checking his notes, Reese scowled. "What can you tell us about your visits with her while she was at Longshore?"

"Her life there—"

The door swung open and in rushed James Benning. His light complexion was flushed, and his hair was askew. "Hello, Judge. Mr. Bishop. Sorry I'm late. Personal emergency." Before he sat, he squeezed his wife's shoulder. From the corner of her eye, Kate saw Reese's gaze narrow on the gesture and his expression became even darker.

"I hope everything's all right," Kate said.

He shrugged. "Sick child."

There was worry on Julia's face as she looked up at her husband. "Did Bret settle down?"

"Once Grandma got there. She's a godsend."

Kate stifled a groan. God she remembered those days. Balancing a baby, a law firm, life.

"So, where are we?" James asked.

"We were just about to discuss your legal visits with Anna Bingham when she was at Longshore." Reese's tone was gruff and his hand gripped the pen he held. "She met with you four times in six months. Can you tell us why?"

"She wanted to scrutinize the trial proceedings. She seemed to think there was a loophole. Apparently she'd been reading up on cases in the prison library where she worked."

"Was there a loophole?"

"Not that we knew of. Truthfully, she was a pain in the butt about it. But her prison advocate kept feeding her incorrect information and she jumped on it."

Reese asked, "Who was the advocate?"

James checked the file, "John Aiken." He glanced at his wife. Distaste was communicated with just a look. "We weren't too crazy about him."

"In any case," Julia put in. "We went over the transcript with her, and sent her the books she wanted."

Reese found a document Kate had highlighted. "Is this list accurate, Julia?" he asked, handing her the record from Barnes & Noble. Prisoners could get orders from bookstores, unopened and paid for by someone else.

Julia reached for her glasses, which weren't in her pocket. Without asking, James got up, crossed to the desk in the corner and retrieved them. Julia read the list and then pulled a paper out of a file on the table and cross-checked them. She read aloud. *"How to Succeed After Prison, Letters and Papers from Prison: One Woman's Story, Major Loopholes and Other Faux Pas of the System, Prison Advocates: What They Can Do For You."* She shook her head. "There's one missing. It was a journal, too—the blank page kind. I remember it because this was always an interesting anomaly about her."

"What was?" Kate asked.

"Apparently she became a writer in jail. She kept journals during her incarceration at Tallahassee, where we had the most contact with her."

Kate and Reese exchanged a surprised look. "Did you ever see the journals?"

"No. But she told us about them. Asked for new blank books."

Reese scrambled for a paper and studied it. "Did she keep one at Longshore? Getting a blank one from Barnes & Noble might indicate she did."

"I don't know."

Kate felt a burst of hope. "Do you have any idea who might have her personal effects?"

"She was divorced twice. Parents are dead. She has a sister. Maybe Nancy Bingham knows." Julia stood. "I'll get you the address."

She left the room, and James had some other suggestions for them to follow up on. Julia returned with the sister's particulars, which she gave to Reese. Then she crossed to get a cup of coffee for her husband. He hadn't asked for it. Her hand went to his sleeve as she set the cup down on the table. She smiled at Kate. "We were up most of the night."

"I remember those days."

Julia cocked her head. "James and I always admired you two."

"Us?" Kate practically choked the word out.

"Yeah, you're quite a legend in this town. Successful practice. Beautiful child. How did you balance it all?"

James grasped her hand. "We're having trouble."

"We did, too," Kate said. "You manage."

"Were there days like these? Where office time was difficult?"

Kate remembered trading off time at home with Reese. "Yes. We played tag team, like you are. We also brought Sofie with us sometimes. Our assistant was only too happy to pitch in."

Reese was stonily silent. He'd even averted his gaze.

"Did you have family to help?"

"Not in town. We were pretty much on our own."

No one mentioned that in the end, Reese and Kate did

not make it after all. When the omission made the air uncomfortable, James touched Julia's hand. "Honey, the
case?"

"Sorry."

They finished their discussions and Kate and Reese
bade good-bye to the Bennings. Kate's mood was somber
when they left the law offices, and as they strode to the
parking lot, Reese's was even blacker than before. With
stiff formality, he opened Kate's door and she slid into the
car. Once he got inside, he reached to start the engine, but
she stayed his hand. "Wait a second."

He checked his watch. "I've got a meeting in a half
hour," he said tightly, not looking at her.

Leaning back against the leather seats of his car, she
cracked a window and let in the warm mid-afternoon air.
"We haven't had much time to talk today. You seem distracted. And angry."

He gave her a sideways glance. "Maybe that's a good
thing."

For some reason she pushed it. "It went well with Sofie
this morning."

"Did it?"

"She fixed me pancakes for breakfast and we took a
walk." Kate snorted. "I should get mugged more often."

He wasn't looking at her. He was staring out the window. "Sometimes it takes a tragedy to remind us of how
much people mean to us."

The words hung heavily in the air.

She tracked his gaze. It was focused on the logo printed
on the law firm's shingle, *Benning and Benning*. "You
never changed your name," he finally said.

"Where did that come from?"

Instead of answering, he shook his head. "Remember
how we fought over it?"

She did. And how they resolved it. "I compromised,
Reese." She'd used Bishop socially, and Renado professionally, which was why Sofie had his name.

He didn't comment.

"What are you thinking about?"

"Them." He nodded to the sign.

"Hits close to home, doesn't it?"

"Too fucking close."

Startled by the vehemence of his expletive, she thought only to say, "I'm sorry."

He gestured outside. "They remind me of us."

"I know. Except they made it."

"Well, the jury's still out on that one. But you're right. They're so close, it's almost tangible." His lips thinned. "We used to have that bond. For a lot of years."

She studied him. "And you're angry about that."

"I'm angry about this whole thing."

"What, exactly? And why today?"

He whirled around in his seat. "Damn you, Kate, don't tell me you don't remember what today is!"

She stilled. She knew all right, but she blocked it, as she did every single year. "I know. I can't think about it; I never talk about it. It's a horrible time for me every year."

"We were married twenty years ago today." He drew in a heavy breath. "I can still see you in that white eyelet dress. Your hair long and curly. You were the most beautiful thing I'd ever seen."

She hated those memories. She hated being forced to remember their wedding, their anniversary. "Stop it, Reese. I won't discuss this with you."

For a moment, he just watched her. Then he reached out, slid his hand over the back of the seat and grasped a few strands of her hair. It was an intimate gesture, especially when he rubbed the strands between his fingers. "Maybe I should just seduce you and force you think about exactly what we had on that day. And lost."

"I'd never do that to Tyler!"

His green eyes glittered. "Otherwise, you'd go to bed with me?"

Time for candor. She shook off his touch, and straightened. "Look, Reese, we know the attraction between us is still there. It would be stupid, and dangerous, to deny it.

What's gone is that closeness that the Bennings have, and the trust. We're no longer bound by that tie."

"Maybe, maybe not. I'm feeling things again, Kate."

She swallowed hard. "This is exactly why I didn't want to spend time with you. I've always been afraid that those *things* that you're feeling would come back."

His gaze was hot. "Would that be so bad?"

"Of course it would. We didn't go through the hell of a divorce, and drive our own daughter away, to say, 'Oops, I made a mistake. Let's try again.'"

"Maybe we did make a mistake."

"If we did, it's one we'll have to live with."

"You heard what Sofie said last night, damn it. She wants her family back." Now, he locked his hand on her neck. Another intimate gesture. "So do I sometimes." He pointed outside. "And that, too. I want that bond back, too."

Please God. Don't let us do this.

"Kate, don't you want it all back sometimes? Be honest, please."

"Yes, Reese, I do. Sometimes, I'd give anything to have back what we had. But A, we're both involved with other people now. And we have responsibilities to them. And B, we've done irrevocable damage to each other emotionally." She bit her lip. "I went to a therapist after we split. I couldn't cope. I couldn't eat or sleep. It took me years to untangle the harm we did to each other. I'm not willing to risk it again." When he didn't respond, just stared at her, she added, "You were practically destroyed, too. I know you were."

"I shut down." He drew his hand back, placed it on the steering wheel and ran his fingers over the gray leather. "I never opened back up really."

"Pollyanna must not like that."

"Don't start on her. Dr. High and Mighty isn't any too happy with you right now."

"See, we're sniping again."

"Jesus Christ, Kate, we're sniping about the other people in our lives. We're fucking jealous."

"No, no. I'm not. They're jealous, and maybe we've given them good reason." She drew in a breath. "I want a pact."

"Kate . . ."

"I want your promise that we won't talk about this again. We won't give in to the temptation just because we have to be together."

He said nothing.

"Reese, please." She touched his arm.

Time strung out. Finally, he said, "All right. I'll give it another shot. I'll try to stop this train wreck." Turning from her, without saying more, he started the engine and began to drive away. Her mind still whirling with all Reese and she had just confessed to each other, she didn't say anything more, either. It was obvious, enough had been said already.

LIKE A MAN possessed, or better yet, like one trying to exorcise the goddamned devil, Reese gripped his racket and smashed the small blue ball into the front wall of the racquetball court. He'd come to The Iron Butterfly, hoping to find a partner and work off some of his frustration, but no one was around, so he pounded the ball in the enclosed space by himself. Perhaps that was for the best. If he killed anybody, it would be himself. Already sweat soaked his shirt, and slicked his skin everywhere.

Racket back. *Smash!* "That's for you, Anna Bingham. For starting this whole fucking thing."

The ball hit the wall and whizzed back at him.

Whoosh! He swung at it again, hard. "And that's for the Bennings. May you have more fucking luck than we did."

He had to run to get the next shot. Racing forward, he picked the ball off just before it hit the floor a second time.

Whack! Inside right corner. The ball lobbed over his head. He ran back, and facing away from the front wall, managed to get a piece of it. "And that's for the goddamned *pact* that she wants," he spat out, sending it spiraling over his head.

He dove for the next shot, missed and skidded across the floor on his knees and arms.

Jesus, he was never this reckless anymore. At forty-five, his body had slowed down considerably. He remembered playing racquetball with Kate. They'd taken lessons together, and she'd picked it up faster than he. They used to career into walls, slide across the floor, and run like the dickens to best each other.

His forearms and elbows stinging, Reese rolled to a sitting position and inched on his butt over to the wall. Leaning against it, he closed his eyes.

Today had been tough. Tougher than previous days when he was forced to be with his ex-wife. Because, if he was honest with himself, he had to admit he was falling back under her spell. In just two short weeks, his whole life seemed to have spun out of control. He could no longer keep at bay these emotions he was feeling for Kate.

The pièce de résistance was the Bennings today. Seeing, played out in living color, who Kate and Reese had been, and what they'd lost, infuriated him. Combined with Sofie's comment yesterday, and the physical attraction he'd been experiencing again for Kate, Reese was about to lose his mind.

"Hey, there, buddy. You still alive?"

Dray had come to the doorway of the court. Dressed in pink sweats, and a pink headband, she looked like a doll.

Reese didn't deserve her. And she certainly didn't deserve his waffling. "Yep." Picking up his racket, he pointed to the wall. "I'm too old for this."

"I was watching you from up there," she said coming toward him and nodding to the glass window where a balcony overlooked the court. "You didn't look old. You looked . . . driven."

He stared up at her. "I needed to let off some steam."

"Did you?"

He wiped sweat from his brow with the hem of his shirt. "I guess." Though not nearly enough to banish Kate from his thoughts.

She dropped down to the floor, and sat cross-legged in front of him.

"Did your aerobics class go well?"

"Uh-huh. My lower back hurts a bit. I think I overdid it, too."

"I'll give you a massage later," he said, winking at her. Man, he had to get out of this ex-wife mode. Dray could do it for him.

"Best offer I had all day."

"In many days." They hadn't made love in a long time.

"It's okay, Reese. I know things are tough right now. We'll get through it."

But in the stark light of the court, Reese had to admit, to himself at least, that his and Dray's relationship might not survive this thing with Kate. Still, he'd try. He would *not* give in to his ex-wife's lure without a fight. He grasped Dray's hand. "Thanks for being so patient."

"Just so I get the prize at the end."

Much as he wanted to, he couldn't promise her that. So he rolled to his feet and helped her up. "You done for tonight?"

She glanced at the clock, trying unsuccessfully to hide her disappointment. "I have to close in an hour."

"I'll head home then. I wanted to call Emily anyway."

"She okay?"

"As okay as ever. I haven't talked to her this week, and I want to touch base. I worry about her."

"You're a good brother, Reese. A good man."

Hell, that twisted the knife. "Not always, babe." But he was trying. "Come on, I think the court's signed up for eight.

Trustingly, Dray put her hand in his. They walked to door and exited the court. He left the gym, giving her just a chaste peck on the cheek. Man, he really needed to talk to his sister.

He didn't wait till he got home. Once in his car, he slid the seat back so he could stretch his legs, whipped out his cell and dialed his sister's number. Staring out at the night, the darkness broken only by a few lamps in the parking lot, he waited impatiently for the connection.

"Hello." Thank you God for letting her answer.

"Hi, kiddo."

"Reese, hi. I was hoping to call you later."

"The boys in bed?"

"Just about." Noise in the background. His name. Away from the mouthpiece, he heard his sister say, "If I let you talk to him, you have to go right to bed afterward."

Cheers. Then, into the phone, "Uncle Reese."

"Jimmy?"

"I lost a tooth."

"Really, did the tooth fairy come?"

"I got a *dollar!*"

"You're a rich man."

"My turn," Reese heard in the background. Then on the line, "Uncle Reese. You comin' to see us?"

"Soon, Jase."

"Bring Aunt Kate. We *miss* her."

Oh, shit. "Maybe."

Emily took the phone. "It's me."

"Shall I call back?" he asked

"No, they know time with you is sacred. They climbed in bed and will go down without a fight if I'm talking to you." She called out, "Good night, guys."

He pictured Emily closing the door, traipsing downstairs. Sitting in her small kitchen. He'd spent a lot of time in her house since her divorce, and they'd even turned a den into a room for his visits. "How are you, Em?"

"Good. I got five orders this week for T-shirts. Business is picking up."

"Tell me about them." Hearing her talk calmed him. Centered him.

He laughed over the two groups who wanted slogans on their shirts—a bunch of psychiatrists who asked for: *I used to be schizophrenic but we're better now.* Apparently they were using the shirts for their basketball team. And a fraternity from a college that wanted *Stud Buds* on their shirts. They talked a bit about cash flow and marketing. Then she said, "So, why do you sound like you did after the divorce, big brother?"

She knew him so well and he never dissembled with her. "It's hard being with Kate so much."

"I knew it would be. Are you making any progress on the case?"

"Some." He filled her in on the details. "This is a hell of a thing, Em. I'm feeling things for her I didn't ever expect to feel again. I . . . want things from her."

"Where does Dray fit into all this?"

"Dray's hurt by it. So is Kate's young stud."

His sister chuckled at his comment. "Sometimes, Reese, you can't stop gravity."

"What do you mean?"

"There's been a force between you and Kate from the beginning, and it draws you back together when you're within range of each other. Truthfully, I'm shocked you could ever resist it."

He peered out the car window at the star-filled sky. He wished for a cigarette, which he'd given up long ago. "Kate says we *can* resist that force."

"You've talked about it?"

"Today."

"Uh-oh. Verbalizing it brings it to a whole other level. Especially for you."

"What do you mean?"

"Reese, you clam up about your feelings all the time since the divorce. You must be pretty raw if you talked to Kate about it."

"Shit."

"What does she say?"

"That nothing's going to happen."

"If she gave you the go-ahead, would something happen?"

"I don't want to answer that."

Emily sighed. "Sorry, you just did."

THE CHAMBER OF Commerce banquet room in downtown Westwood was set up with about fifty circular tables graced with snowy-white linen cloths, navy napkins, and floating candle centerpieces that gave off a vanilla scent. Kate stared into the flickering glow of one, hoping the dim light would hide some of her bruises. She wanted to be here for Tyler, more than ever, but the results of the mugger's attack were still visible on her face.

"So, what do you think of our boy here, Kate?" The question came from the oldest of Tyler's partners in his medical practice. Jonathan Brooke had mentored Tyler and was rightfully thrilled by his accomplishments, which were being honored tonight.

"I'm very proud of him." She smiled over at Tyler. He returned it and squeezed her hand. "Personally, of course." She squeezed his hand back. "But also as a family court judge. What he's doing with children in the program makes my job a lot easier."

Talk about Tyler's Well Child Project continued around the table. Kate sipped her wine and toyed with her salad, enjoying his accolades. She had no idea he'd been asked to go to New York to consult on a clinic that would incorporate some of his practices. Damn, she wasn't paying nearly enough attention to him, and felt bad for it. She nibbled her salad and vowed to be more interested.

People were courteous and friendly to her; they politely skirted the problems Kate was having, the problems plastered all over the newspapers these days. The whole evening had been an oasis from the upheaval of her life, particularly with her ex-husband and his confession, or whatever the hell it was yesterday at the Bennings' law office.

Over spicy shrimp in a cheese sauce, Tyler and she managed some private talk. "You doing all right?" he asked.

"Sure."

"Tired?"

"Some." She patted her face. "I hope I look okay."

"You look beautiful. I particularly like that dress. Is it new?"

Kate glanced down at the little black sheath she'd bought

for tonight. It did look good on her. She liked the way it clung in all the right places. Reese had always been partial to black dresses and used to whisper naughty things in her ear when she wore them out to an event.

Damn it, she was thinking about him again.

"Kaitlyn? I asked you a question."

"Oh, sorry." She touched his hand. "Yes, it's new."

"Did you buy it for me?" His voice was pitched low, and sexy.

Had she? "Of course."

"Mmm. I can't wait—"

The microphone screeched and drew everyone's attention to the podium, where the mayor of Westwood addressed the patrons. "Good evening, everyone. Thanks for coming here tonight. Over dessert, we're going to have this month's speaker. Dr. Tyler Sloan, one of Westwood's innovative pediatricians, is going to tell us about a unique program for children that he's been working on for a couple of years now." He went on to give Tyler's impressive credentials.

Enthusiastic applause followed. Smiling, Tyler squeezed her shoulder as he stood, then made his way to the front of the room. He took the podium with ease, with grace and definitely with charm. "Hello. Thanks for having me here." He pointed to a projector. "I've brought some pictures to go along with my talk so the scenery might keep you awake."

Behind her, Kate heard, "The scenery's just fine as it is."

Another woman chuckled. "God, is he yummy."

He was, of course. Tall, broad shouldered. His wheat-colored hair looked more gold in the lights overhead, just before they dimmed. His runner's body moved assuredly as he turned toward the screen and the PowerPoint presentation came up. His voice seemed huskier, sexier in the dim light.

"We began what became the Well Child Project a few years ago when Westside Medical Associates wanted to renovate their waiting room. I'd done some office-environment study in med school, and, of course, since I was the new kid on the block, I was put in charge of designing the space. We started by sectioning off the existing, traditional Well Child side and provided various activities. We thought if we could keep the kids busy while our always-behind appointments ran into one another, they would have something to do and the parents would be calmer while they waited to see their doctors."

He called up slides of the waiting room, which had partitioned areas for artistic endeavors, music endeavors and movement. "These three areas were roughed out first, but eventually we closed them off as individual rooms—now called the Well Child Zone—because they became so popular and added so much to our practice of medicine."

He went on to show the progress of the rooms—how they expanded, filled with different equipment. "Here's the drawing, painting, clay, etc., room as it looks now."

Everyone laughed at the picture of Tyler with an adorable little girl slathering green paint on his nose. "Sally was terrified of doctors' offices. She particularly hated throat cultures. I noticed that the kids liked the waiting room a lot, so I decided to come out and get the reluctant ones myself and spend a few minutes there with them before their visits. Sally and I drew pictures and talked about her appointment. Then, we took this puppet"—here Tyler showed a new slide, of a puppet and himself doing a throat culture on it. "Treating the doll first made her feel better about the procedure being done to her."

He faced the audience. "Yes, it takes more time and puts us even more behind schedule. But we don't do it with all children; and where this led us is the best part." He called up another slide. "This movement room is great because it allows the kids to let off steam. But it also serves psychological purposes. We find out a lot about a depressed or angry child's state of mind when he's let loose in here. Anxiety in young kids is staggering, and before we prescribe medication, activities of this kind help us to sort out the issues. We now have on staff a part-time art therapist to work in one room, and we have a music person in the other room. We're looking for a movement therapist now."

He showed more slides, then called for the lights. His color was high with excitement and his smile broad. "The upshot of all of it is that we've managed to keep our young patients occupied with these areas before their visits, calm their fears about doctors, and best of all diagnose physical and psychological illnesses, so we can treat them better."

Kate sat back and sighed while he answered questions about his program. He was modest, giving credit to his research and his assistants. He was funny and self-effacing. He was forceful when he asked for volunteers. He was, truly, an ideal man.

Like the women behind her, any female in her right mind would jump at the chance to be his lover, his significant other, his wife. Kate admired him, and cared a great deal for him. Certainly she liked being with him.

She wasn't about to give him up because her ex-husband was feeling *things* for her. She wasn't! She was going to try harder. So she hugged Tyler hard when he came back to the table, and held his hand as he led her out of the room after the evening was over, letting warm feelings for him fill her.

He was slipping her light wrap around her shoulders, and was about to say something, when a man came up to them. "Judge Renado."

It took Kate a second to realize who spoke to her. "Mr. Wick. Nice to see you."

Eddie Wick, Westwood's Clark Kent, nodded to her. He took a bead on Tyler. "Dr. Sloan. Nice speech."

"I hope we'll get a good write up in the *Herald*," Tyler responded easily.

"Oh, you will." Wick studied Kate, as if piecing together something. Then he called over his shoulder, "Joel, come get a picture of the judge and her new prince."

He was referring to the Cinderella Couple comment he'd made during the interview with her and Reese.

And as the camera flashed, just like that, despite her earlier vows, Reese Bishop was part of the picture again.

ELEVEN

IN HIS OFFICE downtown, Chase Sanders was surrounded by file cabinets, a messy desk and piles of books—a fitting backdrop for the interesting private investigator. He addressed Kate and Reese with a neutral expression on his face. "Thanks for meeting me here. I'm sandwiched in-between appointments, but I wanted to talk to you two."

"You said it was important." From where he sat across the desk, Reese leaned forward and linked his hands between his knees. He was still on edge today. "We're both on our lunch breaks."

"Then let's get to it." Chase picked up a folder. "I got nowhere interviewing Anna Bingham's friends. She didn't have that many and nobody particularly cared what had happened to her. However, I did have a meeting with her sister. Nancy Bingham said Anna had been depressed the last several times she visited the prison." He cocked his head and Reese recognized it as the pose of somebody about to deliver bad news. "She believes her sister committed suicide."

Reese ground his hands together. "Fuck."

Beside him, Kate blew out a heavy breath. "This is just great." Her sarcasm lacked oomph. She was as drained as he was. It had been two weeks ago today that the case blew up in their faces.

"Were there any details that might help us?"

"A couple. She said Anna was getting a lot of visitors. Men who seemed to depress her."

Kate shook her head. "It is *so* odd that she had more than one man on the string."

Reese threw Kate a slicing look. She had a lot of nerve making *that* statement.

"I've gone over her visitation list and I'm going to contact the people on it." Chase frowned. "I'd like to see the videotape of the visits."

Kate said, "We put in a request at the prison but haven't gotten the tape yet. It might take a while."

"You said a couple of things about your meeting with Nancy Bingham were important," Reese commented. "What else?"

Sanders expression was hopeful. "She said her sister mentioned some inmates by name—Lena Parks and an Anita Ruiz."

Reese straightened. "What about them?"

"She said they were giving Anna trouble."

"Well that's a lead to go on." And it made Reese feel better. Something had to go their way soon.

"I'll check out both of them," Sanders said.

Kate sat forward. "The Bennings gave us a book order from Barnes & Noble that Bingham received. There was a blank page journal on it. The Bennings say she got into writing in prison. Did her sister mention anything about that?"

"No. Her sister didn't say anything about a journal being among her personal effects."

"Nancy Bingham has her personal effects?"

"Yeah."

"Did you get a look at them?"

The private investigator shook his head. "No, she drew the line there."

"Maybe if we ask her?" Kate suggested.

"Couldn't hurt." He slid the folder over. "You can take the whole thing. It has her numbers in it."

Both Reese and Kate reached for it, their hands making contact on the folder. They stilled. Then Kate snatched her hand back.

Chase Sanders caught the exchange. "Something wrong?"

"No." Reese bit out the word.

Kate said, "We're just strung out over all this."

And other things, Reese thought.

"As you should be." Sanders studied Kate's face. "Your bruises look better today." He grinned at her, making Reese's teeth grind. "I saw your picture in this morning's *Herald.*

"A fund-raiser for my . . ." She hesitated. "The man I'm seeing."

"Yeah, Tyler Sloan. Got a good write up."

Reese had read every word. And had seen Kate in that little black dress. He wondered if Sloan had taken it off of her when they got home. "Can we get back to the case?"

Sanders's gaze sharpened at Reese's curt tone. "Sure nothing's going on here I should know about?"

"Of course." Unable to stay seated, Reese rose and crossed to the window. "I'm just wired," he said from there.

"So where do we go now, Chase?" Kate asked.

"Look at the video when we get it. And I'll be interviewing inmates tomorrow."

"What should *we* do?"

"You can try to make some headway with Bingham's sister. But I think we should implement the next phase, too."

"Which is?" Reese asked.

"You guys take a look at your law cases. Start with the last ones you were on together and work backward. Meanwhile, Kate, you make a list of people from your court who might want to hurt you. Mostly those who could have a grudge against you about a decision you made on the bench."

Kate sighed. "Actually, I've already done that. The police asked for names, so Tyler helped me brainstorm them. I'll send you a copy if you want."

"I do. Asap."

Reese checked his watch. "We have to go." He crossed to Sanders and shook hands. "Thanks. We'll be in touch."

Once again, Sanders lingered over Kate. Reese walked out the door, and couldn't hear what the man said to her.

Outside, they went to their respective cars. When they reached Kate's Mitsubishi first, Reese stopped. "So how do we do this?"

"I don't know. It's going to take an incredible amount of time to go over our case files." Left unsaid was, *Time that we shouldn't be spending together.*

"I could have Yolanda pull the folders for that last year."

Her expression was soft and vulnerable. "I don't want to revisit that last year. It's going to push all kinds of buttons for us personally. Remind us of everything that went wrong."

He banged his hand on the roof of the car. "Fuck."

She studied him. "I hate when you get like this."

"Like what?"

"So coiled up tight that you might blow any minute."

"That's exactly how I feel."

"Then work it off. Play racquetball. Have incredible monkey sex."

The midday air crackled. "You offering?" His tone was not nice.

"I don't play racquetball anymore."

"Good dodge, Kate."

She turned to her car and clicked the lock. He grasped her arm, but she kept her back to him. Again, neither spoke. His hand gentled on her and he began rubbing the sleeve of her deep pink suit. "This is hard."

"Don't make it harder, Reese. Please."

"I'm trying."

"Do better."

"Son of a bitch. You don't give an inch, do you?"

"I have to go."

"Fine, I'll call you when Yolanda gets the files ready."

Since she had the folder, she said, "I'll phone Nancy Bingham and let you know what she says."

Even more frustrated than before, Reese stepped back, watched her get into her little sports car and drive off. He shook his head as it disappeared around the corner. "I think we're kidding ourselves, love. Big time."

HE WAS ALL schmooze and charm. It practically oozed out of him as Kate watched him lay it on thicker than southern honey. Poor Nancy Bingham didn't stand a chance.

"Thank you so much for seeing us, Ms. Bingham." Reese held her hand a little too long.

"You're welcome, Mr. Bishop."

"Reese, please."

The petite blonde—at least he was true to type—smiled at his sexy green gaze and the dimple that sometimes appeared when his face went all soft and tender. "Reese, then. Call me Nancy."

"This is my ex-wife, Kate."

The woman gave her a glance, dismissed her, and focused back on Reese. She sat in an expensive leather wing chair in a fussy room filled with antiques. Her taupe dress was conservative but attractive. "I'm not sure what I can do for you. I've already spoken with that private investigator."

"Chase Sanders. Yes, he said you might let us look at your sister's things."

God, Reese lied so well.

The woman frowned. "No, I told him the opposite. I'd prefer no one go through them."

Reese cocked his head like he did when he was trying a

case and wanted the jury to think he was surprised. "Well, I don't know what to say. We drove up here for that purpose." Again the smile. "I'd never have imposed if . . ."

"Oh, you're not imposing."

Of course he wasn't. She was eating Reese up with her eyes. He did look good today in a light gray windowpane suit that fit his shoulders perfectly. For a change, he was monochromatic, with a dark gray shirt and tie. It made him a bit sinister and a lot sexy.

"Could you just tell me one thing then? Was there a journal among them?"

"No. Why would you ask that?"

"Anna ordered a blank journal from the bookstore. We were wondering if she wrote in it."

"I don't know anything about Anna writing. But it's not out of the question. She used to have a journal when she was young."

"But there wasn't one in her effects?" he asked again.

"No."

Reese looked so disappointed any woman breathing would want to ease it. "Then that's that. We should be going." He pretended to be thoughtful for moment. "If you wouldn't mind, Nancy, could we have some coffee? It's a long drive back to Westwood. We'll get out of your hair and on our way afterward."

"No need to hurry." She stood. "I'll tell Harriet."

Bingham left and Reese whirled on Kate. "You could at least help out here."

"Sorry," Kate said nastily. "I was busy watching the show."

"Do you or do you not want to see those personal effects."

"I do."

"Then play along, goddamn it."

"Don't speak to me like . . ."

"Coffee will be right out."

Sweet as pie, now that Nancy was back, Reese smiled at her, stood and crossed to the fireplace; he picked up a picture on the mantel. "This is you and Anna?"

Nancy joined him, and her hand fluttered to her chest. Oh, great. Feminine wiles were all Reese needed—he was so susceptible to them. "Yes, it is. I'm afraid these photos are hard to look at now."

"When was this one taken?"

"We used to spend our summers at the Jersey shore. That was right after I graduated from college."

"Anna was older than you, right?"

Oh, boy.

"No, no, she was considerably younger."

"Hard to tell." Again the honey molasses grin. "You must miss her."

Chase had said the two sisters were out of contact for years and Reese knew that.

"Oh, I do." She pressed her fingers to her mouth.

Ostensibly out of comfort, Reese pounced on the poor woman and grasped her arm. "I'm sorry for being so frag-ile about this," Nancy said.

Like hell you are, Kate thought.

When the maid brought the tray, they fussed over coffee and Italian biscotti. Kate tried to make conversation, but Nancy Bingham only had eyes for Reese. When enough time passed, Reese stood. "We'll be leaving, I guess." He arched a brow and looked so sexy that even Kate was af-fected. "That is unless I can change your mind about letting us see Anna's personal effects."

Caught in the proverbial hook, line and sinker mode, Bingham shrugged. "Well . . ."

"Oh, Nancy, we'd so appreciate it."

Again a hesitation. "I guess it would be okay." She touched Reese's arm again. "Could you help me bring the boxes down? They're in the attic."

"Of course. And thank you so much."

Kate reiterated the words, but had to keep from rolling her eyes.

Ten minutes later Kate was cooling her heels in the den when they entered with two boxes. Reese's muscles bulged as he set them down on the table. Nancy stood back as

Reese opened the cartons. Kate joined them and helped examine the contents.

"Those are awful things," Nancy said, when Kate drew out the prison khakis.

"Hmm." She noted the patches on them. A lot for six months. Looks like little sister had had some fights that tore her clothing.

Her shoes showed scuffing.

A soft covered Bible. Kate leafed through it. Since the pages stuck together like they were brand-new, it didn't appear that Bingham was concentrating on the afterlife. She wondered why the woman even had the Good Book.

"I gave that to her," Nancy said. "I thought it might, you know, help."

"I'm sorry," Kate said genuinely.

Anna also had a religious medal, and a ring.

Kate picked up a slim silver band. "Is this a wedding ring?"

Nancy shook her head. "Anna wasn't married."

Without asking, Reese took the ring from Kate and looked inside it. Suddenly Kate was reminded of what they'd sentimentally chosen for the inside their wedding bands. *I'll always love you.*

So much for inscriptions.

Reese frowned. "It says 'My love always, DD.' Who's DD?"

"I have no idea."

This was progress, at least, Kate thought.

They waded through the rest of the clothes and personal items, mostly things bought at the commissary. A journal was not among them. Still, Kate studied each item, the last of which was a fingernail clipper. They were heavy. "Reese," she said, unfolding them. "Look."

On the underside of the clipper was taped a small key.

Perfect size for a journal.

* * *

DARKNESS HAD FALLEN by the time they were on the road back to Westwood. In the glare of the headlights, Reese could see Kate's face, set in stern lines. She hadn't said a word since they got in the car.

"What's wrong?" he finally asked, pissed at her detachment.

"Nothing."

Any man worth his salt knew a few things about women's responses. *Nothing* always meant, *If you don't know, I'm not going to tell you.*

"You seem upset."

"I'm fine."

Fine translated to *You have no idea how mad I am.*

"Jesus Christ, Kate, I thought you'd be happy that we got to look at her things. And found the key. At least we know the journal exists."

"I am happy."

"God, I forgot how you could be."

"Oh, just shut up."

Well, some reaction at least.

Silence. For several miles.

"Where do we go from here?" he finally asked.

"I don't know." Her tone said, *I don't care.*

"Look, if you're pissed off about something, spit it out or get over it. I want to save my ass, and damn it, you're going to help."

"Don't you dare yell at me. Just because you used up all your charm on Nancy Bingham . . ."

"Is that what's got your panties in a twist?"

"I couldn't care less about your flirting with every woman on the planet. Just don't complicate this case by playing footsy with somebody involved in it. That's what got us into the whole thing as it is."

"What?" Now he did yell. "You said you believed me!"

She stared out the window and remained stonily silent.

A horn beeped. Reese realized he'd swerved into the other lane.

"Watch your driving. I knew we should have come separately."

"Oh, yeah, an hour trip in separate cars makes a lot of sense. What the hell is wrong with you?"

"Nothing!"

His hands fisted on the steering wheel. Damn her. *Damn* her.

"You sound like a jealous shrew."

"Yeah, that will be the day."

Something about her taunt made him reckless. Spying a scenic view area that look deserted, Reese put on his blinker and pulled off the interstate.

"What the hell are you doing?" Kate asked as he brought the car to a stop.

"I want to talk to you and I'd prefer not to get us killed in the process."

"Damn you, Reese. Don't I have a say in anything?"

"Not this time."

He cut the engine and the silence was deafening. Below them the city where Nancy Bingham lived spread out and the lights twinkled from the valley. Kate huffed out an angry breath and Reese counted to ten before he said, "Kate, talk to me."

Her whole body sagged. She shook her head. "I can't do this. I just can't."

He reached out to squeeze her shoulder.

"Oh, God no, don't do that. Don't touch me."

"Kate . . ."

Thrusting him off, she yanked on the handle, threw the door open and bolted out of the car.

What the hell?

He exited his side and went after her. She was running, in heels, a skirt and suit jacket, which slowed her down. When she stumbled, he caught up to her easily, by a green shingled shed. Grabbing her shoulders, he used force to keep her still.

Her back to him, she struggled. "Let me go."

"No, I did that once and I regret it. I'm not letting you go."

She rounded on him. "Are you *crazy*? What are you saying? We practically destroyed each other. I'm not going to give in to this . . . temptation just because I want to jump your bones again. Just because I hated . . ." She clapped her hand over her mouth, as if realizing what she was admitting and trying to stop the words from tumbling out.

It was all he needed. Her eyes widened as he took a step forward. She backed up but the shed stopped her.

And then Reese was on her.

No, no, no, was all Kate could think when she saw Reese's body move toward hers. His green eyes were dark and dangerous. She put her hands on his chest to push him away, and felt his muscles leap, his heart pound. Her own heartbeat raced to keep up. She opened her mouth to protest, but his lips silenced her.

Ahhhh . . . she remembered that all-male taste of him, his lips firm, demanding. She angled her head for deeper contact, and he growled into her mouth. He dragged her close, so their chests were melded together. The crush of his weight against her breasts, with the shed behind her, made her breath catch. His tongue curled around hers, possessing it, conquering her mouth. She participated, dueled, devoured. His hands on her face, he grasped her roughly, brought her closer. Still the kiss went on. All thought fled, replaced by sensation so acute, so familiar it leveled Kate. She started to slump.

Reese caught her by banding his arms around her back. He lifted her up on tiptoes, still mastering her mouth. Still surrendering to the sweet taste of her, the familiar curves and planes of her. Bracing her against the shed, he slid his hands to her butt, caressed the curves of her bottom, his fingers flexing on her. A moan escaped her lips; he swallowed it, but it fueled his desire. So he grasped her thighs and hoisted her up; almost automatically, she wrapped her legs around him. Brought into intimate contact, he pressed her into the shed, and she bucked right into his groin. He tore his mouth away from hers, and angled his hips forward. "Arrgh . . ." His moan was loud in the relative quiet of the deserted rest area. Her breathing labored, she buried her face in his neck, her teeth scraping his skin. He brushed her hair back so he could get his mouth on her neck, too, as he rubbed her lower half against him.

"Oh, shit . . ." he said, briefly panicking at the thought that he might go off on her, here, right now. His teeth clamped on her bare skin.

"Reese, Reese." Kate bit out the words.

He knew her body so well, knew she was so close to orgasm, all it would take . . .

A car whizzed by, honking its horn. For just a second, Reese stopped grinding her against him. That moment brought sanity.

"Reese," she whispered, her breath still ragged. "Stop. Please, love."

It was the endearment that got to him. That doused some of the desire that demanded hot, sweaty release. He didn't know what hurt more, his physical arousal or the feeling of loss that her words brought. So he stopped. "I'll stop. Don't move, though."

She clung to him, like she'd clung to him a thousand times in the past. Her heart syncopated with his, the heat of her seeped into him. She held on tight.

He didn't know how long it was before he let go of her legs. They slid to the ground. Her face stayed buried in his chest, and his in her hair. Finally their breathing evened out.

He released her in increments. He lifted his head. He dropped his hands. He stepped back, if only fractionally.

Finally she looked up at him. From the rest area's dim lights, he could see her mouth was swollen, her hair a wild tangle. A couple of buttons were undone on her blouse and the swell of breasts that he longed to touch, to take in his mouth, to suckle until she screamed, was visible in the muted light. But her lips were trembling, and her eyes were so sad, he just grasped her arms lightly, swallowed hard, and stared down at her.

Kate held his gaze, still overcome by tasting, touching, reveling in the touch of the only man she had ever loved. She felt chagrined, she felt guilty, but none of those emotions eclipsed the pure joy of raw, intimate contact with him.

"Well," he said softly, sweetly, tenderly. "Well."

"Yeah, well."

He rubbed her arms up and down. "I guess that's where everything was coming from."

"Everything?"

"The sniping. The sarcasm. The jealousy."

"I suppose." She put her hands on his chest but didn't push him away. "Think we got it out of our systems?"

He laughed and yanked her hips closer, pressed his erection against her.

"Oh, I guess not." She chuckled, then sobered and shook her head. "This isn't funny, is it?"

"No, it's damned serious."

"I'm trying not to panic."

"Good luck. I'm halfway there."

She stumbled a bit and he frowned. He glanced down. "Hell, where's your shoe?"

"It fell off when you lifted me . . ." She covered her face with her hands. "Reese, what did we do here?"

Tenderly he brushed her hair back. "You know what happened."

"Too much time together."

"I was afraid of this."

"So were Tyler and Dray."

At the mention of the two people in their lives, they both sucked in breaths.

"Oh, God!" she said.

He frowned.

She shook her head. "This was an aberration. Maybe it was bound to happen. But it doesn't really change where we are in our lives."

"It sure as hell could if we let it."

"We're not going to let it, Reese."

"Some things you can't stop." He motioned to the air around him. "Like this."

"We'll be more careful."

"And how will we do that? We've got hours of work ahead of us, which means hours of time alone. We'll just combust again."

"No." She stepped around him, bent down, and picked up her shoe. "Shit, the heel's broken."

He pivoted. Now that he was more in the light, she swore again. "There's lipstick all over your shirt." She closed her eyes. "And marks on your neck."

"And on yours."

"We didn't try hard enough to resist this."

"Of course we did."

She anchored a fist on her hip. "What do you suggest we do about all this, hotshot?"

"I don't exactly know."

She scowled. "We wouldn't be in this predicament if you kept your promise."

His voice rose. "I tried. You getting jealous of Nancy Bingham would drive a saint to kiss you."

"We need to step back. Reassess. I'm not ready to give up on Tyler." She watched him. "Are you, with Dray?"

"I hate hurting her. But how can things go on as they were, now that this has happened between us?"

"Don't do anything. Just wait and see how we feel to-morrow."

"Tomorrow we're starting our case files. I can't be in the same room with you and pretend this didn't happen, Kate."

"We aren't pretending. We've acknowledged it. Decided it was not the best thing for us. We'll try to get over it."

No answer.

"Reese, please, one more try."

"So what are you suggesting? That we lie to Dray and Sloan?"

"No, we'll tell them. We can put the right spin on it, I think. Make them see it didn't mean anything."

"It *did* mean something or you wouldn't be so upset."

Now it was her turn to be silent.

"At least admit that, Kate. To me."

"Yes, it meant something." She expelled a heavy breath. "We'll tell Tyler and Dray it was a mistake. That our feelings were heightened by the case and we lost control."

"That might be easier to handle." He stepped farther away. "What about tomorrow, and the case files?"

"We'll bring Dray and Tyler. They can help us."

"That is by far the worst idea you've ever had."

"No, no it'll help squelch this . . . thing between us."

"You're wrong."

"I'm right. And I insist we do it."

"You have no idea," he said, lifting his hand and grasping her chin, "how wrong you are. When it blows up in our faces, remember that I warned you."

"It won't." She took in a heavy breath. "Swear to God you'll give this an honest shot. You'll really try to make it work with Dray and keep our interaction . . . platonic."

"All right, I swear to God. Invite young Dr. Kildare to your house tomorrow."

"And you bring Little Bo Peep."

"It oughtta be interesting."

And because she was so sure she wanted to put what had happened between them behind her—and it pissed him off—he leaned over and gave her a hard, possessive kiss on the mouth.

DRAY LAY BACK against the terry-cloth pillow in the three-by-six foot tub in Reese's bathroom and closed her eyes. After a full year of living in this house, she still didn't consider it her own. Oh, she'd made decorating changes, brought in some of her furniture, and stored the rest in the apartment above the gym, but basically, this was Reese's domain. He somehow kept it his, as much as he kept his heart to himself.

Scooping up the bubbles, she blew soap into the air and

watched it scatter. His feelings were as insubstantial as the evaporating froth. And Kate Renado had the power to blow them to the wind, just like this.

He was with her again tonight. They had to travel somewhere to interview Bingham's sister. "I hate you Anna Bingham," Dray said aloud. The woman had brought Kate and Reese together again.

And Dray knew in her heart that Reese was falling in love with his ex again. All that remained undetermined was if Dray was going to fight for him. Tyler contended he'd never give up Kate without the battle of the century. He was such a nice guy, Dray had been wishing lately that *they* were a couple instead. But she had no romantic feelings for Tyler, and though she did find him attractive, her heart belonged to Reese.

She'd called Phoebe again to talk, but her sister wasn't answering, so she'd tried Lacey. But she couldn't lay all this on Lace with the wedding so close. Still, talking to her about normal things helped.

Reese materialized in the archway to the bathroom. She hadn't heard him come in. An automatic smile broached her lips.

"Hi," he said. "I didn't know you were in here." He seemed wound up, though he was casually leaning against the jamb, drink in hand. His tie and suit coat were off, and his light gray shirt was rolled up at the sleeves. There were some smudges on the front of it. She studied him, his flushed face, the odd expression in his eyes.

"How did the visit with Bingham's sister go?"

"Good. She let us look at the personal things." He sipped the amber liquid. "No journal though. She has no idea what happened to it."

Dray asked, "Where do you go from here?"

"Sanders recommended we start scrutinizing the case files from Renado and Bishop, to see if we alienated any clients who might have set us up." He shook his hand. "It's a daunting task."

"Need some help?" She knew he'd say no, that he and

Kate worked best alone. But she asked anyway. Guess she *wasn't* going give him up without a fight.

"As a matter of fact, yes. I was hoping you could help with the files with this weekend."

"Oh. What made you change your mind?"

"Lots of things. Look, I need to shower. I'll use the other bathroom."

Something wasn't right about this sudden change of heart. As Dray climbed out of the tub and dried off, she tried to figure out what it might be. Why, all of a sudden, did he want her with him and his ex? Lathering herself with lotion, she quelled the feeling of unease inside her. This was good news. Wasn't it?

Walking into the bedroom, she saw Reese had dropped his clothes on the chair. She crossed to them to hang up his suit, and put the other things in the laundry. She was just about to stuff his shirt into the wicker basket when she noticed two things: the second button was missing on the front placket. And the smudges she'd seen earlier looked like . . . lipstick. She blew out a breath.

"Dray?"

She turned. He stood in the middle of the room, a navy-blue towel wrapped around his waist. His chest was sprinkled with dark hair that still glistened from the shower.

He frowned at the shirt. "Come over here, honey." He pointed to the bed.

"No, I prefer to stand." She held up the shirt. "This is lipstick, I take it. Kate's lipstick." She shook her head. "It's such a cliché."

He set down his drink and approached her. Grasping her shoulders, he said, "Yes."

"You slept with her."

"No." He swallowed hard and his green eyes were tumultuous. "I kissed her."

"I see." Thick, black emotion churned inside Dray, but she forced control to the forefront. "What exactly does it mean?"

"It means you were right. I shouldn't be spending time alone with her. Things got out of hand."

"Where? How?"

"I don't want to go into details." He was so close she could smell the soap from his shower—and see the marks on his neck. She reached out to touch them, but snatched her hand back at the last minute. "She did this."

"I'm sorry."

She gulped back the bile in her throat. "Damn you!"

His look was full of guilt.

"Why did you ask me to help you two this weekend?"

He ran a hand through his hair. "This thing tonight was a mistake. Kate and I talked about it afterward, and decided it's one we don't want to make again."

"Do you have any idea how unsure of that statement you sound?"

"I'm just trying to figure things out, Dray."

She shook her head.

"I understand if you want to . . . leave." He'd said that before. "But I'm asking you not to."

"Why?"

"Because it would be a mistake for me to reconcile with my ex-wife."

"But you kissed her."

"As I said, things got out of hand."

"I see."

"Do you?"

"More than you, I think."

"What does that mean?"

"Just that I've seen this coming since the Bingham thing broke in the paper. I'm not sure it's something you can stop."

"I can."

She sighed and pulled the robe more tightly around her. "Well, I have a decision to make, don't I?" One that would be a lot easier if he told her he loved her. But, of course, he hadn't. Ever!

He gripped her shoulders and started to pull her close.

She stiffened. "Don't. Not now. I need to think."

"I understand."

"I'm going to sleep in the spare room tonight."

"Whatever you want." He backed away and picked up his drink.

She got some pajamas from the dresser drawer and headed for the doorway.

"Dray?"

When she turned back she found him sitting on the bed, the towel still wrapped around him. "I'm sorry."

She didn't respond. Sometimes, she knew, sorry simply wasn't enough.

KAITLYN CAME TO the bedroom doorway, a broken shoe in one hand, her pretty yellow blouse wrinkled, and her lips swollen. From his place stretched out on the bed, Tyler's hands fisted on the medical journal he was reading. "Well, I guess I don't have to ask what you've been doing."

"I planned to tell you myself." She crossed into the room. "I saw your car. I'm not hiding anything from you."

He set down the journal, determined to stay cool. "Then tell me what happened."

She dropped her things on the couch, and he saw the back of her suit was stained. He bit his tongue to suppress a nasty retort.

Instead of coming to the bed, she sank down on the sofa. "It got a bit out of hand tonight with Reese."

"Define *a bit*."

"We argued. He kissed me."

Tyler raked her with an angry gaze. "You don't look like you were an innocent bystander."

"I wasn't."

The stark words cut to the quick. "Ah, well." His head told him to storm out of here and out of her life. But he loved this woman. "What does all this mean, Kaitlyn?"

"It means nothing. It was a mistake. An aberration."

"Are you saying you won't do it again?"

"Yes, I'm saying I won't. I didn't want to do it *this* time. It just happened."

"Which doesn't bode well for any promises you make about your future actions."

"No, Tyler. You're wrong. I don't want Reese back in my life."

"I won't have you dallying with him until the real deal explodes on both of you and then you come to me and tell me you're sorry you slept with him."

"Reese and I agreed that tonight was a mistake and we won't repeat it."

"Oh, I'll just bet he wanted that."

"Why the sarcasm?"

"Goddamn it, Kaitlyn. He's in love with you. He wants you back."

She shook her head.

"Fuck it. You know very well if you'd told him tonight, after what happened between you, that you wanted to pursue a reconciliation with him, he would have jumped at the chance."

"He's got Dray."

"That's no answer."

"I'm sorry." He could see her composure slipping. "It's the best I can do right now."

Tyler slid off the bed and found his shoes.

"What are you doing?"

"I'm going home. I need to think."

"Wait a second. Reese and I decided we're not going to work on this case alone anymore."

Did she have a clue how much that statement hurt? That they had admitted to each other they couldn't be trusted to be alone?

"This is bullshit."

"No, it isn't, Tyler. We know being alone is dangerous and might lead to something we both don't want."

"And?"

"We want you and Dray to help us with the next phase of this investigation."

"You're joking, right?"

"I never felt less like joking in my life."

"You want Dray Merrill and me to chaperone you two?"

"No, that sounds stupid."

"Because it *is* stupid." He was yelling now.

"It's not. I don't want to throw away what you and I have, just because I'm forced to be with Reese for a few weeks."

"Listen to yourself. It only took two weeks for you two to jump each other's bones in a car, for God's sake." He glanced down. "How did your shoe get broken? And your suit get stained?" He shook his head. "Never mind, I don't want to know."

"Please, Tyler. Give me another chance. I'm sorry this happened. It won't happen again."

He picked up his light suede sports coat that Kaitlyn had bought him for his birthday. "Yeah, well, I'll let you know what I decide." He crossed to her and lifted her chin. He wished he hadn't because he saw the mark Bishop had put on her neck. "Jesus Christ," he said, turned and walked out.

TWELVE

REESE FELT LIKE a first-class fool walking up to Kate's condo, Dray at his side, on this beautiful end-of-April Saturday morning. His gut told him Kate's little plan was a big mistake; he couldn't believe he'd agreed to such a scheme. He also couldn't believe that Dray, after just a few hours of the cold shoulder and contemplation, had also agreed. But then she leaned into him, as if she needed his support, and he remembered why he was doing this. He owed her this much, a good solid attempt to make their relationship work, and to keep Kate out of his life.

At the front stoop, he rang the bell. "You all right?" he asked as they waited.

"Just nifty."

"Dray . . ."

"No, I'm fine. This will be fine. I know it will." She sounded like a little girl trying to convince her friend of something she didn't believe in. Her peacock-blue sweat suit only added to the innocent effect.

Sloan came to the door—staking out the territory, Reese guessed. He would have done the same thing. The younger man's gaze was hostile when it focused on Reese. "Bishop." It turned soft for Dray. "Hi, Dray. Nice to see you again."

"Hi, Tyler."

Stepping aside, Tyler jammed his hands into the back pockets of his jeans. "Come on in." He closed the door after them, and played the good host by hanging up Reese's jacket. "Kaitlyn's in the den." He walked ahead of them, with Dray in the middle. Reese felt like they were going to a goddamned gallows.

Kate was seated at a table in the corner. Another rectangular one had been set up by her desk. She rose, revealing long legs encased in jeans and tennis sneakers, and a pretty red top that hit her mid-hip and accented her coloring. Her hair was pulled back in a ponytail and she wore no makeup. "Hi, Reese." She nodded to Dray. "Thanks for coming, Dray."

Dray said hello only, and didn't respond to the last comment.

"So, how do we do this?" Sloan asked. His hands were cocked on his hips as if he were ready to draw guns from a holster.

Kate looked to Reese.

"I had Yolanda send over the files in groups, for the kinds of cases we handled, beginning with that last year." His gaze momentarily held Kate's. *That last, horrific year.* He crossed to the boxes stacked on the floor near the longer table. "We should get them out."

Sloan asked, as if this was his house, "Anybody want coffee?"

They both did.

"I'll get it." Kate crossed to a pot she'd set up on a high table near the window. She poured two cups. "How do you take yours, Dray?"

"Two sugars. Lots of milk."

Kate didn't ask Reese his preference, and somehow that she knew he took it with just a bit of milk, made this all the harder for him; by the look exchanged between Dray and Sloan, they caught the familiarity, too.

In an effort to banish his discomfort, Reese began laying out piles of folders, as everybody stood around and watched. Then Kate came and helped. They stood on the same side of the table, staring down.

"Okay," Kate said. "We need to pair up. Reese and I should work together and take the drug arrests, the domestic violence cases, and the probation violations."

"Oh?" Sloan asked, "And why is that?"

She shot a glance at Reese and he nodded. "These are the most complicated ones. I figured you two would have trouble with the procedural information."

"I agree," Reese added. "Dray, you and Tyler can do the robbery cases. After we explain a few things, you shouldn't have too much trouble understanding them."

Sloan made a disgusted sound. "Dray—you've got a masters in kinesiology, don't you?"

"Uh-huh."

"And I have a little thing called a doctor of medicine, so I guess we should be able to handle some robbery terms."

Reese's head snapped up. His gaze narrowed. "Fine. Go for it. I just thought if this was all medical terminology, I'd want you to give me the easier ones and help me with specifics."

Kate came around the table with a stack of about a dozen folders. "Here." She nodded to the corner table. "You can work over there. Reese and I will use the end of this long one where the majority of the files are."

"What exactly are we looking for?" Dray asked.

Kate explained. "Chase Sanders said to isolate cases where the defendant got a verdict he didn't like. Then to cross-check each name with Yolanda's notes on current status of that person. For example, if Joe Blow was put away on a felony charge and just got out of prison six months ago, he might be a suspect."

Sloan said, "This sound like a shot in the dark."

"I'd say a shot in pitch-black hell." Kate smiled. "But we're running out of options." She nodded to the files.

"They're arranged by degree. New York State divides robbery into three main categories. Robbery in the first degree is a Class B violent felony. This is the most serious and carries the toughest penalties—twenty-five years max in prison. It's what most people imagine when they think of robbery—done at gunpoint in a store or bank."

Reese half listened as she told them about second-degree robbery, a Class C violent felony, and the next most serious, carrying a fifteen year max sentence. It frequently came up when multiple people worked on a robbery. The last, third degree, was a class D nonviolent felony and carried a seven year max. "I think there's one in there, if I remember correctly, where the guy arrested on a class D robbery didn't get the desk appearance ticket he wanted and he was angry at us."

Reese recalled the case. "A failed desk appearance ticket doesn't warrant somebody going after us."

"No, but then again, whoever is doing this isn't really being rational."

"Yeah, you're right." He said to Dray, "Look for that case, okay? We'll isolate all potential perpetrators."

"Sure. But what's a desk appearance?"

Kate turned her back to them, so Reese explained. "It's when a person commits a misdemeanor, and in lieu of going to jail or court right away, the guy is given a ticket for arraignment. For a court date. He's still arrested, but doesn't have to show up until such and such a time."

Dray smiled at Sloan. "Ready?"

Reese was reminded that she'd spent some time with the guy. He wondered about it. But if he brought that up, they'd have to discuss the real reason for this un-cozy get-together—why exactly Sloan and Dray were with them today. He circled the table to sit next to Kate. Immediately some enticing scent wafted over to him. She used to put perfume on all the places he loved to kiss. When she turned her head, he saw that her neck bore faint red marks. That he'd put there with his teeth. When she was wrapped

around him like a pretzel and he was grinding his mouth
and groin into her. Shit, he thought shifting uncomfortably,
it was going to be long day.

Kate looked up from the file at Reese's intake of breath.
He seemed upset. After checking out the kiddy area, she
leaned in close to him. "You all right?"

He put on his glasses. "I'm fine. Where do you want to
start?"

"Domestic violence is on top. As good a place as any."
She took a file and he did, too.

She read about a young woman requesting a temporary
order of protection, called a TOP; Kate had brought the
case to court. On their second appearance, the complainant
wanted the order rescinded because the couple was living
together again. The guy gloated. Kate remembered coming
home angry about it and Reese wasn't there. He'd been at
Lindsay Farnum's.

"Want to review this?" she asked him. "I don't think it's
anything, but you'd better check it."

He read the file. And she read him. The look on his face
was like newsprint. When he raised his eyes, they were
filled with recrimination. *What the hell were we doing that
year?* his expression asked. But he said, "The guy was sent
to jail twice after that for beating up on their kids.
Yolanda's note says he's out now. It should go in the
possible-suspects pile."

She placed it there, and tried to focus on another file.
She was fine until she came upon a case she had completely put out of her mind. Everybody—police, judges,
prosecutors and defense attorneys—hated to make a mistake in domestic violence cases, fearing that this one would
become *The Case. The Case* was a seemingly minor domestic incident in which the accused walked away, because
someone didn't arrest, prosecute or defend correctly, and
then he or she returns home and murders the partner who
complained.

They'd had one of those, of sorts. Reese had argued in
court that Jack Smith, a rich, successful computer busi-

nessman, was falsely accused of hitting his wife. The evidence supported the defendant: kids' testimony, maid's testimony, parents' testimony. Judy Smith had reported several incidents, but she later confessed that she'd lied about them. All indications were that this newest charge was fabricated. But the woman didn't back down this time. Still, the jury found him innocent. Throughout the proceedings, Reese had confided in Kate that he thought Smith was guilty.

He'd been inordinately restless the night the verdict came in. Things were really bad between him and Kate. They were sleeping in separate rooms. He got up about two a.m. and went out. Kate had heard him leave, had thought he was going to his girlfriend and was furious. Instead, he'd driven to the Smiths' home and found Jack's car parked out front. Though they'd gotten together in the past during a legal separation, Reese had a bad feeling about this. He called the police and when they arrived, they had to burst inside when they heard screaming through the door. Judy Smith had been badly beaten, and Jack would have finished the job if the police hadn't interfered. They arrested Jack—that time it had stuck.

"What's wrong?" he asked.

She cocked her head.

"Which case has the blood draining from your face?"

Tyler's head snapped up; he stood and came over to their table, placing a proprietary hand on her shoulder. "Kaitlyn, are you all right?"

"It's the Smith case." Briefly, she explained what happened to Tyler and Dray, who'd joined them.

"How did you know to go over there?" Dray asked.

"Just a hunch." Reese's voice was raw. "They come to lawyers. We learn to listen to them."

Kate shook her head. "It could have been disaster, but Reese prevented the worst from happening."

Reese's face was dead sober. "I need to stretch my legs." He stood and walked out of the room.

Puzzled, Dray looked after him. Kate said, "It was a

tough one for him. He got Smith off and then the guy beat his wife so badly it took months for her to recover, and then she walked with a permanent limp. The press was not kind to us, despite the fact that Reese probably saved her life by going over there."

Dray nodded and followed Reese out.

Tyler said, "You want a break?"

"No. I want to keep working." And forget.

"Whatever." He went back to his robbery files. Kate tried to concentrate on her own cases, but she couldn't. Because she could still see Reese when he came home at four that morning . . .

She'd met him on the staircase. "I won't stand for this, Reese."

He'd totally disarmed her. "I didn't go where you think."

"Where did you go?"

He told her. She had immediately gone into comfort mode. "Oh, Reese, I'm so sorry."

There were tears in his eyes, and he'd gone to their bedroom, not the spare room where he was sleeping. He sat down on the bed and buried his face in his hands.

She followed and stood before him. "I won't let you take blame here. You did your job. What's more, you saved that woman tonight."

"All along, I felt he was lying through his teeth."

"You can't go on feelings in court. You have to go on facts."

Still he'd been distraught.

"I won't let you do this to yourself." She dropped down to her knees and grasped his hands. "You did nothing wrong."

He'd just stared at her. Then, he'd tugged her onto his lap. They hadn't made love since she'd found out about his affair. But that night, she fell into his arms and let him do whatever he wanted.

Which was to strip her, explore her—roughly with his mouth and hands—and thrust into her like a madman.

They both came with violent, shuddering force. Just the memory made her go damp.

It changed nothing between them though . . .

"Kaitlyn?"

She looked up at Tyler. "What?"

"You moaned. What's going on? Are you finding suspects?"

"No. No. I just don't . . ." She bit her lip. If she told him reading these files reminded her of those last years of her marriage to Reese, he'd flip again. He'd barely calmed down as it was; he'd agreed to come here today because, bottom line, he wanted to salvage their relationship. He'd made it clear, though, that he wasn't happy about any of it. So she bluffed. "I'm discouraged. I just can't believe we're going to find any answers here."

Still, she went back to the file. Oh, no. Jack Smith was out on bail. As of six months ago. She put the folder in the possible stack. And opened another case. Which only brought on another memory.

How on earth was she going to survive this process?

THEY WORKED UNTIL noon, in awkward, awful tension. Tyler's neck hurt from it. When the clock in the foyer chimed twelve, he stood. "I'm hungry. And I need a break. I also have to call my office."

Dray stood, too. "I've got to leave for a bit. I have to go over to the gym to bring in next week's schedule."

Both Kaitlyn and Reese looked up. Kaitlyn seemed annoyed, which pissed him off. "Okay. What did we decide for food?"

"Subs," Tyler said.

"I can get them on the way back," Dray offered, when Tyler whipped out his cell and went into the foyer to make his call. He was back in seconds. "I need to stop in at my office, too."

Unspoken was the *don't leave Kate and Reese alone* edict—the reason they were all here together. What the hell? Tyler was tired of elephants in the room. "So," he said somewhat nastily. "Is it safe to leave you two alone?"

Bishop's face reddened, and he gripped the file he held. "Fuck you, Sloan."

"Hey, we all know what we're doing here."

"Tyler." Kaitlyn's voice was hoarse. Shit.

"Maybe it's just better to get it out in the open." This from Dray. "It's been like a morgue in here all morning."

Bishop leaned back in his chair and nailed Tyler with an insolent look. "Well, as long as we're being honest, you and Dray seem to be pretty chummy with each other. Jillian Jenkins saw you at Starbucks together. What was going on there?"

Dray raised her chin. "Tyler and I have a lot in common. I don't think I need to spell out what." She faced Tyler. "Since Reese drove me over here, why don't you and I go together? I'll only be a minute at the gym, then we can go to your office."

"Fine by me." He gave Kate and Reese one last disgusted look and headed out the door.

They were in his car before Tyler spoke. "Did I make a mistake bringing it out in the open?" he asked, pulling his Blazer out to the street.

"No, *you* didn't make any mistake."

"Oh, that's right. *They* did. That's why we're all together." He hit the steering wheel. "Is this as bizarre as I think it is?"

"Yep." Dray crossed her legs. "But since the alternative is giving up on my relationship with Reese, I decided to come. What do we have to lose, Tyler?"

"Our pride. We're goddamned chaperones."

"It's probably not even going to work anyway." Dray laid her head on the back of the seat, looking exhausted.

"What do you think about their *big mistake*—the infamous kiss?"

Her blue eyes shadowed with pain. "It makes me sick. But I knew it could happen." She reached out and squeezed his arm. "So did you, Tyler."

"Maybe it's best they fucked up. Now they'll be more careful."

"I hope so."

But Tyler didn't believe what he said and he'd bet his medical license that Dray didn't, either.

When they reached The Iron Butterfly, Dray turned to him and asked, "Want to come inside and see the place?"

He smiled. "Sure."

The gym was huge. It had several rooms, each devoted to an activity. Upbeat music sounded from one area where Tyler could see an aerobics class in progress. The clank of weights came from another. As Dray went to her office, he checked out the dance room, where a yoga class was being held. Everything was state-of-the-art, slick and contemporary. He was absurdly proud of all Dray had accomplished here. It made him wonder why she was putting up with Bishop's shit.

"I'm very impressed," he told her on their way to the car.

"Yeah, I work hard. It pays off."

On the drive to his office, he talked about his Well Child Project.

"My sister's into all that." She told him about Phoebe, studying all over the world in music and movement therapy. "I'd like to see the room—what did you call it—the Zone, firsthand."

"Come in with me then."

She accompanied him into the building. Since they had office hours until noon on Saturday, only a few of the staff remained. He went back to the offices and she wandered into each area of *the Zone*. She was in the movement room when he came out. "All set?"

She smiled over at him. "Tyler, this is great." She ran her hand along a barre. "I took some courses in dance therapy at Butler when I was there. And some workshops given here in Westwood."

"Really?" His wheat-colored brows rose. He looked cool, in his Georgetown long-sleeved cotton shirt and black jeans. But he seemed confident and professional, too. "Want a job?"

She grinned. "No, I have one." She looked over at a jungle-gym thing. "But I could volunteer a few hours a week. Phoebe would love it."

"Hey, that would be great." He squeezed her arm, this time not letting go. "You're terrific, you know that?"

"Sure I am." She smiled. "So are you. What the hell's wrong with Reese and Kate that they don't see that as clearly as we do?"

He chuckled. Then turned serious. "Actually I think they see it. I also think they're genuinely trying to work this out. For us, as couples."

"Maybe," she said as they went out to the car. "I don't hold a lot of hope for it."

Once they were on their way, he said, "It's hard to watch them together, isn't it? They don't even realize how they gravitate toward each other."

"They touch, unconsciously."

"Maybe this is futile. Not to mention demoralizing. I feel like a jerk."

"So do I."

He headed to the sub shop. "But, as you said, what do we have to lose?"

"GOT ANY BEER?" Reese asked Kate when he finished the file he was working on. "The kids" had been gone about ten minutes.

"Yep." She stood and arched her back. "Let's go out to the kitchen."

He followed her, blanking his mind, which was cluttered with cases, and tension and plain old confusion. She got them two Coronas, and squeezed lime into each. Sipping the beer, he leaned against a counter, and she butted up against the one facing him. "So," he finally said. "How'd the morning go, do you think?"

"Awkward, tense, stupid, like you said it would be." She sipped. "I'm sorry I didn't listen to you."

He peeled the label off his bottle. Without looking at her he said, "It's the other stuff that's harder for me."

She watched him as she drank. "It's why I didn't want to go through those old files."

"I can't help but remember, in 3-D Technicolor, what went on that last year between us."

"God, it was so up and down. One minute we were screaming at each other and the next, we were clawing at each other in bed."

"I was thinking about the Smith case." He sighed. "And how we made love that night."

Shaking her head, she sighed, too. "We were both overwrought."

He laughed, but the sound wasn't happy. "We used to make love every time one of us was overwrought." Setting his beer down, he pushed away from the counter and crossed to her. He reached out and brushed a fingertip down the inside of her collar. "What did he say about this?" Even to his own ears, his voice was loverlike.

"He flipped, as you might expect." She shook her head. "What about Dray? Did she see the telltale evidence?"

"Teeth marks on my shoulder." He rubbed the spot. "They're still there."

"What were we thinking, Reese?"

"We weren't. Thinking."

"I'm scared."

He scowled. "Of me?"

"No, of us together. That's why I came up with this desperate scheme. I'm scared we'll hurt each other again and Tyler and Dray, and worse, hurt Sofie even more in the process. You know she can't handle much wavering on our part. We can't give her false hope."

Backing away, he went to stand by the window, looking out at her sterile yard. "I know we have to do this for Sofie." He turned around. "So, maybe I was wrong. Maybe today wasn't such a bad idea."

"Maybe."

* * *

ONCE AGAIN, KATE doubted that bringing the four of them together today was a good idea when she watched Dray and Reese together over lunch; she was totally stunned at her own reaction to seeing them interact. She cringed inwardly as Reese broke off a piece of his meatball sub and gave it to Dray. Apparently America's Sweetheart didn't eat meat, but cheated once in a while. The intimacy of the gesture, automatic and tender, hurt to watch. As did the unconscious way she petted him—a hand on his arm, leaning into him, brushing fingertips down his back. Every single gesture stung. It was then that it hit Kate: Even now, if they managed to stay away from each other, she was going to get hurt by Reese Bishop again. Big time.

Tyler, who'd gotten up to get her some water, set the bottles down next to her, and placed his hands on her shoulders. "You're tense." He began to rub there.

She closed her eyes. "That feels good." When she opened them, she caught sight of Reese staring at them. Oh, shit. His feelings mirrored hers: It was torture watching someone else care for each of them. A bottomless sense of loss flooded her. She shook her head, moved in her seat to ease it.

Finally Reese asked, "We ready to get back to work?"

The afternoon was just as grueling as the morning. Tyler and Dray found an interesting case where a girl was charged with robbery but contended she was just along for the ride. Kate had tried to convince the jury of that, but the law was clear. It was a Class B felony to be in the car with someone who committed the crime. The girl's mother had raged at Reese and Kate for not doing more to help her daughter.

Kate herself found a case on drug possession. A group of college boys were arrested when the police stopped them and found almost an ounce of cocaine in the trunk. Everybody in the car had been charged with a B felony, and had gotten one to three years in jail. She scrutinized the file.

"Reese, look at this." She edged in close so they could both see it. "Harry Jones's father was furious at us because we couldn't get his son off scot-free. We managed a reduced sentence and some probation. He was worried his kid wouldn't get into Harvard."

"He didn't, did he?"

Kate pulled out a newspaper article. "Nope. Yolanda must have clipped this." The kid had gone to SUNY Brockport, dropped out and had other run-ins with the law. "Think Harry, Sr., blames us? Would he come after us?"

"Who knows?"

"Kaitlyn!" She looked up to see Tyler coming toward them. He handed her a file. "Look at this."

She opened it and Reese read it over her shoulder. "Shit, the garage mugger. I'd forgotten."

"How could you forget that?" Tyler asked. "You defended him on charges exactly like your own assault."

Reese bristled next to her. "She forgot because we got him off. He'd have no grudge against her."

Now Tyler bristled. "I don't care about that. It's too similar to what happened to her the other night. Some of the details are the same."

"I don't think it's relevant." Reese's tone was condescending.

Hell, now they were having a pissing contest.

"Oh, for God's sake, stop it you two." This from across the room, from Dray. "Reese, just give it to the police and investigator without arguing. Tyler, stop trying to one-up him." She threw down her own folder. "As a matter of fact, I'm done with all this. We've pretty much exhausted these files, and quite frankly, I'm tired of the stress level in this room."

"Well," Kate said nastily, "Sorry if my career and reputation being on the line kicks up your stress level."

Like an angry goddess, Dray strode over to Kate. "The

stress I'm referring to has nothing to do with the Bingham case. And you damn well know it. Don't try to treat me like some imbecile, Kate. I may be a jock, and not a judge, but anyone can see what's going on here."

Kate jutted out her chin. "You forget, today was my idea, to circumvent *what's going on here*."

Dray cocked her head. "Then maybe you're the imbecile." She looked to Reese. "Can we go?"

He glanced down. "We haven't even touched the probation violations or the DUI's yet." He glanced at his watch. "It's only three."

Dray's whole body seemed to sag into itself. "I see." She faced Tyler. Something passed between them.

He said, "I'm done here, too. I've had about all I can take watching you two together." He said to Dray, "Let's go." On his way out, he glared at Kate. "This really *was* a stupid idea."

Kate watched them leave; Reese also gawked as they exited. When the door shut, none too softly, she turned to him. "Well, here we are, hotshot, alone again."

THIRTEEN

❧

AT FOUR ON Wednesday afternoon, Reese studied the kid across from him. Mitchell Crane was a slight, stoop-shouldered, pimply-faced boy who, one ordinary morning, after months of harassment, had brought a small handgun into school and shot one of his tormentors in the gym locker room. He'd inflicted only a small flesh wound to the shoulder, but the consequences were dire. The case would go to trial soon, and so far, Reese wasn't feeling good about getting the kid a light sentence. He caught the eye of Greg Abbott, the thirty-five-year-old lawyer from his firm, whom he'd asked to be on this case with him because Greg was dynamite with kids. Reese nodded for his associate to take the reins.

"Mitchell, we're going to need more from you than what you've given us." Greg held up his notes. "The boy you shot was one of three who stuffed you in a locker, tripped you in the hall and repeatedly dumped your lunch tray. Can you think of anything else that might help us—something more threatening?"

Mitchell Crane pressed his glasses into the bridge of his nose. "I dunno."

Abbott leaned over. "Think about why you took action on that particular day. Where you were? What was happening? Or maybe something happened on the day before that precipitated what you did."

"Oh, yeah. We had swimming. I hated swimming because they always did stuff to me in the pool."

Calmly, though this could be big, Greg asked, "What did they do in the pool?"

"They used to hold me under water. One of them would distract the teacher and the other two would dunk me." The kid got tears in his eyes. "I couldn't breathe. I had to do something."

Reese's phone beeped, startling him. He nodded to Abbott. "Go ahead, Greg. Get this testimony. Tape it so I can hear it later."

Excusing himself, he left the room, pleased as hell at this new information. It would be a godsend for the defense if the kid's life had been endangered. "Bishop here," he said, catching the call on the third ring.

"Mr. Bishop. This is Lauren Evans from Longshore."

"Warden Evans." His heartbeat escalated. The Anna Bingham case was not going well, nor was Reese's personal life. He and Kate needed a break.

"I have some good news, I think, for you."

Thank you Lord. "We could use some."

"We found the journal your wife called me about." After the visit with Nancy Bingham, Kate had phoned the prison to inquire about the missing journal. Warden Evans had said she'd check into it.

"That *is* good news."

"For you maybe. Not the prison. Apparently, the journal was confiscated by a guard, Nell Sorenson, who gathered Bingham's personal effects, ostensibly because some of them were contraband. But our employee never reported finding a journal. We discovered it in her—the guard's—locker."

"Why is that the bad news for the prison?"

"The locker was abandoned, and Sorenson quit, abruptly. I can't reach her by phone."

"Ah, the plot thickens."

"My thoughts exactly. In any event, I called the New Jersey police, and they weren't particularly interested in a prisoner's journal. The case is closed as far as they're concerned. Then I called Nancy Bingham, who told me to give it to you. That's what she'd do anyway."

"Warden, I can't tell you what this means to us. Have you read it?"

"No, but I will. You can come and get it asap, if you want."

"Can I send someone?"

"I'm afraid not. You or your wife has to collect it. Nancy Bingham gave me permission to turn it over only to either of you."

Reese didn't correct her use of the term "wife." "One of us will be there." He checked his watch. "By what time?"

"I'll be staying till six."

He'd have to leave Westwood before four. This was a problem. They had depositions to take from other witnesses in the Crane case. "See you by then."

Clicking off, he punched in Kate's cell phone number. Maybe she could drive up and get it. He'd rather they go together, but that probably wouldn't be such a good idea because of Tyler and Dray. Though Kate had told him Sloan left yesterday for a conference in Cancun, where she was joining him on Friday.

Cancun. He hated the thought of her going away with the guy. After the fiasco Saturday, both of them had managed to soothe ruffled feathers. This little jaunt to Cancun was supposed to be makeup time for Kate and her man. As was Reese's trip to New York with Dray to attend her sister's wedding. Which he wasn't looking forward to. Things were unbelievably strained between him and Dray. He wondered if the same was true for Kate and Sloan. He didn't know, because he and Kate hadn't worked together on the files this week. They had split up what was left and reviewed them alone, and had planned to meet about them later today.

Surprisingly, he got Kate on the phone. Her voice came across the lines, exasperated.

"Kate, it's Reese. I didn't expect you to answer."

"I'm on a break from the courtroom and the defense attorney from hell."

He chuckled.

"What's up?"

He explained about the journal.

"Wow. It's about time we got a break."

"My feeling exactly. But the warden will only turn it over to one of us."

"Hmm. I'm in a hearing right now. If it goes the way it appears to be heading, I'll be able to leave by four. If it gets more complicated, I'll be tied up the rest of the day."

"We were meeting at six anyway. I wish we could take the trip together and use that time on the case."

"Can you get away?"

"I planned to take depositions all day. But Abbott could finish up after four. We could go together."

"Together? Alone?"

"Damn it, we're adults, we can take a fucking two-hour ride together, without getting permission."

"Things were a mess with Tyler before he left. But I'm feeling the same kind of frustration you obviously are."

No response.

"Are you frustrated? With Dray?"

"Like you wouldn't believe." She'd been angry and upset Saturday night, and he'd accused her of overreacting. They'd fought bitterly, but eventually she'd calmed down. "Truthfully, I'm getting tired of defending myself."

Abbott stuck his head out. "Reese, you need to come in."

"I have to go. Hell, plan to meet me at three-thirty in the lobby of the courthouse. If you're not done, call me and I'll go alone."

"All right." A hesitation. "This is good news, don't you think?"

"I do, babe. See you later."

BABE. KATE CLICKED off the phone and headed back to court, thinking about Reese's call. He didn't even realize what he said. Just like he didn't realize a lot of things. But Tyler had noticed all of them . . .

He touches you all the time . . . You lean into him . . . Hell, you even communicate with just a look. The rubber's met the road, Kate. You have to stay away from him. And you'd better meet me in Cancun, no matter what's going on with the case. We need these four days together . . .

Fuck it. Finding the journal was a huge boon, and she was going to take pleasure in the discovery. She reentered her courtroom on that positive note.

"All rise. Judge Kaitlyn Renado in session." Kate sat on the bench and looked at the respondent's table. The defense lawyer was in big trouble. She'd prolonged the hearing on drug possession, and probable drug sales, with hesitations, rechecking notes, lengthy pauses. Kate had called a recess and told her to get her act together.

"Ms. Frank, I assume you're ready now."

The lawyer pinched her nose. She'd told Kate she had a headache. Geez. "Yes, Your Honor."

"We need to hear from the respondent, before I remand this to fact-finding."

Tommy Toledo took the stand. He was a pudgy little guy, with baggy jeans and a shirt that was way too tight. An expensive-looking leather jacket completed the outfit.

Frank said, "Tommy, you heard Officer Steiner testify that you were running away from the scene of the drug bust and when he chased and caught you, you had two vials of cocaine in your hands that you dropped on the ground. You were still holding five hundred dollars. Is this what happened?"

"No, ma'am. I don't know how those things got on the ground."

The lawyer looked confused again.

So Kate asked, "Were you stepping on the vials?"

"Um . . ." The kid turned beet red. "No, ma'am."

"I see." Kate did see. Her gut told her Toledo was lying, but she tried not to overanalyze. "Go ahead, Ms. Frank."

"Could you tell us where you got the five hundred dollars you were holding? Mr. Jacobs contends you'd sold the vials, but the police came before you could hand them over. Then you dropped them so the cops wouldn't find them in your possession."

"No, ma'am. That's not true. My ma gave it to me, the money."

Kate asked, "For what?"

"I was gonna use it to buy shoes."

"Five hundred dollars is a lot of money for shoes," Kate commented. "And you were holding it, right, Mr. Toledo? It wasn't in your pocket?"

The kid shrugged.

"Were you planning to buy the shoes at eleven at night?" the prosecutor followed up with.

"Ah, no. The next day."

Kate let Toledo's testimony go on, heard from the mother, a few other character witnesses, and Officer Steiner again, whom she had some pertinent questions for.

By two, it was clear they were spinning their wheels. "I'd like to meet with counselors in my chambers." She declared a recess. Once they gathered inside, she said, "All right, Mr. Jacobs. Is there an offer?"

"What do you mean?"

"That you're not going to make us go through all this in fact-finding again, are you?" If the case went to trial, the same confusing situation would occur.

"No, I guess not. I'll take possession, with maximum penalty. We'll drop intent to sell."

"Ms. Frank?"

"I'll ask my client."

By three, Tommy Toledo had allocuted to the charge of possession, and Kate had set the sentence hearing for three weeks away. Meanwhile, she'd mull over the appropriate punishment.

She phoned Reese and left a message that she was indeed free and would meet him at three-thirty.

Maybe this journal thing would be a miracle and end the whole Bingham case today. Then she could fly to Cancun on Friday, free of the accusations the dead woman had made, and free of Reese. If she felt a twinge of regret—all right, more than a twinge—that Reese would be out of her life once again, she'd deal with it. It would be the best for everybody.

It would.

ONCE AGAIN THEY were in the car, headed for Longshore. The day was sunny, even at 4:00 p.m. They'd both put on their sunglasses because of the glare off the pavement, and had rolled down the windows to let in the warm breeze.

They'd been driving about a half hour when Reese said, "I'm going to stop at that rest area. I need some coffee. Want some?"

"Sure." Kate held one of the files from two years before the divorce on her lap. No sooner had they gotten in the car, than they said, almost simultaneously, "Let's review more files." It was obvious they both wanted to avoid personal talk.

He swerved into the parking lot, cut the engine, but didn't get out. Draping a hand over the wheel, he stared through the windshield.

"What's wrong, Reese?" she asked.

"I was just thinking how things work out."

"What do you mean?"

Tossing his glasses on the dash, he turned to her. He'd removed his suit coat and tie, and rolled up the sleeves of his light green shirt. She could see sprinkles of chest hair peeking out from the unbuttoned vee at his throat. "I'd say that you and I have about reached our limit in being together, without doing something stupid, wouldn't you?"

Removing her sunglasses, she met his gaze directly. "I think all four of us pretty much agreed on that." Her tone was dry, but he was right.

"You're going off to Cancun with Sloan in a few days, and I'm going to the Hamptons with Dray for a long weekend."

"Uh-huh."

"Now the journal turns up. Maybe it'll clear us. Today. And this whole thing will be over. You and I won't have reason to be together anymore."

"I know. Though I hate to count our chickens, so to speak."

"I have to ask you something, before we're cleared, if that happens."

"Go ahead."

"Are you sure this is what you want? For us to go our separate ways again?"

"Are you?"

He swallowed hard. "Honestly, Kate, I don't know anymore."

"I'm not sure of what I want, either. I think it's probably for the best to go back to what our relationship was like before the Bingham thing. For all the reasons we've enumerated a million times. The primary one is Sofie, of course."

"Sofie would want us to try again."

"And if we failed, it would send her into a real tailspin." She leaned back in the seat. "Besides, I promised Tyler that you and I wouldn't get back together. And you promised Dray."

"You're probably right. We've survived five years without each other." His voice sounded sad though.

"Yes." Some of them had been really awful, but Kate's life had been on the upswing when the Bingham case exploded.

His gaze was made more intense by the color of his shirt. "Will you marry him?"

"I don't know." She watched Reese. "Will you marry Dray?"

"Probably. I'm sure her sister's wedding, as well as this whole mess with you and me, are going to prompt some ultimatums."

"You were never good with ultimatums."

He chuckled. "No, I wasn't. But it may be time to compromise." He cleared his throat. "And marry her."

Kate's heart did a nosedive at the words he spoke. Still she said, "Probably."

"What about you? Are you going to make Sloan a happy man and have the wedding he's wanted all along?"

"I'm not sure . . . I . . . I guess."

The lack of enthusiasm in their answers was pitiful and they both knew it.

Reese sighed. "So, I guess that's it." He nodded to the building. "Now that's answered, I'll get coffee."

Watching him walk out to the store, Kate felt a tightness in her chest. Is this what she really wanted? For Reese to walk out of her life forever? Was she doing what was best for other people, and not for herself and Reese? The tightness turned into panic. Did she just give the only man she ever loved his walking papers for a second time? "Oh, God," she whispered out loud.

A shrill inside the car startled her. Reese's cell lay on the console between the two front seats. She scowled. Should she answer it? What if it was Dray? That would really go over big. She let it ring, until it stopped. Seconds later, it shrilled again. Maybe he had caller ID. Sure enough, when she picked it up, the screen read, *Pa.*

Bill Bishop. Hmm, that was a safe bet then. Kate would say hello to Pa and take a message for Reese. She pressed send. "Hi, Pa. It's Kate, not Reese."

"K-Kate?" The old man's voice sounded horrible.

"Pa, are you all right?"

"No, no I'm not. Oh, Kate, something awful . . ." Bill began to cry. Hard.

Kate felt a black fear, deep in her belly.

"I gotta tell Reese. But I don't know how."

"Then tell, me, and I'll tell him."

"I . . . I . . ." More sobs.

"Pa. Tell me."

CARRYING A CARDBOARD tray with cups of coffee for him and Kate, Reese swallowed back the lump of regret in his throat. The path for ending this thing between him and Kate might just be cleared today, and he could get back to his sedate, easy life with Dray. Which he wasn't so sure he wanted anymore. Did he, in reality, simply want his wife back but told her otherwise, for all the wrong reasons?

He scowled when he saw that Kate had gotten out of the car and was standing by a tree near where they'd parked. Though they were in a hurry, he took the time to watch her. God she was lovely. She was still in her judge clothes, beautifully tailored wine pants and jacket. She looked tall and strong and very desirable.

But her shoulders seemed stiff. And she was holding her arms crossed, gripping her elbows with opposite hands, like she used to do when she was upset. Hell, he was upset, too, at the ending of what was between them. But as he got closer, he saw her face. It was ravaged. Something had happened. Something bad. She caught sight of him and clapped a hand over her mouth. In her other hand, she held his cell.

"Katie? What . . . did I get a call?"

She nodded.

His first thought was Sofie. "Is everything all right with Sofie?"

She nodded. And just like that all vulnerability fled. He'd seen it before when she was devastated and determined to be strong. Her reaction scared the hell out of him. She straightened, slipped the phone in her pocket, and came toward him. She took his free hand. "Reese, your father just called." Her voice was funereal.

"Something bad happened, didn't it?"

"Yes. Oh, Reese, I'm sorry, but Emily had a car accident. She . . . didn't make it."

He just stared at her. "Emily? You don't mean . . ." The coffee fell out of his hand, and landed with a *thud* on the ground. His ears began to ring. "You don't mean . . ."

"Yes, Reese, I do. I'm sorry. Emily's dead."

"No, no, that can't be. She's my sister. My *baby* sister. She can't be dead."

Kate gripped his other hand. "I'm sorry. She is, Reese."

It was when he saw the tears in Kate's eyes that the truth of her statement sunk in. "Dead? Emmy's dead?"

Kate bit her lip. "Her car was hit by a truck when she was going to work at the diner."

"I . . . I told her she didn't need that job. That I could send her more money."

"I know you did."

"She works too hard. She needs . . . oh, God, she's . . . Katie, my *sister*?"

Emotions ambushed him from all sides, taking uppercuts and jabs everywhere in his body. Kate stepped closer, let go of his hands, and drew him close. His own arms banded around her, and in just a few seconds, he came apart.

KATE PULLED REESE'S Mustang into the driveway of his house, and shut off the engine. On the half-hour drive back to Westwood, he'd been mostly silent. His meltdown seemed to have drained all of the emotion out of him, which was probably good. He'd have a lot to deal with in the next few days. She herself was hanging on by a thread, but wouldn't let Reese see it. She'd be strong for him, but oh God, she loved Emily like a sister. Still, she'd stifled her grief all the way here and would continue to do so.

She'd suggested Reese call his father but he said he had to wait until he felt stronger. She asked what she could do for him, and he'd said only, "Stay with me." Now, at his home, she waited to take her cue from him.

When he didn't get out of the car, she asked again, "What can I do?"

His gaze flew to hers. "I told you, stay with me." He gripped her hand. "You have to stay with me. Promise me you will."

"I promise." Though she had no idea what that meant. "I promise. I'll do whatever you want."

He stared out the window. "I have to pack, right?"

"Yes."

"For a funeral." His throat worked convulsively. "Oh, God."

"Want some help?"

"Yes. Come in. Help me pack."

She wondered if Dray was home. What would the younger woman do if she saw Kate and Reese together. The hell with it. Reese was Kate's primary concern now. She opened the garage door with the remote and exited the car, walked around the front and opened Reese's door. When he just sat there, she leaned in, released his seat belt and tugged on his hand. He didn't let hers go as they walked up the driveway. They entered his house through the garage. The interior was still, and empty, Kate hoped. Reese stood in the kitchen, just looked around. Dazed.

"Come on, let's go to your bedroom."

The huge master suite was lovely. Dray was a good decorator. God, what was Kate doing, thinking about room décor? Reese came in behind her. When he just stood there, she took his hand and led him to the bed. "Sit. I'll pack for you."

He dropped down on the bed, saying nothing. Just watching her. She ran a hand down his hair. His eyes were so bleak, she could barely stand it. But she beat back her own emotions. "Where are your suitcases?"

"The closet."

Opening the louvered doors, she was momentarily startled to see Dray's clothes hanging at one end and his at the other. A crazy reaction. The woman lived here. She found a large leather bag, a carry-on and a hanging suit cover on shelves at one end and dragged them out. Glancing over at Reese, she asked, "Want me to pick things out?"

He nodded, then just sat there staring at the floor. Kate chose a dark suit, trousers and a sports coat. A few dress shirts. Wingtip shoes. Within ten minutes, she had one case packed. Setting it on the bed, she made quick work of getting underwear, jeans, shirts, from his dresser. She was in his bathroom scooping up toiletries when she heard, "Reese? What are you doing just sitting there?"

Kate came out of the bathroom.

Dray frowned at her. "What's going on? Why are you in our bedroom?"

Setting down the small case, Kate crossed to Dray and grasped the younger woman's arm. "Dray, something's happened." Kate could barely choke out the words, and when she did, Reese moaned, bolted off the bed, and crossed to the window, totally ignoring Dray—who began to cry right away.

After a moment, Dray crossed to him. "Reese?" She touched his arm. Tried to turn him around.

He flung her off. "Don't!"

She stumbled back and looked to Kate for help.

"He's been quiet all the way here."

"All the way here? Where was he? And why did he call *you*?"

Kate explained the situation.

Dray drew herself up. "I see. You can go now, Kate. I'll take care of him."

"No!" Reese whipped around. "No, Kate, don't leave."

She froze. Dray turned to him. "Reese, honey, it's okay. I'll do whatever you need to be done."

His expression didn't change but he cocked his head, as if he didn't even recognize her. "Emily's dead."

"I know."

His gaze transferred to Kate. "We have to go to North Falls."

She didn't respond.

"You have to come with me, Kate. You promised."

"Reese," Dray pleaded. "You're not thinking straight. I'll go with you."

He looked at Dray finally. "Of course I am. The boys." His voice cracked. "They'll need me . . . and Kate."

Dray stood there, dumbfounded.

Kate intervened. "Look, Dray, I can drive Reese to North Falls. You can come along—"

"No, she can't." He faced Dray again. "Your sister's wedding is in two days."

"I can miss that."

"You're maid of honor." He nodded to already-packed luggage in the corner that Kate hadn't noticed. "You were going to New York tonight."

"I can't leave you now."

"I have Kate."

Dray's eyes widened. "No, no Reese. Don't say that."

"For God's sake, Dray, don't make this about us. My little sister's dead. Can't you for once think outside that box of yours."

Again, Dray burst into tears. Kate crossed to her. "Dray, he doesn't mean what he's saying. Cut him some slack." In truth, Kate was angry at the younger woman's selfishness. But a catfight wouldn't help Reese.

"He wants to be with you."

"I know Bill. The boys." Her own voice cracked and she felt tears welling up; once again, she quelled them. "Please, let me drive him home tonight. We'll sort all this out later."

Dray drew back. She watched Kate, and said, "Well, I guess you've won."

"Nobody's won today," Kate said, shaking her head. "Can't you see that everybody's lost?" When Dray said no more, Kate shook her head. The hell with her. She'd tried to be kind. "I'm taking Reese to North Falls." Picking up the carry-on and hanging bag, she crossed to Reese and said, "Here, take these."

Rotely, he did.

Then she took the heavier one and led Reese out of the

bedroom, leaving Dray standing alone in the middle of it. Kate blocked out the sight. She had more pressing problems than Dray Merrill's insecurities now.

Like how on earth to help Reese through the next few hours when she herself was dying inside. She'd loved Emily, too.

REESE STAYED CLOSE to Kate as they walked out of his house into the garage. Before he rounded the car, he said, "Give me the keys."

"Not on your life. I'm driving."

He halted abruptly. It was important to stay in control. He needed to snap out of this daze. If he let himself feel, think, he would only . . . Oh, God, his little sister was dead. Sucking in a breath, he said, "No you're not."

She bypassed him and got in the car; he swore vilely. But he slid into the passenger side. When they pulled out onto the street, and she took a left instead of right, he frowned. "What are you doing?"

"Going to the interstate."

"We have to drive to your house first. Get your things."

"Reese . . ."

"You'll need stuff for several days."

She drew in a breath. "Are you sure you want me there, to do this?"

"Don't you want to be?"

"Of course I do." Her voice was raw and he realized she was hurting.

"Please, Katie, don't argue about this. You have to come with me. We'll get through it together."

"I will. I want to. We'll stop at my place."

She turned the car around and headed toward her house.

"Do you have a black dress?" He didn't know why he asked that. "For the funer . . . oh God, oh, Christ . . ." He buried his face in his hands.

The car swerved and jolted to a halt. He felt her hand on his back. "It's okay, Reese, let it out."

He shook his head. "I can't."

"You have to."

"I need to be strong. For my dad and the bo . . ." He couldn't finish. Just the thought of Emily's boys, alone now, destroyed him. Kate's hand went to his neck, and she must have somehow come up on her knees because she pulled him to her chest. He buried himself there, just for a minute. She crooned, "It's okay, it's okay."

Once more he broke into sobs. He didn't know how long later, he pulled back. Drew in a heavy breath. Shook his head. Okay, so he had lost it with her. With Kate. That was all right. "Let's go. I'm better."

She kissed the top of his head, slid back behind the wheel and started to drive. At her house, she insisted he come in. Mindlessly he walked into the foyer with her. He'd followed her upstairs before he asked, "Jesus, what am I doing?"

She grasped his hand. "You just need human company." She started to pull him to the door to her bedroom.

He tugged her back. "I need *your* company. Is that all right?"

Her gaze was penetrating. "Yes, I wouldn't want to be with anyone but you at a time like this."

"We've done it before."

"When my dad died. And your best friend from college. Remember that. We'll get through this again, Reese, together."

Soothed by her calm assurances, he sat on her bed while she packed. His mind whirled. Funeral . . . his dad . . . Jimmy and Jason . . . Kate staying with him.

"I'm ready." He looked up at her. "You need to call your dad, Reese, and your office."

Yes, he needed to do both. "I can't. Will you do it?"

"Of course." He gave her Greg's number. "Tell him what happened, that he has to take over the Crane case. Tell him to give the details to Yolanda. Tell him . . ."

"Shh, I know what to do." He heard her punch in numbers. Talk to Yolanda then to Greg. Then she called his dad.

"Bill, it's Kate." A pause. "Yes, I told him. No, he doesn't want to talk to you yet." She turned her back but he could still hear her words. "I think he needs to gather himself before he talks to you. Of course I'm coming with him." A sniffle. "I loved her, too, Pa." Silence. "Uh-huh. We're leaving right now. An hour, max. No, of course I won't speed. I promise I'll be careful."

Once they were on the road, Reese laid his head back and closed his eyes. That was a mistake. Pictures ran through his mind like a filmstrip and he couldn't stop them.

"Will it help to talk about what you're thinking?"

"Nothing will help."

"Share it, anyway."

In a voice he didn't recognize, he began to speak. "I remember the day Mom brought her home from the hospital. She was so tiny. I was six and felt like a giant . . . She didn't want to go to kindergarten. Mom had gotten sick by then, so I had to walk her to school before I went to sixth grade. My buddies teased me, but I held her hand all the way . . ." He swallowed hard. "The night Mom died, I let Emily sleep in my bed. I told her I'd always be there for her . . . always." He swiped at his cheeks. "Fuck."

"You kept your promise, Reese."

"I suppose. I know this was out of my control . . ."

"Of course it was."

Leaning back, he closed his eyes again, reached over and took Kate's free hand in his. The next thing he knew Kate was shaking his arm.

"Reese, we're here."

He startled awake. "What?" He looked over. "Kate, what . . . where . . ." Then he remembered. Emmy. Dead. His head fell back. "Oh, shit."

She'd pulled into his dad's driveway, and cut the engine.

He said, "Wait a sec, okay, before we go in."

In the dim light from the driveway lamps, he saw her smile sadly. "We can wait as long as you need."

His hand dropped to her knee. "I slept."

"Self-preservation, I guess. You'll need your strength to face that." She nodded to the house.

"I'm not sure I can do this. Say the right thing, take care of the boys."

"Mostly, you just have to be with them."

"Are you sure?"

"Hey, I'm a judge. I know from whence I speak."

"I made you come to North Falls with me."

"No, I wanted to."

"Your job . . . Sloan . . ." He hit his head. "God, you're supposed to go to Cancun Friday."

Leaning over, she kissed his cheek. "I'm not going anywhere, love, but into that house with you."

Maybe he *could* do this. If she was there with him. If he had her for support. "All right, let's go in."

IT WAS ALL bravado. Kate hung on to Reese's hand, needing him as much as he needed her. Her heart hurt so much for him, for the boys, for Pa, whom she loved as much as her own father. But she'd do anything to help them through this, even pretend she had the strength to do it.

The side entrance door to the kitchen still creaked when it opened. The house still smelled of coffee and the homemade bread Emily often baked for Pa. Kate heard a low rumble of voices and got a glimpse of people at the old Formica table in the corner before anyone noticed them.

"Oh." An older woman Kate vaguely recognized saw them first. "Bill." She nodded to the doorway.

Bill glanced over his shoulder, then threw back his chair. He strode to Reese and enveloped him a big bear hug.

"Pa . . . Pa . . ."

Bill said nothing. He just sobbed in his son's arms. Kate could see the struggle on Reese's face. He was trying so hard not to give in to the grief again. Finally, he lost the battle. He cried as hard as he had earlier, with his arms locked around his dad.

When they pulled apart, Bill wiped his eyes, blew his nose, then turned to Kate. He yanked her to him. "Kate . . . my baby . . ."

"I know, Pa. I know." Much as she'd done with Reese, she patted his back. Tears misted in her eyes but she battled them back.

Bill finally pulled away. Reese was at the table talking to the older couple there. "Kate, come here." She approached Reese; he slid his arm around her waist and leaned into her. "You remember Nat and Merle Gates. Charlie's parents. This is my wife, Kate."

Kate said, "Sorry to see you again under these circumstances."

"Me, too." This from Nat. She glanced at Reese. "I . . . I thought you two were divorced."

A blank look came over Reese's face.

"We are," Kate said. "I'm his ex-wife."

As if that explained things.

"Emily was like another sister to me." She was amazed at how strong she sounded. "I loved her very much."

"Where are the boys?" Reese asked.

"In the den. I put on a video." Merle shook his head. "They're dazed."

Reese looked toward the sound of cartoons. "I want to see them."

Bill shot Kate a worried look.

"I'll go with you." Kate knew this would be the hardest of everything—seeing the kids for the first time, finding something to say. Again, she held Reese's hand as they walked into the other room. His grip was so tight it hurt.

The boys were on the couch, arms entwined, covered with a blanket. Jimmy was sucking his thumb, a habit she knew he'd given up long ago. Jason held a stuffed bear at his side. They both looked up when they saw someone enter. "Uncle Reese," they said simultaneously and, again together, they both burst into tears.

Kate said, "Take one," as she circled to the left side and

Reese to the right. Jason leaped into her arms. Jimmy threw himself at Reese. "Uncle Reese, Mommy's dead. She's gone to heaven, Papa said."

Reese held Jimmy close, his face layered with anguish. "I know, buddy. I'm sorry."

Jason burrowed into Kate. "Aunt Kate, I want my mommy."

She held him tight and stumbled back into a chair. "I know, honey. I do, too."

Reese took a seat with Jimmy still in a headlock, and for a long time, they just hugged the kids, who finally cried themselves out.

When they were done, Jimmy drew back. "Who's gonna take care of us? Grandma Gates says we're orphans now."

Jason scrunched up his face. "She says we're gonna go live with them, Aunt Kate. I don't want to."

For this she looked to Reese.

"No," he said so firmly, it even comforted her. "You're going to live with me."

Kate knew Emily had named Reese as legal guardian. Actually, she'd named both of them, though Em had changed her will after their divorce.

Reese straightened and became the competent adult. "Look at me, both of you." When they did, he said, "I know your mom talked to you about this. She said if anything happened to her, you would live with me. Remember?"

"I do." A small smile Jason's face. "With you, and with Aunt Kate. I remember."

"Oh, honey . . ." Again, she looked to Reese. Should the boys be told the truth now? If they waited till later, would they feel betrayed?

He stared at Kate a minute, then said to the boys, "We can figure out the particulars later. Just know that Aunt Kate and I love you very much, and we'll both take care of you, no matter what."

Kate relaxed. That was a good answer. They could all deal with *the particulars* later. It was important to just get through one minute at a time.

FOURTEEN

KATE HELD HER breath as she closed the door to the boys' room. Jason and Jimmy had finally fallen asleep when Kate and Reese lay down with them, one on each of their beds. Just ahead of her in the dim hallway of Emily's house, Reese turned and looked at her. "Think they'll sleep?"

"I hope to God they do."

"I'm sorry about this." He waved to indicate the house where they'd been forced into staying.

"I don't mind."

"Who are you kidding? You love five-star hotels."

A small smile escaped her. Jimmy and Jason had thrown a tantrum when the Gates grandparents tried to take the boys home with them. They'd even resisted Bill Bishop's offer to stay at his house. The only way they'd quiet was when Reese agreed to sleep at their own house with them. His features had gotten even more ravaged as he made the offer, and Kate knew being surrounded by Emily's things would be excruciating. She was just about to suggest she go with him and the boys, when Jason attached himself to her waist and wouldn't let go. "Aunt Kate, too," he said stubbornly.

Which was how they ended up here.

He glanced down the corridor, where there were two more bedrooms. "I can't . . ." He drew in a breath. "I can't stay in Emily's room."

"You don't have to. I will. Where do you usually sleep when you're here?"

"After Charlie moved out, they turned his den into a bedroom for me."

It made her heart ache to be reminded of how close Emily and Reese were. Had been.

He said, "I'll get the bags."

She watched him trudge downstairs to the foyer, where they'd dumped their suitcases earlier, come back up, and approach the bedroom to the right. He pushed open the door but didn't go inside. Instead, he set her bag down at the threshold. "It's stupid, I know. Cowardly."

"It's not, either. Give yourself a break, Reese." She laid a hand on his arm. "Are you tired?"

"I guess."

"Go on to your room. Unpack. Try to get some sleep."

"I want to shower first."

"Okay. I have to make some calls."

Reese's face hardened. "To Sloan?"

"To Jill . . . and to Tyler."

Reese's shoulders sagged, and he shook his head. "He'll have a fit that you're here."

Reaching up, she caressed his jaw. "No, he won't. He'll pull through because this is a tragedy." When Reese still looked skeptical, she added, "It doesn't matter, anyway. I'm here for the duration."

He grasped her hand and kissed it. Then he turned, picked up his suitcases and crossed into the room a few feet down the hall.

Kate entered Emily's room and, after dumping her bags on the floor, shut the door sank down on Emily's bed and closed her eyes. It took her a minute, but she gathered strength from inside her and began to unpack. When she went to the dresser to put away some clothes, and saw the pictures Emily had set out, her heart constricted so hard in her chest, with so much pressure, Kate didn't think she'd be able to stand it. She traced her sister-in-law's features: Emily with the boys, laughing. Emily with Reese, on a boat somewhere. But the sight of her as a child, holding hands with her big brother, overwhelmed Kate.

She heard the shower go on.

Okay, so it was safe.

Hugging the childhood picture to her breasts, she crossed to the bed, laid down, and let go. She sobbed into the pillows for Emily, for the boys, and especially for Reese.

Five minutes later—thank you God for letting Reese like long showers—Kate was calm again. She even felt marginally better. Enough to call Tyler at his hotel in Cancun.

Using Emily's phone, she pressed buttons and waited for the overseas transmission. Hoping like hell he was in his room—she really needed his comfort tonight—she waited. And waited. Finally he answered. "Sloan." He was a bit breathless.

"Tyler, it's Kaitlyn."

"Hey, gorgeous. I just got in. I'm so glad you called."

"How's the conference?"

"Really good, I gave my speech today."

"Speech?"

"Yeah, I was the luncheon keynote, remember?"

No, she'd forgotten. "How did it go?"

"Kaitlyn, what's wrong? You sound odd."

A few tears escaped. She swiped them back. "Something's happened."

His tone was tense. "What?"

"Tyler, Reese's sister, Emily, was killed in a car accident today."

"Oh no. Oh, honey, I'm so sorry."

"It's awful. Reese is beside himself with grief. Jimmy and Jason are confused, and crying all the time. Bill Bishop's walking around like a zombie."

A silence. "Jimmy and Jason? Bill Bishop? How do you know all that? Did Reese call you?"

"Um, no. I'm in North Falls with him."

An even longer pause. "Why is that, Kaitlyn?"

"We were on our way to Longshore when he got the call from Pa about his sister's death. I couldn't let him drive down here by himself." Which was a bit of a lie.

Tyler was quick to catch on. "Where was Dray? Had she already left for her sister's wedding?"

Odd that he should know about the wedding. "No."

"No?"

"It's a long story. Tyler, please, this is so awful. I need some support from you."

"All right. What's the plan?"

"Plan?"

"When's the funeral?"

"They're going to see the undertaker tomorrow. Bill thinks calling hours will be Saturday and the funeral on Monday."

"I see."

The cold tone angered her.

"Ty, I can't come to Cancun."

"Of course you can. It's only Wednesday night. Stay with the boys and the Bishops all day tomorrow, then drive back to Westwood and catch your plane Friday morning like you planned."

"I can't do that."

"Why?"

"Well, for one thing, somebody's got to go get Sofie."

"Let someone else do it."

"Tyler, she's my child. Her aunt just died. She loves those boys like they're her brothers. I have to be here for her."

"Just for her?"

She didn't answer.

"You want to stay there, don't you?"

Kate said, "Yes, I want to stay. I loved Emily, too." Her voice broke on the last word.

When Tyler didn't say anything, tears leaked from her

eyes, out of frustration, and pain, and loneliness. Damn it, she needed comfort, too, and expected to get it from him.

Instead, he asked, "Where are you staying?" Again no warmth in his voice.

"What?"

"Where are you? Right now."

"I'm at Emily's house. I told you, the boys are over-wrought."

"And is Reese there?"

"Yes."

No response.

"Tyler, please."

"Please what? Give you carte blanche to sleep with your ex-husband so you can comfort him? Well, you know what, Kaitlyn. Go ahead. Seal the deal. Console your ex. I'm done with all this."

"How can you be so callous? A lovely, thirty-nine-year-old, woman is dead. Everyone is beside themselves with grief. Including me."

Still, no answer.

"Please, Tyler." Now she began to cry in earnest. "Don't do this!"

But he'd already hung up.

Leveled, Kate just sat on the bed and stared at the phone in her hand. The water was still running in the bathroom, and after a while, she got up, got out some necessities and headed downstairs. Charlie had put in a small bathroom off the kitchen, and she showered quickly, forcing her mind to blank like she had after the divorce from Reese. Dressing in red cotton pajamas, she came out of the tiny space under the staircase and caught sight of the kitchen. "I need a drink," she said aloud.

She rummaged around until she found Reese's favorite brand of scotch. She poured herself one, then glanced up-stairs, noticing the sound of the water had gone off. "What the hell?" she said, and poured another.

Back on the second level, she saw Reese's door was closed. She crossed to it and knocked.

"Just a second." She waited. "Come on in, Kate."

He was standing by the window, dressed in a light knit robe she'd packed for him. It was dark green and paisley. She'd wondered if Pollyanna had given it to him. He nodded to the drinks. "Is one of those for me?"

She smiled and approached him. "Here you go."

He took the glass and grabbed her waist with his other hand. "Do you have any idea what this means to me, that you're here?"

"I want to be here."

"I know. And that means even more."

"Drink your scotch."

He sank down into a stuffed chair, and she sat on the edge of the bed. After a few sips, he looked over at her, his green eyes narrow. "You okay?"

"As well as can be expected."

"You look like you've been crying." He rolled his eyes. "Of course you've been crying." He shook his head. "I've been selfish in my grief."

"I'm fine, Reese."

He angled his head. "Did you call Jill?"

"Um, no." Truthfully, she'd forgotten after Tyler's unkind words.

"Sloan?"

"Yep."

"I'll bet this went over big. You coming here."

"Don't worry about Tyler."

"Kate—"

"Shh, Reese. Just try to relax."

They made small talk about what would happen tomorrow.

"While you're making the arrangements," Kate told him, "I'll go get Sofie. Unless you want me to come to the funeral parlor with you."

"No, Pa and I can do that." He took in a deep breath. "Should we call Sofie first?"

"I don't think so. I want to be with her when I tell her."

His mouth thinned. "She'll be devastated."

"We all are, Reese. Don't worry. I'll take care of her."

He finished the last of his drink, set the empty glass on the table and laid his head back against the chair. "I feel so bad. Even worse than I did after the divorce. I never thought anything could hurt more than that."

Kate watched him wrestle with his feelings. She had a quick flash to the past, to times when one of them was hurting so badly, they thought it would never stop. And what they did for each other, to briefly extinguish the pain.

She finished her drink, set it on the nightstand and switched off the light, so all that illuminated the room was a small lamp on the dresser across the room. Without thinking, without considering the ramifications of her actions, she went to stand before him. He opened his eyes and looked up at her.

Long moments, full of meaning, passed. Then he reached out his hand and tugged on hers. She shook her head, and instead knelt before him.

"Kate—what . . ."

"Shh," she said softly sliding her hands up his thighs. "You remember."

"I . . ." An anguished chuckle. "Oh, man, of course I do. When something bad happened. One of us would . . ."

"Comfort the other." She brushed a hand across his groin. "Like this."

"Sometimes I pretended that I felt rotten, just so you'd do this."

"You did not!"

An easier chuckle. "No, but I was tempted." He stroked her hair. "Sweetheart, are you sure?"

Was she? Staring up at him, seeing the grief etched in his face, remembering the past, she gave him a sad smile. "I'm sure. At least right now."

Then she reached for the belt of his robe.

NUDGED FROM SLEEP by a sound, Reese opened his eyes to semidarkness and the smell and feel of Kate in his arms. He snuggled into her back. They were sleeping together? In his bed? It took a split second for him to remember. No, no. Emily was dead. The cold weight of grief returned. He'd been overcome with its slicing pain. And as Kate had done in the past, she'd comforted him with physical release.

And it had helped. Afterward, he asked her to sleep with him, and she hadn't refused. Burying his face in the flowery smell of her hair, he let himself breathe in the feminine scent of her. He heard the noise again; reluctantly, he eased away and slipped out of bed. Putting on a robe, he found his way to Jason and Jimmy. They were in one bed, their backs against each other, seeking contact and comfort. Jimmy was moaning.

Swallowing hard, Reese crossed to them and knelt down. He brushed back Jimmy's hair, kissed his forehead, and stayed there until the boy quieted. He watched them for a few seconds, overcome with despair. Emily. Dead. He just couldn't believe it.

Finally he went back to his room. Kate was asleep on her side. He smiled at her, all wrapped up in red cotton. Her hair was tousled, her breathing even. He sat on the edge of her side of the bed and simply watched her chest rise and fall. And in that stark moment of life and death, of recognition of his mortality, and of hers, he admitted some things to himself.

He was in love with her. He'd never stopped loving her. Everything they'd done to each other hadn't been able to destroy the tie between them.

And he believed she felt the same.

Yes, they had Sofie to consider. Yes, they'd done perhaps unforgettable damage to each other. But in the early hours of the morning, blanketed by sorrow, Reese couldn't dissemble. He wanted her back as his wife. He wanted Sofie home, and Emily's boys with them. Maybe even his dad.

He drew in a breath. This was a big deal. Not one to be made lightly, maybe not in the midst of unendurable grief. Kate stirred, and he brushed his hand down her cheek. She opened her eyes. Slumberous, and sexy, she smiled up at him, grasped his hand and brought it to her breast. His fingers flexed on the supple flesh. "Hmm. I love when you touch me."

She didn't remember where she was, or *when* it was. "Katie . . ."

Moving to her back, she held his hand on her, and came awake by degrees. "Oh." Awareness dawned . . . about Emily, first, given the sadness that flushed her face. "I forgot."

"I did, too, when I awoke."

"Are the boys okay?"

"I just checked."

She looked down at his hand. He didn't remove it. "Are you all right?"

Again, his hand flexed on her. He nodded his head to the chair by the window. "That helped. Do you remember?"

"Yes."

"Do you regret it?"

She squeezed his hand. "No."

"Will you make love with me, now? Not a mercy fuck, but real just-you-and-me lovemaking."

Without hesitation, she said, "Yes, Reese. I will."

Her consent pushed away the sadness. He knew it wouldn't last, that he'd fall back into the black abyss, but he'd allow himself this respite. "Give me a second." He rose, went to the bathroom, and retrieved a condom from his shaving kit. When he returned, she smiled up at him. He smiled back and sat on the mattress.

Slowly he undid the top button of her pajamas. "Let's pretend."

"Pretend what?"

Two buttons. "That we're still married. We're in our bedroom at the farmhouse. Sofie's asleep down the hall." Leaning over, he kissed the flesh he'd bared.

When he drew back, her eyes were filled with tears. "Sometimes, I want that so much I ache."

Another button. "Me, too, love."

"All right. For a few hours, we'll have it back."

The shirt undone, he drew it apart. She lifted off the bed so he could remove it and surprised him by raising her arms so she could grasp the headboard. Her breasts were full and feminine. She had some tiny lines on them from childbirth and breast-feeding, but he couldn't see them in the dim light. Her nipples beckoned. He lowered his head and took one in his mouth. Caressed it with his tongue. Scraped it with his teeth. Suckled.

She squirmed on the bed and her fingers tightened on the wooden slats. "Ah, Reese."

"So sensitive there," he said as he transferred his mouth to the other breast. "Still."

His hand slid to the waist of the pj's. He worked them down her hips like he'd been doing this every night for the last five years. She angled her hips to help him along. He drew back and eased off the bottoms.

And there she was, bared to him in all her loveliness.

He relearned her curves, and found that he hadn't forgotten much. The soft slope of her shoulder. The indentation at her waist. The little roundness of her belly.

Her thighs and calves were firmer than before. He traced each muscle. "So beautiful, so taut," he said as he kissed her foot.

He watched her as he kneaded her instep.

She closed her eyes to savor the sensation. "Mmm . . ."

He leaned over and kissed the triangle of curls between her thighs. "Oh, yeah, mmm."

Her hands came down from the headboard and entwined in his hair. "Reese, I . . . I love this . . . I love how you touch me."

"I love how you smell." He nuzzled her dark curls. "Everywhere." After long moments, he lifted his head. His hand replaced his mouth, and he rubbed his palm against her. She groaned. "You like?" he asked.

"Oh, God."

He felt his own body heat at her arousal. It always happened this way. Her desire fueled his own. His skin itched, and his muscles rippled. He parted her legs for better access and slipped a finger inside her. She lurched. His other hand gentled her shoulder. "Shh. Just feel."

She came on one long rising crest of emotion. And when she did, she called out his name. It was the absolute best sound in the world.

KATE LOOKED UP at Reese, who was poised over her. His first thrust into her was hard and complete. He filled her fully. She'd forgotten how perfectly matched they were. Still humming from her orgasm, a rush of renewed stimulation shot through her. She groaned. Bracing his arms on either side of her, he grinned. "That's music to my ears, love."

He moved slowly at first. Her insides clenched around him. A bit faster, and she felt the muscles of his shoulders tighten. He swelled inside her, wonderfully. He pushed harder. His hands went to her shoulders, and he seemed to sink into her, wanting the closeness, the total possession.

"Katie, you make me . . . Arrgh . . ."

"Reese . . ."

He withdrew, then plunged, then withdrew again.

At the third powerful thrust, her mind blanked and pleasure exploded inside her. She screamed his name. His release came on the heels of that. As if in pain, he moaned, called out for her, and let go.

The next thing she was aware of was the weight of him, heavy on her chest and thighs. He didn't move though, and she was able to raise her hands and smooth them down his back. He buried his face in her neck. After a few moments, he rolled to the side, carefully taking her with him, so they were still joined. They'd perfected that little twist and turn over the years, because they didn't want to be separated after such cataclysmic joining.

They waited until their breathing evened out before speaking.

"I guess we still got it, Katie."

She chuckled. "Damn right we do, hotshot." She nestled further into his chest.

"I can't believe how much of this I still remember. After five years."

"Shh. It was just yesterday, remember. We're in our bed in the farmhouse."

"Ah, yes."

She didn't want to face reality yet.

He held her close. She inhaled his scent, musky and male, tinted with the sex they just shared. It was that—his smell and the familiarity of it—which made her admit some things. One thing, really. That she still loved him.

"We need some more sleep," he said, his voice hoarse. "To deal with tomorrow."

"We do."

He tipped her chin. "Look at me."

She did.

"I love you, Katie," he said simply. "I never stopped."

"I love you, too, Reese. No matter what's happened, I never stopped, either."

His grin was so poignant, so tender. "That's all I need right now." He tugged her back to his chest.

They lay that way until their breathing slowed. Kate's eyes closed while she was still in the dream world of yesterday. It felt good and right and exactly what they needed now.

THE BLACKNESS OF loss descended on them the minute Kate and Reese awoke. Thank God they were both covered because Jimmy and Jason, clothed in Spider-Man pajamas, were standing by the bed. And crying.

"I want my mommy," Jimmy wailed.

"Uncle Reese."

The kids climbed onto the bed, and Kate and Reese cuddled them.

Reese looked over at her. "It's real," he said.

"I'm so sorry."

The boys finally calmed and Reese managed to slip out

of bed, get his robe and, hand-in-hand, the three of them left the bedroom; she heard them traipse downstairs. Kate took in a deep breath, and let the grief swamp her. Emily. Poor Emily.

And Reese. Oh, Lord. What she was feeling? No guilt, surprisingly. It was like she had made love with her husband. Flinging off the covers, she got out of bed, strode to Emily's room, found a robe and slippers and, after using the bathroom, went downstairs to join them in the kitchen. The boys were eating Cheerios, and the smell of strong coffee filled the sunny room. Reese was sipping from a mug, once again looking haggard and devastated. When he saw her, his expression lightened, and she wondered how she'd ever feel guilty about what happened last night, if it helped him through this tragic time. He poured her coffee, and when she crossed to him to get it, he kissed her briefly on the lips.

"Second thoughts?" he asked somberly.

She shook her head, holding his gaze. "I don't know what all of it means, but no, no second thoughts."

"We'll figure it out."

The doorbell rang before she could say more. After exchanging a questioning look, Reese went to answer it. Kate sat down with the boys, but they didn't say anything, just ate morosely.

Nat and Merle Gates preceded Reese into the kitchen. When she caught sight of Reese's face, he was scowling.

Nat rushed to the table. "There they are. My poor little boys." She tried to hug Jimmy, but he pulled away. Jason rose immediately from his chair and launched himself at Reese. Taking his cue, Jimmy threw back his chair, and Kate had just enough time to pull away from the table before the little boy tumbled into her lap.

Merle said sternly, "Boys, come to your grandparents."

Neither child would even look up.

Reese said softly, "They're overwrought, Merle. Give them some time."

"Best they get used to us, and not you two." This from Nat, who looked affronted.

"Can we talk about this later?" Kate asked.

"No," Merle said. "We'll talk about it now, before the boys get any mistaken impression." He took some papers out of his pocket.

Reese interrupted him. "Jase, Jim, how about watching a few cartoons while the grown-ups talk?"

Once the boys were tucked away in the living room, and Reese returned, Merle held out his papers. "This is Charlie's will. He names us as legal guardians if something happened to him."

Reese looked utterly weary. Kate straightened. "Mr. Gates, in the event of one parent's death, the other parent automatically becomes the legal guardian. She, and only she, then makes decisions on the child's future, if nothing contrary to that was specified in the divorce agreement."

Reese put in, "Emily left me full custody."

"Well, we'll see about that."

"I think you'd better leave my sister's house now. This isn't helping anybody."

Both older people were startled. "I don't get it," Nat said. "You can't provide a two-parent home for them. You don't live together anymore." He scowled as she studied their attire. "Or am I mistaken?"

"It doesn't matter if we live together or not," Kate explained. "The terms of Emily's will, which I can assure you *does* take precedence over Charlie's, names Reese as legal guardian. And, of course, I live in the same town and will help out."

"You're a criminal lawyer," Merle pointed out. "She's a judge. You don't have time for the boys. We're retired. We do."

"We'll make time."

"You sent your own daughter to boarding school. We won't have the boys live like that."

"They won't." He looked to Kate. For assurance.

"Of course they won't," she said. "We'll work something out."

"Well." Nat stood. "I still don't like this."

Merle added, "We'll talk to the lawyer again, Nattie."

Kate blew out a heavy breath. "Nat, Merle. Can't you just let this go at least until the next few days are over with? We're all beside ourselves with grief."

They exchanged looks. "Maybe. We'll leave now, I guess. But don't think this is over." With that they swept out of the room.

Kate shook her head. "What next?"

Reese swallowed hard. "Sofie." He drew in a breath. "I wish I could come with you. But I don't want to leave Pa or the boys."

"I can do it myself."

"You're so strong, Kate. I'd forgotten."

"So are you. Don't forget *that*."

"Not as long as you're here to remind me."

"I'm here." For now, at least. But she didn't say that to Reese. Instead, she reached across the table and took his hand.

SOFIE WAS ABOUT to take a toke from Jax when a loud knock sounded on the door of her dorm room.

"Don't answer it," Jax whispered, from the floor beside the bed.

She frowned, but nodded. Whoever it was could go away.

"Sofie."

She recognized the voice right away. Her mother.

"I know you're in there. I heard you. And your friend Allison said you weren't feeling well."

Jax shook his head.

But Sofie stood and smoothed down the denim capris she wore with a T-shirt. "Put it out." She waited till he butted the joint and stuffed it in his pocket. If her mother was here, something was wrong.

She whipped open the door. Her mother stood in the entryway, wearing simple jeans and a red top. Her hair was in a ponytail . . . and her face—oh, no, she had that horrible look she got when something bad happened—like the divorce, her friend Jillian's breast cancer, when Aunt Patty had had a really bad car accident. "What happened?"

Reaching out, Kate smoothed down Sofie's hair. "Oh, honey." She stepped inside before Sofie could stop her. Ever alert, the judge took in her surroundings, studied Jax. Then sniffed the unmistakable odor of weed.

Sofie waited for her mother to blow. Instead, she bit her lip. "Jax, could you leave us alone for a minute?"

He looked to Sofie.

"Go."

"Sure, whatever." Rolling to his feet, he leaned over, kissed Sofie on the cheek, said, "Catch you later," and was gone.

Her mother closed the door and leaned against it.

"Why aren't you mad?"

"I am." She swallowed hard. "But something else takes precedence."

When she took Sofie's hand and sat down on the bed, Sofie panicked with a sudden horrible thought. "It's Daddy, isn't it? Something's happened to him."

"Daddy's fine physically. But Aunt Emily . . . Oh, baby, she died in a car accident yesterday."

"What?" Sofie couldn't take it in. "What? Oh, no." She clapped her hand over her mouth.

Her mother tugged her close. "I'm sorry, sweetie, it's awful."

"Oh, no, Mama." She buried her face in her mother's breast, like she used to when she was little. And she let herself cry. Like she hadn't cried since that night her parents told her about the divorce.

"It's okay, baby, get it out."

Her mother held her a long time. Sofie drew back finally. Wiped her face. "Daddy must be devastated."

"He is."

Sofie clapped a hand over her mouth. "Oh, no, Jimmy and Jason."

"Pretty much everybody's leveled."

She stared at her mother. "You seem pretty cool."

Her mom looked like she'd slapped her. "I'm desolate, Sof. But I'm keeping it together for your dad and the boys."

"I'm sorry. I know that's the right thing to do." She raised her chin. "I will, too. I promise."

"Good." Her mother stood. "You need to pack some clothes. Nice ones, okay? You'll be gone until at least Tuesday."

"All right." She just sat there.

"Sofie?"

Tears clouded her eyes. "Will you help me, Mama?"

"Of course. I'll help you with this, with anything." She nodded to the floor. "We'll talk about all that later. But don't tell you father, please. He has enough to deal with."

Sofie felt like a shit. Still she said, "Okay, I won't. And thanks for coming to get me."

"Of course I'd come to get you. I'm your mother and no matter what you think, I love you more than anything else in this world."

The thought comforted Sofie. Her mother was here. She'd help her dad and the boys. They could get through this. So she stood, but before she got her suitcase, she hugged her mother. "Thanks, Mama."

AT ONE O'CLOCK, Reese was mindlessly putting out lunch fixings that a neighbor had brought to his father's house when he heard the front door open. Sofie's voice sounded, higher pitched than Kate's. He bit his lip and prayed for the strength not to break down in front of his little girl. She'd need help through all this. He'd just put down the salad when they both appeared in the entryway.

"Oh, Daddy," Sofie said rushing to him. "It's so awful."

He held her tight as she clung to him. "I know, princess. I know."

She surprised him by drawing back. "Are you all right? How can I help?"

Over her head he saw Kate smile sadly. Their child had

her mother's grit. "Just you being here helps." He caressed her cheek. "And you can be with Jimmy and Jason."

"Oh, Daddy. What's going to happen to them? Their father's dead, too."

Reese grinned. This was the old Sofie, who cared deeply about people and showed it. "They're coming to live with us."

"Us? You and *Dray*?"

"I meant you and me. Honey, your mom and I will take good care of the boys."

"How can you? You're not married anymore."

Kate came up to them and touched Sofie's arm. "Sweetie, Dad's exhausted. And I'm starved. Can we table this now? Just know that we're all going to take care of Jimmy and Jason as best we can."

"Oh. Oh! That's great. I always wanted a brother."

Kate swallowed hard and averted her gaze. Reese squeezed her shoulder, silently telling her to leave the past in the past. Then he walked to the hallway and called out, "Hey, guys, lunch is ready."

Noise sounded on the steps as Jimmy and Jason trundled down.

Reese said, "I got a surprise for you. A good one."

"Sofie . . ." they called out simultaneously when they raced to the kitchen.

Sofie bent down so she could hold on to both boys.

Together, the three of them cried. Reese went to stand by Kate, and put his arm around her, tugging her close. She leaned into him.

The back door opening made everybody draw back. Sofie stood and saw her grandfather, who never looked as old or vulnerable as he did today. Reese thought about how he'd feel if he lost Sofie and emotion for his father clogged his throat.

Sofie flung herself at her grandpa. "Oh, Papa. I'm so sorry."

Bill Bishop cried again, this time in his granddaughter's arms. Jimmy and Jason looked on solemnly.

Once the moment passed, they all made their way to the table for lunch. Though somber, they felt the comfort of having family around. Kate and Reese volunteered to clean up while Sofie and Bill took the boys to a nearby park for some fresh air.

"She seems okay," Reese said as soon as they were alone.

"She's got her dad's heart. It's nice to see again."

Leaning against the counter, he grunted. He was wearing blue jeans and a golf shirt, but he was pale, and his eyes were grim.

"How did it go this morning?" she asked.

"Horrific."

She touched his arm.

"We picked out a pretty . . ." He couldn't finish. Memory of the oak casket with blue lining, Emily's favorite color, ambushed him.

Kate reached up and put her arms around his neck.

He held on, shocked at his sudden weakness. Shocked at the strength this woman gave him. When he was composed, he pulled back. "I thought I was better. I'm still a wreck."

"It will come and go. Just accept it."

He nodded, but grasped on to her arm when she tried to pull away. "Kate? Last night? It meant a lot to me. And it's helping me through all this."

"I'm so glad."

He cocked his head. "That wasn't just why you did it, was it?"

"No."

"Good." He turned and began loading the dishwasher.

"What's the time line, Reese?" she asked as she arranged glasses on the top shelf.

"Just what we thought. The calling hours won't be until Saturday. And Catholics won't bury on Sunday. So the funeral will be Monday."

She put soap in the compartment while he washed some pans in the sink. "Are you going to call Dray?"

"I hadn't thought about it." He stilled. "I know I treated her badly when I left."

"She should understand."

"Did Sloan?"

"Truthfully?"

"I think we're past anything else."

"He was really angry I wasn't coming to Cancun."

"He should understand, too."

"I know."

When they finished cleaning up, Reese took Kate's hands in his. Leaning over, he kissed her gently, possessively, as if he had a right to. A knock startled them. The kitchen door had a glass window at the top. They looked through it and saw Jillian Jenkins on the other side.

KATE BARELY MADE it to the car before she burst into tears. Ostensibly going out for coffee, Jillian had taken one look at Kate and made excuses to get her away for a respite as soon as Bill and the kids returned.

She wept in Jill's arms. "You didn't come down here for me to cry all over you."

"That's exactly why I came down. I know you. You'll be strong for everybody else and nobody will take care of you." She held on to Kate, and smoothed down her hair. "Like you did when I had cancer."

"Oh, Jill, it's so awful." More sobs.

"Of course it is."

After a few moments, Kate calmed, and felt a lot better. She sat back and leaned against the seat. "What a nightmare this has been."

"Tell me."

Kate filled her in on the call from Pa, the horrific drive to North Falls, the tense exchanges with Tyler and Dray. "About the only good thing that happened was Sofie rising to the occasion. She's really put all her rebellion aside to help her dad."

Jill drove the car down the quaint street, heading for a coffee shop. "The only good thing?"

A pause. "You saw Reese and me together."

"Looked pretty chummy to me."

"We made love last night."

"Wow!"

"It wasn't just a mercy fuck, either."

Jill chuckled. "I don't imagine it was. How are you feeling about it?"

"It was like coming home, Jill. I know that sounds like a cliché, but it was . . . spiritual almost. Like we'd broken a sacred bond and for a little while, we were able to mend it."

"You did break a sacred bond, honey. Vows you made in marriage."

"I guess."

"You don't seem too upset."

"How can I when being with him was so wonderful?"

Jill didn't respond.

"I know I've done an awful thing to Tyler, something I said I'd never do. But it's hard to see it that way, since I feel like I made love with my husband."

"And being with Tyler was always a little like cheating on Reese?"

"Oh, hell. That's pretty complicated."

"Nothing about your relationship with Reese Bishop has ever been simple."

"I know. I feel so bad for him, Jill."

"What's going to happen with Dray and Tyler?"

"I have no idea. And I decided this morning that I'll deal with that after Monday."

"Sounds sane. What can I do?"

"Nothing more. You coming here today was a godsend."

"I'm glad. I'll be down for the funeral. And I'll take Sofie back to school when it's all over, if you want."

"Maybe. Let's see what happens."

"One last thing? What are you going to do if Tyler and Dray come to the funeral?"

"Tyler's in Cancun. Dray's in New York. They won't come."

"Ah, well, just in case. Prepare yourself."

Kate blew out a heavy breath. She'd given no thought to that occurring at all.

FIFTEEN

"I HOPE WE'RE doing the right thing." Dray glanced across the front seat of Tyler's Blazer as he drove down Interstate 90. Commiserating with her, worrying with her, was wearing thin on both of them.

"We are." He shook his head in disgust, squelching his resentment, in light of the tragedy that had happened in the Bishop family. Still some remnants remained—he and Kaitlyn should have been walking the hot beaches of Cancun now. "I feel bad about how I reacted when Kaitlyn told me she was in North Falls with Reese the night Emily died. I was a jerk about it." He tugged on the striped tie he wore with a navy blazer and tan slacks. "I gave her ultimatums."

Dray squeezed his arm. "I'm sorry. If it's any consolation, I reacted badly, too. I cried like a freakin' baby, while Kate was stalwart and strong." She shook her head. "She always outshines me, no matter what the circumstances."

"No, it isn't any consolation at all. You're usually so unselfish. This whole thing with Reese and Kaitlyn has made us both so . . . fragile. And needy."

Leaning back into the leather seat, she smiled sadly.

"Funny, I don't picture you as fragile. You're so successful, so sure of yourself."

"Not always." He drove for a bit then asked, "You talked to Reese after he left, right?"

"Uh-huh. He called me a couple of times—and told me not to come until today, to stay with my family for the post-wedding celebrations."

"And that hurt?"

"Of course it did. I could have flown down early Sunday morning. He didn't want me there, but I'm sure he won't let Kate out of his sight." She swore. "Oh, shit, Tyler. I *hate* being like this. Emily's death isn't about me. I know that. I feel so stupidly selfish."

Glancing in the rearview mirror, Tyler signaled and pulled into the outer lane. "When faced with losing someone you love, Dray, people tend to act selfishly. I do, too."

"Not their daughter, for change. Reese said Sofie's being a doll." She waited a beat. "That makes all this worse, doesn't it?"

"What do you mean?"

"Their whole family is reunited."

"I guess." When she said no more, he decided to change the subject. "Speaking of family, how was the wedding?"

"It was terrific seeing Phoebe, and Lacey made a beautiful bride. Phoebe was fascinated by what I told her about your work."

"That's nice."

"The service and reception were lovely."

"But . . ."

"All I could think about was would I ever have a wedding with Reese."

"It's not out of the question." Briefly he glanced at her. "I'm not ready to give up on Kaitlyn. She'll be back in Westwood soon. The Bingham thing has to end—they found the journal, did you know that?"

"What journal?"

"Anna Bingham kept a journal in prison. The warden

called Reese on Wednesday. He and Kate were heading to Longshore when they got the news."

"No, I didn't know any of that."

"I'm sorry."

"Just another piece of evidence, Tyler. We're not getting them back."

"Yes, we are."

Tyler's statement echoed in his mind as he pulled into the parking lot of St. Mary's Catholic Church a half hour later. His resolve was mostly for Dray's sake, as every conversation he'd had with Kaitlyn since the initial one when she'd called him in Cancun, had been stilted. It might have been from grief, but she sounded so distant. He wondered if that's how she got when something really bad happened. Or if she was removed only from him out of anger. Was she was confiding in Reese?

"Ready?" he asked as he shut off the engine and opened his door.

"Yes." Dray soothed down the black suit she wore. "Thanks for listening to me, Tyler, and driving today."

"You're welcome."

The church was long and high-ceiled, though well lit. Emily's casket had already been brought in, and occupied the space just where the pews ended and before the altar began. The church was nearly full and they were early; but Tyler could see down the aisle clearly.

The tableau halted his steps and dented his confidence. Lined up in the front pew was Emily's family. Bill Bishop sat in the middle, Jason and Jimmy flanking him. Then Sofie and Reese off to the left. Kaitlyn was on the other end. Organ music played softly in the background.

"Where should we sit?" Dray asked.

"I'm going to let Kaitlyn know I'm here. You do the same with Reese. Take your cue from him."

"I don't want to intrude."

"You live with Reese, Dray."

She shook back her hair. "You're right." She headed

down the middle aisle and he strode down the one on the right side.

When he reached the family pew, he saw that all of them were holding hands. Sofie was crying softly on Reese's shoulder. Kaitlyn had Jimmy's hand in both of hers. When she looked up at Tyler, he saw that her face was haggard. Surprise showed in her expression. "Oh."

From the corner of his eye, he saw Reese startle, too. Then he stood and hugged Dray.

As Tyler inched into the pew, Kaitlyn stood. "Ty, hi. I didn't expect you." A great big hug. He felt her tremble. Though her words made him angry—she didn't *expect* him to come—he held her close and said only, "I'm so sorry, honey."

She hung on tight as if she needed his strength. "I know you said you'd come. I'm glad you did."

He saw Jimmy tug on the jacket of her navy suit. "Aunt Kate? I need you."

"Go ahead," Tyler told her. "I just wanted you to know I was here."

"Sit with us." She indicated an empty seat in the pew. "Here."

He smiled and dropped down next to her. He noticed Dray had also been invited to join the family. Maybe this was a good idea after all, he thought, taking Kaitlyn's other hand. Reese took Dray's, too.

But Tyler's confidence wavered when he saw Reese stare down the pew, and Kaitlyn look over at him. A lot transpired in that silent exchange.

"AMAZING GRACE . . ."

The mournful hymn filled the church. Standing, gripping Sofie's hand, Reese choked on the words. He focused on the casket where his little sister lay.

The smell of incense . . .

The instrument clanked as the altar boy released the holy scent into the church.

The flickering of candles . . .

"Emily Bishop Gates was a lovely woman. A member of our church . . ."

The priest's low voice rumbled through the pews as he praised the life Emily had led. As Reese let himself absorb the eulogy, tears fell unchecked, and the constriction in his heart tightened. He closed his eyes to contain the reactions, to be able to breathe. But images of Emily had been haunting him through the brutal calling hours, the prayers before the funeral, and now the final good-bye. He pictured his sister laughing with her boys last summer when she and the kids ganged up on him with water balloons . . . How she sat up with Reese the last time she visited, and they watched horror movies until the early hours . . . How she'd taken up ice skating in the winter and was getting pretty good at it . . .

Somehow they were all standing. The casket was being wheeled out and Reese was aware of people moving around him. Sofie touched his shoulder. "Go on, Daddy."

Dray pulled at him, too, and they made their way out of the church to the street. The bright light of the sun shocked him. How could warm rays be beaming down on them when he was burying his sister? It was obscene. He felt himself stumble on the way to the black limo. Funeral home staff surrounded them, directing them to the right cars. Dray kissed him on the cheek, let go of his hand, and faded away.

The limo was plush inside. He moved to the right and felt a hand reach for his. Kate. He bypassed her hand and slid his arm around her instead, keeping her close, finding a microchip of comfort in her presence. He hugged Sofie with his other arm. Across the seat, his dad huddled with the two little boys.

Again bright sunlight . . . gravel crunching under his feet . . . people milling . . . someone handed him a rose, and he approached his little sister's casket. Setting the flower on the lid, he whispered, "Good-bye, Emmy."

He knew he was crying, and couldn't stop it. He glanced

over, saw tears from Kate, his daughter, the boys, his father. Grief consumed them all as they bid their last
farewells.

And Reese knew in his heart nothing would ever be the
same again.

THE SMALL RESTAURANT in downtown North Falls was
filled with people who'd come to pay their respects to the
Bishop family. Flanked by Jillian and Kate's sister, Patty,
who'd flown in from Arizona on Friday, Kate sipped her
wine and watched Reese.

Patty tracked her gaze. "He's holding up pretty well."

"He's a wreck." He looked pale in the dark suit he wore.
She turned to her sister. "I still can't believe you came."

"Of course I came. Dee and Joan would have, too, except they're in Europe together." She nodded to Sofie, who
hadn't left her dad's side. "Besides, your daughter made it
clear I should come."

Kate was surprised, and pleased, that Sofie had taken it
upon herself to call Kate's sisters and ask them to fly in.

Jillian chuckled. "That kid can be daunting."

"Are you sure you can't stay, Patty? Come back to Westwood with me. I'm off till Thursday."

"Sorry. I only get a few days leave from work." She was
a reading teacher in Phoenix and had taken three days of
family bereavement time.

Reese scanned the room. His gaze fell on Kate,
stopped, then he looked back to the neighbor who was
talking to him.

"He's done that all day," Patty said.

"What?"

"Look for you."

"I'm glad I could help."

Jillian and Patty exchanged some silent message but Kate
ignored it. Drained from the funeral—they were always the
worst because of their finality—she blanked her mind.

Jillian nodded across the room. "Dray and Tyler seem like they have a lot to talk about."

Kate saw the two of them sitting at a table. She'd been shocked to see Tyler this morning. Things between them weren't good the last time they talked. And he was supposed to be in Cancun. She was supposed to be there, too. But she should have known he'd come. She wasn't thinking clearly.

"I should go over there."

Her friend grasped her arm. "Do what's best for you, Kate."

"Who the *hell* knows what that is?"

Patty shook her head. They'd stayed up late talking last night about what had happened with Reese and what that meant for the future. With the arrival of Sofie and then Patty, any physical comfort Kate could give Reese had been precluded. Sofie had stayed at the Gates' house with her father and Kate had gone to bunk with her sister at the hotel. She'd barely had a moment alone with Reese.

Excusing herself, she crossed to Tyler. He stood when she approached and kissed her cheek. She looked down. "Hello, Dray. Sorry I didn't greet you sooner."

"No problem. How are you holding up?"

"I feel like I'm put together with static cling."

Tyler's arm slid around her. Pulled her close. It felt odd.

"Did you get enough to eat?" she asked them, falling into the hostess role.

"Yes, thanks."

"Sit down, Kaitlyn. I—"

Someone approached from behind. "Kate, I need to see you."

Turning, she found Reese. "Sure? What is it?"

"Come with me." He said to Tyler, "You don't mind, do you, Sloan?"

"Of course not, Reese. I'm sorry about Emily."

"Thanks."

Dray stood. "Can I help?"

Kate felt sorry for her. Reese was ignoring her, but he was barely conscious of his actions, he was so mired in his grief.

"No, thanks." He touched Dray's shoulder. "We'll only be a minute."

With a proprietary hand on Kate's back, Reese urged her to the back entrance of the restaurant. She went without question or comment. Once outside, he led her to a tree where a picnic table had been set.

She didn't say anything, just sat down.

He loosened the striped tie that she'd packed for him and braced a foot on the bench of the table. "I needed a minute alone with you."

It was warm out, so she pushed up the sleeves of her black dress and smiled at him. "I need to be with you, too."

He stuck his hands in his pockets, removed them. Staring off into space, he said, "I can't believe it."

"It'll take a while for it to sink in."

He shook his head. Then focused on her. "What will you do now?"

"What do you mean?"

"When will you go back to Westwood?"

"I'm not sure. What do you want me to do?"

"Now there's a question." His smile, meager though it was, warmed her.

"Jillian's taking Sofie back to school tonight."

Reese nodded. "I know. She has a track meet tomorrow, and I told her to go. She needs some respite from the weight of all this."

"Patty's flying out tonight, too."

"So that leaves just you and Tyler, me and Dray."

"Once again," she said dryly.

"Dray wants to stay overnight here."

"Tyler does, too."

"I don't want her to." He kicked the table. "I want to sleep with you tonight."

"Reese . . ."

"You want that, too, I know it."

"I do."

"But you'll sleep with Tyler and I'll sleep with Dray."

"Maybe I should just go back to Westwood with him. Remove myself for a while so you can figure things out."

"You can't. I have that appointment with the lawyers and the Gates tomorrow. About custody of the boys. I want you there."

"It's a moot point, Reese." Glad to be back on safer ground, she said, "Unless Charlie's wishes were specified in the divorce agreement, Emily's custody arrangement stands."

"The agreement didn't make those specifications. I went over the papers up myself."

"Then there's nothing to worry about. I don't have to be there tomorrow."

"I *want* you there."

She hesitated only briefly. "I'll stay. Tyler and I will drive back after the meeting. Patty didn't cancel the hotel room just in case. I'll stay there."

"With Sloan?"

She nodded.

Reese's face reddened; he pushed off from the table and went to stand by the tree. His back to her, he braced his hand against the trunk of the big maple and pulled a few leaves off a branch. After a moment, she followed him. From behind, she rested her cheek on his back and slid her arms around his waist. "This is awkward."

His muscles tightened, and she could feel the struggle within him. "Don't have sex with him."

"What?"

"Don't have sex with Sloan. Not after making love with me Wednesday night."

"I don't think we should be making any decisions or promises today, love."

He whirled around, and grasped her arms. "No decisions. No promises. Just a pact. Don't . . ." He pulled her to him. "Please, Katie. I can't bear the thought. Not now. Maybe never. We have to talk, when this is over and we're more sane. But I need to hear that you won't have sex with him in the meantime."

They were digging themselves deeper into the emotional hole they'd created when they made love again. What to do?

His hand came to her neck; he kissed the top of her head.

And she said words that she feared would alter her life forever. "I won't have sex him." She looked up. "You, too, right?"

The corners of his mouth quirked. "Sloan's not my type, sweetheart."

"Funny."

"Say the words, Katie."

"I don't want you to sleep with Dray Merrill. At least not until we've had time to figure out what we're going to do."

"Good. I won't. Now that's settled."

He took her hand and led her back to the restaurant. He only let go once other people came into view.

EARL ATKINS, THE lawyer Reese had recommended to Emily, sat behind a cherry desk and looked over at the cast assembled before him. "I'm sorry, Mr. and Mrs. Gates. But Reese was right in what he told you. Since designation of legal guardianship was not part of the divorce agreement, Emily got to make the choice."

The older couple sat stiffly on one side of him, with Kate on the other. "They're all we have left of Charlie."

"Nat, because Reese has them," Kate said, "doesn't mean they won't be part of your lives."

"You'll bring them back to Westwood. Take them away from us."

"It's only an hour's drive."

The boys' grandmother sniffed.

Kate leaned forward in her seat. She looked haggard today, and Reese chided himself for wondering, in the midst of his grief and these life-altering decisions that were being made, what happened last night in that hotel room. "We promise you'll get to see them. We'll drive them here, if necessary."

Merle said gruffly, "Appreciate that."

The lawyer straightened. "There's one more thing. I gathered from this interchange that there's something you don't know about Emily's will."

"What could that be?" Reese asked.

"You recommended Emily make some changes in her will a few years back. She made all of them but one."

"Which one?"

His gaze shifted from Reese to Kate and back again to Reese. "She didn't take Judge Renado's name off the guardianship."

Kate sat up straight. *"What?"*

"You're still legal guardian, Kate."

Her gaze snapped to Reese.

He held up his hands. "I recommended she take you off. She said she'd talk to you about it and then change the will. I didn't have any idea she hadn't done what I asked her to."

"She did talk to me. I told her I thought it best to take my name off of it."

"Are you protesting the guardianship?" the lawyer asked. "You don't want the boys?"

"Of course I do. I'm just shocked Emily left it this way without telling any of us."

The lawyer seemed to understand. "When I asked about your divorce, in relation to the custody agreement, she said she didn't care that you were split up. She wanted you both to have legal guardianship of the boys."

Reese thought, *As if she always knew we'd get back together.*

When that had sunk in, the lawyer straightened. "I think that's about all of it."

"One more thing." This from Merle. "What about school? The little guys have another month left this year."

"I'll get them tutoring in Westwood," Reese said.

"Maybe they can finish out here," Merle suggested.

"Stay with us until then."

"No." This from Reese.

"Reese." Kate touched his arm. "That might be a good idea. They won't have to be uprooted. They'll have your dad and their other grandparents around. We can see them on weekends. In June, they'll come and live with us."

"With us?"

"I mean . . . whatever arrangements you and I make."

"Maybe you're right. I'll have to talk to them and Pa first."

The Gates looked relieved.

Reese and Kate parted company with the lawyer and the Gates and they headed for Reese's car. He circled around the driver's side. At least he was capable of functioning a bit more normally, though he feared the ache in his heart would never go away. He slid in beside Kate.

He didn't start the engine, just sat staring through the window. "It's a good resolution, isn't it?"

"I think so."

"What about the rest?" he asked turning to face her.

"I have no idea. I'm shocked about the guardianship."

"I can't say I'm that surprised. In retrospect, Emily always wanted us to get back together." He waited a beat. "I have to ask you something. Don't take offense at this."

"What?"

"You said you didn't want any more kids. That's why you . . ." He cleared his throat. "I don't want to burden you with the boys if you don't want them in your life."

"I want them in my life!" She sounded offended. "How can you even ask me that? Especially after what's happened between us?"

"I'm not getting on you about the past, Kate. I just need to know what you want now."

"I want the boys. I'm different from who I was at the end of our marriage."

Smiling, he brushed his knuckles down her cheek. "I think we both are."

She blew out a heavy breath and grasped his wrist. "I

guess we have to take this one day at a time."

"Or one night." He sat back, his gaze was intense, piercing. "How'd it go with you two?"

"It was unbelievably awkward. Things are really strained between me and Tyler. Neither of us slept well."

"Join the club. It was a nightmare for me. I was afraid I'd wake up and reach for you. Call your name." He looked thoughtful. "We have to tell them what happened."

"I know. I'd like some time though."

"Yeah." His tapped his fingers on the steering wheel. "How are we ever going to pick up on the Bingham case? It's the last thing I want to be thrust back into now."

Kate the judge emerged. "I thought maybe Tyler and I would stop by the prison and get the journal."

"Good idea."

"How long will you stay here, Reese?"

"Another day or two. Then I have to get back to work."

"I know. I'm due in court Thursday."

"Should we meet on the journal when I get back?"

"Yes." She grabbed his hand. "This is going to be big, Reese. I have a feeling this journal is going to reveal things we need to know."

"And the other? You and me?"

"I don't know. Honestly, I'm afraid of what's happened between us."

"Rightly so. We have a lot to lose."

"Well, nothing needs to be decided now." She checked her watch. "We should go. Tyler and Dray are waiting."

Without censoring his actions, he leaned over and took her mouth. It was soft and yielding and for a few blissful seconds, he lost himself in the sweet taste of her.

If he had this, he might very well survive the loss of his sister.

SIXTEEN

STILL WEARING HER pajamas—bright blue-and-yellow
flowered bottoms from Old Navy and a yellow T-shirt—
Kate took her coffee and Anna Bingham's journal into the
den and sat at her desk. She wanted to have an analysis
done for Reese before he returned from North Falls. As the
sun streamed in through the window, Kate basked in its
warm rays and allowed herself to think about him before
she got to work. It was no longer painful to let her ex-
husband into her thoughts.

He'd been so sad when she left yesterday. He'd stood
with Dray on the sidewalk of his father's house and hugged
Kate, then watched as she drove away with Tyler. Kate's
own emotions were in turmoil, and the trip back to Westwood had been tense. They'd stopped at the prison and gotten the journal from Lauren Evans, who said she'd read it,
and had contacted the prison authorities about the information. She sounded very unhappy about what Anna Bingham had written.

For the entire drive, Tyler was morose, sensing, she
guessed, that things were in flux. When they arrived at her

house, he'd asked her to have dinner with him. She refused, claiming exhaustion. Instead she ate pizza by herself, climbed into bed and planned to skim the journal so she could get a sense of what it contained. But by then it was late and she fell asleep with the book on her lap; she dreamed about Reese making love to her.

Tyler was still on vacation from work, but he hadn't asked to spend today with her; instead, he said he needed some time alone to sort things out in his mind. Thinking about the fact that they should have been renewing their relationship in Cancun gave her a twinge of guilt, but damn it, none of that was her fault.

It's your fault you made love with Reese. Yes, it was, and she'd take full responsibility for what she'd done. Right now, she wanted to hunker down and get this journal thing in place.

The book itself was interesting: It was an eight-by-ten volume, with thick vinyl front and back. First, she skimmed through it. The entries seemed to deal with certain areas; she decided to section it off by content, so Reese could see an organized chunk of information, and they could then scrutinize it together and decide what it all meant. The fact that the pages were perforated and easy to tear out made her task easier.

Section one she labeled: Bingham's anger over the differences between life in a federal prison camp vs. life in a federal correctional institution. She read each entry carefully this time to decide which to pull for examination later. She tore out a few that exemplified Bingham's distress.

The first entry . . .

I'm fucked! This place is the pitts. The dormitories I stayed in at Danbury have been replaced by eight-by-eight concrete cells. The toilet is right out in the open. The ratio of guards to inmates is high. I'm in with goddamned drug addicts and convicted felons. There's no freedom to move about. I thought I was going to go crazy at Danbury, but this is a whole new ball game. Five years of this? I don't think so.

That last sentiment made Kate cringe. It indicated suicide as a strong possibility. If indeed that's what happened, how could she and Reese ever be cleared?

No use in panicking, Katie, Reese would say. She wished he was here to center her. She went on to the next section, which she labeled *Shopping.* There were several entries about that. She removed the first . . .

> Shopped at the commissary today. It sure as hell isn't Rodeo Drive. You get $175 per MONTH—I spent more than that on a friggin' blouse when I was on the outside. The place to requisition goods looks like a drive-thru window—inmates on outside, clerk on inside. The line to shop—and I use that term loosely—snaked out into the hall. I finally got my turn and gave them my order for the few things you can purchase—tennis shoes, a watch. I had both when I came here, but the prison dicks took them away. Other inmates say the officials do that so you'll spend money at the commissary: Some refuse to purchase the duplicates inside. Who gives a flying fuck? While you wait, you get to socialize with your fellow prisoners—now that was fun. What a bunch of losers.

Kate found several more entries that dealt with shopping and clipped them together. One in particular stood out . . .

> I got into trouble today for questioning my commissary order after I accepted it. Apparently, if you don't agree with how they filled your order, you have to protest it right when you get it. Lena dared me to make a fuss, and I got a shot for it, but it was fucking A to see the guards get mad. Especially that asshole Sorensen.

Well, this was good information. Kate scribbled on a legal pad, names: Parks, Sorenson. She'd keep a tally of who Bingham mentioned.

The next section dealt with her entries about recreation and entertainment.

They took away my movie privileges for a month because of the commissary thing. Who the hell cares? They don't show any R rated ones, so all of them are bland airline-type flicks. There's no sex scenes, but the shows are full of fast money, fast women and drug running. Ironic, huh? Just what these bozos inside need to be seeing in their spare time. Bet they identify with the characters, ha-ha.

Another sampling . . .

I saved a seat for Lena today at the Super Bowl party. I don't have a group—translate gang—like most people, though anybody will gamble with me. Anyway, this Chicano chick Anita Ruiz wanted Lena's chair. I told her to go to hell. I got a split lip and she got a big fat bruise on her boob but by the time the guards got there, we were sweet as pie to each other. Nobody rats inside, and we cover up fights routinely.

So, this was the reason why no confrontations with other prisoners were recorded in the disciplinary reports. The inmates had their own code of honor. Unfortunately, that secrecy would make Kate and Reese's job harder. She added Anita Ruiz—the inmate also named by Nancy Bingham—to the list of those mentioned in the journal.

Other entries Kate pulled from this category revolved around sports. Seemed like Bingham had been good at baseball. Just like Reese.

Reese. Taking a break, Kate leaned back in her chair, propped her feet up and closed her eyes. He'd called late last night. He was at Emily's house with the boys, and apparently Dray was asleep . . .

"I wish you were here," he'd said, the rawness of his voice scraping her nerves.

"I do, too."

"I need to be with *you*."

"Reese, we shouldn't belabor our situation." But she'd weakened and asked, "Is Dray in your bed?"

"No, I made some excuse about the boys being around."

"Oh."

"We were good there, in my bed the other night, weren't we, Katie?"

"Really good." She chuckled. "You haven't lost your touch, hotshot."

That dragged a laugh out of him . . .

Forcing her mind from Reese, Kate sat up again and zeroed in on the entries about Bingham's cellmate, Lena Parks. It seemed like they had a love/hate relationship.

The first on this subject . . .

Lena's cool. She bought us some blow from Blackie—get it? Her black market supplier. We got stoned into blissful oblivion.

Another . . .

Lena's cranky these days. Her guy on the outside didn't come to visit. Somebody else came up, though, who told her he'd seen good old Randolf with some broad. I told her not to sweat it with men—they're only good for two things, and I can take out my own garbage. Ha-ha!

A final entry . . .

Don't know how I feel about all this. Lena crawled into my bunk last night . . .

Bingham had gone on to explain the sexual encounter in great detail. Kate had read where healthy men and women in prison made sexual adjustments. The primary form of gratification was masturbation, but consensual homosexuality abounded.

When she'd had enough of those entries, Kate broke for lunch, and called Sofie.

She caught her daughter just heading out for the dining hall. "Hey, Mama," Sofie had said, actually sounding like she was glad to hear from Kate. Obviously, things had changed for her, too.

"How are you, honey?"

"Sad. How's Daddy?"

"Sad, too. He called me last night."

"You didn't stay in North Falls with him?" Her tone was accusatory.

"No. I came back with Tyler."

Silence. Then in a little girl voice, her daughter admitted, "I was hoping you two would get back together . . . you know . . . you were so close at Grandpa's. I saw you hugging all the time."

Oh, God, just what they'd feared. Sofie getting her hopes up. And nothing had been decided. Kate didn't even know if they were going to try to make their relationship work again.

"Sof, now's not the time to talk about something that life altering. Dad's grief is coloring his outlook."

"What about you?"

"I feel bad, too. A lot. Can we just leave it at the fact that your dad and I are trying to help each other through this?"

A long pause. "Okay."

After a moment, Kate asked, "How's everything going at school?"

"I'm behaving myself, Mom."

Kate had found time to talk to Sofie about what she'd witnessed with Jax in Sofie's dorm room. Her daughter contended she'd been experimenting with a few drugs. Kate had come down hard on her about that, and Sofie promised she'd stop. Kate still hadn't told Reese, but she would eventually.

"No more drugs, right?"

"Right."

"And if you feel tempted, you need to talk to Dad and me about it."

"I will. He still doesn't know, right?"

"Not yet. But I'm going to tell him."

"I know." Sofie's voice lightened. "Tell me about the boys."

She was elated to hear they would be living in West-wood and overjoyed that Kate had legal custody, too.

Finally, Kate said, "I'll let you go eat. I just wanted to check in with you." She hesitated. "I love you, Sof."

"I love you, too, Mama."

Tears threatened as Kate hung up. She couldn't remember the last time Sofie had said those words to her. Was it only because she had hopes for a reconciliation between her parents? What if that didn't work out? Her heart had done a two-step when Sofie said she loved her. Kate didn't want to lose that.

To avoid worrying about Sofie's reactions, Kate returned to the journal. She tackled the visitation information next. This had stood out when she skimmed it . . .

"A" came today.

Kate cross-checked the list Reese had put on the computer. Arnie Anders was designated as a visitor, and the recipient of several phone calls and outgoing pieces of mail.

Bingham continued,

He looked so good in his new suit. He held my hand across the table. God I wanted to fuck him right there. Lena can't hold a candle.

Another . . .

"B" came for visit.

Bernie Benson, also on the lists.

I like the mustache. It makes him look different. (Ha-Ha!) He put his hand down my blouse and the fuckin' guard Sorensen made him leave.

There were more entries about "A" and "B". Kate sat back in the chair and stared at the visitor group of entries from the journal. Something was really odd here. When she remembered Anna Bingham's ring, Kate realized what it was. The names. The beginning letters of each guy's name were *A* and *B*, and all the first and last names were alliterative. Just like the *DD* in the ring. Could the visitors' identities be for real? Yet, all visitors needed to be on a list, prepared immediately upon the incarceration; they had to fill out an Information Form, and provide an acceptable mode of ID. They were subjected to searches, asked questions and went through metal detectors. Hmm. Then, she had another thought. DD had not come to see Anna at all. Why, when he'd given her a ring?

She wished Reese was here. He'd have some insights. Just then the phone rang; Kate checked the caller ID. It was Tyler. She needed to see him, needed to talk to him. If for nothing else, to tell him about what happened with Reese.

Time to face the music, she thought, and answered her phone.

FROM THE DOORWAY of Emily's guest room, Dray watched Reese hang up the phone with a sigh, sit back on the bed and close his eyes. Dressed in dark shorts and a golf shirt, he looked older in the late afternoon sunlight, his face lined with sadness and grief. She was trying hard not to add to it. To just comfort him, as Kate had done.

"Hey." She stepped into the room when he glanced over and smiled at her.

"Hi. I didn't see you there."

"Nap time?"

He shook his head. "I can't sleep. Couldn't last night, either."

She crossed to him and sat down on the edge of the mattress, took his hand and kissed it. The familiar, sexy smell of his aftershave surrounded her. "I could help you sleep," she said hopefully. He'd barely touched her, even casually, since she'd gotten to North Falls. She knew some men lost total interest in sex when they were grieving, but some men wanted to do it a lot, to reaffirm life.

He caressed her cheek. "I'm sorry, Dray. No."

"It's okay."

"No, it's not. I have to talk to you."

Sensing she wouldn't like what he had to say, she shook her head. "No, Reese, we aren't going to have this discussion when you're so overwrought."

"Yes, honey, we are."

Abruptly she stood, strode to the window, and looked out at the pretty backyard. "I don't want to, Reese, not now. People say things they don't mean in times of tragedy. They don't think clearly."

Before he could continue, Jason and Jimmy burst into the room. Ignoring her, they bounded onto the bed. In her peripheral view, she saw them cuddle into Reese, one on each side; he kissed their heads and held each of them tightly.

"Wish Aunt Kate was here," Jimmy said, glancing at Dray with mutinous eyes.

"Like she was when Mommy died," Jason added. "How come Aunt Kate doesn't sleep in here like that anymore?"

The air backstopped in Dray's lungs. This was exactly what she did *not* want to hear. Damn it!

Reese spoke softly to the boys and shuffled them out, then he came to her side. He grasped her arm. "Dray, please, we have to talk."

Facing him fully, she nodded to the bed. "You slept with Kate, didn't you? That's what the boys meant."

"Yes, it's what I wanted to tell you."

"Did you just sleep in the same bed? Was it like the night she was attacked?" She cursed the hope in her voice, the near begging tone. What had *happened* to her?

"No, Dray, it wasn't like that. We made love. I'm sorry."

She wanted to fling herself into his arms. But she didn't. Instead, she threw back her shoulders and asked, coldly, "You said you'd never cheat on me."

"I . . . weakened."

"Because of Emily and your grief? Did it cloud your judgment?"

He drew back and stared down at her. His green eyes were turbulent. "Maybe some. But that's not the only reason I did this. I'm sorry, I'm still in love with Kate."

"You never told me you loved me."

"Dray . . ."

She wanted to bawl like a baby. She wanted to pound on his chest, rail at fate. But she knew, in that moment, she had to take care of herself now, protect herself, and falling apart, begging, wasn't what was best for her. So she gathered her strength. "I guess this is the end of us then."

He didn't object, didn't beg for another chance, and that hurt most of all.

She glared at him. "For the record, I hate you for sleeping with her before you told me we were through. It was wrong, no matter how upset you are."

"You're right. I deserve your contempt."

"I'll move out of your house." She watched his face, saw the lines of grief, now accompanied by guilt and regret. She knew she shouldn't be doing this, but the pain of his rejection eclipsed everything else. "When will you go back Westwood?"

"Tomorrow. The boys are coming in with Dad on Saturday. But you can stay at the house until you find a place to live. I don't want you out on the street." He moved toward her, to touch her.

She stepped back abruptly. "Don't."

He recoiled.

She lifted her chin. "I won't stay with you now! I'll move into the apartment over the gym. It's empty."

"If that's what you want."

"And what do *you* want, Reese? To have Kate back in your life?"

"There's a lot to consider."

He was so obviously dodging the question.

"What does Kate want?"

"She's as confused as I am. We didn't mean for this to happen. Kate's really broken up about telling Tyler."

Tears did moisten her eyes now. "Oh, poor Tyler. This will kill him. He loves her so much."

She saw Reese's mouth tighten and his eyes flame green fire.

It was all the evidence Dray needed. Despite his hedging words, it was obvious in that instant exactly what Reese wanted.

FEELING A SENSE of dread, Tyler showed up at Kaitlyn's house about six. He'd gone golfing today, to think things through, to decide what he really wanted and how to get it. Now, he was ready to say a few things to her. Using his key, he let himself into her house, and found her on the phone in the kitchen. She hung up quickly.

Dressed in jeans and a long-sleeved T-shirt, she smiled, but didn't come toward him. He stayed in the doorway. "Hi."

"Hi." He nodded to the phone. "Was that Reese?"

"Jason and Jimmy. I think it helps them to talk to me. A woman, you know."

"Hmm."

"Come in and sit. Want something to drink?"

He noticed a bottle of red wine open on the counter, and a glass half full next to it. "I'll have some of that."

She poured him a glass and brought it to him; he took a seat and sipped his wine, wondering how to open this discussion. She started to speak, but he held up his hand. "I have some things to say before you talk."

"Ty—"

"No, let me." He cocked his head. "Something's happened with you and Reese, I can sense it. Maybe not physical but . . ."

Her blush, and the way she averted her gaze, told him otherwise.

"Shit." He raised his eyes to the ceiling. "You promised you wouldn't cheat on me, Kaitlyn."

She said only, "I'm sorry."

He remembered voicing his fears when this whole thing with Bingham began. *I'm afraid you're still in love with him. That he'll get you in the sack, then take you away from me.* He'd been right on target.

"Are you? Sorry?"

"Of course, what I've done is an unconscionable betrayal of trust."

"It was." He drew in a breath. "You know, if this is just a slip up, I might be able to forgive you. He's not good for you." He watched her for some reaction. Her face told him nothing. "It's not a slip up, though, is it? You're in love with him."

She stared at him, her chocolate-brown eyes full of feeling.

"This is it, Kaitlyn. Your next words decide our fate. Tell me you don't love him. Tell me this is an aberration, that what happened physically was all because of the Bingham case and Emily's death. We'll go from here and forge a future together."

Still no response.

"It's what I want to hear!"

Finally, her eyes filled with tears. "I can't tell you any of that. I'm sorry. I'm still in love with Reese."

DRAY PULLED THE rented car into Reese's driveway and shut off the engine. She got out, slammed the door, and stalked inside through the front door. "Son a bitch. Damn him. How *dare* he?" She kept up the diatribe as she stomped down the basement steps to get boxes, then up to their bedroom. *His* bedroom.

When she saw the bed, her throat tightened. But she held back the response. Time to be strong, she reminded herself. She flung her clothes into suitcases. Stripped the walls of the paintings she had put there. In the bathroom, she swept all of her things into small traveling bags she used for trips. Her cell phone rang an hour after she'd arrived home.

She didn't let herself hope it was Reese.

"Hello."

"Dray?" It was Tyler. He sounded awful. "Can you talk?"

"Yes. I gather she had her little chat with you, too?"

"Kaitlyn? Yes, how did you know?"

Holding her phone, she took the stairs down to the kitchen, and began ferreting out her things. "Take a wild guess."

"Fuck." A pause. "What's that banging in the background?"

"I'm home, well, at Reese's house, which has never really been mine."

"Is Reese there with you?"

"No. I rented a car and drove back myself. I'm moving out of this godforsaken place right now."

"Dray . . ."

"No, I'm done with this. I have an apartment over the gym. It's small, but enough till I can get my own place. I can't stay in this house another night. Not now."

"Want some help?"

"Only if we don't talk about Reese and Kate. I'm done with all that."

"Yeah. So am I." He sounded as sure as she.

"Good. Come on over. I can use some help with boxes. Your truck would be good to transport my stuff."

After she hung up, she finished packing the kitchen things that were hers, and some of her favorite pieces they'd bought together, like the ceramics they'd gotten in Mexico. Her heart ached when she packed the teapots she'd collected, most of which Reese had brought her. She remembered one time . . . *No, no, don't do this*, she told herself.

She was removing some original prints from the walls in the living room when the doorbell rang. She found Tyler on the porch. He looked like he'd been hit with an emotional sledgehammer. Leaning against the door, hands in his pockets, he swallowed hard. "Thanks for letting me come over."

"No problem." She stood aside to let him in. "I'm glad for the help, and the company."

He wore an old sweatshirt and jeans—moving clothes. "Can I start putting boxes in the truck?"

"Yes, that would be great."

He grabbed her shoulder as she turned away. "Wait a sec. You okay?"

The muscles of her face hurt from staying composed. "I told you I don't want to talk about them."

"This isn't about them. It's about you."

His blue eyes were so sincere. "No, of course I'm not all right. I'm hurt and pissed as hell at them. And I want *out of here*. I want my own life back, one where I don't walk on eggshells worrying that the man I love is going to go back to his ex-wife. Christ, I can't believe I took this shit for so long!" Her voice rose on the last words.

"Well, don't hold back, Dray." His eyes twinkled. It was better than the gravity in them when he arrived.

She smiled sadly. "How are you?"

"Ditto."

She shrugged. "We've known for a long time that this was going to happen, didn't we, Tyler?"

He scanned the room as if looking for answers. "That doesn't make it hurt less."

Squeezing his arm, she said softly, "Nothing will for a while." She drew in a huge breath. "Now, let's finish packing so I can get out of here, and start my life over. You, too," she added.

When they finished an hour later, Dray had wiped every trace of herself from Reese's house. He'd done the same thing—gotten her out of his life completely—by sleeping with Kate.

TYLER WAS EXHAUSTED by the time he brought in the last of the boxes. The loft over the gym was up two flights of steps, and Dray didn't pack lightly. She meant it when she said she was done with Reese for good. Tyler flopped himself on the bed she'd just made up with dark green sheets and a geometric print comforter and threw his arms over his head. "I'm whipped."

She dropped down beside him. "Me, too." They watched the overhead fan whirl around, its low hum the only sound in the room.

"What time is it?" he asked, too tired to raise his arm.

"It's martini time!"

"What?"

"I brought the fixings for raspberry martinis from Reese's. He never liked them anyway."

Tyler sighed. "I don't drink much more than wine or beer."

"Well, big guy, you're in for a treat." She rolled off the bed and said, "Stay here, I'll be right back."

He did. He knew it was late, but he didn't care. He wasn't due into work until tomorrow afternoon, as this was supposed to be his vacation. He was *supposed* to walking the beaches with Kaitlyn, drinking rum concoctions with little paper umbrellas in them, taking moonlight swims.

And making love.

Shit! Instead, she'd fucked her ex-husband.

He wasn't going to do this! He sat up and moved to lean against the headboard. This place was small, but cute. He could see Dray's touches in it. Like her touches in Reese's house. She had a nice sense of style.

"Here we go." Dray returned with a tray. On it was a huge pitcher of martinis, some fruit and cheese.

He laughed. "Hey, pretty lady, we drink those and we'll be smashed by midnight."

"There you go. That's the first good idea I've heard all day."

"Why not? I can always sleep on the couch, right?"

"Right." She poured him an oversize glassful and one for herself. They sat on the bed, sipped the tasty drinks and nibbled on sharp cheese.

An hour later, they were giggling over the silly jokes

they were telling each other. Tyler lost track of how many martinis he'd downed.

Another hour, and too many drinks later, Tyler's eyes began to close. Dray was drooping on the other side of the bed herself, humming some silly song she remembered from childhood.

When Tyler awoke to light streaming in from the window, he was still on Dray's bed. Only, now he wasn't clothed. Turning his head to the side, he gasped at the pain radiating from his brain to all of his nerve endings.

And also at what he found next to him.

Dray, still zonked out.

And from her bare shoulders, visible from under the sheets, he was pretty sure she was as naked as he was.

Holy hell, what had they done?

SEVENTEEN

HIS HEART HEAVY, Reese pulled into Kate's driveway at 7:00 p.m. on Wednesday night. She'd set up a meeting with Chase Sanders to review the journal entries, and Reese was trying to be interested in what she'd found to help their case. But it was hard to muster the enthusiasm. Nothing had as much significance as it had before Emily's death.

As soon as he'd hit the city limits, he'd wanted to drive right over to Kate's, but he knew intuitively trying to rush things with her was the wrong move. He didn't even know if she'd talked to Tyler yet. So he'd gone home and found his house had been wiped clean of all traces of Dray. It was bad enough when he'd discovered she'd rented a car and driven back on her own; he'd tried to reach her but she didn't answer or return his calls. The stark emptiness of his house only accented the grief he felt when he arrived home. He'd lost so much in his life—Emily, of course; his mother at a young age; Kate and Sofie to a degree; and now Dray; he didn't know what to do with the emptiness inside him.

While he sat in the car and stared off into space, the door to her condo opened, and Kate stepped out on the porch. A little smile and a wave, a questioning look—why was he sitting out there in the driveway? He took a moment to study her—hair loose around her shoulders, casual black capri pants and a pretty multicolored striped top. Her body language was wholly open and welcoming, not tense and forbidding as before. Saying a small prayer of thanks for that, he exited the car, and strode to the porch. The early May air was warm and a slight breeze rustled the trees around him. He took no joy in summer, though, and his steps were heavy.

"Hi." Kate studied him and he knew she was seeing the haggard lines at his eyes and grooves at his mouth; then she embraced him right there on the porch. "I'm glad you're back."

He held on tight, losing himself in the scent of her perfume, the texture of her hair against his cheek. It felt so good to be enveloped in her strong grasp. Once again he was hit by the notion that if Kate stayed in his life, he might survive the loss of Emily.

Please, God, don't let me use that to orchestrate a reconciliation. She had to come to him willingly, without being emotionally blackmailed into it. Because he knew if he did get her back, he'd never survive the loss of her again.

Kate drew away and seemed to read his mind. "Don't think too much right now, Reese. Just come inside, and we'll talk about the journal." She linked her arm with his. "We're not making any big decisions tonight."

"Okay." He accompanied her into the house and back to the kitchen.

"Want something?"

"A scotch. Neat." He sank down in a chair at the table while she went to the counter. His fingers drummed on the granite surface. "I have to know some things before we start with the case again."

Pivoting, she held the Johnnie Walker bottle in one hand and two glasses in the other. She crossed to the table, sat, and as she poured, said, "I think I know what." They'd spoken on the phone, but hadn't inquired about Dray and Tyler. Neither had volunteered information then.

"Did you talk to him?" Reese said simply.

"Yes. It was horrid." She bit her lip. "Did you talk to Dray?"

He nodded. "It was equally as hard. I feel rotten about hurting her."

"I know." He saw tears in her eyes. "It about killed me to tell Tyler what we'd done."

"You broke it off, though, didn't you?"

"Yes. He was willing to forgive me if sleeping with you was just a slip up." She shook her head. "Even after I betrayed him."

"I guess infidelity isn't the death knell of every relationship."

Instead of anger, hurt shadowed her face. "Are you saying I should have been more understanding about your affair?"

"I don't know, maybe."

"I wanted to. You were so furious at me, and couldn't forgive what I'd done."

"I guess we were both wrong." He ran a restless hand through his hair. "Let's make a pact and not rehash the past again. We'll never be able to go forward if we keep doing that." And he'd realized, with Emily's premature death, time on this earth could be short.

"You're on."

"What did you finally tell him?"

She met his gaze directly. "That it wasn't a slip up, that I'd never stopped loving you."

"Good." He heard the masculine satisfaction in his voice, but didn't care.

She ran her finger around the rim of the glass. "What did you tell Dray?"

He was moved by the vulnerability in her voice. "That I was in love with you, too. That I couldn't continue a relationship with her."

"How did she react?"

"She got angry. She stormed out, rented a car and drove home by herself. When I got there a few hours ago, all her stuff was gone."

"Wow, that's uncharacteristic behavior for her."

"I guess she'd finally had enough of my waffling." He took a gulp of scotch for reinforcement. "So, where do we go from here? In our relationship?"

"I think we should just get through this thing with Bingham and adjust to life without . . . with the boys. Too many decisions have to be made there to clutter the present with anything else."

"Some of those decisions will depend on what happens with us."

She raked back her hair. "I know."

"But you're right. We don't need to make life-altering choices tonight." He leaned over and kissed her forehead. "Just being with you helps."

"I'm glad. It's the same for me."

He sipped his scotch and relaxed. "Let me take a look at the journal before Sanders gets here. What time is he coming?"

"Soon."

Kate rose and got Anna Bingham's book out of the drawer in the corner desk and brought it back to the table. Reese studied the heavy black back and front, then frowned.

"What's wrong?"

"I'm not sure. Odd bindings, maybe. Or something else I can't put my finger on."

The doorbell rang. "That must be Chase," Kate said, standing. "God, I wish we could solve this case. I'm tired of having that monkey on our backs."

"Well, let's go try."

They greeted Sanders at the door and settled in the den again, with the private investigator facing them. "Before I read the journal, I took the names of Bingham's visitors that you sent me by email and had a cop run them through his files."

"What did you find out about the men?" Kate asked.

"That they don't exist."

"Excuse me?"

"Arnie Anders and Bernie Benson don't exist. They have no Social Security numbers, no credit cards, no trace of anything to say they're real people."

Reese shifted in his seat. "What does this mean?"

"That Bingham's visitors at Longshore provided false identities."

"Why would they do that?"

"I don't know. It's a lead though. Something's not right about her life there."

Kate leaned forward in her chair. "What do we do next?"

"Take a look at the tapes of these guys' visitations. I called the warden and she said that the okay came through for us to view them."

"Terrific."

The private investigator's eyes danced. "There's something else. That guard mentioned in the journal—Nell Sorenson. She and Lena Parks knew each other from when Parks was imprisoned in Atlanta and Sorenson had just been hired as a guard in that very same institution. Also, when I went out to Longshore to talk to some of the inmates, I found out Sorensen was a black-market provider." He paused for effect. "Of drugs."

"She could have gotten the pills Bingham took." Reese shook his head. "But that doesn't rule out suicide."

"One thing at a time." Sanders checked his notes. "I'm going to the prison tomorrow to get the tapes. And I plan to talk to this Anita Ruiz that Bingham had some run-ins with. She might be able to link everything together."

"Well, that would make my day." Reese's voice was tinged with sadness, despite his words.

"By the weekend, we might have some good news."

"We could use that," Kate said, squeezing Reese's hand.

"I'm sorry about your sister, Reese. I meant to say something earlier."

Reese nodded. "This bright spot in the case helps."

"Good then." Sanders stood. "I'll be on my way." He touched Kate's arm and gave her a very male smile before he headed out.

"He's attracted to you," Reese told her in the foyer after Sanders left.

"What?"

"I can tell." Reese placed his hands on her arms and rubbed up and down. "I recognize the signs, I guess."

She chuckled. "Do you now?"

"Uh-huh." He tugged her close and his middle bumped with hers. "I'm *intimately* acquainted with what if feels like to be under your spell. We said no decisions should be made now. Does that preclude this?" His erection pressed against her.

She tilted her hips forward. "Not in my book. How about yours?"

"It reads the same way, babe." He met her forehead with his. "I want you, Katie. I want the oblivion that making love with you brings. And I need to be close to you." He sighed. "Is it awful to want that when my sister just died?"

"No, of course not." She drew away, took his hand, and led him up the steps.

When they reached the bedroom, Kate felt unaccountably shy. She and Reese had made love hundreds of times, and once recently, so she wasn't worried that he'd notice the sags here and there, or less muscle tone in places. But that last time they were together, in Emily's home, had been in a blur of pain. Now, tonight, was clearer, more real—both of them had their wits about them. Making love was a conscious, I-know-what-I'm-doing decision. Her heart pounded with the thought as she went to the bathroom to get condoms.

"What is it, love?" he asked when she came to the bed and dropped the foil packets on the nightstand. "You're frowning."

"I don't know. I'm . . . scared, I think."

"Of us together." His words weren't a question, but a statement of fact. "I feel it, too."

"Why, I wonder?"

He kissed her shoulder. "Maybe because we aren't doing this out of grief. Maybe because we're free from other commitments, and nothing's keeping us from each other. Maybe because we can really be together now."

"I suppose. I'm terrified of getting hurt, of hurting you and Sofie again."

He eased open the front button of her pretty striped top. Then the second, stopping to kiss the skin he exposed. Kate closed her eyes and steeped herself in his touch. The brush of his fingertips. His mouth on her ear. She let herself drown in the sensations of what he was doing to her—kneeling on the floor, tugging off her pants, seating her on the bed and removing her shoes, underwear, everything.

Then he stood. His grin turned a bit cocky, reminding her of the boy he used to be. She realized with blinding force that she wanted that boy back! He yanked his navy golf shirt over his head, baring sleek muscles and chest hair placed perfectly, as if by God. His hands went to his beltless jeans, and she watched, enthralled.

Snap, snap.

The *whoosh* of the zipper.

The *thunk* of his shoes as he kicked them off.

She got a peek at tight blue boxers before he pushed them down with his jeans. Now they were both bare. Exposed. Physically, yes. But emotionally, even more so. After he rolled on a condom, he knelt again, kissed her navel, her breasts. When he looked up his eyes were shining with surrender. To whatever was between them now.

She was eased back on the bed.

Then stretched out.

His touch was gentle, increasing in urgency by increments.

When she was ready, and he was more than, he entered her. She cried out, not in pain, not even in ecstasy, but with a deep sense of coming home, of finding what they had lost five long years ago. And she held on to him—this man who had been her husband, felt him push and plunge, thrust and parry, until they both lost themselves in each other.

On Thursday morning, at Bishop Associates, once again Reese felt a sense of disorientation. It had subsided briefly while he was with Kate, but now, being here wasn't the same because of Emily's death; the sense of loss threatened to overwhelm him.

Yolanda met him at the door. She took his briefcase and hugged him. "Are you sure you should be here so soon? It's only been a week."

Could that be true? It felt like a lifetime. "I need to work. I've taken so much time off."

"Things are running smoothly here."

"I don't doubt that." He'd been touched when she and most of his staff came to Emily's funeral. He reiterated his thanks for that. "And I appreciate your concern now, but I'm all right." He checked his watch. "I need to call Jason and Jimmy before they go to school." He'd promised them he'd talk to them every day.

"Go ahead, I'll bring you coffee."

Inside his office, Reese sat down at his desk and picked up the phone. Though the boys were staying mostly with the Gates, they'd spent last night with his father. He got the little guys just before the bus arrived. They were lackluster on this first day back to school. He knew exactly how they felt. Returning to the routine of daily living seemed blasphemous to the hugeness of the loss they'd experienced.

Pa got on the phone once the kids left. "You doin' okay, Son?"

"As well as can be expected. You?"

"I . . ." A choking sound. "I miss her."

Those few wrenching words stretched Reese's control. He barely held on to it for his dad. "Me, too. You're coming this weekend, right?"

"Saturday."

"Why don't you drive over tomorrow instead, as soon as the guys get out of school?"

"They'd like that." His father cleared his throat. "So would I, Reese. It . . . helps to be with you."

"I know, Pa. For me, too."

"Will Kate be around?"

"Yes, she wants to spend as much time as she can with the boys."

"Just the boys?"

He knew what his father was asking. He didn't want to give his dad false hope, but Bill Bishop could use some good news. "No, for you, too. And me. As you might guess, things have changed between us."

A male chuckle. "The little ones told me all about finding you two in bed together."

"Put a muzzle on them, will you? I don't want the whole world to know." Which wasn't quite true. "Nothing's been decided, Dad."

"Doesn't have to be now. It's not the best time to make big changes, anyway."

"I know. In any case, you'll get to see a lot of Kate."

"Good. Take care of yourself until I get there."

"Back at ya, Pa."

He felt better after talking with his father. It was amazing how people sharing their grief could shore up each other.

Throughout the morning, his colleagues stopped by, and he finally left the door open so they could offer condolences. When Greg Abbott came in, Reese asked him to sit down.

"Bring me up to speed on the Crane case. I'm sorry I dumped it into your lap."

"No problem. Good news, I think. I tracked down the gym teacher. Seems she had a hell of a time with the boys who tormented Mitchell."

"She document it?"

"Every single time. There's a whole paper trail of incriminating material. It'll go a long way when you present it at the trial. The school should have done something about this."

He watched Greg. The younger man would be wanting a partnership soon. "How about if you take over this case, Greg?"

"Really? I'd jump at the chance."

"You've done a lot of the legwork, anyway." He smiled. "It'll look great on your résumé."

Greg knew what Reese was saying. Bring this one home with the least amount of damage and his partnership was looking good. "I'll do my best, Reese. I think I can get minimum detention, probation, and counseling."

"That would be the best we could expect. Do it and things will go well here for you."

"Thanks." He stood. "You okay?"

"Yeah. I'm rethinking my priorities."

"If there's anything else I can do, holler."

"Just holding down the fort here means a lot to me. You and the others."

"You can count on us."

No sooner had Greg left than the phone rang. He let Yolanda get it. She was at his door promptly. "Reese, Jane Summers is on the line."

He drew a blank.

"From the nominating committee. For the criminal court judgeship."

Shit, he'd forgotten all about that. The head of the committee was probably calling to tell him that because the Bingham case had dragged on so long, his name had been withdrawn. Somehow getting the judgeship didn't mean as much anymore, so he took the call with calm resignation. "Hello, Jane."

"Reese. I'm calling to offer my condolences about your sister."

"Oh. Thanks."

They made small talk.

"There's something else," she said.

Here it comes.

"I want to assure you, especially now since things must be tough all around, that you're still on the nomination ticket. The Bingham situation needs to be settled in your favor, of course. But when it is, I believe the appointment will go through."

Under ordinary circumstances, he would have been elated. But the emotion just wasn't there. However, the vote of confidence felt good. "Jane, thanks so much for calling to tell me this."

"I thought you could use some good news."

Reese hung up and turned to his computer. But he couldn't stop thinking about Abbott and the call from Jane. He was shocked to feel apathy about assigning one of his cases to a younger man and giving him all the kudos that would accompany the outcome. And it surprised him to suspect, deep in his heart, that the judgeship carried little weight now. He could live without it.

Maybe it was just the yawning expanse of loss he felt about Emily.

But maybe not. Maybe his priorities *were* changing, just like he'd told Greg. He pictured his robust father leveled by the loss of Emily; he pictured Sofie's face, Jason and Jimmy, and now Kate.

And Reese wondered if in death, life took on new meaning.

AT FOUR O'CLOCK, Kate sat on the bench in her courtroom and faced a man who was seeking custody of his children. This was a hearing to determine if the case would go forward to trial.

Kate focused on the petitioner's lawyer. "All right, Mr. Clarke. Tell me why your client is here."

The petitioner himself, an Edward Riker, spoke instead. "She's a damned lesbian. She's corrupting my girls."

"Mr. Jones, please inform your client that sexual-orientation slurs will get him nowhere. And may harm his case."

The lawyer spoke softly to his client.

"Go ahead, Mr. Clarke."

"My client contends that his ex-wife's lifestyle is unhealthy for his daughters."

Kate checked the notes. "And his daughters are thirteen and fifteen?"

"Yes, Your Honor."

"I don't see any negative reports from CWA. They are in good health, doing well in school, no record of police intervention at the home." She looked up, faking surprise. She knew exactly what was going on here. Bigotry. "What's the problem?"

"My client is worried their mother's lifestyle will rub off on them." Even Kevin Clarke seemed embarrassed.

"Do the girls object to their mother's lifestyle?"

"No, Your Honor."

"Because she lets them get away with murder." Again, Riker spoke out of turn.

"Are the daughters here?" Kate asked.

"No, Judge Renado, they're in school."

"First off, I need to speak with the girls." Kate turned to the mother, a beautiful woman who looked a little like Princess Di. "Ms. Ackerman. Would you like to make a comment?"

"Yes, Your Honor. Our family is all female. My partner, Josie, has two girls, who also live with us. We all love each other and are getting along fine."

"Oh, great. One big happy homo family."

"Mr. Riker! I will not listen to this harassment."

"She's a pig!"

"Mr. Riker!"

"Makin' my girls into dykes . . ."

"That's it." Kate pounded the gavel. "I want him in a cell for contempt."

Riker bolted off his chair. "You can't do this to me. She's the one you should lock up."

Again Kate used the gavel to shut him up. "And I'm fining you one hundred dollars." She turned to the attorneys.

"I'm ordering a CWA investigation into the matter, and I expect to speak to the girls asap. Ms. Ackerman, we'll see you in . . ."

"Two weeks," Portia said.

The guards dragged the man out kicking and screaming at Kate. Something about his diatribe was familiar. She was trying to place it, when Portia leaned over. "Hell. Just like that Buckman case five months ago."

"Ah, yes. The Buckman case." She pictured a large man. Remembered a gravelly voice. Something about the memory tugged at her. "Herbert Buckman didn't get personal like this one though. He wasn't happy, but he was mostly full of hot air."

"No, Judge, he *threatened* you. You were leaving for your chambers, but we all heard it."

"I didn't hear it. Must be I was out of the courtroom by then." She thought for a moment. "Oh, no, Portia. I didn't put Buckman on my list of suspects when I was assaulted."

"Oh, Lord. I'm so sorry. I honestly thought you heard it. We didn't talk about it afterward, because we had an emergency right away. But I'm sure he threatened you."

"What did he say?"

"Something along the lines of . . . he'd get you. When you least expected it."

She drew in a breath to calm herself. "I need a recess to call the police."

Kate rushed to her chambers and called the detective in charge of her case. It would go a long way to cheering her up if Buckman was found to be the one who assaulted her two weeks ago—and she wouldn't need an escort to and from where she parked.

At the end of the workday, she got her wish. The police found Buckman, and because he was drunk, he admitted to the whole thing to them. Kate had put his son in protective custody because of his drinking and Buckman was striking out at her. His plan had been to rough her up enough to scare her. He'd succeeded.

She dialed Reese's number right away.

"Bishop," he said into the phone, sounding weary.

"Reese, it's Kate."

"It's good to hear your voice."

"I have some good news."

"Really? I do, too."

"You go first."

He told her about the judgeship.

She told him about her attacker. "This means no more escorts needed to and from the parking garage."

"I'm glad. But still be careful."

"Maybe things are finally looking up," she said.

"Maybe. With any luck Sanders will make some headway today, too." A beep sounded. "Can you hold on a second? I'm afraid that's the boys."

She waited on the line until he came back.

"More good news. Sanders says that Warden Evans has the tape of visitors for the last few months. It took a while to find the ones where Bingham was videoed. She released it to him for us. He's going to drive up and get it. We can watch it tomorrow night after the boys go to bed."

"Wonderful." She hesitated. "Um, what about tonight?"

He waited a beat. "What about it, Katie?" She loved the tease in his voice. Maybe "that boy" really could come back.

"I want to see you, hotshot."

"I love hearing that. I'm swamped here though."

"I'm done for the day. I'll head home, and you can come over when you finish. I'll cook."

"Don't cook. We'll order out. Just like old times."

And that, Kate thought, was the heart of the matter. Everything did indeed seem like old times.

FRIDAY NIGHT WAS the piéce de résistance. They sat in Reese's family room in front of the TV. The boys were asleep—after an exhausting reunion with Reese and Kate, and a dinner where the fondness wore off and they got cranky. Reese had wrestled them into the shower, then to bed, and looked weary himself. Bill Bishop was in the den where he was sleeping on the pull-out couch.

They put in the videotape of A's and B's visits and watched it run. Chase Sanders had already seen it, and earmarked the spots that were important, so they got to see the men consecutively. He was excited, but wouldn't tell them why. He said he needed their confirmation for what he thought he saw in the tapes.

Reese caught on quickly. "Arnie Anders has the same watch on as Bernie Benson."

Clued in now, Kate looked for similarities. "And they're the same height and build.

By the time they'd seen all the tapes, one fact became clear.

Reese vocalized it. "Both men on the tapes are the same person. They're in disguise—or at least one is, but I'd bet both are concealing their identities."

Kate frowned. "How did they manage that?"

"They must have had fake ID's," Reese guessed.

"But why, Chase? Why would the same person disguise himself two different ways? Visits aren't limited to how many times one person can go to the prison."

Sanders said, "If we can answer that question, I think we'll have solved this case."

"Where do we go from here?" Reese shook his head. "I know this must be a breakthrough, but I don't understand how."

"Truthfully, I don't, either. I'm going to take these tapes home and review them over the weekend. I suggest you scrutinize the journal again in that time also. We might have missed something."

"Speaking of the journal, did you talk to Anita Ruiz, the prisoner who tangled with Bingham?"

"No she was in solitary confinement."

Reese looked up sharply. "Interesting coincidence."

"I thought so, too. I'll go back up next week when she gets out. Meanwhile"—Sanders nodded to the TV—"this has to be real headway. We don't know yet how it fits into the Bingham puzzle, but it has to. Be happy about this."

Kate smiled at him. "We are."

Reese showed Sanders out and returned to the family room. "That's something, isn't it?"

"Yeah. I don't know what to make of it though."

"We just have to have faith."

She stared up at him.

"In everything, Katie."

"All right. I'll have faith."

"Good, I will, too."

A shout from upstairs in the boys' room had them both running. It was probably a good thing, Reese thought, as he followed Kate up. Like he'd said yesterday, this was no time for promises.

Eighteen

Just like one big happy family, they walked into West-wood Lanes for an afternoon of bowling. The crack of balls hitting pins, the shouts of good play, and the buzz of machinery resonated around them. Reese hung on to Jason's hand, Kate to Jimmy's; Pa had his arm around Sofie, who'd surprised them by taking the train home for the weekend. As it was early May, she only had a few weeks of school left.

Kate smiled over at Reese. He smiled back. They were being very careful about physical contact, about these kinds of intimate glances. They had to be circumspect so Pa, the boys and Sofie wouldn't expect too much. But it was hard for Kate not to touch Reese. Not only were they still dealing with their own unsorted emotions for each other, but since Jimmy and Jason arrived yesterday, they'd been a handful. Pa was at his wit's end. Reese's suggestion to get everybody out of the house today seemed good at the time.

"I don't wanna bowl," Jimmy whined, shrugging off Kate's grasp.

"Oh, sweetie, at home, you said you did." Kate was unsure of how much to push and be firm, or whether she should just be patient and let the boys act out.

"Jimmy's not bowling?" Sofie turned back and feigned shock. "Then I won't have a partner." She gave him what Reese used to call his daughter's *you're dead meat* look.

"'Kay. I will," Jimmy said.

Sofie grabbed his hand and Jason's and said to the others, "Beat you to lane fifteen." Together, the three of them loped down the alley.

Kate moved in closer to Reese and, since no one was watching them, touched his forearm. It was bare, as he wore an oversize check shirt with black jeans. She was dressed casually, too, in a white blouse and capri jeans. "Another disaster averted."

"They're cranky because they didn't get enough sleep." Reese looked worn, too. "I finally let them come into my room and lie down with me at about three. I forgot how much work kids were."

Pa slowed his steps and walked with them. "They're gonna live with you, Son, you best get used to it."

"He will, Pa," Kate told her ex-father-in-law. "It's just going to take adjustment."

"I wish school was done." Bill Bishop gave them a defeated look. "I think they're better with you two than they are with me or the Gates."

"I can get a tutor," Reese offered as they neared the lanes designated for their use. Sofie and the boys were off to the side of the alley picking out balls.

Pa shook his head, frowning. "No. The original plan's best. The Gates deserve their time with the boys. Besides, I don't know what I'm going to do when they leave North Falls." His voice cracked and he glanced away.

Reese stopped short and watched his father. "I do."

His face ragged, Pa looked at Reese. Kate's heart broke at the sight of the man's suffering. He was totally lost. "You know what I'm going to do?" he asked his son.

"Uh-huh. You're coming to Westwood with them, Pa."

"What?"

"You're going to live with us. Permanently."

"Nonsense. I got a life in North Falls. Friends. A house."

"You can go visit your friends anytime you want. You can sell your house. You belong with us, Pa. And I need you here."

"You do?" The older man's tone was so hopeful, Kate's eyes misted.

"I've been giving this a lot of thought. Family should be together." His glance to Kate was meaningful. "It's how you survive the bad times."

"I guess I wouldn't mind." Pa's brightened expression told Kate that was an understatement. "That couch in the den's okay."

Reese grinned, his own expression lightening. "I think we can do better than that. We'll iron out the details later."

Pa gave Reese a huge hug. "Can't tell you how much this means to me, Son."

"I want this, too."

"Can I tell the boys?" he asked, like a little kid himself.

"Go ahead."

When Pa drew back, he slid an arm around Kate and hugged her close. "Don't this beat all, Kate?"

She had trouble speaking past the lump in her throat. "It does."

Pa hurried ahead. Reese started after him, but Kate remained rooted to the spot. "What's wrong?" Reese asked when he realized she'd stilled.

She shook her head.

"Don't you think I should have done that?" His face blanked. "Oh, shit, should I have asked you first? In case we get back . . . ah, Kate, I'm not thinking right."

"You're thinking just fine."

"Then what are you . . . ?" His expression turned curious. "You're looking at me the way you used to when we were young."

"That's because I'm thinking what a good man you are.

Somehow I lost sight of that. I want you to know, Reese Bishop, if there was any doubt in my mind that I was still in love with you, it's all gone now."

He crossed to her, blocking the view of the rest of the family. He locked his hand at her neck and kissed her head. "Me, too, baby. These last few days have made me sure about how I feel, too."

Pa's news lifted everybody's mood, and bowling turned out to be fun. When Reese and his dad were up on opposite lanes and the boys were drawing on the score sheet, Sofie came to sit by Kate: She was dressed normally in a short denim skirt and a pretty pink T-shirt. "Mama?"

"What, sweetie?"

"Do you think you can take me to Margaret's salon after bowling?"

Margaret was Kate's hairdresser, and used to be Sofie's.

"I can call and see if she'll squeeze you in," Kate said carefully nonchalant. "Why?"

Sofie's hand crept to her hair. "I . . ." She looked directly at Kate. The baby Kate had birthed, the toddler she'd raised, the teenager who used to love her, surfaced. Sofie wrinkled her nose. "I hate this," she said. "I don't know why I did it."

"Anger at me and Dad, rebellion against something you couldn't control."

"It was stupid."

"Some things in life are fixable, honey." Kate squeezed her daughter's shoulder. "We're lucky this is one of them."

Sofie nodded to her dad. "He's better when you're around. This morning, when I got to his house and you were at your place, he was so depressed, it scared me. As soon as you came over, he cheered up."

"Sofie, nothing's been decided about me and Dad. There are still things we need to work out."

So much like her dad, Sofie gave her a skeptical look: "But you're thinking about getting back together, aren't you?"

"It's come up."

"You still sleeping with Tyler?"

"Honey, that's private."

Sofie went on in that irrepressible way teenagers have even when they'd invaded personal territory. "I know Dray moved out. Just tell me if you're still seeing Tyler?"

"No, I'm not, but Sofie, don't get your hopes up."

"Okay. That's all I need right now." She leaned over and kissed Kate's cheek. "I'll wait and see."

When it was her turn to bowl, Sofie went up to the lane. Pa began to give her pointers, and Reese came back to sit with Kate.

"What was that all about?" he asked.

Kate reiterated the conversation. "Without meaning to, I think we got her hopes up."

Reese squeezed her hand and didn't let go. "She's not the only one."

The words frightened Kate. But not enough to make her back away. She held Reese's hand tightly, and watched Sofie get a strike. Maybe everybody would be as lucky as her daughter.

"I WANNA EAT!" This time, Jason was acting up, while Reese was trying to fix dinner. Kate had taken Sofie to the beauty salon and his dad and Jimmy were napping.

"Soon, buddy."

"Where's Sofie?"

"With Aunt Kate at the hairdresser."

"Mommy used to take us to the hairdresser when she went." And with that memory, Jason burst into tears.

"Aw, buddy." Reese quickly crossed to his nephew, picked him up and hugged him. "I know it hurts."

The boy buried his face in Reese's chest. "I want Mommy."

"You know she's in heaven."

"Why?"

Dropping down on a chair, he rocked Jason. His own heart was torn to shreds by his nephew's despair. "I don't know, Jase. I just don't know."

When the emotional moment passed, Reese set the boy down. "As soon as I finish with the sauce, I'll color with you while it cooks."

"We brought our crayons and paper."

"Good, go get your stuff and I'll meet you in the family room."

Reese made quick work of browning the meatballs he'd made and got the sauce simmering. He found Jason in the family room, at the coffee table, a big box of crayons spilled out over sheets of papers. He was scowling and scribbling at the same time.

When Reese reached him, he saw that Jimmy was coloring the pages Kate had ripped out of Anna Bingham's journal for him to look at. Jesus Christ.

He bit his tongue not to snap the boy. What did it matter anyway? They'd gotten copies made. "Hey, buddy, that's state's evidence there. Let's substitute some drawing paper for it."

Jason looked up at Reese with rebellious eyes. Reese was reminded of Emily when she was little. "I wanna color in the secret 'partment, but I can't open it."

"A secret compartment?"

"Uh-huh. I found it when the book dropped to the floor." His eyes misted. "I didn't mean to Uncle Reese, honest. I think I ruined it. Some shiny stuff came off."

"No harm done, Jase." Reese's heartbeat escalated. "Just show me, okay?"

And as soon as Reese picked up the journal, he realized what had been bothering him when he'd first seen it. Nancy Bingham had given him the key found in her sister's personal effects. But the journal the warden had provided didn't have a lock on the front.

However, the secret compartment, visible only when Jimmy dropped the journal and dislodged the false backing—the shiny stuff—did indeed have a little steel locking device.

Hurrying to his den, Reese tiptoed in so as not to awaken his father and found the key in his desk. Back in the family room, he tried it on the journal and, sure enough, it opened the lock. Inside Reese found several pages of entries.

And he knew in his heart, he'd just struck gold.

SOFIE LIKED HER hair a lot better, now that it was back to its natural color. Margaret had scolded her for bleaching it, but that was cool. Sofie deserved it. She wished she could undo other damage she'd done with just a color and cut. The house smelled of spaghetti sauce and garlic bread when she walked in beside her mom. In the dining room ahead the table was set, but her father was nowhere in sight.

"Where's Daddy?" she wondered aloud.

"In here." He called out from the family room. "Bring Mom."

They'd come in the front door and stepped into family room. Jason was coloring at the coffee table, and her dad was on the floor, papers sprawled out before him. When he looked up, Sofie saw his face was animated like it hadn't been since before Aunt Emily died.

"Hey, princess, you look terrific. Like my little girl again."

She crossed to him and kissed his cheek. "I know, Daddy."

"What's happened?" her mother asked, coming up to them. Her rigid stance said she expected bad news. But Sofie was seeing something different in her father's expression.

Jason said, "I found the secret 'partment, Aunt Kate. Uncle Reese says I saved the day."

Her mom sent her dad a puzzled expression.

"He did, Katie." He held up some kind of book. "Anna Bingham's journal had a secret compartment."

"Oh my God."

Her father grinned.

"You said something was niggling at you about the journal."

"Yeah, no lock. At least not in the front part. But the secret compartment was locked. That's why the book has such a thick backing."

"Good news?"

"Uh-huh. Seems like Mr. Alphabet Man was blackmailing Anna Bingham."

"For what?"

"I don't know yet. She calls him DD. But says he's the same as the two guys who visited."

"DD as in the ring."

"Yep."

"Does she identify him?"

"No, she was about to, but the entries stopped just before she could."

"Come color with me, Sofie." This from her cousin.

"Cool, Dad." Sofie sat down to play with Jason, but listened to her parents' conversation.

"DD was in collusion with the guard, Nell Sorenson. They got evidence of some bad behavior that could extend Bingham's sentence. For a fee, which Bingham could very well afford on the outside, the guard was willing to overlook it."

"Did she pay them?"

"Some. To stall them. But she was furious. These entries plot just how she was going to outsmart this DD."

"Does it implicate the guy in her death?"

"No. But it sure as hell implies that she didn't commit suicide. The last entry was the day before she died. She's mad as hell, but not depressed."

"This is big, isn't it, Reese?"

"Yeah, sweetheart, this is big!"

Sofie watched them. Man, it was good to see them click like this, help and support each other. *That* looked pretty big to her, too.

THEY SHARED THE discovery of the hidden journal entries with Chase Sanders over the phone on Sunday morning when Pa took the boys to St. Peter's for church.

Sanders asked for copies to be faxed to him; he wanted to wait to meet with them until Monday night, after he'd visited Longshore. He also wanted the warden to see the journal entries. His comments were self-effacing and pithy. "Hell of a thing that an eight-year-old finds the jackpot when a lawyer, judge and private investigator missed any trace of it."

Kate volunteered to fax the papers to Chase while Reese showered. She wanted to read the entries for herself anyway. Last night had been busy with the boys and Sofie and Pa. Reese had summarized the contents for her, but she wanted to see firsthand what was going on. When she finished faxing, she sat down and scrutinized Anna's Bingham's words. Several salient points stood out.

First . . .

Do you fucking believe it? DD's blackmailing me. Says he's got proof from one of the guards of my *misbehavior*, and I won't see the world anytime soon if that so-called information makes itself into the warden's hands. Damn it. He told me the disguises were to mislead the guards and the prison. But they were really for this, so nobody knows his real identity. Who the hell is in on this with him?

Next . . .

It's Sorensen; she caught Lena and me snorting some coke. Of course, she provided the stuff, then took pictures of us doing it. We're fucked, big time.

Another . . .

We'll see who has the last laugh. I got a plan . . .

A fourth entry . . .

Lena's acting funny. She says it's just the blackmail. She wants me to give in.

A fifth . . .

I had a scuffle with Ruiz. Then a picture of us rolling on the floor turns up in my bunk. He's playing dirty. Must be Sorensen is working me, too. I could kill her.

A final one . . .

I'm in the infirmary. I tripped and fell. Lena says Ruiz did it when I walked by her in the chow room. I hate to say this, but now I'm scared. I need to tell somebody who he is.

The last entry was never finished.

Reese came into the family room, carrying some coffee and the morning paper. His hair was damp and his feet bare. He wore a plain white T-shirt and sweatpants. And he smelled wonderful. Kate was hit by a sudden bolt of lust for her ex-husband, and it made her smile.

"Why the grin?"

"No reason you need to know."

He cocked his head, and when she said no more, he nodded to the entries she still held. "They're something else, aren't they?"

She accepted the coffee. "Thanks. Yes, they are. It's all got to mean something for the case, right? Bingham was being blackmailed, so maybe DD killed her to keep it quiet."

"That's my conclusion. But I still can't figure out how this involves us. We don't know any of the parties involved. And looking for DD is a long shot."

"We've got to be connected somehow."

They discussed possibilities for a while, but when they came to a wall, they left it to relax before the boys returned. Reese picked up the World News section of the newspaper, and Kate opted for the Local section. Funny, how they fell back into old patterns.

She scanned the front page. "Damn it. Eddie Wick's got an article on the guy they arrested for assaulting me. I wish he'd back off. I hate this notoriety."

"Hmm. He's a busy guy. Here's his byline on an article in the National News section. Why would he . . ." Reese's eyes widened. "Shit, I didn't even look at the headline."

Alarmed, Kate put down the paper. "What is it?"

"SECOND INMATE DIES IN PRISON." Reese skimmed the words. "Kate, it's from Longshore."

"Who was killed?"

"Anita Ruiz."

"Oh, no."

He read further. "It mentions us. That's why Wick wrote it."

"Hell, Reese, what's next?"

"I have feeling the whole thing's all coming to a head."

"I can't believe—"

The doorbell rang. Reese looked over at her. "I don't want to answer that. Lord knows what piece of the sky is going to fall next."

"Maybe we don't have to. Pa, the boys and Sofie aren't due back from church for a while."

One more peal of the bell and the front door opened, then closed. A shuffling. Into the family room walked Dray Merrill. Her gaze shifted turned from Reese to Kate, then back to Reese. "You didn't waste any time."

"Dray." He stood. "Are you all right?"

"Just peachy. I came over to get some papers of mine in your safe. I forgot them when I left. Since you're here, I'll give you back your house keys." She set them on a side table.

Kate stood. "I'll leave you two alone."

Dray gave her a searing look. For some reason Kate asked, "Have you seen Tyler?"

"Yes. He's miserable. You could have called him. To see how he is." She focused on Reese, and tossed back skeins of light hair. "You should have called me, too."

"I'm sorry."

"Same old, same old."

"I'll call Tyler right now." Kate left Dray with Reese

and went into the kitchen. She punched in Tyler's cell phone number from there. He answered right away. "Sloan."

"Tyler, it's Kate."

No response.

"I called to see how you were."

"Oh, just fine." He still sounded angry.

"I'm sorry I didn't call before."

"Why did you now?"

"Lots of reasons." She wasn't about to tell him Dray Merrill had shamed her into remembering to do it. "Dray just stopped by to get stuff out of Reese's safe. I asked how you were, then I decided to call and see for myself."

"Dray's there?"

"Yes."

"How is she? I've been trying to reach her and can't get her."

"She seems sad, and upset. Do you want to talk to her?"

"Yes."

"Before you do, I just wanted to say I'm sorry. Again."

"Understood. Now get Dray."

God this was strange. But Kate went back into the family room. Reese was just removing papers from the safe; Kate handed Dray the phone. "Tyler wants to talk to you."

At the questioning look from Reese, Kate shrugged. Who the hell knew what this was all about?

Dray took the phone gingerly. "Hello."

Tyler must be talking.

"No, I can't today. I'm looking at houses . . . Yes, I know I can't . . . Oh, all right, I'll meet you at Starbucks . . . Fine, then."

She clicked off. Kate quelled a question and it seemed as if Reese did, too. Dray took the papers from him, and turned away. "I'm going."

"I'll walk you to the door." Reese took her arm, but she shrugged it off. Still he followed her out.

"Good-bye, Dray," Kate called after them.

She didn't respond. No surprise there.

DRAY SEEMED DETERMINED to bolt as fast as she could, but Reese tugged her back just as she opened the door. "Wait a second, Dray."

Her back to him, her shoulders stiffened in the pretty pink summer blouse she was wearing. "I don't have anything more to say to you."

"I know. I have something to say to you." He tugged her around.

"If it's more of the I-don't-know-what-I'm-doing stuff, forget it, we're through."

"I know we are. I just wanted to say good-bye."

Her blue eyes moistened. "So you've decided to marry Kate."

"Nothing's gone that far. We're embroiled in new developments from the case."

"Are you going to be able to prove your innocence?"

"I think so."

Her expression softened. "I'm glad, Reese. I knew you didn't do anything wrong."

"Thanks for believing in me." He shifted from one foot to the other, uncomfortable in her presence because he was ashamed of what he'd done. "Dray, I wish I could have given you what you wanted."

She nodded to the family room. "She was always between us, Reese. I knew it all along."

"Honestly, I didn't."

"I realize that. It's the only thing that makes me not hate you."

"I'm glad you don't. Good luck, honey. In finding a house, in everything."

"I'll be fine. I hope you're happy."

"Thanks." He didn't spout platitudes, like she was a wonderful person, or someday she'd find love. He always hated those candy-ass sentiments.

Surprising him, she stood on her toes and kissed his cheek. Then she walked out of his life. He watched her go, again feeling deep regret for hurting her.

When he returned to the family room, Kate looked up from the paper. "Did you say good-bye?"

"Yes. It was . . . tough."

She gave him a weak smile.

"What the hell was all that about with her and Tyler, do you think?"

"Who knows?" Kate pushed her hair off her face. She was wearing it down and curly most days now. Along with a soft green outfit made of linen, she looked young. "That whole thing was odd."

"Damn it, Kate, everything's off." He nodded to the newspaper. "What do you think it means about Ruiz getting killed?"

"I don't know, but I'm going to call Chase again."

"We're ruining his Sunday."

"Ours isn't shaping up so well, either, Reese." She looked after Dray. "I feel bad for her. And Tyler."

"I know. I feel like a shit." He ran his hand through his hair. "Let's call Chase Sanders again."

TYLER SIPPED HIS latte and watched Dray enter Starbucks. She seemed slight in stonewashed jeans and a baby pink blouse. When she got close, he could see she'd been crying.

"What did that bastard do to you now?" he asked without even greeting her.

"Nothing. And hello to you, too."

He gave her a sheepish look. "I'm sorry." He leaned over and gave her a kiss on the cheek. "Hello. Are you all right?"

"As well as can be expected." She sat and smiled at the coffee he'd ordered, just like old times when they were trying to keep Kate and Reese apart. They'd failed, miserably. "To answer your question, Reese did nothing to me. I went over his house, hoping he wasn't home. I needed my papers from the safe for buying a house. Anyway, when he didn't answer the doorbell, I let myself in. He and Kate were in the family room, like a married couple, having coffee, reading the Sunday paper."

"I'm sorry." That's exactly what Tyler and Kaitlyn used to do, but he pushed away the thought.

"Did you talk to Kate?" Dray asked.

"Briefly. Did you tell her to call me?"

"No." She was lying, but Tyler let that slide.

"It doesn't matter now." He sipped his coffee, too, then reached out and grasped her hand. "Why haven't you returned my calls?"

She twisted the thermal holder on her cup. "I . . . I was embarrassed."

"I am, too."

On Wednesday morning, when they'd awakened together in bed, she'd asked him to leave right away, without talking about anything that had happened the night before. He'd gone because he was chagrined by what they'd done, too, and he had a hangover and he didn't know what to say to her anyway. During the week, he'd tried to call her though.

"Tyler? I asked why you wanted to see me."

"I can't leave things between us like this, Dray."

She blushed. "We were pretty drunk. Do you . . . remember what we did?"

"Of course. Finally, I remembered why."

She shook back her hair. "I did, too. We were comforting each other. We took solace in a little recreational sex, so what was the harm?"

"No harm in it, as far as I'm concerned. I was afraid you regretted it."

"I only regret it if I've lost you as a friend."

"You haven't. I'll always be your friend."

Dray watched Tyler's eyes turn a deeper blue. They did that when something hurt him. He was such a kind, sensitive, sympathetic man. If the situation were different, they might have been able to build something together.

"What are you thinking? You look so sad."

"Honestly?"

"Please."

"I was thinking that if things were different, we might have been able to have something together. I like you, Tyler, and truthfully, the sex—what I remember of it—was great."

"Any relationship between us could never work, I know. The last thing you need is another man in your life who's hung up on Kaitlyn Renado."

"And the last thing you need is another woman in love with Reese."

"Been there, done that," he joked.

At least he still had his sense of humor. "I should have taken your calls; you always make me feel better."

"You do that for me, too."

"So, I guess we're square?"

He grinned. "Uh-huh." He smiled. "You're looking for a house?"

"Yes, I got some listings from the newspaper. I'm heading over to see a couple this afternoon."

"Want company?"

"I'd love some."

He held out his hand. "Friends?"

She took it, feeling marginally better. "Friends." As they stood to go, Dray felt a twinge of regret. Tyler was off limits because of Kate Renado.

Damn the woman.

NINETEEN

AFTER COURT ON Monday morning, Kate headed for the courthouse cafeteria for lunch. She smiled sadly, thinking how Tyler had often brought her food, and they'd spend a short half hour together. In truth, she missed him, but she couldn't regret what had happened. Apparently she had always loved Reese—something Tyler had feared and repeatedly voiced to her; it wasn't fair to pretend otherwise with a good man like him. She intended to call him today and ask to see him one more time to say a final good-bye.

She was halfway through her BLT when she looked up and saw Reese heading toward her table. He wore a beautiful light tan suit that went well with his coloring. There was spring in his step; he appeared more rested. "Hi," he said when he reached her.

"Hi."

His green eyes were mischievous. There was a glimpse of that boy she had married again. "Do you have any idea how much I want to lean over this table and kiss you?"

She giggled, like a schoolgirl, not a judge. "I think I do. But it would surely shock the assembled crowd here to see that. Try to control yourself." Then low and sultry, she added, "At least for right now."

"Ah, I'd forgotten how lethal you are when you flirt." He sat down and placed a bag on the table.

She said, "I didn't know you were in court today."

"I'm not. I brought you something."

She focused on the bag. "What is it?"

"Insurance." He smiled, a bit self-effacingly. "Open it."

Inside she found something which resembled brass knuckles and a canister of some kind. "Not exactly hearts and flowers."

"You want hearts and flowers, I'll send them later. These are equally important."

She studied the devices. "Pepper spray and a key ring with a weapon on it?"

His casual pose, leaning back in the chair, was deceptive. His gaze had intensified. "You going to and from the parking garage alone doesn't sit well with me."

"Reese, they caught the guy who attacked me. He's in jail."

"I know. But humor me. This might be one of those lawyer hunches we talked about. Or it might just be paranoia. In any case, I'm unnerved by what happened to you before." He nodded to the weapons. "It won't hurt you to carry them."

She rolled her eyes. "All right."

"Give me your car keys."

She fished them out of her purse, handed them over, and watched him attach the brass knuckles. "These have holes for your fingers, but they'll only work if you have your keys in your hand when you need them." He finished the task and slid them on his own hand to show her how they worked. "I want you to promise me you'll use them every time you go into that garage. At least for a while."

"I guess."

"And carry the pepper spray in your hand, too; don't leave it in your purse or briefcase."

At her skeptical expression, his face darkened. "I know

it sounds extreme, but so much has happened, Kate. And I'm still uneasy about this whole Bingham thing. At least carry these until the case is solved. I don't want to lose you now that we've . . ." He trailed off.

She knew the finish line. *Now that we've found each other again.*

"I promise." He'd lost so much, even though he hadn't played that card on her.

He reached over and squeezed her hand. "Now, can I have some of that lemon meringue pie?"

She grinned. "You can have anything you want, Reese."

His eyes flared hotly. "Now there's a thought. Hold it until we can be alone."

For the rest of the day, Kate did indeed hold thoughts of her ex-husband, in her mind and close to her heart. It wasn't until she left her courtroom after the last session that she realized that for five years, her goal was to keep thoughts of him out of courtroom. She wasn't able to do that anymore because she believed in her heart they might just have a chance to make it work between them again. And she was going to take the opportunity when the time was right.

Because she was still thinking about him, as she packed files and her purse in her briefcase, she remembered to take out the pepper spray along with her keys. Then she left her chambers and took the elevator down to the ground floor parking.

As soon as the elevator opened at the garage level, she slid the new chain on her hand—it was bulky and awkward—and held on to the spray. She was also more alert, more watchful of her surroundings. Maybe Reese had spooked her, but he was right, she wouldn't take chances with her safety.

She met John, the guard, coming toward the elevator.

"Hi, John."

"Hello, Judge."

"I don't need an escort today."

He grinned. "Sure am glad they caught the guy." He

held up jumper cables. "Judge Jenkins's car won't start, so I'm heading over to the other side to help her out."

"I'll drive around to where she parks, and make sure she gets going."

"Don't think you need to, but go ahead."

Kate made her way down the second aisle to where her car was parked. At nearly seven, the garage was well lit and daylight still streamed from the windows. She was thinking about spring, and how nice it was to have the warm weather; she'd just popped the lock on her Eclipse, when a shadow from behind blocked the light.

Her heart beat faster; dropping the briefcase on the ground, and gripping the key ring and pepper spray, she whirled around. When she saw the man in the ski mask, she thought *Not this time* and raised her arm. But before she released the pepper spray into his eyes, the man grabbed her wrist. The canister fell to the concrete with a clank. She saw him grin at the triumph of disarming her, and felt adrenaline flow into her body as his grip released fractionally. She yanked the hand he held out of his grasp and with her other, she sliced the jagged edges of the key chain down the side his face. He growled in pain as metal cut through the knit material and his skin. When he recoiled, Kate pulled at the mask. Though his hand had clapped to one side of his face, and there was a lot of blood, she got a good look at the guy before he managed to push her away and turn tail and run.

REESE WAS LIKE a caged tiger at the police station. He waited in a conference room with Kate, pacing and swearing. At least she wasn't hurt this time, though she was shaken. Her face was pale against her red linen dress and her hands trembled a bit. His heart had practically stopped when he got her call telling him about another attack in the garage.

"Jesus Christ, Kate, this can't be a coincidence."

"No, it was intentional. The police detective said the

first guy's still locked up." She drew in a heavy breath. "Apparently someone else is after me."

"Are you sure you recognized him?"

"Yes, but I have no idea from where. It could have been my courtroom, or from our practice. But I have feeling it was more fleeting than that since I can't place him. For some reason, I think I just saw him for a few minutes." She shook her head. "I'm not sure I'll be able to nail this down though."

He stopped behind her and kneaded her shoulders, letting the flowery scent of her hair soothe him. "I guess I should just be glad you're all right."

"It was your hunch."

"What?"

"I was thinking about your hunch. I got the pepper spray out and put the key chain on, but even unconsciously, I had my wits about me enough to react quickly." She shook her head. "So instead of just spooking me, you may have saved my life."

"Thank God." He ran a hand down her hair. "I don't know what I would have done . . ." He shook his head and dropped down into a chair beside her. "The hell with waiting until things are settled. I love you. We're getting back together now and giving our marriage another shot. I won't take no for an answer."

Before she could respond—damn it—a detective entered the room. "Judge Renado." He nodded to Reese. "I'm Detective Pike."

"Reese Bishop, Kate's husband."

Pike addressed Kate. "I need to go over the statement you gave to the officer on the scene. Then I'd like you to work with a police sketch artist. You got a good look at the guy, right?"

"Yes. I can do that. And I'm sure I know him from somewhere."

"Are you feeling up to this? The best time to do these sketches is right after the contact. Victims remember more."

"Now is fine."

Reese said, "This is going to take a while. I'll call Sanders and change our meeting till tomorrow." He headed out the door, but looked back through the glass window once he had closed it. She seemed in control and calm now, but he couldn't shake the thought of what could have happened to her.

Chase Sanders had the same thought. "This has to be related to the case. I'll be interested to see the police sketch."

An hour later, Reese got a look at the finished product. His breath caught in his throat. "Holy hell. I recognize him, too."

"Who is it?" the detective asked.

"I can't place him, either. But I'm sure I've seen him before."

"This is good news." Pike stood and thanked the artist who left them alone. "The fact that you both recognize him establishes a connection between you two and the attacker."

Kate shook her head. "But if it was a case we handled together, we'd remember him more clearly. We wouldn't forget a client we worked with for any period of time."

"Still, there's a tie between you two and this guy."

"Again," Reese said thoughtfully. "There's another tie between us."

KATE FACED REESE across her kitchen table and lifted her chin. "I'm not going to change my mind. You can yell all you like, though I suggest you get rid of that temper before Chase arrives."

"Temper? You think this is just temper?" Reese threw back his chair, stood and slapped his hand on the table. "God save me from stubborn females who are careless with their own fucking safety."

"I am *not* being careless with my safety just because I won't move in with you. I stayed at your house last night because you wanted me to. Today I made other arrangements."

"What? Having Jillian here? That's a fine solution! The

thought of the two of you against some lunatic will really make me sleep better at night."

"I have an alarm system. And the police are going to cruise by regularly."

"It's not enough."

She slapped *her* hand down on the table. "Stop it, Reese. I'll make my own decisions."

His face shadowed with hurt, but his tone was still belligerent. "Well, I guess I've been jumping the gun here. I thought we were making important decisions together these days."

"We are. But the fact remains, that if I move in with you like you're demanding, we'll just get everybody's hopes up, including our own."

"Would that be so bad?"

"Yes, we can't afford to fall back into this relationship because we're grieving over Emily or because we're frightened about this turn of events with the Bingham case."

"I love you! I told you at the police station it was time to stop pussyfooting around."

"You were upset. Now you're just mad. *You're* the one who's being stubborn."

"Well, pardon me for wanting you safe."

The doorbell again.

She stood. "That's probably Jillian."

Reese let loose more expletives and turned to pour himself a drink. Shaking her head, Kate headed to the foyer. She found Jillian on the doorstep.

"Hey, girlfriend," Jill said. "Ready for our sleepover?"

Kate smiled. "I am, but Reese is here and furious because I won't move in with him." Kate took Jillian's suitcase from her, and they found their way to the spare room to put it there. She filled Jill in on the situation as they went back to the kitchen. Reese wasn't in any better mood.

"Hi, Reese," Jill said.

He didn't even greet her. "I suppose you agree with this little plan?"

Jillian cocked her head. "It's what Kate wants. She chooses."

He rolled his eyes to the ceiling.

"But for what it's worth, much as I want to spend time with my best friend, I do think she should move in with you for a while."

"Jillian!"

"Sorry, Kate. We've always been honest with each other."

Kate sniffed. "If you don't want to be here, you don't have to stay."

Jill shook her head. "Don't be an ass. I'm staying here because you asked me to, and I'd do anything for you. I can't help it if Reese's right. And while we're at it, let me say I'm glad you two are finding your way back together. You've never gotten over him, Kate. I know that, and so do you." She shook her head. "Now, I'm going upstairs to unpack. I'll let you two finish fighting before your private investigator gets here."

Jillian left and Reese glared at Kate over his drink. He was leaning against the counter, dressed in faded blue jeans and a navy shirt. She just started to say something when the doorbell rang again. Kate gave him a long look then headed out to the foyer. She felt him follow behind her.

On the front stoop, Chase Sanders was more animated than Kate had ever seen him. "Kate." He looked over her shoulder. "Reese."

"Come on in, Chase."

Without greeting the private investigator, Reese grunted and walked back to the den ahead of them.

"What's that all about?" Chase whispered to Kate.

"Don't ask." She closed the door and led them back to the den where they'd worked with Tyler and Dray that awful day.

When they were all seated, Chase pulled a tape out of his briefcase, along with some papers.

"So where do we start?" Kate asked.

"With Warden Evans. She's pissed as hell about the accusations in the journal, and is taking measures to see if these things really happened. The fact that the guard Sorenson is nowhere to be found is incriminating. Evans has launched a full-fledged investigation. Yesterday, we started with Lena Parks. Evans called her in again, and she was cool as a cucumber. Too cool." He nodded to the tape. "So I took a look at this."

"The tape of Bingham's visitors?"

"Nope, of Parks's visitors."

"And?" Kate asked.

"Watch."

He put the tape in the deck and pressed play. "This is only one of several tapes of the woman and her visitors. I cross-checked the dates and the guy you're going to see only came to visit Parks when Bingham didn't have company."

They watched the scene unfold. At first Kate suspected Chase had found the Alphabet Man on the tape, but he didn't. "It's not Mr. AB."

"No, but it's the same man, using a different alias. Chuck Cramer. We got Mr. *C.* Look closely."

Both she and Reese leaned in. She said, "The same watch again."

"Shit." Reese scowled. "This guy really gets around."

"He does. And if he's meeting with Parks, maybe she was in on this blackmail with Sorenson."

Kate stared at the screen. "Can you freeze it?"

"Sure."

She got up and crossed to the desk, ferreting out the police sketch she'd done that afternoon. Crossing to Chase, she handed him the picture. "Look at this. Same shape of the face, though he's disguised himself. Same height and build, I think. Hell. This might be the guy that attacked me. Do you still have the tape of his meetings with Bingham?"

"Yeah." He put it in the machine.

They watched carefully.

"It's the same guy." Sanders sat back in his chair. "Now, the only thing we have to do is figure out who he is."

"Or get Lena Parks to ID him." This from Reese.

"The warden's working on her." Sanders watched them. "Meanwhile, you two will have to go back to your files and take another look-see. Go through them with a fine-tooth comb. I think the answer's there somewhere."

"Oh, great," Kate said, glancing at Reese who had been stone faced the whole night. "We'd love to spend every free minute together again."

REESE SAT IN his office, waiting for Kate to join him to start scrutinizing the fucking files again. Sneakered feet up on his desk, dressed in sweats because he'd worked out earlier, he closed his eyes and tried to center himself. He had to be honest about why he was acting like a jerk. Down deep, he knew what he was doing. Going back into self-preservation mode. Because Kate wouldn't move in with him, he took it as a sign that she was backing out of the relationship. He knew he wasn't thinking clearly, but why the hell should he? Maybe he'd call Emily. She always . . .

Oh, Lord, he thought, a lump forming in his throat. He still did this once in a while. Thought about calling his sister. He even reached for the phone occasionally. His grief was still there, a heavy load in his chest that seemed as if it would never go away. Maybe his feelings of loss were why he was being such an ass with Kate.

Or maybe she *was* just being a damned stubborn female.

"Hi." His stubborn female's voice came from the doorway. He opened his eyes to find her standing there in a lightweight red sweat suit.

"Did you go *running*?" he asked without greeting her.

She sighed and leaned against the doorjamb. "Not alone. I went with Jillian. We left work early, when it was still daylight and we ran on public streets." She scowled at him. "Lay off, Reese."

His feet thumped to the floor. "Fine, forget it." He rose and crossed to a tall built-in wooden cabinet. "Luckily, Yolanda kept all the files we were working on grouped to-

gether. She put them in here." He opened one of the doors,
removed the folders, then turned to find her staring at him.
"What?" he asked.

"Are you going to stay mad at me all night?"

"Yes." He put the files on the conference table and went
back for more. "Maybe longer."

"Hmm."

Something smirking about that sound. Something dar-
ing. He turned to face her.

She walked into the office.

Shut the door.

Locked it?

He watched her, wondering what the hell she was up to.
Then she hit the switch on the wall, plunging them into
semidarkness. He could still see her from the light sneak-
ing in under the door, and the overhead windows. Street-
lamps from below also illuminated the room. She fumbled
in her purse, then dropped all her stuff on the floor.

"What the hell are you doing, Kate?"

She didn't answer. She didn't have to.

He *saw* what she was doing. First the zippered sweatshirt came off and dropped to the rug. Her top went over
her head, then it, too, joined the jacket. She leaned down
and, after a moment, he heard her sneakers hit the floor.
Her long pants puddled on the carpet; she stepped out of
them and came up to him. He was standing openmouthed
by the cabinet when she reached behind her and unsnapped
her bra. Black lace, it matched panties that she also slith-
ered off. She was naked. Beautifully naked. Gorgeously
naked.

He grabbed her before she could speak. A driving need
to possess her overtook him. Having her plastered against
him, in the buff, while he was completely clothed, fueled
the feeling, which was accompanied by mind-blanking
lust. His hand flexed on her bare bottom as he took her
mouth. Devoured it. He turned around with her in his arms;
shoving the cabinet door closed, he pushed her up against
the cold wood.

She headlocked him as he hiked her up. Just before her legs went around him, he managed to push his sweatpants and briefs down far enough.

She dragged her mouth away. "Wait." She slapped a condom in his hand. Shit, she'd planned this. He rolled it on.

"Reese, I—"

"Shut up." He took her mouth again, as he reached between them and touched her. It didn't take long before he felt her legs tremble, her body tense. She was close.

He drew his hand away and she whimpered. Then he replaced it with his cock and thrust inside her.

She screamed.

He groaned, swore, shouted her name.

It was over in—maybe ninety seconds.

Barely breathing, he met her forehead with his. "Jesus, Kate."

"Hmm." She tilted her hips forward.

"Ahhhh . . ."

She laughed.

"Damn it. This isn't funny."

"I thought it was great."

And then, because he loved her, because she wanted to lighten his spirits and knew exactly how to do it, he let go a begrudging chuckle.

A BOTTLE OF wine, Italian subs, and the great sex from three hours earlier mellowed them both. They were amiably summarizing each case aloud from their third year together.

"Okay, John Chilton." Kate's eyes narrowed on the file. "We defended him for fraud."

From a comfortable leather chair, Reese asked. "Anything unusual about the case?"

She was lying on his couch with a file propped up on her chest. "Yeah, looks that way. We got into the courtroom and the judge recognized him. The judge's name was Reiner. I think he's retired now. He had to recuse himself from Chilton's case. It got postponed for months. We were mad because we had to cancel vacation plans when it was ready to be tried. Then Chilton pleaded out. We—"

"Oh, hell. I know where we recognize the mugger from." Reese bolted out of his chair, and strode to the file drawers.

Kate quickly joined him. He'd bent down and opened the drawer marked 2002. "Reese, we weren't working together then."

"I know. We were divorced. But we saw each other in court once."

Kate thought back. And was practically knocked off balance by the knowledge that hit her. He'd just yanked out the file and, still on his knees, he opened it. "Here it is. Dave Demming."

"DD," Kate breathed. "The guy on the ring. And the Alphabet Man."

"He was accused of fraud, and Greg Abbott was defending him. But Greg's mother died, and I took the case to court."

She whispered. "I was trying my hand at criminal court. Just to see if I liked it. I was filling in for somebody, and pulled this case, last minute."

Reese shook his head. "I don't get it though." He sat down on the floor and she plunked herself down across from him; he handed her the file. "There's no reason for Demming to have a vendetta against us. You recused yourself, and his court date got postponed. By the time it came up again, Greg handled it. I didn't do anything harmful to him, and neither did you."

"It doesn't make sense."

"Why would he attack you? Even if he is the Alphabet Man—and who knows what his connection to Bingham would be—why would he want to hurt us?"

"I have no idea. This just keeps getting more and more weird."

"Yes." Reese placed his hand on her neck. "But we're close to solving this. I can feel it." Then his fingers tightened and she saw determination in his gaze. And something cute . . . and sexy. "If you think for one second that mind-blowing sex against the cabinet is going to soothe ruffled feathers, think again. As soon as this is settled, and that could be any day now because of this"—he glanced at the file—"you're going to have to commit. And I warn you, Katie, I'll fight as dirty as you just did against the cabinet."

As threats went, it was a pretty good one. But since her body was still humming from its earlier connection with his, she felt safe and secure as she leaned into him.

TWENTY

ｿ✿ઝ

"THANKS FOR COMING in, Judge Renado." Detective Pike nodded to Reese. "You, too, Bishop."

"We want this solved." Reese glanced to the room where Kate would meet with an investigator who did not know the identity of the accused. There, she'd be shown mug shots, one at a time, of possible perpetrators. The TV lineup concept of several suspects in a dark room, with height markers and lights shining on them, wasn't used much anymore. All of these new methods were based on research for identifying suspects with the most accuracy.

"The police are anxious to catch this guy, too. We have a suspect if custody. If you ID him, you can watch us talk to him in an interrogation room with two-way glass."

"How did you find him?"

"Actually, it was Chase Sanders who gave us the clue."

"Really?" Kate was nervous, wrapping her arms around her waist. She wore a lightweight taupe suit that Reese thought made her eyes look almost hazel.

"Hell of a thing. Sanders went on the Internet. Seems

Demming has a website in his own name, as a prison advocate."

Ah, the connection to Bingham. "And I'll bet he helped out our girl, Anna."

"Yep. We tracked him down and subpoenaed his files. Seems he has a whole drawer full of women he helped. We're stumped on the disguise thing. We might be able to get him for fraud on that, but if you identify him as your attacker, Judge, we'll pile up the counts—blackmail, too, if we can nail him with the journal."

The lights went on in the small room and Reese took Kate's hand. It was warm and firm. "Scared, love?"

"Are you kidding? I'm pissed as hell that some guy did all this to us, and we don't even know why."

"That's my girl."

An older man wearing a suit approached the three of them. "Hello. I'm Detective Joe Johnson."

Pike introduced everyone.

The detective escorted Kate into the room. Reese watched through the small window. Johnson smiled at her and they sat down at a table. One by one, he put out five-by-seven mug shots, taking back the previous one. Kate had her judge face on as she looked at each of them. After she was done, she said, "He's number four."

Johnson picked up the photo and nodded. "This is him?"

"Yes."

"Are you sure?"

"No question, Detective. This is the man who attacked me."

From beside Reese, Pike said, "Bingo!"

The investigator rose and called them in.

Reese put his hand on her shoulder. "You all right?"

"Fine."

Pike said, "You've identified David L. Demming."

"Well, good. It's a match with our files."

It only took ten minutes to set up the interrogation. Soon, Reese and Kate were watching Pike question Demming.

Standing over the seated suspect, Detective Pike asked, "Are you sure you don't want a lawyer, Mr. Demming?"

"I got nothing to hide."

"Is that a no?"

"For now."

"Where were you two nights ago at seven p.m.?"

He made pretense of thinking. "Home with my girlfriend."

"Will she testify to that?"

He laughed. "What do you think?"

Pike studied him. "Were did you get that cut on your right cheek?"

"A little sex play. You oughtta try it sometime, Detective."

Pike ignored the comment and thrust still photos in front of the man. "Wanna tell us why you dressed in these getups to visit your clients at Longshore Federal Correctional Institution?"

The man's face paled. Clearly he thought they'd only caught on to the assault. "I want my lawyer now," Demming said abruptly.

"I thought you might." Pike smiled. "You're going down, Demming. And all the attorneys in the world aren't gonna stop it." He stood. "I'll be back."

"I AIN'T GOIN' down alone." This from Lena Parks, who fidgeted in the chair, tugging on the collar of her khakis.

Pike had requested a visit to Anna Bingham's cellmate after their interview with Demming. The next day, Kate and Reese once again watched from behind the mirror. Warden Evans stood beside them fuming.

Pike towered over the accused. "Demming says you killed Bingham on your own. All he hired you to do was to get something on her for his blackmail scheme."

"Yeah, man, that's how it started out. He blackmails alotta the chicks he takes on as clients. That's why he wears all those disguises, sometimes more than one per customer so the guards don't take notice. The rich bitches, he called them. Like Bingham. She thought she was such hot shit."

Casually, Pike asked, "What happened with the blackmail?"

"Bingham wouldn't go along with it like the others did."

"Can you give us names of others?"

"Uh-huh." She swallowed hard. Her eyes looked slightly panicked. "For a deal, right?"

Warden Evans swore. "I hate this."

"I don't blame you," Kate told her.

Reese's hands fisted as Lena Parks listed the names of the women just in Longshore that Demming had connections with. "There are more in other prisons."

"So, Lena," Pike asked. "You kill Bingham?"

"Fuckin' no. I didn't kill nobody. My guess is Demming got to Ruiz."

"Anita Ruiz?"

Kate and Reese had told the detective about the coincidence of Ruiz being in solitary confinement when Sanders visited the prison to talk to her, and how they thought her subsequent death was suspicious.

"Yeah, that's her. I stopped cooperatin' with Sorenson and Demming when they brought up murder. So they hit on Ruiz. Sorenson got the beef on her bad. Ruiz picked fights left and right with Bingham. I'd bet money that she put those pills in Bingham's food."

"How'd she get pills?"

"From Sorenson."

Kate sat back and sighed. "This is all well and good. It's evidence against Demming, though any judge will be suspect about a prisoner's testimony. I still don't know how it relates to us."

Evans said, "They're looking for Sorenson now. She's on the run. And we can track Ruiz's actions until she died. Now that we've got a probable scenario, I bet it'll fall into place. But I don't know how this concerns you two, either. Why did they implicate you, if Demming had her killed here by Ruiz or anyone, for that matter?"

"Maybe to set it up better as a suicide," Kate suggested. "It still doesn't explain why us."

Evans sighed. "At least you're off the hook on the suicide note. If it wasn't suicide, the accusation's invalid."

"Still, our reputation will be sullied if we don't get the connection and tie this all up."

"It's gotta come out," Reese said, sounding confident.

"Not soon enough for me," Kate told him. "I want to get on with our lives."

TWO NIGHTS LATER, the doorbell rang at Reese's house. He and Kate were fixing dinner, still shell-shocked from the events of the last few days. Earlier, Chase Sanders had called and asked if he could come over. But Reese, with Kate at his elbow, was surprised to find Chase at the door with Eddie Wick, the newspaper reporter. Since the reporter's account of the situation, in the paper this morning, was friendly to Kate and Reese, he was glad to see the man.

Reese asked them into the family room.

"What's up?" Reese asked, standing behind Kate, when she sat in a chair.

"We think we got the connection," Chase said without preamble. "Thanks to my good buddy here, we were able to piece it all together."

Reese grasped Kate's shoulders, encased in a thin blue T-shirt. "Tell me we're free and clear."

"You're free and clear." Chase smiled at Kate. "Good news, Kate." He faced the reporter.

Wick pulled out a flip pad. "When I did the story on Demming's arrest for today's paper, something niggled at me. I knew I'd heard or seen something that involved him in the past. So I went back to my notes." He held up the pad which looked worn. "It was in here, dated 2002, June 5." He read from his pad: " 'Routine courthouse coverage duty today. The presiding judge, sick. The defense attorney's mother died. Perp accused of fraud. It was like a circus.

The judge was openmouthed to see her ex stride in as the defendant's lawyer. Husband stopped dead in his tracks when he saw her on the bench. The animosity was so thick you could cut it with the proverbial knife. As if that wasn't bad enough, the prosecution raised all kinds of hell, objecting loudly before either of them got their wits about them. Note: Stupid of the guy to embarrass those people. It was obvious this had a simple solution.'"

Kate looked over her shoulder at Reese. "It was so awful. I was embarrassed, and sad." She grasped his hand where it still rested on her shoulder, as if to soothe the memory.

"My feelings exactly."

Wick watched them with shrewd eyes. The last interview they had had with him, they had been estranged.

He said, "Maybe this'll take the sting away. 'Demming was an asshole. I eavesdropped at the drinking fountain, and heard him bitching to his girlfriend about the delay. Then he said, "Sure was a show in there. With those two in the limelight, a perp could get away with anything."' "

Kate gasped. Reese was circumspect.

Chase smiled. "We think that maybe he gave himself an idea. I'd bet my license he used you guys as red herrings to draw attention away from the fact that it might be a murder, not a suicide."

"We thought maybe Bingham's note—her suicide— might all be a ruse," Kate commented, "But it's hard to believe."

Wick shrugged. "Not so hard. Because it worked, didn't it? If it hadn't been for your tenacity, which he obviously didn't count on, because divorce doesn't breed good partners, he might have gotten away with it."

Reese shook his head. How ironic: falling back in love had saved their careers. "What a chain of events. It seems so far-fetched."

Sanders shrugged. "Just because you're the victims."

"What should we do with all this?" Kate asked. "It's not

exactly hard evidence, and it would never stand up in court."

"You don't need hard evidence. You just need the connection. Take it to the police. It'll help build their case. And it'll give them the connection to you two that they need."

They discussed who should do what, and afterward Reese called Pike. The detective asked Wick to meet him at the precinct. As the men were leaving, Chase turned to Kate. "Happy?" he asked, all too friendly.

She reached out and squeezed his arm. "I am," she said. "Thanks to you."

"I'll be seeing you, I hope," he added.

"Maybe." Reese tugged her close and slid an arm around her waist. "Maybe not."

Wick socked Sanders on the arm, and they left.

When Reese closed the door and turned to her, she placed her hands on his shoulders and his went naturally to her hips. "What was that all about?" she asked.

"He was hitting on you."

"Hmm. You short-circuited it."

"Damn right."

She grinned broadly. His matched it. He picked her up and swirled her around. "Looks like it's over, love, if this is the connection."

"It's enough of a reason for me," she said smiling.

"Come on . . ." He pulled her to the kitchen and found a bottle of champagne in the wine rack. Its pop was loud and the fizz spouted out; Reese poured them each some.

"Here's to victory," he said, clanking his glass with hers.

"How sweet it is."

Reese drank, she drank and then he leaned over and kissed her. Her lips tasted like the dry bubbly. "Nothing compared to how sweet the future's going to be. And before you stiffen up, remember what I said in my office the night we identified Demming. The gloves are off. I'm going to play dirty. Make no mistake, Katie. You're going to be mine in no time."

"Back off, hotshot. Let's just savor one victory at a time." She saluted him with her champagne.

"All right." After he drained his glass, he took hers out of her grasp, set it on the table and, bending over, slid one arm under her legs, one at her back and scooped her up into a carry.

"Hey, what are you doing?"

"Take a wild guess."

"What about the champagne?"

"We'll finish it later," he said making his way to the staircase: "A lot later."

REESE FILLED HIS father in on how the case with Anna Bingham had been unraveled as they drove up to get Sofie from Connor Prep. It was the end of May and the school year was over. Summer had come, and the sun was shining down brightly on the blacktop. Everything on the roadside was green and lush. They'd taken Pa's van, so the boys and his dad could come along, and still fit his daughter's belongings in its rear end.

Pa shook his head after Reese gave him a summary of the story. "Sounds like one of those TV shows. Hard to believe this Demming guy didn't have it out for you."

"It's bizarre." Reese put on his blinker and passed a car. "All those nights we spent reviewing our files, reading through material on Anna Bingham, when it had nothing to do someone we'd offended or pissed off in our practice or her courtroom."

The case had busted wide open after Wick and Sanders had met with the police. It was a short journey from that conversation to the truth: Lena Parks's testimony, as well as the investigation into Anita Ruiz's prison life, involvement in the blackmail, and her death—which, ironically, *was* a suicide. The crowning glory came when the police found Nell Sorenson. She confirmed Demming's plans and the reason for his false identities. When Sorenson had questioned him about Bishop and Renado, Demming had told her what he was up to. All of it led to Kate and Reese being exonerated.

"Wouldn't say those nights together were for nothing though." Pa glanced at the backseat where the boys each wore the headphones Reese had bought them; Pa probably wanted to be sure they wouldn't be heard. "Things seem pretty good with you and Kate."

"They are now. She hasn't said outright she wants to get married again, but she'll get there. And soon."

"Is that what you want?"

Reese watched the road, sure of one thing. "It's what I always wanted. All it took was being with her a few weeks to make me realize I am still in love with her."

"Where'd she go this morning? You just said she couldn't come with us to pick up Sofie."

"Tying up loose ends." She was seeing Tyler to say good-bye. Reese grinned. "I got a surprise for all of you, hopefully for this afternoon."

Pa said, "You're getting the judgeship?"

"Ah, not exactly."

He recounted to Pa the conversation he'd had with Jane Summers, the chair of the nominating committee . . .

They'd met in her chambers, a few days after the story had broken. She'd smiled at him from behind her desk. "Reese, thanks for coming. I wanted to see you in person to congratulate you on solving the Bingham case."

He'd politely thanked her, but didn't know what else to expect. In any case, he'd been ready.

"Turns out instead of hurting your appointment to the bench, the case helped. The panel was impressed by how you figured out the unusual chain of events that led to Bingham's accusation. The members think you'll make a great criminal judge." Jane checked her calendar. "It shouldn't take more than a couple of months to get your sworn in."

Reese had looked around at Summers's swank chambers—much nicer than those of Kate, who had been right about family court being the stepchild of the justice system. All this could be his, if he wanted it.

Trouble was, he didn't.

"Thanks, Jane. I appreciate the vote of confidence, but

I'm afraid I'm going to have to ask you to withdraw my name."

The woman's eyes rounded with surprise. "Why on earth would you do that?"

Out of courtesy, he told her about Emily, and the promises he'd made to his sister about taking care of her children. He told her about wanting to spend time more time with his daughter. He talked about his father growing older and Reese's desire for quality time with Pa. Basically, he'd said that in the last few months other things had become more important to him than the judgeship, which had always been his ultimate goal.

Jane Summers had been disappointed, but he could see in her eyes an understanding of his shift in priorities . . .

From Pa's expression, when Reese finished the story, his father was equally as surprised—and pleased as punch.

They pulled into Connor Prep just before noon. Sofie was sitting outside her dorm on the steps. She looked young and cute in plain white shorts and a little blue top. Now that her hair color was back to normal, she resembled Kate again.

As soon as the van stopped, the boys burst out and threw themselves at her. She grabbed one in each arm and held them close. As Pa and Reese approached the trio, Reese was even more confident that he'd made the right decisions about his future. About all their futures.

"Hi, Daddy. Grandpa." Sofie let go of the boys and hugged each of them. "I didn't know you guys were all coming to pick me up."

Reese tugged her close, warmed by the weather and by Sofie's lack of inhibition for showing affection these days. "They wanted to surprise you."

Pa was frowning. "Nice place. Looks like a college." Under his breath he murmured, "Plenty of time for that." His father had been vocal in his protest of Sofie going away for high school.

"So," Sofie said. "Everybody can help bring my boxes to storage, then we can go home."

"Not so fast." Reese glanced at his dad. "Watch the boys, would you, Pa?" He drew Sofie away, under the shade of a leafy maple tree.

"What's up?" she asked. Gone was the scowl and teenage sarcasm that had flavored most of their contact for the last year. Her smile was big and bright.

"I don't want to put your boxes in storage, princess."

"It's stupid to take all that stuff home. We'll just have to drag it back up here again in the fall."

"I don't want to do that, either."

Her eyes narrowed. "What's going on, Daddy?"

He grasped her arms and rubbed them up and down from shoulder to elbow. "I want you to go to school in Westwood next year, honey. I want you to live with me and Pa and the boys."

Hope sprang into those eyes which were so much like his. "You do?"

"Uh-huh. As a matter of fact, I'm going to have to insist you come home."

A half smile. Then a frown. "What about Mom?"

"You know things have changed between us. Truthfully, I'm hoping that she agrees to live with us, too. But, Sof, even if she doesn't, I don't want you up here. Since Aunt Emily died, I see things differently. I want you with me until you go away to college." He ruffled her hair. "Even then, it'll be hard. But I want these next two years as a family."

Sofie glanced at the car where Pa and the boys stood. A grin came to her face. She turned to him with mischief in her eyes. "We aren't all gonna fit in that small house of yours."

"We won't have to. I'll tell you more about that later."

"What the heck?" She threw her arms around him and hugged him like she used to when she was little. He held on tight. "You're on, Daddy." Drawing back, she gripped his hand. "Come on, let's go tell the boys and Pa."

"In a second." He held her close again, and rested his chin on her head to savor the moment. He also said a prayer of thanks. Emily had been lost to him, and he'd grieve over that his whole life, but he took joy in the notion that his daughter had found her way back to him.

CARRYING A BOX with the last of the things Tyler had left at her house, Kate walked into the modern building housing Westside Medical Associates; her heart was heavy. She'd called and asked to see Tyler this morning, and since he was working till noon, he suggested she meet him there after lunch. She needed to say good-bye properly.

Mostly everyone was gone; Kate set the box down on a table and took a minute to study the outer offices. The place was huge and airy with counters and padded seats and several aquariums. She spotted his Well Child Zone and crossed to it. She hadn't been there in a while, and the area had expanded. She was ashamed that she hadn't taken more interest in his work since the Anna Bingham thing broke, and before that, too. She peeked inside. "Oh, I didn't expect to find . . ." Kate hesitated at the doorway. "Dray? What are you doing here?"

"Hello, Kate." Reese's ex-girlfriend was stacking some kind of brightly colored foam blocks in a corner. She looked young and innocent in her leotard, tights and dance skirt. "I'm volunteering with the Project."

Kate was speechless.

"I minored in movement therapy at Ithaca College. I have a degree in fitness training, as well." She lifted her chin. "I'm not the dumb blonde I appear to be."

"I never thought you were dumb. I'm sorry if I gave you that impression."

Emotion filled Dray's eyes. "How is he?"

No need to dissemble. "Still sad over Emily. He'll be better when the boys and Pa move up from North Falls."

"And you? Will you move in with them?"

Kate hedged. She didn't know how much to say, or what would hurt Dray to hear. They'd done enough to her. "That hasn't been decided yet."

The other woman shook her head, and gave Kate a pitying look. "What's *wrong* with you?"

"Excuse me?"

"You were always there between him and me, and because of that, I couldn't make it work for us." She gestured out the door. "And it's why you couldn't make a go of it with Tyler. Stop being so stupid about it. Give Reese what he needs."

"Which is?"

"You. It's the only thing he's ever really needed." She drew herself up. "Now, if you'll excuse me, I've got an aerobics class to teach at one."

Kate watched Dray Merrill leave the Well Child Zone and heard the outer door close softly. Who would have thought? She was still pondering the younger woman's words when Tyler, wearing his white doctor's coat, came out of the back area into the outer offices. Reading something on a clipboard, he didn't immediately see her.

The feeling of sadness she'd experienced earlier intensified. He was so handsome, so talented, so kind. As if he felt her stare, he looked up. "Oh, Kaitlyn, I didn't know you were here yet." He walked to the doorway.

"I just arrived."

He glanced behind her. "Did you see Dray?"

"Yes."

A scowl. "I hope you didn't upset her. I thought she'd be gone by the time you got here."

"Tyler, is something going on between you and Dray?"

His blue eyes were sad. "No, nothing's going on. Rebound relationships aren't a good idea. We *have* become friends though."

"Is she all right?"

He motioned for them to sit a table and joined her. "She's heartbroken, like me. But broken hearts mend. I know." He gave her a little smile. "I'm a doctor."

She watched him.

"Why are you here?"

"I wanted to say good-bye." She nodded to the box in the hallway. "I brought you some things you left at my place."

"So," he said, stretching out his legs, "this is it."

"Tyler, I'm so sorry I've hurt you. Believe me when I say I didn't mean to."

"I believe that. I know you didn't do this on purpose." He leaned back and crossed his arms over his chest. "I was right all along, wasn't I?"

"I'm afraid so. Honestly, I didn't know how I still felt about Reese."

"I can accept that. Will you remarry him?"

"Ah, the big question."

He shook his head and anger fired in his eyes. "Don't do this, Kaitlyn. Don't hurt Dray and me like this, disrupt all our lives, for nothing."

"You want me to go back with Reese?"

"I want you to be happy. And I don't want our relationships—yours and mine, Reese and Dray's—to end with *no* one coming out happily."

She shook her head. "You're a nice guy, you know that?"

"Hmm. Somehow that proverb, 'nice guys finish last' is cold comfort."

"I have a feeling you'll be leading the pack again, soon."

"I suppose I will. It'll just take a while."

"Good luck with all this," she said, encompassing the area with a sweep of her hand. "It's a great venture."

"I know. I'm taking a leave of absence from this practice to go to New York City and consult on that special clinic I told you about."

"You'll be wonderful at it. Someday you'll be world famous."

"I don't know about that." He stood, signaling he wanted to end the conversation. "Good-bye, Kaitlyn."

She stood, too, moved closer, and hugged him. Tears moistened her eyes as he held on tight to her. "Good-bye, Tyler. I hope you have a happy life."

* * *

"JASON, DON'T PEEK. You'll spoil the surprise." Sofie sat in the third seat of Pa's van with the two boys and scolded them like a big sister. The kids were all dressed similarly today, with denim shorts and T-shirts. "Dad made us promise," Sofie added.

He winked at her in the rearview mirror. "How do you know they're peeking, princess, if you got your eyes closed?"

Giggles from all of them.

Reese heard his father, who sat in the middle seat, grumble about Reese's request for all of them to close their eyes when they neared the edge of town.

Sofie said, "I think it's Pa you have to worry about."

Again, Pa grumbled.

"How's Mom's doing up there? She couldn't ever sit still for something like this."

"Mom's doing great."

But Reese wasn't so sure about his statement. Ever since they'd returned home from Connor Prep and found Kate, back from seeing Tyler, she'd been quiet. He knew she was sad, the way he'd been after saying good-bye to Dray, and so he'd waited until this morning for the surprise. They'd all gone to church, just like a real family, and he was hoping that was a good omen.

They reached the city limits and turned down a secluded road. His heartbeat escalated as they were crossing the familiar terrain—and in apprehension of what he was about to do. He was hoping he hadn't jumped the gun on this one. But damn it, he wasn't wasting any more time in his life.

Forcing himself to be positive, he pulled up to his destination. "Okay," he said taking in a deep breath. "You can open your eyes."

He kept his gaze on Kate, despite the cacophony of sounds going on around him . . .

"Omigod. Our *house*." This from Sofie as she threw open the door.

"This is where we used to stay. I *love* it here," Jimmy added, right on her heels.

Halfway out the car, Jason quipped, "Let's go see if the tree house is still there."

Pa remained in the van for a minute. Reese felt his dad's hand on his shoulder with a squeeze of approval, and maybe good luck. Then Pa headed after the kids.

Reese couldn't see Kate's face, as she was staring out the window. "Sweetheart? You okay?"

She nodded.

He slid an arm around her shoulder. "Katie?"

Finally she turned. Her cheeks were streaked with tears. "Aw, shit."

She swiped at her face, then glanced back to the farmhouse. "It looks empty."

"It is."

"How did this happen?"

He shrugged, sheepishly. "I never sold it."

"Of course you did. I drove out here more than once. A family was living in it."

He brushed his knuckles down her cheek. He'd never known she'd gone near the place they'd loved with all their hearts. "I rented it to them. Their lease was up in March, and I told them a while ago I wouldn't be renting it again."

"March? Before the Bingham thing?"

"Yes. I'd decided to sell it and wanted to get it ready before spring. I guess I'd given up on living here again."

She sighed. "I'm afraid to go inside, Reese."

"Don't be afraid, love. I'll be with you."

Solemnly they got out of the car. Reese took her hand and led her to the front door. Memories came with each step . . .

What are you doing? She'd asked when they'd first moved in, four years after they were married.

Bringing my bride home. He'd scooped her up like a new bridegroom and crossed the threshold with flourish . . .

She touched the door reverently before she opened it. The downstairs was empty, and cleaners had come in to spruce it up. The house smelled like furniture polish and lemon.

A huge room opened up to the left. High ceilings. Built-in oak bookcases. And a fieldstone fireplace at one end . . .

Come here, Katie. I want to make love to my wife in front of the fireplace our first night in the house . . .

Kate crossed to the floor-to-ceiling structure. Touched the mantel, the uneven stones. Light reflected off of them from the expanse of windows across the front where they'd once hung pretty curtains.

The kitchen brought more memories . . . cooking together, late-night snacks when they couldn't sleep . . . once making love on the table. That little indiscretion had been where Sofie was conceived. Kate solemnly walked to the bay windows where the beautiful oval oak table had been; the spot looked out at the backyard.

Reese came up behind her. Over her head, he could see that the boys were in the tree house he'd built, and Pa was pushing Sofie on the sturdy swing set she'd used until she was a teenager. "That's good to see."

His hands rested on Kate's shoulders. "Too much?"

She covered a hand with hers. "No. I want to see it all. I want to remember."

They toured the wing off to the left where Emily and the boys had stayed when they visited. Reese swallowed hard, picturing his sister, in the home he'd loved.

I could live here, buddy, it's so big. Me and the boys.

Even then, he'd said, *You can, honey. Anytime.*

Kate linked her arm with his, reading the sadness in his expression. "Emily loved these rooms. You were a good brother to her, Reese."

They took the open oak staircase up to the second floor. Sofie's room was on the right.

Reese swallowed hard when they reached the doorway . . .

Reese, you're putting the spindles on wrong; would you please read the directions. I don't want her falling out of the crib . . . Then later, *Oh, Reese, look at her sleep. She's an angel . . .*

Kate turned her face into his shoulder and he held her there.

The final stop would be the hardest, he knew. They walked slowly down the hall to their bedroom. Tears misted his eyes, and Kate cried in earnest when they stepped inside . . .

Why are we putting oak and skylights on the ceiling? he'd teased. *I'd rather have mirrors.*

Kate detached herself from him. She crossed to the built-in dressers, checked out the bathroom they'd had put in for privacy, went to stand where their big brass bed had been . . .

I love you, so much, Reese. Swear to God you'll never leave me . . .

She was more composed after they'd seen everything. She faced him with an odd expression on her face. "You said you'd fight dirty. This is dirty."

He jammed his hands in his pockets. "I want our life back."

His heart rammed in his chest when a look so sad came over her face. "We can't have it back, Reese."

Oh, no . . . He'd been so sure this would work . . . she was almost there and he'd thought a final push would . . .

"But we can build a new one." The odd expression turned into a thousand-watt smile. "You, me, Sofie, the boys and Pa. It'll be even better."

Relief caused his body to sag. She crossed to him. "Didn't you think I'd say yes?"

"Thinking it and hearing it are two different things."

She slid her arms around his waist. "Then hear this. I love you. I'll never do anything to hurt you . . . I'll protect you from others who want to do you harm . . . I'll cherish every day we have together . . . I'll give you everything I have and always put your needs above mine . . . I'll stay with you no matter how tough life gets and rejoice in the good things . . ."

He was unbelievably moved at her reiteration of the wedding vows they'd made to each other.

She continued with new words of promise. "I want to marry you again, Reese. I want to be with you here or any-where. And this time, I'll support you no matter what."

She was referring to the judgeship. Later, he'd tell her he'd turned it down. And that Sofie wasn't going back to Connor Prep for school. But right now he didn't want to cloud the moment.

So he said only, "Is that a pact?"

"It's a pact."

His head bent, he began to lower his mouth to hers when they heard a door slam downstairs.

"Mom? Dad?"

"Uncle Reese?" Twice repeated.

So instead of kissing Kate senseless, he hugged her close. Cocooned in the warmth and safety of the home they'd built together, Reese vowed that this time they'd make things work. He'd learned from his sister's death that life was too precious to waste.

After another shout from below, he whispered, "Let's go tell the kids, Katie."

She buried her face in his chest and said, "You're on, hotshot."

Turn the page for a special preview of
Kathryn Shay's next novel

CLOSE TO YOU

Coming soon from Berkley Sensation!

SECRET SERVICE AGENT CJ Ludzecky, along with three of her colleagues, hustled into New York City's Memorial Hospital on the heels of the Second Lady and the Vice President of the United States. Though CJ kept all her emotions at bay when she was on the job, she couldn't help but empathize with Bailey O'Neil, the Vice President's wife of two years. CJ remembered only too well the night her father had died in an institution far too similar to this one. She'd been fifteen, and she and her brother, Lukasz, had taken it hardest, probably because they were the oldest of his eight children. Briefly, CJ wondered how Bailey's brothers were faring. Embedded in her memory was the image of holding a weeping Luke in her arms. His vulnerability had crushed her. She thought, for a moment, of saying a prayer for this family, but dismissed it; she didn't believe in all that anymore.

The group of six reached the admittance desk and were met by a man dressed in an impeccable suit. "Mr. Vice President. Ms. O'Neil. I'm sorry to meet you under these circumstances. I'm James Jones. I manage New York Memorial."

Bailey and Wainwright shook hands with the administrator. "Thank you for meeting us at this hour," the Vice President said.

CJ watched Wainwright slide his arm around his wife's shoulders; Bailey leaned into him. They had to be the most demonstrative political couple she'd ever encountered in the eight years she'd been with the Service. Their open affection for each other was a topic of discussion among the Who's Who in Washington—and much of it not always kind.

Automatically, CJ scanned the reception area. The other three agents did the same, though she noted her partner, Mitch Calloway, and Jenkins, one of Wainwright's bodyguards, moved in close to the couple.

The hospital administrator noticed. His voice was strained when he said, "I'll show you two the way." He shrugged. "All of you, I guess."

Calloway glanced over at CJ. About forty, Calloway had shrewd blue eyes and a touch of gray at the temples. Nodding to the other side of the hospital reception area, he signaled CJ to take note. A red-headed woman was having an argument with a . . . uh oh, a man with a camera. Damn it, how had the media gotten wind of the Vice President's midnight trek on Marine Two, the VP helicopter, from DC to New York? And how did they get past the two uniformed guards at the entrance to the hospital? True, the agents hadn't had much time to do any advance work because this was an emergency. But, still . . .

CJ strode across the room. When she reached the pair, they were disagreeing.

The female stood tall on her three-inch heels. Apparently she was digging them in. "I said no, Ross. We're not intruding on them. We're leaving right now."

"Yes," CJ said, drawing herself up to her full five-foot eight-inch height. "You are."

The camera man, a wiry wrestler-type, peered over half glasses at her. "Yeah? Who says?"

Brushing back the tailored jacket of her black suit, she

exposed her semiautomatic, then flashed her badge. They'd know who she was anyway by her suit and the Secret Service lapel pin, but a little show of force never hurt. "The United States Secret Service. No media here, hotshot." She shook her head and let her usually even temper spike. "Can't you people be humane for once? This is a family emergency."

"First Amendment gives us—"

The woman stepped forward, sending a fall of auburn hair into her eyes and a whiff of perfume—even this late—toward CJ. "I'm Rachel Scott. Our TV station got a tip that the VP and his wife had arrived in town and were headed to Memorial. But we won't intrude. Obviously a family member is ill. We'll be leaving."

"Thank you. I'll follow you out." Her comment was neutral, as she'd been trained to respond to questions.

Don't confirm or deny the press's comments. Usually they're on a fishing expedition. Her first boss, David Anderson, often gave her sage advice that she stored in her photographic memory. David had been her mentor until he turned on her, which still made her furious. But it had led to her working with Mitch in the D.C. field office. When Mitch had gotten into the coveted VPPD, the vice presidential protective detail, he'd often called on her to substitute for agents or when extras were needed. When one of the Second Lady's personal agents was transferred, Bailey O'Neil had asked for CJ as a permanent guard. That was how she'd come to such a plum position with not even a decade in the Service under her belt.

CJ saw to it that the press exited through the front door without taking any detours, turning them over to the uniformed agents standing post outside, then had to find her own way to the ICU. As she traversed the corridors, she spoke into her shoulder unit, part of the Service's restrictive radio network. "Reporters are history. I'm on my way back."

"Got ya," Mitch said. "We're at the ICU with Bulldog and Bright Star." Code names were given to protectees, usually indicative of their personalities. Clay Wainwright was know as a bulldog in fighting for the rights of others, and Bailey was a breath of fresh air on the hill because she didn't play politics.

The smell of hospital assaulted CJ as she made her way upstairs. Antiseptic, ripe food and something best left unidentified abused her senses. She remembered the odors too well. She always associated them with death. For Bailey's sake, CJ hoped her own visceral reaction was wrong this time.

CJ found her three colleagues, Wainwright, and Bailey in the ICU corridor talking to a doctor whose tag read, ED-WARD CRANE, CHIEF OF CARDIOLOGY. The Vice President of the most powerful country in the world commanded attention. CJ came up next to Mitch, who threw her a quick nod.

"He's resting now. We've given him a sedative." The doctor's voice was soothing. "We've run some tests to assess his condition and make a determination on how to proceed. I've called in our best cardiac surgeon and his team." Glancing at his watch, he added, "I expect them any minute."

Bailey clung to Clay. His grip was tight on her shoulders. "What's the prognosis?" she asked.

CJ had to smile, despite the circumstances. Though she'd only been the Second Lady's permanent shadow for a few months, she'd followed the news accounts of the woman's whirlwind career as the wife of the VP. Apparently, Bailey and Wainwright had a history; first, as a young DA, he'd put her in jail for harboring a criminal. After that, for almost a decade, they'd disagreed on the best way to stop youth gangs, and had battled out their different views in the newspapers. But two years ago, when they were assigned to the same task force by the governor of New York, they'd fallen hard for each other, and thumbed their noses at the political world. From what CJ understood, they'd fought like hell to be together. Though she'd seen that kind of devotion in her brother and his wife, she didn't believe it would ever come around to her. In any case, Bailey O'Neil was a perfect role model for teenage girls and women alike. CJ truly valued her assignment protecting the Second Lady, even though there had been some nasty gossip about how she'd gotten the position.

The doctor continued analyzing the patient's condition. "It appears Mr. O'Neil had a major heart attack. Your brother tells us he had the classic symptoms of an attack—chest pain, shortness of breath, discomfort in his arm. Mr. O'Neil, the son, called 911 and administered aspirin, which helped."

"Will he be all right?" Bailey asked.

"We won't know that for a while. We've already done some tests to determine the amount of blockage. It wore him out, which is why he's sleeping. The cardiologist and his team will determine the extent of the heart disease and a course of action."

"What might that include?"

The doctor glanced at Wainwright when he asked the question. "It depends on the amount of blockage. It could mean angioplasty or some form of surgery. But we're getting ahead of ourselves. I really hate to commit, Vice President Wainwright, until the surgeon can give us his opinion."

A woman who'd hovered behind them—she wore a hospital badge which read JANICE DENNY—cleared her throat. "I'll show you to the private waiting room where the rest of your family is, Ms. O'Neil."

Bailey looked at Clay.

He said, "Can't she see him first?"

"Yes, of course." The doctor's smile was sympathetic. "One person at a time is allowed into the room. He's alone now, as your mother took a break. Try not to wake him up, though."

"Hold on." Mitch spoke with the air of a man used to being obeyed. "An agent will have to accompany Ms. O'Neil."

"Into ICU?" the doctor asked.

"Yes, I'm afraid so, since we had no time to do thorough advance checks."

Jenkins said, "One of you should go to the waiting room and check it out, while Ms. O'Neil is in with her father. We'll stay here with the Vice President until you let us know all's clear."

"CJ can come with me," Bailey said. She seemed to accept the protection of the Secret Service willingly—only the Vice President himself was required by law to have it—but on occasion the Second Lady let it slip in conversation that it was hard for her to have the agents around. She knew the need to protect her and her children, especially because she was so high profile due to her gang work in New York. And she did her best not to take her annoyance out on the agents. Mitch had told CJ horror stories about presidents like LBJ mistreating his protectives, and even some VP's wives trying to outsmart them.

CJ stepped forward, her face blank. "Whatever you want, Ms. O'Neil."

The doctor opened the door to the private ICU room, a privilege given to them because of the vice presidency. When the doctor moved back, Bailey and CJ stepped inside. Bailey hovered by the door and stared over at the bed. Then, she grasped CJ's hand. The Second Lady was such a toucher, it often shocked CJ.

Still, CJ squeezed her fingers. "It's all right. Go on over."

A nurse sat by the bed. CJ followed Bailey and stopped a discreet distance away, while Bailey went to her father's side. Machines at the head of the bed beeped and whooshed; the soft sounds of muted phones and footsteps filtered in from the corridor.

"Hi, Papa," Bailey whispered, lightly touching Patrick O'Neil's limp hand. There were tears in her eyes. "It's me, your little girl. I'm here in New York, and I'm going to stay until you get better." Some sniffling. "I love you so much. Please, come out of this. Get better. I'm not ready for you to leave us yet." She placed a hand on her stomach. "Clay and I are having another boy. We're going to name him after you." Reverently, she kissed her father's head. "Please, Pa."

Before she lost control, even a modicum of it, CJ averted her gaze. She was used to quelling her personal feelings, though she'd known this trip to New York would test that skill. Ever since she'd joined the Secret Service, become estranged from her entire family, and been subjected to unfair rumors, she'd learned to harden her heart. Being weepy and sentimental about the situation had no place in her life now.

AIDAN O'NEIL STOOD by a window in the private waiting room with its stuffed couches and subtle lighting, staring down ten floors at the taxis and stalwart motorists who braved New York City at midnight; he heard a commotion behind him. Drawing in a breath, he steeled himself for this encounter. He'd been holding it together all night, but he knew Bailey's arrival would be a test of his strength. And right now, he was afraid he'd fail miserably.

Pivoting, he watched his baby sister come into the room; he had to smile at the sight of her. The Second Lady of the United States of America was dressed in jeans and a light blue top that revealed her just-beginning-to-swell stomach. Her hair was in a messy braid. The Vice President wore jeans and a sweater.

His sister went right to their mother; the two women hugged, then Bailey sat down and held Ma's hand. Before long, Aidan's brothers approached them. By order of age, they hugged their sister. Aidan grinned thinking of the nicknames Bailey had given them all. Patrick, the oldest, enveloped Bailey in his strong arms. He was physically bigger than all of them, but had the same dark hair, blue eyes, and Irish wit they all shared. He was dubbed The Fighter. Dylan, the next oldest, sported the broadest shoulders, and he dwarfed Bailey when he kissed her head. She called him The Taunter. Tall and lanky, Liam, The Manipulator, held Bailey in a death grip. Also the most sensitive of them, he wiped his eyes when he drew back. There were murmurs and more touching among them.

Aidan noticed the bodyguards lined like soldiers up behind the foursome. He'd met all of them but the woman,
who'd just been permanently assigned to Bailey three
months ago. The men were his height, a touch over six feet,
and were muscular. So was she. About five-eight, with
steely blond hair pulled off her face, she stood poker-
straight in her black suit and severe white blouse, rarely
taking her eyes off Bailey.

When his sister spotted him on the other side of the
room, she broke away from their brothers and crossed to
him.

*Please don't let me break down. It wouldn't be good for
Bailey.*

As always, Bailey enveloped him in an embrace. She
smelled the same, like lilacs, though she felt a bit heavier.
She always gained a lot of weight with a pregnancy. They
shared the hug wordlessly. No need to talk. He and his sister were still as much on the same page as they'd always
been, despite her two-year sojourn in D.C. Finally they
drew back. When he caught sight of tears on her cheeks, he
wiped them away with his thumbs. "Pregnancy makin'
your hormones wacky again, B?"

"Yeah." She cradled his cheek in her palm. "You don't
have to be so strong, you know. You can cry, too."

"I've had my moments."

"It's bad, isn't it? The guys . . ." she nodded across the
room "are putting up a front for Ma, but . . ."

"Yeah, honey, it's bad."

He'd heard the EMT's. *Myocardial infarction.* Which
meant part of the heart had died.

"You were with him?"

Aidan felt his pulse pound like a thousand drums. Of
anyone, he could tell this woman the truth. But he wouldn't
lay it on her now. "Uh-huh." He glanced over Bailey's
shoulder to see the female agent standing a discreet distance away. "I don't think I've met your new watchdog."

"What? Oh, no, you haven't." She turned and smiled at
the woman. "CJ, come here."

Long strides brought the agent to them. CJ? What the hell kind of name was that for a girl? The fairer sex should be named Adriana, Lorena, Sophia.

"CJ Ludzecky, this is my brother Aidan. He's the youngest of them."

A small smile softened the agent's mouth. "Nice to meet you, Mr. O'Neil."

He snorted. "Better not call me that, you'll have all of us doin' a heads up. Aidan, please."

"Thanks, but I prefer Mr. O'Neil." He noticed she didn't offer her own first name. What was he supposed to call her, Agent Ludzecky? Shit, what the hell did it matter? Where was his *mind*? His father lay dying in the hospital room right down the corridor and Aidan was wondering about formalities.

Clay came up to them and gave Aidan a bear hug. From their open affection for each other, a spectator would never guess Aidan had once decked the future vice president in Bailey's living room because he thought Clay was playing her. "You okay, buddy?"

"Yeah."

Turning to his wife, Clay said, "You have to sit down." She didn't move. "Now."

"I want to know what happened."

Clay nudged Aidan. "Help me out here."

"Let's sit and we'll talk."

They chose a furniture grouping away from the others; Aidan took a chair and Bailey and Clay sank down onto a sofa. Again, the agent stood several feet away.

"Where, when, and how?" Bailey asked. "Paddy didn't have details on the phone."

To stem the rush of guilt, Aidan took a deep breath. "Pa and I were in the backroom of the pub." The O'Neils owned and ran Bailey's Irish Pub on MacDougal Street. "We were having a beer, watching over Shea and Mikey." The sons and daughters of his brothers often accompanied their dads to the pub. A bedroom/play area was set up in the back for them, and the adults took turns standing guard.

Though Aidan was the only sibling who'd never married, nor had kids of his own, he often babysat. "We were talking and watching the end of the Knicks game."

Aidan swallowed hard. Ever vigilant, and because she knew him too well, Bailey would sense something in him if he wasn't careful with his words; she could be a pit bull when she wanted information. "We got into it, like we usually do. As always, Pa got himself all stirred up. And then he clutched his heart. Started to sweat. He said his arm was feeling funny." Damn it. Aidan's voice cracked on the last word.

Because he could still see his father, furious at him . . .

"You want to leave the pub? To take *pictures*?"

"Pa, it's more than taking pictures. I want to be a photographer full time, to do that with my life. I don't want to work at the pub anymore. Besides, if I leave, Dylan and Liam might be able to give up their second jobs."

"You can't make a living taking pictures."

Usually, Aidan was careful to quell his anger at Pa's dismissal of his talent. This time it had bubbled to the surface. "Damn it, Pa. I can. I worked at it after college when I stayed in Rochester for a year. I've sold photos to different magazines for years now. Last month, I won this prize, and was contacted by . . ."

He never finished explaining the coveted national photography accolade he'd won. The heart attack had come fast and furious, taking down his big, robust father within seconds. Mother Nature could strike vehemently, and that night she'd been in top form.

Bailey said, "Aidan? Are you all right?"

"Yeah, sure."

His sister shook her head, rose, and knelt before him. She grasped both his hands in hers. "A, you're not blaming yourself, are you? We all get into it with Pa. Your fight was about the stupid Knicks."

He tried to lighten the mood. "Watch your mouth, girl. The Knicks are sacred ground."

"Aidan." She squeezed his fingers.

"No, no, I'm not feelin' guilty. I do feel bad, though."

She stayed squatted before him, studying his face.

Then Clay was by her side. "Up, woman."

"I'm not an invalid, Clay. For God's sake, I'm pregnant."

"I know, love. But you need a keeper. And I'm the man to do it. Now get up, and sit on that couch. Put your feet up."

His sister stood, and squared off with her husband. Aidan usually loved to watch these little tirades, but not tonight. Clay cut it off at the pass, anyway. "Sweetheart, it's going to be a long night." His tone was tender. "Conserve your energy."

She leaned into him. "You're right. Before I sit, though, I have to use the ladies room." She peered down at Aidan. "But we're not done with this."

"Okay. Go for now."

Aidan knew he'd tell Bailey the truth eventually, but for tonight, no one but him needed to deal with the fact that he might very well have killed his own father.

DAWN WAS BREAKING, but CJ surveyed the waiting room area with crisp alertness. Bailey lay stretched out on a couch, her head resting on the Vice President's lap, sound asleep. Wainwright had propped his legs up on a table, his head thrown back; he was dozing, too. At six am, most of the O'Neils were either sleeping or resting quietly with their thoughts. Liam had his arm around his mother, and snugged her head tight to his shoulder. The support and love in this room was tangible. It made CJ sad to be around what she once had and lost, by her own making.

When the homey scene became suffocating, she crossed to Mitch. "I'm going to the john."

Wide awake, too, he rubbed his hand over his stubbly jaw. "Do me a favor?"

"Maybe. If you're nice."

Even though he was the SAIC, special agent in charge of the VP detail, and technically, she worked for him, she could tease him because they had a special bond. He was one of the few people in the Service who knew her whole history. Since he'd once been in the interrogation division, over the five years she'd known him, he'd dragged everything out of her.

"Check up on Aidan. He's been gone a half hour."

"You don't think he's in any danger, do you?"

"No, I don't. But since the media was here, other people might know we're all in town by now. Mason is checking the morning news to see if it's on there. I'd like to keep track of this whole family for a while."

"Sure. Any idea where he is?"

Dylan had awakened and was crossing to the coffee pot. He must have overheard them. "My guess is in the chapel."

Hmm, that surprised her. It shouldn't though. These people were Irish and Catholic. Not unlike her Polish family, who prayed before every meal and went to church every single Sunday.

CJ hit the ladies room, then went in search of the chapel. She found a small one, almost like an anteroom, down a ways from the private waiting area. The space housed only four pews, an altar, and a wooden cross. Like many churches, the scent of candles hovered in the air. Aidan sat in one of the pews, his shoulders slumped and his head bent, his blue thermal top stretching across broad shoulders. She was about to go inside when she realized he was talking.

She should leave, he was safe, but she didn't. For some reason, his words, spoken aloud mesmerized her. So she stepped into the shadows and blatantly eavesdropped.

"I'm sorry." His voice was sandpapery. "I didn't think . . . I didn't know . . . Oh, hell, I knew Pa would be pissed that I wanted to leave the business, but I thought he'd understand. I thought he'd fuss, but in the end give me his blessing. Damn it!"

CJ hadn't ever heard anybody swear at God.

"If you let him be okay, I'll stay. I'll forget all about the stupid prize. The chance to do my photography full time. I promise, I . . ."

As she listened to his words, caught the hoarse tone of his voice, CJ's throat got tight. She was well acquainted with the kind of deal he was trying to make with God. When her brother was a Secret Service agent, she'd done the same thing. *If Lukasz is okay and calls this Monday like always, I'll go to Mass an extra day . . . If he comes home for a little while, I'll be nicer to the twins.* And then that heart-stopping time when he was undercover trying to ferret out suspected school violence and was beaten badly by some punks. *Please, please God, if you let him recover, I'll stay in New York and take care of Matka.*

That was a promise she'd broken. Lukasz had gotten better, then the roof caved in a few months later when CJ told her family that instead of continuing her work at the UN, she had new career plans she'd been putting in place for months. Because they couldn't understand her choices, she'd left home under strained circumstances. Apparently, the weeping man in the front pew had tried to find his own way by breaking off from the family business, and now felt he caused his father's heart attack. That was dumb, but guilt, CJ knew, could be as irrational as hope.

She knocked on the half-open door to make her presence known. "Mr. O'Neil, I've come to see if you're all right."

No answer. She waited. "Mr. O'Neil?"

"Come in a minute."

Again she hesitated. The *thing* inside her that made her such a top notch agent—knowing when to check out someone in a crowd, when to draw her piece—stirred inside her. Talking to this man alone wasn't a good idea. Still, she made the short trip down the aisle. He scooted over, signaling for her to sit. "I'll go back . . . oh, shit, has something changed with Pa?"

"No, no. My partner wanted me to check on you. We're

being overly vigilant, but there was a reporter in the reception area when we came in, and," she shrugged, "we'd rather be safe than sorry."

"Glad to hear that. My sister's welfare is . . . vital to me."

She wanted to comment on how close they all seemed, but didn't. *Stay detached,* she warned herself. *Stay distant from these people who were filled with so much love it was tangible.*

As if he knew her thoughts, he said, "We're all so close. It's spooky sometimes."

Smiling, she remembered Luke's words . . . *Christ, Cat, you can read my mind. That's spooky.*

Aidan glanced over at the woman beside him. He'd watched her all night and was intrigued by her demeanor. Truthfully, he'd appreciated the distraction from his worry over Pa that she'd provided. "Do you have family, Agent Ludzecky?"

For a minute she'd relaxed, but now all the starch stiffened up her body again. "I, um, I yes. Of course, I do."

"Where?"

"Where what?"

"Where are you from?"

"Here, New York. Queens."

"Will you see your family this trip?"

She'd been staring ahead, but now she looked at him. "No, I don't have time off like regular people. I . . ." She stopped herself, as if she'd said more than she wanted to. "It's not protocol to talk about my personal life with you."

Her brows, now furrowed, were thick, unplucked and wheat colored. Up close he could see that her eyes were a light brown, almost amber, with flecks of green sprinkled in. Their shape was unique. He'd love to photograph just those eyes.

He said finally, "Surely your . . . code, or whatever it is, doesn't forbid chitchat."

"It's recommended we don't get friendly with protectees or their families."

"I can't believe Bailey lets you get away with that."

A chuckle escaped her throat. "No, she doesn't like distance. But mostly it's the little ones . . ."

When she trailed off, Aidan seized on her slip. "How are my niece and nephew? I assume Anika is taking care of them." Their Polish nanny was a delight.

"Yes, she is."

"I helped raise Rory, you know. You call him Bruiser, right?"

"You shouldn't know that," she said scowling.

"I do. Apt name."

"We had him designated at Buddy, but he found out and wanted a more manly name. He's a pistol." CJ shook her head, looking more woman than agent. "He hounds the Vice President all the time to tag along with him. Mr. Wainwright takes Rory everywhere he can and the staff has to scuttle to accommodate them. They love the kid, of course; he's become sort of a mascot at the office."

Since she seemed more comfortable with this topic, he pursued it. "How about Angel?" He winked at CJ. "Blue Eyes, right?"

Her gaze narrowed on him.

"I don't get to spend much time with her, but she seems as mischievous as Ror."

"She's beautiful." So was Agent Ludzecky's face, when it got all soft and feminine, like when she began talking about Angel. "She's walking now, you know."

"Yeah, Bay called me when she took her first steps. Angel was late in doing that, wasn't she?"

"Hmm. That's because everybody *does* everything for her. I remember when my sister Elizabeta was born. We all jumped when she wanted food or a toy . . ."

Again, she drifted off.

"Elizabeta is a beautiful name. What does CJ stand for?"

"Huh?" Shoulders tensed. Agent Ludzecky resurfaced.

He wondered what kind of woman hid beneath the light wool suit, was tucked away in the knot she'd pulled her hair into.

"I asked what CJ stood for."

Abruptly she stood. "I should be getting back. I—"

There was movement in the doorway. They both pivoted around. CJ's hand slipped inside her suit coat. Aidan caught a glint of silver at her hip.

Bailey's other guard, Mitch, was poised in the back of the chapel. Aidan had spent some time in his presence before CJ came on board and liked him. "Aidan, Ludzecky, come quick."

Alarmed, Aidan bolted up. "Is, is . . ." He reached out and grabbed CJ's arm. Clutched it.

"Everybody's fine. The cardiologist is ready to talk to you. The team has a diagnosis."

Aidan's body felt ready to implode. "Any good news?"

"I really don't know, Aidan. The Vice President's agent radioed me when I went to do a sweep of the halls."

Mitch walked halfway down the aisle and his eyes narrowed on Aidan's grip on CJ.

She said, "Come on, Mr. O'Neil. Let's go see what's happening with your father."